T0267710

RUNE OF LAZARUS

S.I. VERTELLER

Print ISBN: 979-8-35095-645-0
E-book ISBN: 979-8-35095-646-7

Printed in the United States of America.

First Edition

CONTENTS

RUNE OF
LAZARUS

ALGIEBA
UNKNOWN FOREST
UNKNOWN
LAND

AMIA
STRENG
Cygnus
MySomATARIAN

CHAPTER 1

The Elf Hunt

Clotilda held her balance as she slid down the slope. Pebbles crackled and parted from the toes of her pink boots like a wave of water as she slid gracefully down it as if skiing. She giggled as she held her wooden sword in her outstretched arm and hugged her elf doll, Anstice, close to her chest as she pretended to charge into an imaginary battle.

Her descent gradually slowed to a stop as the ground leveled and opened to a large rock outcrop, and a cliff stretched out before her, with their jagged edges and craggy surfaces that were weathered by the elements over time. The towering trees of the surrounding forest were colossal, like castle towers, with their leaves rustling gently in the morning breeze like banners. The air was fresh, with the scent of pine needles and damp earth filling her senses, and the melodic chorus of birds and fairies graced her hearing in a soothing ambiance. She had never ventured this far in the forest before but was glad she did. This area was beautiful, with pure tranquility that would allow her to play for a while before she had to return to her village for lunch.

As she admired the natural beauty around her, her fiery, orange irises, framed by her soft bangs, locked onto something nestled on the slope's edge. The elf girl narrowed her eyes to see what looked to be a cave. But there was something inside it that ignited her curiosity like a sunrise.

Clotilda walked on the tips of her toes as she crept toward it, seeing a small firepit with faintly glowing embers at the cave entrance. Her fairy wing–shaped, pointed ears perked, and she became alert as the rays of sunlight basked over a dark figure lying against the stone wall of the cave.

Studying the broad shoulders, the muscular arms folded across his firm, strong chest, and the fairy wing–shaped, pointed ears poking out of holes in the fabric of the black hood, she could tell that he was an adult elf. Unfortunately, the upper half of his face was completely hidden under the hood, so she couldn't tell which elven species he was. He physically looked to be in his mid or late twenties by the looks of the youthful contour of his jawline and lips, but due to elves having eternal youth and beauty, it wasn't easy for her to know how old he was.

Clotilda wondered why he was out here on his own. The forest of Mysomatarian was beautiful during the day, but after ten years of living in the village of Cygnus, which is surrounded by these woods, she knew how dangerous it was during the night. Her Lazarus elf father, Cadmar, and Airavata elf mother, Bathilda, cautioned her whenever she played alone in the forest. They warned her not to wander too far or go out at night. But there was one warning they were strongly stern about. *"Beware of the lions that stalk prey in the forest's shadows."* Clotilda always found it odd that her parents told her to stay away from an animal she usually wouldn't see in a forest. But she obeyed them, and whenever she went out, she kept her eyes open for a giant cat that wore a majestic crown of golden fur.

Standing a few feet from the cave, Clotilda silently stared at the sleeping elf. Where did he come from? Who is he? As she wondered, she tucked the loose strands of her hip-length, rose-gold hair behind her ears.

Clotilda was hesitant to disturb his peaceful slumber. She took a step back, her movements slow and measured so as not to make any noise. She lifted her feet carefully, avoiding any rocks or fallen branches that might make a loud sound to wake him. The forest was quiet, save for the occasional rustle of leaves and the songs of the winged singers in the distant treetops. Clotilda paused every few seconds, listening intently for any signs that she had made a sound. Her eyes never left the sleeping figure in front of her, watching for any movement that might indicate he was waking up. When she was sure that she had retreated far enough, she turned to the slope from which she came, ready to run up it to make her way home, when she heard something that made her pause.

Clotilda heard footsteps and tumbling rocks coming from the nearby rock outcrop, and she quickly turned her head toward the direction of the noise. She wasn't sure who or what was approaching, so she ran toward a thick cluster of bushes growing along the cave like a garland. Once she got there, she hid behind the leaves and branches and lowered them to see who was approaching.

A group of teal-skinned, purple-haired elves wearing gray cloaks descended the narrow path of the outcrop.

"Seax elves? What are they doing here?" she whispered to herself.

The male leader of the group, wearing a thick pair of deep red gloves, held out his right hand to silently signal his followers to stop in their tracks. He slowly kneeled on one knee, carefully examining the ground beneath him. After studying the terrain briefly, he stood up and looked back at his group. With a commanding presence, he addressed them with a firm voice, conveying his observations.

"He's here," he whispered as he pointed toward the cave.

Silently, like a cougar stalking prey, the leader crept toward the sleeping elf. His right hand's golden weapon hand chain glowed as magic arose, and he summoned a long sword. Panic bloomed in Clotilda's chest as fear took her! Her mother and father had always warned her about these menacing assassins. From the look of their scorpion-designed armor, adorned with scarlet plating like blood stains, they were from the Graffias clan, one of the most dangerous and notorious groups of elven killers.

Clotilda trembled. She didn't know why the Graffias Assassins wanted to kill the hooded elf, but she couldn't stand back and watch him get murdered! She had to do something!

Her eyes swiftly scanned around for something she could use as a weapon. Unfortunately, she didn't have a weapon hand chain and wasn't allowed one until she turned eleven, as part of the elven tradition. She only had her doll, a wooden sword, a purple-and-pink beaded choker necklace, and two matching bracelets she had made. She had nothing to help him! Then, her gaze fell upon the bracelets once more.

Making do with what she had and knowing that she could always make new beaded bracelets later, Clotilda ripped the bracelet off her right wrist! She bit into the sweet pea vine of the jewelry, pooled the beads into her palm, and tied the ends around the tips of her index and middle fingers of her left hand. The leader neared the slumbering elf, and the sword blade gleamed in the sunlight as he readied his weapon for the kill. The frightened ten-year-old girl slipped one of the pink beads in front of the vine of the broken bracelet and pulled it back like a slingshot. She fought to steel her trembling arms, and her ears rang with the drumming of her racing pulse as she aimed at the sleeping elf, preparing to fire.

"Please . . . wake up! Wake up!" she whispered a prayer before releasing her hold on the bead.

The sweet pea vine rebounded as it launched the bead through the air. The bead charted through the air like a comet, hitting the sleeping elf on his left cheek, causing him to grunt and hunch his shoulders as he stirred from his deep slumber. Clotilda watched as he awoke, seeing him catch the falling bead she had fired with his gloved hand. She nearly screamed to warn him of the assassin, but her words got caught in her throat as he jerked his head up to see the blade nearing his neck. He snarled, baring his sharp fangs, before the lion-shaped cobalt gem of his silver hand chain, looping around his middle finger like a lion's claw, glowed as blue magic ribboned from it to form a large sword.

The air shrieked as the two blades clashed. Despite him sitting down, Clotilda could see that the hooded elf held back his attacker with one arm and defended himself with strength she had never seen before.

"Kill him now!" the leader ordered his followers.

Heeding their leader's command, the assassins summoned swords from their hand chains and charged after him. The hooded elf dug the heels of his boots into the ground and kicked himself back, using his powers as an elf to melt through the stone wall of the cave as if he were enveloped in water.

"You won't escape from us this time, you filth!" the leader snarled as he and his comrades ran through the cave wall after him.

Clotilda quickly stood up and used her powers to run through the cave wall. She poked halfway out through the other side of the stone wall and looked out to see the group of assassins and the hooded elf facing each other.

Clotilda had never seen an elf grow as tall as the hooded warrior. Comparing his height, she guessed that he was around seven feet. His reversible cape was the color of blackberries and had a hidden color of blue inside that framed his muscular body.

He clenched his hood tightly over his face with his free hand as he stood his ground, waiting for the attackers to make the first move. The Graffias group banished their swords into their hand chains, summoned bows from them, and fired arrows at him. He sliced through the approaching arrows with his sword before turning on his heels and sprinting away with the group chasing him along the slope.

Clotilda slipped back into the cave wall and hurried toward the bushes to grab her belongings before running up the sloping trail. She grasped the broken bracelet in her hand, stuffed her doll into one of the pink waist packs she was wearing, and used her free hand to fish the rest of the beads from her pant pocket, ready to fire another shot as she followed them.

From the higher grounds, Clotilda watched as the hooded elf charted a path through the forest trail. His cape whipped behind him like a pair of wings, and he banished his sword back into his hand chain as he pumped his arms to gain more speed. He ran with the grace and speed of a sailfish hunting for a school of prey, quickly creating a pregnant distance between himself and his attackers. Clotilda ran as fast as her short legs could carry her, trying to avoid running into trees as she watched the chase. As she ran, low-hanging branches brushed against her dark-brown pants and snagged a little on the puffy sleeves of her light-brown shirt.

Arrows rained down from the group of assassins, puncturing the ground near the fleeing elf. Clotilda worried for him. She could see that he was fast, but the arrows were getting closer to him, and she feared they might pierce his feet. Deciding to try to slow the assassins down, she skidded to a halt.

Clotilda peeked over the bushes and saw that the leader had stopped atop a large boulder, drawing his bow back as he aimed for the hooded elf. She tightly grabbed her sword with both hands until the wood whined, and her bird-scaled knuckles turned white like mist before she threw it down toward him, striking him on the head. The leader grunted in surprise as the little wooden sword hit his temple, which snapped in half. She could feel the anger radiating from him like a forest fire.

"Who dares?" he snarled, firing an arrow blindly toward her.

The arrow tore through the leaves of the bushes and sliced through the skin of her right bicep before spearing a tree trunk behind her. Blood dotted the leaves of the bushes like garnets, and pain ripped through her body like lightning. A scream spilled uncontrollably from her lips, and she threw her hand over her mouth as she quickly hid behind the closest tree. Now that they had heard her, the Graffias Assassins would find her! They were void of remorse or mercy and had been known to kill anyone, whether adult or child.

Warm blood streamed down Clotilda's arm, and she quickly ripped a piece of her pink scarf from around her waist, tying it tightly around her bicep to stop the bleeding. Then, she slowly and cautiously poked around the tree to see that the hooded elf was no longer running. He was standing his ground, with a bow summoned from his hand chain, and the assassin leader who fired at her was a limp corpse on the boulder where he once stood, with an arrow through his head.

Clotilda tore her gaze from the corpse and looked around to see that the other assassins were nowhere in sight. She looked at the surrounding trees below for movement but only saw the hooded elf looking around for them. The thought of the Graffias group fleeing after the death of their leader crossed Clotilda's mind, but she knew they wouldn't. Seax elves were known to be cunning and vengeful and had the power to turn invisible. Because of this, they were ideal for the roles of thieves and assassins and would never withdraw or retreat without spilling the blood of the ones who took the lives of their comrades.

The glimmer of an arrowhead peeking from behind a tree and pointing right at the hooded elf ensnared her eye. Clotilda drew the vine of her bracelet and armed it with one of her purple beads before aiming at the hidden archer and firing. The bead shot through the air and struck the archer in the junction of his wrist, causing him to grunt. The hooded elf jerked his head toward the archer as soon as he heard him, then fired an arrow and pierced his skull.

Arrows screamed through the air and speared the ground around him as the male elf dodged them with fluid movements. He sharply grunted in pain as one of the arrows pierced his right thigh, creating a black stain of blood on his dark-brown pants that grew bigger and bigger. Clotilda drew her bracelet, using the enemy arrows' directions to find the assassins, and fired her beads at them to reveal them. The hooded elf pulled the arrow out of his thigh, blood streaming down his fingers and bow as he fired it back at one of the assassins and killed him.

The three remaining Seax elves burst out from hiding and charged toward the hooded elf with daggers and swords. He banished his bow into his left-hand chain and summoned a sword in its place and another one from his right-hand chain.

Dual-hand chain wearers weren't uncommon to Clotilda. Her father had two of his own that he would wear every day. She knew it took great skill to use them, and the hooded elf was no exception. She was in awe watching him. Judging from how he fought, she could tell that he wasn't ambidextrous like her father, but he wielded them with balance and skill that looked to be from hundreds of years of practice and experience. He swung the swords in the air, cutting through the last three enemies as if they were blades of grass.

Clotilda silently watched as the hooded elf stared at the bodies littering the ground around his feet. Beads of sweat rolled down his cheeks and brows, and his shoulders heaved heavily as he panted. She heard him inhale deeply through his nose before he looked up toward the slope.

Clotilda gasped as she quickly hid behind the tree. Her heart pounded so hard against her lungs that she felt like they were being bruised. Trying to calm her breathing in fear of him hearing her, she shoved her bracelet into her pant pocket and pressed her hand over her injured arm and steeled herself for what might come before slowly poking her head around the tree trunk.

The male elf stood there as if he were a marble statue. He silently looked in her direction before transforming one of the swords into a silver shield resembling a lion's head and cautiously began walking up the slope. Clotilda watched him nervously. She didn't want him to see her and feared what would happen if he found her. She didn't want to take any chances. She had to act fast!

Prying herself from the tree, she crept behind the bushes. Clotilda knew she had to be careful and stay hidden, or he would see her. She hurried as she heard his heavy steps nearing the top of the slope. Hoping not to be seen, she leaped into a sprint to return to the safety of her home, not realizing that her broken bracelet had slipped out of her pocket and spilled a trail of beads onto the forest floor.

CHAPTER 2

Commander of the Royal Guard

The grown Clotilda gazed through the crystal visors of her concealed, serpent-designed knight helmet as she marched into the royal ballroom. She led her troops down the long violet carpet, feeling the eyes of the ocean of guests following their movements as they made their way toward the royal Dominus elf family.

Clotilda was dressed in a suit of Dominus elven armor, made entirely of tarnished silver, and had been through numerous battles and harsh weather conditions. The chest guard of her armor fit her hourglass figure, revealing her toned but feminine body underneath it. The chest guard was designed to look like rows of protective snake scales that covered her torso but was only open at the stomach area to show the fabric of her chainmail and was held together with a corset of silver wire, adding elegance to her appearance. She wore round, silver shoulder guards as smooth as horseshoe crab shells, serpent-design armbands, and elbow-length gauntlets. Her attire also included long, thigh-high, armored high-heeled boots that were elegant but functional for fighting and running and a worn ankle-length train that was gray like the chainmail fabric she wore under her armor. The only visible skin on her was her collarbone and chest, which showed a little of her cleavage.

Clotilda's pearl-like skin shone in the light of the golden gems that illuminated the room and grew from the ceiling. She cringed a little when her sensitive eardrums rattled to the heavy and loud clunking of their armored greaves that echoed off the crystal walls.

The heels of her boots clicked as she climbed up the marble staircase. She saw the high seats of the thrones breach the top steps like dorsal shark fins as she and her troops neared the royal family. Yet even with her face covered by the helmet, she kept her gaze stern and stoic as she approached the elven king and princess.

Clotilda ceased her march, causing her troops to stop behind her. She held out her right hand; the rose-pink gem on her phoenix-designed hand chain glowed as bands of magic erupted to form her weapon. Her weapon, Universeel, which she named many years ago, was decorated with graceful, crescent pink blades attached to the top and bottom of the staff-like base and had purple gems of various shapes and sizes. The harp strings on the weapon glimmered like a spiderweb's delicate threads, and the blades hummed as she gently waved it in the air and held it vertically against her breastplate in a salute. She glanced at the royal family, seeing King Thierry sitting proudly on his throne with his right arm on the armrest of the empty throne where his late queen once sat.

Like all male and female elves, King Thierry looked to be in his twenties and had eternal youth untouched by time. His long black hair was pulled back and tucked under his golden crown, his teal eyes were stern, and like all Dominus elves, his skin was a cold, light grayish beige that looked like stone. His amber-colored regal clothing embraced his lean body, and he wore a golden cape that glowed as if it were trying to rival the sun. Princess Malvolia was adorned in her finest silver dress, with a long, white ribbon around her narrow waist. Her hair was rose gold like Clotilda's and grew to her hips. It had white gems through it that looked as if she had plucked the stars from the evening sky and wove them into her locks. The princess smiled as she flirtatiously stared at the male mage, Bandus, among the troops.

Bandus was a half-Airavata and half-Dominus elf hybrid. He had pearl-like skin like an Airavata elf, mixed with his grayish complexion and neck-length, platinum-blond hair, and pale blue eyes. He had a muscular body; it wasn't from years of training, but rather the magic he used to make himself more buff to attract the ladies, and he did not mind the princess's interested attention on him.

Clotilda fought the urge to roll her eyes or shake her head at the princess's actions. Even though the princess was betrothed to an elven prince from a neighboring kingdom, Malvolia kept flirting with any man who caught her eye. She would tease him in a twisted game of flirtation until he became infatuated with her, and she would quickly move on to the next man as if he were a new piece of jewelry. As much as Clotilda disapproved of Malvolia's actions, it was not her place to say anything. She could only follow her duties as a guard if it meant not bringing trouble to her loved ones.

King Thierry roughly crushed the letter he read into a crumpled ball.

"Burn it! The capital of Streng doesn't help outsiders!" he said as he shoved it onto the silver tray that one of his female servants standing next to him held. He turned his gaze to Clotilda, his glare unfazed as his eyes laid upon her. "Lady Clotilda . . . step forward," he ordered as he waved his hand to gesture to her to approach.

She obeyed as she drew closer to her leader and kneeled before him. She removed her helmet, and her long, ankle-length hair, styled in a half-up and half-down bun, spilled over her slender frame and pooled on the marble floor. She brushed the loose locks behind her pointed ears, revealing a stab wound scar on her left cheek. The old wound spread vertically from the bottom of her cheekbone to the back molars of her bottom jaw. The mark was the color of white chalk and shone dully in comparison to her Airavata skin. She rested her helmet on the ground next to her and planted the bottom of her weapon on the floor.

The king looked at her from top to bottom, studying her as if she were being inspected. He looked down at one of the papers in his hand; a letter with the wax seal of the military of Streng made him shake his head. She recognized the seal from one of her commanding officers and saw it was a letter of promotion. She watched as the king read the letter quietly, a scowl prominent on his face. Clotilda felt it was a promotion of some kind, knowing that the king always made that same disapproval expression every time it was. The king lifted his gaze from the paper, looking over her head as he spoke.

"You came to us one hundred and thirty years ago as a lone orphan, and today, my military wants to promote you to the title of Commander of the Royal Guard for your service to the crown." He said the words as if he had rehearsed them before sitting on the throne.

"Thank you, Your Grace," Clotilda said politely as she bowed her head.

"We expect you to continue your duties as you have been doing. Do not fail us, Commander." He said the last words with slight mockery and a hint of warning.

The king's rudeness toward her wasn't uncommon to the newly promoted commander. Ever since her arrival to the capital of Streng when she was a child, the king quickly disliked her. She later learned from the castle guards how the king birthed a hatred for her people when a Lazarus elf murdered his queen.

The Lazarus elves treasured art and family, an essential part of their culture. They needed to create! Whether it was making a painting, a poem or a story, a dance, a piece of music, or a recipe, they needed to nurture their creativity. Their artwork wasn't hurting anyone, but King Thierry and his queen considered it a waste of time and banned art from the capital. Without the ability to create their works, many Lazarus elves transformed into decaying, vicious, bird-like creatures known as Hollows. As a result, many in the castle were attacked, one of the victims being the queen. Fearing for his own life, King Thierry had no choice but to give the Lazarus elves their freedom to create art again. The Hollows reverted to their elven forms upon the return of art, but the king developed an intense hatred for them.

Being half-Lazarus, Clotilda didn't want the same fate to happen to her. She didn't want to lose her creative ability and kept her musical compositions a secret from the royal family. She was already feeling a little emotional since she woke up this morning because today marked the deaths of her blood family. She wanted her unpleasant visit with the king and princess finished immediately.

"Is there anything else, Your Highness?" Clotilda asked as calmly as she could.

"No, you may go," he said flatly, waving her off to dismiss her.

She silently obeyed and stood up before walking back toward her troops. As she walked past them, the male and female elven soldiers parted for her, and they followed close behind her.

Exiting the ballroom, Clotilda let out a shaky sigh as she banished her weapon into her hand chain, and her eyes stung at the threat of tears as the painful memories nipped at her. Today was the sorrowful anniversary of her family's death. It always brought heavy sadness to her every year as she missed them profoundly and was haunted by the images of their undeserved deaths. She wanted to leave the castle to retreat to the comfort of her piano that called to her. She could feel that she was beginning to decay on the inside. She would transform into a Hollow if she didn't exercise her art and immortalize the memory of her family and a boy from her childhood in her music.

"Clo?" a male voice pulled her from her painful thoughts and caused her to glance at the corner of her eye to see Bandus walking beside her. "What's wrong? Why the frown?"

"I have a lot on my mind right now," she replied without looking at him.

"About?" he arched one of his blond eyebrows at her.

"Memories of my childhood. I suppose I'm a little tired as well," she said with a shrug.

"I don't doubt that. You go to sleep late every night. You need your rest now that you've been promoted to commander."

"I know. But nightfall is the only time I have to write my music." She paused as she walked down the spiral stairs of the grand foyer while holding the rail.

Bandus sighed softly, Clotilda catching a hint of frustration in his breath.

"You've been writing music since we grew up in the orphanage. I think it's time for you to stop with your silly musical nonsense. You're not a musician, you know."

His words made her abruptly stop on one of the steps and glance sharply at the mage.

"You're wrong about that," she glared at him, causing him to step away from her as if she were an angry animal. "Music is a part of who I am. I don't see anything wrong with being both a guard and a musician. Even though my free time is limited because of my duties, I need to compose something, even if it's one page. Art is significant to me!"

"But Clo . . ." he tried to protest but was cut off by her.

"I had never forgotten that you stole my music journal when we were children," she said with a glare that caused him to stare at her with wide eyes. She tore her angry gaze from him and glanced back at her troops with a smile. "The rest of you go and take some time off. There's something I need to attend to. May the Father God smile upon you!"

Her troops held their weapons to her in salute. She turned to walk down the stairs when Bandus ran down a few steps and blocked her path.

"Wait!" he said.

"What is it?" she sighed softly in frustration, her smile dropping as if it were never there.

"I was thinking . . . well . . . your promotion to commander was underappreciated, so . . . I thought you and I could go to the tavern to celebrate it. I'll buy you one of those nectar milk drinks you like."

"No, thank you."

"But . . ."

"Bandus . . ." she arched one of her eyebrows at him. "I made a promise to meet up with someone already. I don't want to keep him waiting."

"Who might that be?" he frowned.

"I'm meeting Garth at the orphanage where you and I grew up," she replied flatly.

"Oh. Will I see you later then?"

"I need to get going," she said as she grasped his shoulder and pushed him aside as she continued to walk down the stairs.

She could hear whispering as she descended the steps. She recognized one of her male Dominus elf troops as Ivan, whispering to Bandus disapprovingly.

Ivan was a shield and spear bearer who served as a tower guard and occasionally traveled with her and her troops whenever they needed to patrol the kingdom. Ivan was nineteen years old, the youngest member of the royal guard. He was a handsome, lean young man with short, silver hair pulled back in a low ponytail, and his eyes were purple like amethysts.

"Nicely done. Telling her to give up on something she enjoys?" Ivan whispered, but Clotilda could sense his anger toward the mage.

"Shut up!" Bandus hissed through his clenched teeth.

CHAPTER 3

Rumors from the Fire Jotnar

Clotilda breathed a sigh of relief as she slipped off her heavy armor in the barracks, stripping down to the light-brown jumpsuit she wore underneath, with her long, dark-brown, elbow-length gloves and matching thigh-high boots. She put on a dark-brown choker to hide the scar where her throat was slit open and a long waist bag that hooked around the left high heel of her boot and strapped it around her narrow waist. She put her hand chain back on her right wrist and the loop of the chain around her index finger, an elven tradition of showing her rank as one of the leaders of the elven military.

She gently brushed the pad of her thumb over the pink, enchanted gem of the bracelet resting on her knuckles. Then she walked over to one of the small wooden nightstands by one of the beds and opened the top drawer. She reached into the drawer, carefully pulling out a red leather book with gold-painted lettering and a seal that resembled a crossbow and a wilting wreath of flowers. Looking down at the novel, a nostalgic smile spread across her face. She had happy memories of reading it countless times as a child and telling the heroic and inspiring stories to the children in the orphanage over the years. She couldn't wait to give it to Garth, knowing he would enjoy it as much as she did. She gently patted the book before slipping it into the upper, most enormous bag of her waist pack, where her water-resistant music journal and quill pen were.

Packing her armor in wraps of leather into a tight bundle, Clotilda grunted as she lifted it off the carpeted floor and made her way out of the empty barracks. She continued outside to a pond that was in a small garden nearby. The aquatic surface was decorated with giant blue water lilies and green pads as big as wooden painting palettes. She placed the leather bundle on the ground before kneeling and pulling the long glove off her left hand. She dipped her fingers into the cool water, submerging the small webbings between her five fingers and the bird-like scales on her knuckles and fingers. She glanced around the pond, noticing a swirling shape inside the murky depths.

"That's where you're hiding," she chuckled as she stood up and softly blew into a pegasus-designed whistle she fished out from her pack to call forth the lurker in the pond.

Bubbles erupted, and a gurgled neigh echoed in the water. The tranquil wake exploded as a steed broke through the surface. A mare covered in a soft plumage of fuchsia scales and feathers emerged from the shower of droplets. Her delicate but strong, webbed wings were transparent and barbed with beads on the tips that looked like pearls. Her long, white-and-pink mane billowed in the air, and her mermaid-like tail swayed back and forth instead of an average horse's tail as she galloped towards the shore. Her claws tapped against the pebbles, and she neighed happily as she neared her master.

Clotilda smiled as she approached the mare, embraced the beast's powerful neck, and hugged her. The aquatic pegasus snorted happily and pressed her head against Clotilda's shoulder to return the hug. She broke the embrace and gently patted the steed's wet muzzle.

"Thank you for waiting, Coralina. It turned out the promotion didn't take as long as I thought. Here, I brought you something," she said, pulling an apple from her waist pack and holding it in her outstretched hand to her steed. Coralina's webbed ears perked with interest and hunger. She sniffed the apple's red-and-yellow painted skin before tenderly plucking the fruit from her master's hand with her sharp, shark-like fangs.

Securely packing the armor on Coralina's back, Clotilda walked ahead, allowing Coralina to rest her head on her shoulder as she followed. As they navigated the busy market, Clotilda couldn't help but smile as she noticed the lively crowd of children of many species, from elves, Jotnars, goblins, and fairies, playing and laughing along the streets. The sound of merchants calling out to customers, the displays of worldly goods, and the tantalizing smells of food wafting through the air all added to the vibrant atmosphere. Clotilda kept a firm grip on Coralina's muzzle, sensing the pegasus's fascination with the sights and sounds around her. They strolled past several vendors selling various fruits and fresh seafood, and Coralina's nostrils flared with interest as she took in the delicious scents.

"No, Coralina. I'll feed you when we get back home," Clotilda said. She tried to continue their walk, but her steed wouldn't take another step. She turned to scold her, only to see the hunger in the pegasus's black pearl eyes. "All right, my friend. You've convinced me. I'll buy you some food to hold you until we return home," she smiled as she gently patted Coralina's forehead before making her way to the food stands and tying Coralina's reins to a hitching post nearby.

Coralina had always been a curious soul since she was a colt and had a habit of wandering around and getting into places she wasn't supposed to. With the market filled with some of her steed's favorite foods, Clotilda knew that her horse would binge, and she didn't want to have a sick pegasus, let alone pay for all the food she consumed.

The commander gazed upon the wide assortment of fruits and proteins, feeling hungry as she eyed the food. She placed her gloved hand over her growling stomach, trying to silence it as she explored the display for something for both her and her pegasus to eat.

A large shape emerged through the dark mouth of the giant door to the shop, and the heavy stomps of the titan's feet caused the ground to quake. A Fire Jotnar with a long, full mustache and beard of kindling fire and lava spilling over his muscular stomach and torso stood before the food stand. His fiery, orange hair was styled in a long rat-tail, and his irises were orange and gold like fireflies. He had a robust body, and he wore a long, orange tunic, thick brown pants, and leather-wrapped boots that made him look like he was going into battle, and his muscular arms wielded two large crates of fruits and vegetables.

Clotilda tore her attention from the fruit stands and tilted her head back as she looked upon the fourteen-foot-tall Jotnar, who easily towered over her six-foot-five tall height.

"How are you doing today, Ignis?" she said with a smile.

Ignis's eyes shot wide as he saw her. He beamed a smile, revealing his crooked teeth, and dropped the food crates to the ground next to his feet. The various fruits and vegetables bounced out of the boxes and scattered all over the ground.

"Clo!" he bellowed cheerfully, causing her ribcage to rattle from the powerful volume of his voice, and she fought the urge to throw her hands over her ringing ears. Ignis walked around the food stand to her, giving her an apologetic look. "Sorry about that. I keep forgetting you elves have sensitive hearing. It's been a while. Came over to see an old Jotnar, like me?"

"Oh, you're not old, Ignis. You look like you're in your thirties," she softly scolded him.

"You hardly changed yourself since we first met one hundred and twenty years ago. Well . . . you've grown more beautiful over the years, I should say," he said with a chuckle.

"Thank you," she smiled at his compliment. "I was twenty years old and still training for the guard when I first met you."

"That's right, and I was ten years old when I moved to Streng with my mother and father," he recounted the memory with her.

"After all these years, I'm glad we've held our friendship."

"Me too," he said, clapping his hands softly, trying to avoid hurting his female friend's hearing again. "Is there anything I can do for you since you're here?"

Clotilda felt a ping of guilt piercing her insides like needles. She could tell that Ignis missed her, and she missed him as well. Her duties as a guard kept her strictly busy, offering her little time to write her music and spend precious time with her friends and family. Being apart from them for an extended time contributed to her festering decay. She glanced up at her friend, her eyes filled with apology.

"I'm sorry I haven't been able to see you for a while. But I was able to take the opportunity today to come over and maybe . . . get a hug from you," she said with a shy smile and a shrug.

"Bring it on, Royal Guard!" he said happily as he gently grasped her waist and carefully picked her up like a porcelain doll until she was up at his fiery beard.

Clotilda outstretched her slender arms, wrapped them around his muscular neck, and pulled herself into an embrace. Flames from his beard licked the bottom of her chin, and a soothing warmth resonated in her from the comfort of his hug.

A sharp, pitchy voice caused Ignis and Clotilda to break the hug and drop their gazes to see a tiny female Beetje elf standing at the doorway, staring down at the spilled fruit and vegetables.

The female Beetje elf stood four feet tall, the same height as a male Beetje elf. She had an hourglass figure, wore a cobalt dress, and had a soft, round face, which made her look more like a teenager than a grown woman. She had tiny blue flowers in her blonde hair, neatly pulled back in a low bun. Like all Beetje elves, she had a pair of fairy wings sprouting from her back that were the size of butterfly wings and, though useless for flight, fluttered rapidly to express her growing anger.

The petite elf shot a deadly glare at Ignis as she pointed sternly at the spilled mess on the ground.

"Ignis! What have you done?"

Clotilda and Ignis' eyes popped open in surprise at the Beetje elf's powerful voice.

"I'm sorry, Soora, I didn't mean to drop those," he apologized sheepishly as he gave her a toothy grin.

"These are our newest supplies, and they are all over the ground!" She paused as she kneeled and picked up a few fallen fruits to examine. "Thank the Father God that they are not bruised!" She stood up and pointed her index finger at Clotilda while holding the fruit in her hand. "Now, you put her down before you burn her with your whiskers, you clumsy fool!"

"You needn't worry," Clotilda politely smiled in reassurance as she pulled away, displaying the exposed skin of her collarbone and the brown leather of her sweetheart neck top, both void of burns. "I'm half Lazarus elf. I'm resistant to fire and heat."

"That's right," Ignis said happily. "Clotilda is great to hug because I don't have to worry about burning her. Besides, I will return to work soon. I need to tell her something important first."

"Very well, make your visit with your lady friend quick," Soora sighed as she marched back into the shop and stopped by the door frame, her blue wings fluttering angrily. "I swear, Ignis, if you drop more of our produce, I will call the largest bear in the forest and tell him to maul you to the ground until you are a pile of ash!"

"I won't anymore. I promise," he said with a chuckle as he watched her disappear back into the shop.

"I'm sorry I caused you some trouble," Clotilda said as she tucked a few strands of her hair behind her ears.

"It's not your fault," he said as he lowered her to the ground. "I'm just glad that you came to visit. I hope I see you again sooner than later."

"I will work on that, I promise," she said with a smile. "What was it that you wanted to tell me?"

"Oh right," he realized before kneeling to her and whispering. "Have you heard about the rumors lately?"

"What rumors?" she asked in a whisper.

"There's been some rumors that Battle Komodons are prowling the rooftops of the villagers' homes at night."

"Battle Komodons? Here in Streng?" she asked, unsettled by what she heard and fighting to keep her voice down.

"Yes. This is the first time I know of Battle Komodons ever coming here. Do you know how to take one of those creatures down?"

"I do," she nodded. "I read books about them and found their weakness. But the first time I fought one . . ." she paused as she reached behind her back and rubbed a large stab wound scar between her shoulder blades. "It didn't end very well for me," she cringed.

"I'm glad you know how to take one down. They are hard to kill with all those armored scales covering their bodies."

"I agree. But why are they here? The capital of Streng is invisible to outsiders behind the magical barrier. They shouldn't have been able to find it . . . unless they have a Seal of Serpentis," she said hesitantly. The sickening thought of them probably killing someone to obtain one of the sacred and rare seals caused her stomach to churn.

The Seals of Serpentis were only given to those King Thierry wanted to have in his capital. Clotilda's late father, Cadmar, was given one of the seals, but he refused to go, let alone bring his family there, not wanting to have them trapped there like caged birds. But in the desperate last minutes of his life, he gave it to Clotilda, hoping she would be safe in Streng, and the one who killed him and his wife would never find their daughter.

"It's a possibility. Not sure why they're here. Unless they're looking for something."

"What could they be looking for?" she asked.

"I don't know," he said with a shrug.

"How long have they been here?"

"I'm not sure. Last night was the first time that someone saw them."

"I'll speak with the king as soon as possible and tell him about the Battle Komodons. Maybe he can set up a nightly patrol for us soon."

"Just be careful out there," he said as he gently placed his hands on her slender shoulders. "I don't want anything bad to happen to you or otherwise . . . I'm going to go berserk on anyone foolish enough to try," he said with a snarl, and his eyes flickered like geysers of lava from an erupting volcano.

CHAPTER 4

The Orphanage

Ignis carefully plucked eight apples from the fruit stand with his large thumb and index finger into a basket and held his other hand as Clotilda placed seven golden tree seeds, the elven currency, in his palm as payment. He smiled at her as he put the golden seeds in his front coin bag and handed her the apples.

"Thank you again, Ignis. I'll see you next time," she said, returning the smile.

"Hopefully, next time is soon," he said with a wink. "Be careful when you go out tonight."

"I will," she said as she waved farewell to him and returned to Coralina, who looked at her with excitement as soon as she laid eyes on the basket. Clotilda plucked an apple from it and hand-fed it to her hungry steed before grabbing a second apple for herself and taking a bite out of it. She untied the reins from the hitching post and patted Coralina's forehead before continuing their trek to the orphanage while hand-feeding the mare one apple at a time.

The sound of children laughing signaled that she was close. Clotilda took faster steps in excitement to return to where she grew up and where her adopted family waited for her. She turned the corner of the market to see the orphanage carved into the trunk of a large tree, with children of many species playing together outside in the small woodland playground. She walked through the vine-woven gate, the children quickly turning their heads to her at the sound of her approach. Smiles of flat, tusked, and sharp teeth gleamed on the children's faces as soon as their eyes fell upon the approaching female elf.

"Clotilda!" they cheered as they sprinted toward her and hugged her waist.

"Clotilda! You're back," one of the elven girls said.

"Glad to be back," Clotilda replied, gently patting the top of the children's heads.

"Can we see Universeel?"

"You may, but you can't touch or hold it because it is very sharp."

She waved her right hand high in the air, causing the magic within the pink gem of her hand chain to ribbon out and form into Universeel. The children marveled in awe as they looked upon her trusted weapon.

"It's incredible," one of the boys said as he studied the design but frowned slightly. "But I don't like the color."

Clotilda giggled at the comment before banishing her weapon back into the confines of her hand chain.

"Where did you get the pink jewel from, Clo?" one of the goblin girls asked as she gazed at the hand chain with sparkles in her brown eyes.

"It was a gift from a boy I met when I was little."

"A boy? Like a boyfriend?" she asked, with a smirk on her green lips.

"Well . . ." Clotilda said as she placed her gloved hand over her cheek, hoping to hide her spreading blush from the children.

"All right, you dust bunnies!" a deep and sharp feminine voice pierced the air, causing Clotilda and the orphans to jerk their heads toward the front door of the orphanage to see a female hobgoblin standing by the doorframe with her arms crossed above her swollen, pregnant stomach and her right hand clenching a broomstick.

Rose Hip and her husband, Stump, were the hobgoblins who ran the orphanage. Rose Hip was four feet tall and had emerald-green skin like all hobgoblins, but she made up for her short size with her bossy nature! Despite being hardworking around the house and teaming up with her husband to get some of the dirtiest jobs cleaned up, Rose Hip always wore a light dusting of make-up that enhanced her natural, goblin beauty and a delicate, clean dress every day, either red or green, which were her favorite colors, with her signature orange apron that she was never seen without. Her long, dark blonde hair reached the ground, and she allowed it to drag behind her like a wedding veil as she walked around doing her chores. Her hair was always brushed back in a bubble braid held securely with numerous green ribbons, and each strand was decorated with red constellations of rose hip berries.

"It's time for all of you to come back inside!" Rose Hip called out to them as she scowled at the outdoor air.

"Aww! Can't we stay outside a little longer," one of the elven boys groaned as he looked at her with pleading eyes.

"So be it! If you want your lunch to get cold," she said as she swept along the front step.

"Lunch?" the orphans asked in unison before they ran toward the doorway.

Clotilda giggled as she watched the children run to the orphanage, remembering when she was their age and was always excited whenever Rose Hip made one of her splendidly tasty meals.

"Clotilda?" She heard Rose Hip calling out to her as she held her free hand horizontally over her thick brows like a sun vizor. Her brown eyes widened as soon as they laid eyes on the commander. "Clo? It's about time you've decided to come back," she called out as she dropped the broom, grabbed the wooden railing for support, and tenderly cradled her pregnant stomach as she carefully walked down the stairs.

"Stay there, Mom! I'm coming over," Clotilda called out before she tied the reins to the gate so Coralina wouldn't wander around and ran toward her mother.

Rose Hip shuddered at the feeling of the blades of grass under her leather-wrapped shoes and bore her pointed teeth at birds chirping. Then, as she reached the bottom of the stairs, she growled as she grasped a handful of large rocks on the corner of the step and threw them toward a flock of songbirds. The rocks shot through the air and rammed into one of the birds, and it torpedoed toward the ground.

"That should shut you up, you little pests," Rose Hip growled as she sneered at the birds as they fled and hid in the treetops.

"That was unnecessary, Mom," Clotilda softly scolded her in disapproval as she approached. "I know you and Father are not fond of being outside, but that doesn't mean you can hurt or kill any animal that's not bothering us. So next time, you can wait for me to come inside."

"I can bear it if it means seeing my daughter! Besides . . . I missed you!"

"I missed you guys too," Clotilda giggled softly.

"So what was King Thierry calling you for?" Rose Hip asked.

"It was a promotion to becoming Commander of the Royal Guard."

"A promotion? Well, that's just great! We missed your celebration!"

"Well, no, you didn't miss anything," Clotilda reassured her.

"What do you mean? Was there a celebration for you? Becoming a commander is a big deal," her mother asked as she gave her a puzzled look.

"No, it was just short," she replied, shaking her head.

"Short? What did he do? Just say you're now Commander and told you to leave?"

"Pretty much," Clotilda replied.

"What is wrong with that king," her mother shrieked angrily as she balled her hands into tight fists. "For over one hundred years, you served him; he disgraces you like that?"

"We both know he's as fond of me as much as you are with the outdoors."

"Clo . . ." the hobgoblin paused as she slapped her palm on her forehead. "I can't see why anyone would not like you. You have sacrificed much to serve that fool and protect . . . the power you have," she dropped her voice into a whisper to the last words.

Clotilda groaned softly as she felt the inside of her ribcage getting brushed and rubbed her gloved hand below her collarbone to ease it.

"Calm down. Calm down," she whispered.

"Are you all right?" Rose Hip's worried question caused her to drop her hand from her collarbone and glance back at her mother.

"I'm fine. Anyway," she continued as she rested her hands on her hips. "Despite the king's behavior, I am grateful he allowed me to stay here in Streng, as long as I didn't cross the enchanted barrier."

"That's not a good excuse for him! He is such a wretched scumbag," Rose Hip glared.

"Mom, please keep your voice down. No one must hear you insult the king, and you need to be careful with the baby. I don't want you to get too worked up," she said softly.

"I know, but it makes me so angry that he mistreats you. I'm glad he hasn't banished you like a complete idiot. If he did, there would be a rebellion with us!"

"I appreciate you for watching out for me, but can we please not talk about it anymore? Besides . . . today is the day," she said sadly.

"You mean . . . it's the anniversary?" she asked as her angry expression softened.

Clotilda nodded in reply.

"If I may, I want to devote a prayer and a new piece of music to my blood mother and father. Is it all right if I go to the woodland area here to play my tribute to them?"

"Of course, you can," she spoke softly. "But . . . will you be coming inside once you're done? Garth has been talking about you all morning, and I've made plenty of food for everyone."

"I would love to," she replied with a smile.

"Good! I will make sure your food stays warm until you come in to join us."

"I appreciate that," she said as she kneeled to her mother, giving her a quick but loving embrace.

She helped Rose Hip up the stairs and started making her way to the small woodland playground of the orphanage.

"One more thing," Rose Hip called out to her from the orphanage entrance, causing Clotilda to stop and look over her shoulder at her. "If you so happen to find that pesky songbird, tell it that it won't be the first time I'm going to knock it out of the sky!"

"All right! I'll warn him, you brutal mother of mine," she called back with a tease, noticing the hobgoblin shaking her head and laughing in response.

Clotilda chuckled softly before she turned back to the woodland playground and continued her way into the wooded barrier, looking for a quiet place to write and pray.

CHAPTER 5

Memories of the Elf Boy

Beams of sunlight broke through the overlapping tree branches overhead and stamped irregular diamond shadows on Clotilda's hair as she walked under them. She brushed the arrow wound scar on her right bicep and remembered the memories of returning home to her village when she fled from the forest all those years ago. She eyed the blades of grass on the ground, coming to a stop when she saw the rocks Rose Hip threw and the lifeless body of the songbird beside them.

"You poor thing," she said softly as she kneeled, tenderly scooped the bird into her hands, and pressed her thumbs against its still, feathered chest. "Come back, little one," she said as glowing, orange runes appeared beneath her skin and spread down the skeleton of her forearms to the tips of her fingers, and her ribs groaned as something pushed against them, trying to break free. Clotilda felt her heart race as the markings spread down the rest of her skeleton. Her eyes glowed orange like the sun, and the skin on her chest began to crack open like magma. "No! No, I need a little of your power to restore this life. That's all," she said urgently to the creature within her.

She shut her glowing eyes and pressed one of her hands against her chest, hoping to keep the being within her at bay. To her relief, the magma crack disappeared, and the spreading of the rune markings ceased but remained only on her arms as magic sipped into the bird's lifeless body.

The bird's eyes glowed orange momentarily as it gasped deeply, and his tiny chest rose rapidly with life. The bird fluttered his deep brown eyes open, and soft tweets emerged from his throat. Clotilda smiled as she cupped the bird in her hands, and he looked up at her as if she were the first living thing he had ever met.

"Welcome back. Take care of yourself, and don't fly too close to my hobgoblin mother again," she said with a smile.

The bird opened his wings and flew around her in a joyous dance before flying up to the treetops. She stared at the branches where the bird flew, smiling before standing up and continuing her trek.

Clotilda dropped her gaze down to see a halo of hand-painted rocks on the ground by the toes of her boots. She stared at the pieces of art created by the orphans before carefully stepping inside the ring. She sat down with her legs folded under her, reached into her waist pack to pull out the music journal, and laid it on her lap. She opened it and brushed her gloved fingers over the blank music sheet, hearing the melodies hum inside her. Clotilda fished out her inkwell and quill pen and placed the well on the soft moss beside her.

In her artistic barrier of solitude, her mind began to fill with the melody of the song she had created. It was a tribute song that told a story about her blood mother and father's first meeting on the battlefield. She allowed the quill to guide her fingers, the stem of the feather skating on the paper as she created the chain of notes. She softly hummed her song as she drew each one.

The beginning of the melody carried strongly like a war drum as she thought of her father, Cadmar, charging through a battle with his allies, the Phoenixian Guild. Then the music escalated to a strong beat; she imagined it as if it was her father's powerful heart racing when he spotted her mother. Bathilda fell, injured from an arrow wound in her shoulder, as she fought along with her fellow Airvata priests and priestesses. Cadmar rushed over to help her. Then, the rhythm turned soft and serene, like the fluttering of a swarm of butterflies, as she imagined her parents' growing love.

Clotilda's eyes stung, and her vision blurred as tears rolled down her face, pooling at the bottom of the scar on her left cheek and spilling on her trembling, gloved hand as it clenched the quill. She raised her left hand and rubbed the tears from her eyes, leaving wet streaks in the worn fabric. Clotilda swallowed the salt of her tears before steadying her grip on the quill and continued writing her music. Nearing the end of her piece, her mind began to slip into a cloud of one of her memories—a memory of when she first met him.

Feeling safe as soon as she returned to her home from her adventure in the forest, the young Clotilda felt the watchful eyes of the Lazarus and Airavata elf guards on her as they stood on top of hovering islands of ice floating over the wall of water and kindling fire that surrounded the village of Cygnus.

She mended her arrow wound, using the healing remedies from her father's supplies and covering it with a leaf bandage. She wanted to forget the encounter with the Graffias Assassins and the hooded elf. Clotilda gathered her doll and music journal and walked through the market toward the apple tree orchard, accidentally bumping into one of the hooded male travelers. She politely excused herself to the elven man before continuing her trek.

She found a necklace of delicate white lilies, her favorite spot in the entire orchard, and a peaceful place to create her music and feel safe behind the wall while she wrote. She carefully stepped over the flowers and sat down in the middle of the ring with her doll sitting on a rock beside her that she found for him.

The apple trees and Anstice were her only company as she wrote her music, and she hummed the cheerful melodies playing in her mind. As much as she enjoyed music, she wanted so badly to have friends around her age. Part of it was she was an only child, and many children in the village were teenagers who weren't interested in playing and were busy learning from their parents about the arts and essential tasks for growing up. Clotilda wanted to have someone to play with. Someone who could run around with her in the forest, play games with her, and someone she could share her music.

A sudden loud noise of a twig snapping ripped her from her concentration, and a startled gasp escaped her throat. She recoiled the quill pen from the paper, nearly scratching it across the music sheet. She scooped up her journal and doll and pressed them to her chest like a mother protecting her children.

"Hello? Is someone there?" she called out timidly, wishing she still had her wooden sword to provide protection.

Her eyes focused on the rustling of flowering bushes in front of her. The blue fabric of a cape spilled from the parting branches as an elf boy, who looked to be ten years old like her, appeared. He was slightly taller than her, and his skin was pale like freshly fallen snow. His short hair grew to the middle of his neck and was silver as stardust. Beneath the blades of his split bangs were his eyes, which were celestial blue, and his pupils were slitted like a feline. The elf boy wore dark brown pants and a white, long-sleeved shirt with tears and dark stains that looked like he had been playing in the harshest terrains. His reservable cape was blue like a glacier and was ebony as blackberries on the inside. The elf boy was very handsome, but he had a hidden presence behind his eyes, making him look more adult to her than a child.

"Am I bothering you?" he asked politely.

"W-what," she squeaked, causing the boy to smile at her softly. "No. I was writing. Why are you here?"

"I heard music, so I was curious to see where it originated. Are you a singer?"

"No. I play piano and the harp, and I enjoy writing music too. See," she smiled as she turned her journal around and showed the boy the sheet of newly written music.

His feline eyes carefully studied the page of her music before they met her eyes once again.

"You wrote that?" he asked with a smile.

"Yes, I did," she nodded.

"It's beautiful."

"Really?" her eyes widened at his compliment.

"I have little knowledge of music, but how you write, it looks beautifully presented and professionally written. Nicely done."

"Thank you! That means a lot. My name is Clotilda. What's yours?"

She noticed how his eyes widened before his soft smile spread, becoming a beaming one.

"My name is Cyril," he said, dipping into a bow to her.

As she conversed with the boy, Clotilda couldn't help but feel drawn to the possibility of him being a potential playmate. So she asked him if he wanted to play with her, and much to her excitement, he politely but shyly accepted.

From that day, Clotilda and Cyril played together in the orchard. He taught her how to fence using the wooden swords they made together and showed her essential techniques for battle. His talents were not that of any child she knew. He was masterful and disciplined as if he had many years of practice.

Running games was the boy's favorite. Despite happily playing it with him, it always resulted in him winning with incredible speed that excelled beyond that of any Lazarus or Airavata elf. But every game they played pushed her to do her best, a challenge she took head-on! Every improvement she made, every experimental run in a different direction and quick sharp turns, would serve her well when she grew up. She could sense that Cyril was having fun like an invisible heavy weight that had long since been on his shoulders was no longer there.

When they weren't playing games, they would enjoy peaceful talks together, and she played the piano for him when he came to visit her at her window. She brought lunch to him after they took a break from playing, but she noticed that he ate the food as if starving. When she wanted him to meet her parents, he hesitated.

Clotilda enjoyed her time with Cyril and felt her heart flutter the more she spent time with him. But little did she know it would be the last time she would see him.

"Clotilda," the boy said as he stood before her in the orchard, a saddened expression on his face as he spoke. "I . . . I have to get going."

"Going? Going where?" she asked as she tightly hugged her doll close to her chest.

"I have to go back home," he said apologetically.

"How far is your home?" she asked him.

"It's far. But I promise I will return when my home is no longer in danger."

"Your home is in danger?" she asked with concern.

"Yes," he replied with a nod. "That's why I must go back and mend the damage done to my people. You do realize that I am a Regulus elf, right?"

"I knew when I first met you," she said with a sincere nod. "It doesn't matter what you are, but who you are that counts. You're nice and fun, and I wanted to be with you."

He smiled warmly at her words.

"It means a lot to hear that from you. But many elves and other creatures are fearful of my kind because the current king of the Regulus elves is abusing his power and ordering other Regulus elves to attack and conquer innocent villages."

"That's why you didn't want to see my parents," she said in realization.

"That's right. That tyrant must be stopped, and you gave me the strength I needed to do so. But before I depart, I need to ask you something."

"What is it?"

The boy hesitated, glancing briefly at the ground before meeting her eyes again.

"When you reach adulthood . . . would you consider marriage?"

Clotilda's eyes widened in surprise. The question made her heart beat faster than it had ever done before. Did she have a crush on Cyril? She wondered if this feeling was what her parents had felt when they had become attracted to each other.

"Yes. It would be great to be married someday."

"Then . . . when I return to you when you reach adulthood, would you marry me?"

Clotilda felt like her heart was going to burst with joy! Marriage was beautiful, but it was too quick, and she only knew Cyril for a couple of days. She wanted to learn more about him and convince him to stay longer.

"Um . . ." she bashfully paused before a playful grin spread on her lips as she thought of a plan to keep him around. "Not until we face each other in a duel," she said as she pulled her wooden sword from her belt and held it up as if ready to face an opponent. "That way, we know we are truly worthy of each other," she said before she lowered her weapon until it pointed to the ground.

"Very well then," he said with a chuckle. "If I were to complete that task, would you marry me?"

Clotilda's playful smile dropped before she glanced at her home and then back to him. She loved her family, and the thought of being away from them stung her heart as if a swarm of wasps engulfed it.

"What about my family? Will I ever see them again?"

"Your family is as important to me as they are to you. They can live with us if we get married since they will be my family too. There's plenty of room for them."

"You mean that?" she asked as relief engulfed her like a soothing spring.

"Yes. Anything for you," he nodded. "You don't have to give me an answer right now. I will wait until I return to you," he said as he gently grasped her hand and placed a pink gem in her palm.

Her eyes widened when she gazed upon the jewel before looking up at Cyril.

"Is this a . . .?"

"It is. It's an enchanted gem we elves use for weapon hand chains. This is my gift to you, for your hand chain and the magic within it to wield and name a weapon of your own."

"I will use it! Thank you so much," she said, closing her hand over the gem and bringing it to her chest.

"You're welcome. I will return to you," he said as he turned to leave, but Clotilda quickly reached out and gently grabbed his gloved wrist to stop him.

"Wait, I have a gift for you too," she said as she held her doll to him.

"You don't have to give me, Anstice, Clotilda. He's your favorite doll."

"I know, but I want you to have him. So, you can remember me, and I will give you my answer when we meet again. I know he will be in good hands with you."

He smiled at her as he reached for the doll and accepted it.

"I will take good care of him for you," he said as he carefully tucked the doll into a pocket of his reversible cape.

"I'll see you soon, right?" she asked through her quivering voice, tears beginning to well at the corners of her eyes.

"Of course. I will never forget you," he said before gently grasping her right hand, kissing her knuckles, and turning it to kiss the inside of her palm.

A blush bloomed on her rosy cheeks. Then she pulled him into a loving embrace as he pulled his lips away from her hand. She felt him return the hug as she softly sobbed against his chest and felt his hand gently patting her back to comfort her.

"It's all right. This farewell is not forever. I promise," he vowed.

"I won't forget you. I promise," she sobbed as she tightened her arms around him.

Clotilda gently tapped her index finger over the paper to ensure the ink had dried before closing her journal and standing up. She gently shook out her legs, which had fallen asleep from sitting on them for an extended time. Her heart twisted painfully at the thought of the one hundred and thirty years since she last saw Cyril. She missed him profoundly and longed to see him again. But she would continue to wait for him.

She held her right hand up, looking at the pink gem of her hand chain. She gently brushed her thumb over it, remembering how she had made it after he had given her the jewel and named it "Universeel."

"I hope you are well, Cyril. Wherever you are, I have not forgotten you," she whispered as tears spilled down her cheeks.

CHAPTER 6

Garth

After praying to her mother and father and playing the new song she wrote for them on the harp strings of Universeel, Clotilda packed her music journal in her waist pack and made her way back to the orphanage to join her adopted mother, father, and the rest of the orphans for lunch.

Clotilda went to the dining room, where all the orphans and her parents waited for her at a long, wooden dining table decorated with dishes of warm meat, cabbage soup, and freshly baked bread. She sat on the small wooden chair next to her mother, who sat beside her husband, Stump, who claimed the head of the table.

Stump was four feet tall and had a big, rounded belly that made him look like an old tree stump. Unlike his wife, he wore worn and tattered, brownish-green clothes, which were old—baggy pants and a long-sleeved linen shirt laced with dust from his hard day's work in the attic of the orphanage. He wore his favorite brown cap, a gift from Rose Hip when they were still dating three hundred years ago, and it reeked of ash and soot from cleaning the fireplace. He had shaggy black hair that framed his plump face, and the sharp, greasy spikes of his sideburns stuck out like the barbs of a hedgehog. He had muscular arms from years of helping his wife with heavy lifting and chopping firewood despite his reluctance to go outside. He had a pair of green eyes that were the color of rosemary and a big, round nose like his wife's.

Clotilda giggled softly as she saw the soft glare on Rose Hip's face as she looked at her husband. She knew that her mother loved her father deeply, but Rose Hip despised it whenever he ate at the table when he was dirty.

Clotilda rested her knees on the floor and sat awkwardly on the small chair as she tried to sit at the table. The chairs were a lot easier for her to sit on as a child, but now, as a tall elven woman, it was tricky, and her knees were protesting for her to change position. She shifted her legs to the side of the chair, only to find herself sitting like a frog on a lily pad. She could hear some of the orphans giggling as they watched her. She laughed a little in embarrassment as she slid her legs back under the table. She would have to wait until no one was watching before she tried to find a comfortable sitting position.

"Clo! You made it," a small male voice called out, causing her to look over her shoulders to see a skinny, six-year-old faun walking into the dining room. The faun stood upright on his thin hind legs and was three feet tall. His fur was white and painted with light brown spots, and his eyes were deep blue like a pair of diamonds. Two short horns grew from his forehead, his linen clothes were brown and loose on his timid frame, and he wore no shoes since he had cloven hooves for feet.

He cheered with joy, his pitchy laughs sounding like bleats, as he ran to the side of Clotilda's chair and wrapped his arms around her neck in a loving embrace.

"I made sure I kept my promise to you, Garth," she said as she shifted awkwardly in her chair and wrapped her arms around him to return his hug. "It's good to see you again."

"Come and sit down, Garth," Rose Hip said to the excited faun. "Your food will get cold."

"Yes, Rose Hip," he said as he broke the hug and sat in the empty chair next to Clotilda.

Stump loudly cleared his throat, picked up his wooden cup, and held it over his forehead.

"A toast to Clotilda's promotion to Commander and to have her with us today," he said as everyone held their wooden cups in the air and cheered for her. Then Stump turned his cup to his adopted daughter and tapped her cup with his. "Your mother and I are delighted that you can join us. We are very proud of all you have done over the years."

"Thank you, Dad," Clotilda smiled at him and sipped from the nectar milk in her cup.

After helping Rose Hip clear the table and clean the dishes, Clotilda walked around the connected rooms near the kitchen and the dining room until she came to the great room. Her eyes locked onto the wooden piano in the center of the room. She made her way to it, her high heels clicking on the floorboards as she carefully walked around toys and dolls as she approached the piano.

Clotilda stopped before the piano, gently brushing her gloved hand over the polished wood. She lightly pressed the tips of her fingers on the keys, hearing the soft tune of the piano like a heartbeat. She planted herself on the piano bench and began to play. Her mind's ear resonated with the piano's intertwined melodies with a pan flute. She raised her second hand over the keys, allowing her fingers to guide her hands as she played a music piece with a frolicking tune resembling a leaping lamb, then slowed to a woodland lullaby.

"That's beautiful, Clo," Garth said.

Her hands paused, and she turned to see Garth standing behind her.

"Thank you. I didn't realize you were there," she said with a smile.

"I'm sorry if I disturbed you," he said apologetically.

"You didn't," she said, patting her hand on the bench. "Come sit next to me."

The young faun obeyed happily and sat next to her.

"I didn't know you knew the Lullaby of the Faun."

"Xanthus taught me," she replied, resting her hands on her lap.

"Xanthus?" he asked as he cocked his head to the side.

"He was a faun like you. Xanthus was the first orphan I met when I first came here. I remember playing duets with him a lot when I was a child. He played the pan flute while I played the piano. We would do recitals on special occasions, and I had a great time with him. He was like an older brother to me. But he didn't like it when I stayed up late," she giggled softly. "Whenever I was up late at night, he would trick me into letting him play a song on his flute, and before I realized it, I fell asleep because of his spell. The next thing I knew, I woke up tucked in my bed the next morning."

"So what happened to him?"

"He was seventeen when I first met him. Once he turned eighteen, he was getting ready to leave the orphanage."

"Why didn't he get adopted? Did no one want him?"

"Oh no, he was outstanding and well-mannered. But he didn't want to get adopted. Many good fathers and mothers wanted to have him as their son, but he kindly refused. Despite the law by King Thierry to stay in the barrier once you come into this capital, Xanthus didn't want to stay here for the rest of his life. He wanted to return to his birth home, Sheratan Forest."

"But how did he convince the king to let him return to Sheratan?"

"He didn't. He knew the king wouldn't let him, even if he asked for permission. So he decided to escape during the night."

"Did you ever see him again?"

"No, I didn't," she said softly as she shook her head. "The last time I saw him, he woke me up in the middle of the night to hug me and bid me farewell. I have prayed that he made it to his homeland safely ever since."

"Have you ever thought of . . . leaving too?" he asked as his ears folded back.

Clotilda was silent for a moment before she slowly nodded.

"I've thought about it before, but . . . I decided not to."

"Why? Do you miss your home?"

"I do. But I don't have a home anymore. Unlike Xanthus, I lost mine along with my blood mother and father. So even if I did manage to escape, it's not home without you guys. You're my family and the reason I stay here."

"Are you happy here with us?" he asked.

"Of course I am," she smiled reassuringly at him. "If I didn't have you, the orphans, Rose Hip and Stump, Ignis, my music, my memories of my loved ones, I probably would have become a Hollow by now."

"A Hollow?"

"It's a . . ." her voice quivered a bit. "It's a horrible state for a Lazarus, even a half-Lazarus elf like me, to transform into. But let's not talk about it," she said as she reached into her waist pack, fished out the red leather book, and held it to him. "Here, I have something for you."

"Thank you! I wanted to read this book for a while," he cheered as he excitedly accepted the novel from her and brushed his hoofed fingers over its golden seal on the front cover.

"I'm glad you're excited about it. This book is special because it tells the noble tales of brave heroes and heroines of Nortamia. I know you want to be a warrior when you grow up, and I hope these stories will help guide you. So, take excellent care of this book."

"I will! I promise," he said as he hugged her.

Clotilda returned the hug and combed her fingers through his hair.

"You're welcome, Garth. It's one of my favorite books growing up," she said softly, remembering how she became inspired by the bold tales of the brave souls on the pages, and her blood mother and father's stories were among them.

CHAPTER 7

Battle Komodons

A chill lingered in the midnight summer air. Clotilda had stayed with her family longer than she had planned, but it was worth it, and she was grateful for what they did for her to celebrate her promotion. But it was time for her to return to her house and wake up early tomorrow morning to continue her guard duties at the castle. She also wanted to talk to King Thierry tomorrow to investigate the kingdom and see if the rumors of Battle Komodons here in Streng were true. She didn't doubt Ignis's warning about the rumors but hoped they weren't true. She needed to be ready to fight the Battle Komodons, and this time, she wouldn't let herself be killed by them again.

Clotilda stood on the porch of the front door to the orphanage, using the bright light of the full moon to search the playground for intruders. Much to her relief, there were none, only Coralina grazing along the entrance gate she was still tied to.

"Are you sure you will be all right?" Rose Hip asked as she stood by the doorframe with a green shawl over her shoulders.

"Oh yes, I'll be back to my normal self by tomorrow," Clotilda said as she smiled reassuringly. "It's just that today was my downiest."

"Well, get yourself back on track," the hobgoblin demanded as she planted her hands on her hips. "Your father and I don't like it when you're miserable!"

"I will," she chuckled before she kneeled and embraced her mother. "Thank you so much for today. All of you helped lift my spirit."

"Well . . ." Rose Hip smiled warmly as she returned her daughter's hug. "All we did was do what we've been doing for years."

"But it means a great deal for me to be with all of you," she said as she pulled away from the hug. "I'll return as soon as I have some free time."

"You better," her mother said as she pointed her index finger at her with a smirk on her lips. "Be careful on your way back home. It's dark out there, and I'm uncomfortable with all the rumors spreading."

"I'll keep my eyes open," Clotilda said. "I'll arrange a meeting with the king as soon as possible. Good-night, Mom."

"Good-night, Clo," Rose Hip said as she waved at her daughter as Clotilda made her way over to her awaiting steed. "Be careful out there!"

"I will," she waved back as she untied the reins before pulling herself on Coralina's saddle and clicking her tongue as she ushered her steed through the gate and onto the darkened streets.

With the full moon's light, Clotilda could see the empty streets of the market without using a torch or her fire magic to light the way. She could see that the doors and windows of the villagers' homes were securely closed and were void of lights, telling her that they were sound asleep.

The alleyways and underbellies of wagons were the only places that remained untouched by moonlight. Clotilda held out her right hand, using her Lazarus magic to summon a pulsing flame in her palm to illuminate the darkness as she searched the alleyways and wagons as she rode. She moved the pulsing flame in her hand with her eyes as she scanned around and lifted her arm as she glanced up at the rooftops for any prowling, reptilian shadows. She tightened her grip on the reins as she searched for the slightest, beastly movements of a Battle Komodon. The stab wound scar on her back throbbed at the thought of the creatures, and her stomach churned as she remembered her first encounter with one. Acanthus was his name, and she could feel the phantom pains of the blade tip of his armored tail tear through the tissue of her heart and splinter through the bones of her rib cage. It was a painful death, but she was grateful that Acanthus didn't see her resurrect with her hidden power.

Coralina's soft, nervous neigh pulled her back from her thoughts. Clotilda snapped her hand shut to diminish the flame when she heard the tapping of large claws from the alleyway closest to her. She pulled back on the rein to stop her steed and pat Coralina to calm her as she perked her ears and listened. Whispers echoed from the alleyway accompanied by the glow of a torchlight. Clotilda dismounted Coralina, softly shushing her to keep quiet as she walked on the tips of her toes to prevent her high heels from clicking on the ground as she crept toward the alleyway.

She pressed her back against the wooden exterior of the house on the right side of the alleyway and slowly peaked halfway around the corner until she saw two figures. Her eyes widened in recognition as she saw a male Seax elf wearing scorpion-designed armor with a gray cloak. He was holding a torch as he stood facing a giant anthropomorphic Komodo dragon . . . a Battle Komodon! A chill rushed up Clotilda's spine.

"Graffias Assassin," she whispered under her breath. She turned her gaze to the Battle Komodon, who stood face-to-face with the assailant. She glared at him, her hand curling into a tight fist. "Oh no, not you again, Acanthus."

Acanthus stood ten feet tall, and his muscular body was covered with thick plates of blackish-red scales with gold on the tips, and his long tail was armed with a sharp pointed end. He had spikes and plates covering his broad shoulders and mid-back. His reptilian hands were armed with splintered talons that had collided with many swords and shields over his lifetime, and he had rows of jagged teeth behind the lips of his pointed dragon-like snout.

"What are you doing here?" Acanthus hissed sharply like an alligator as he glared at the Seax elf with his glowing green eyes. "No one disturbs my hunt for new gladiators!"

"Keep your voice down!" the Graffias Assassin demanded between a whisper and a snarl as he summoned a dagger from his hand chain. "I know you aren't just after new fighters for the Slachten Arena. You're after the same weapon as we are."

"Perhaps, and perhaps not," Acanthus shrugged with a smirk.

"You can banish that plan from your thoughts. My leader wants to recover the Graffias Manticore, and no one will stop us!"

"The Graffias Manticore? It's a fitting title for our former champion. But it's a shame that I must kill him. Anyone who escapes from the Slachten Arena must pay with their life!"

"I don't think so," the assassin snarled, pointing his dagger at the beast.

"Do you honestly think your weapon would work on me? Have you even slayed a Battle Komodon before?"

Clotilda could sense the assassin's hesitation. She remembered fighting Acanthus and how she struggled to pierce Universeel through his armored scales. She looked him over, seeing the scales were decorated with scratches and dents, but there were no scars from deep lacerations or stab wounds. There was only one weak spot, and from the look on the Graffias Assassin's face, he didn't know what it was, but she did.

The assassin growled, sighing before returning the dagger to his hand chain.

"How about an offer?"

"What's your offer?" Acanthus hissed with intrigue.

"I propose a partnership. Once we obtain the Graffias Manticore, we want him back alive. If I'm not mistaken, he must have brought you and your audience riches and entertainment for all the battles he fought. So he is more valuable to you alive than dead."

"That is true."

"So, as part of our agreement, we will share the Manticore with you. He will serve us when we have him, and you can have him part of the time to fight in the arena as your returning champion. What do you say?"

Clotilda silently listened with intrigue. Who was the Graffias Manticore? Was he a creature, or was he a warrior? The Slachten Arena sounded familiar to her. She read about it in books and remembered her blood mother and father telling her about it. But would the Graffias Manticore come to this capital? Was he already here? She felt a nervous chill rush up her spine. She had to find out more about the Graffias Manticore in case he came here and be ready to fight him.

Acanthus jerked his head up in attention and sniffed the air.

"Looks like we're not alone," he hissed as his forked tongue slithered out of his mouth.

Clotilda felt every muscle in her body grow taut like the chains of a drawbridge, and her eardrums rang with her racing pulse. She took a deep breath as she summoned Universeel from her hand chain. She clenched her weapon tightly in her grasp until the leather of her gloves strained, readying herself to strike at her enemy.

Much to her surprise, Acanthus turned to the other end of the alleyway and crept down it like a hunting predator. She perked her pointed ears in confusion and arched one of her eyebrows at his plated back as he disappeared into the darkness.

A scream erupted, causing Clotilda's heart to jump to her throat. The torchlight captured Acanthus's shadow that glided over the alleyway wall with a smaller, squirming shadow in his grasp. She threw her hand over her mouth. Her veins swelled with rage, and her protective nature reached boiling point when she saw that he had Garth in his grasp!

"Looks like we got ourselves a little spy," Acanthus hissed as he held the struggling faun in his large, scaly hand.

The assassin smirked as he approached Garth.

"There is one rule that we Graffias Assassins strictly follow . . ." he said as he summoned the dagger from his hand chain. "We don't let spies live."

Clotilda saw red! She knitted her brows together, and adrenaline raced through her bloodstream. She sharply turned the corner of the alleyway and charged toward them like a mother bear protecting her cubs. She held Universeel in her grasp, seeing the Seax elf's hooded face jerk toward her in surprise before she plunged her weapon's elegant, curved blade into his chest. Blood sprayed from his deep wound, splattering her hair, chin, and scarred cheek. The Graffias Assassin let out a pained cry before collapsing backward onto the ground.

She quickly pried Universeel from the corpse and pointed it to Acanthus.

"Let him go, Acanthus!" she snarled, giving him her deadliest glare as if ready to turn him to stone.

Acanthus' puzzled expression morphed into a smirk that made her skin crawl. Garth looked at her pleadingly and tried to free himself by clawing his dull, hooved fingernails on his captor's tightly clenched hand.

"My, if it isn't the brave battle maiden? I felt ashamed of what I did the last time I encountered you. But it looks like you had another chance in life. You Lazarus elves may be able to resurrect once after you die, but you can't do it the second time," he snarled as he whipped his long, armored tail toward her.

"Clotilda! Look out!" Garth bleated as he struggled harder to free himself.

The commander held her weapon securely with both hands as she dodged the attack, leaped to the narrow alleyway wall, and kicked off until she maneuvered behind Acanthus's back. She plunged one of Universeel's large, top blades on the only golden scale between Acanthus's shoulders and tore it off to reveal soft, pulsing tissue . . . his weakness! The only way to kill a Battle Komodon! Acanthus gasped sharply in panic and leaped away from her. He stopped at the end of the alleyway, creating a pregnant distance between them.

"I'm impressed. You have gotten stronger and more agile since the first time we met, and I now know your name, Clotilda," he spoke with a salivated hiss, causing her stomach to churn in disgust from hearing him speak her name. "I must go now, my dear Clotilda, and I'll take this snack with me," he said with a smirk as he held Garth up before running off.

"Stop!" she yelled before sprinting down the alleyway, quickly leaping onto Coralina's back and galloping after him.

Clotilda banished Universeel back into her hand chain and tightly gripped the reins as she and Coralina raced down the streets.

"Hurry, Coralina!" she said, and her steed grunted in reply.

Coralina galloped as fast as she could and was quick on land and in the air, but Acanthus was quicker. How was Clotilda going to save Garth? Maybe she could shoot at Acanthus with an arrow. But the thought of archery made Clotilda tremble. Of all the weapons she had learned to use during her training to become a guard, the bow and arrow were her archenemies. It had been years since she used one, and she was horrible at it, resulting in more arrows fired at the ground than at the archery range targets. But she had to give it a try!

Pink magic ribboned from her hand chain as she transformed Universeel into a bow. Clotilda grasped the bow and crafted an arrow from the magic in her hand chain as she readied her weapon. The rapid movement of Coralina's gallop made the arrow waver as if refusing to be drawn.

"Come on, Clo!" Clotilda growled at herself in frustration as she fought to steady her hand.

She roughly pulled the arrow back until it pressed against the bowstring, and she fought as she drew it back. Her arms trembled as she pulled back on the bow. But before she could aim at Acanthus, the arrow dropped out of her grasp, falling to the ground and disappearing into ribbons of magic. Clotilda cursed under her breath as she summoned another arrow and tried again. She released her hold on the arrow, shooting it through the air and striking the ground behind Acanthus. Clotilda drew a shaky breath as she summoned a third arrow and pulled it back. She aimed and fired, only to hit the ground behind the Battle Komodon again. Her blood roared as she shook her head in disapproval of her lack of experience with the bow before dismissing it back into her hand chain. With how bad she was as an archer, Clotilda might hit Garth instead of Acanthus. She couldn't take that chance. A slingshot made from a broken bracelet was easier to use!

Clotilda focused her gaze on Acanthus as he continued to flee until he started sprinting upward. Clotilda jerked her head up, seeing they had reached the kingdom's surrounding stone wall.

"Take flight!" she called out to Coralina while she kept her eyes on Acanthus. She held on tightly to the reins as her steed spread her wings and took to the air.

The ground fell rapidly below them as they soared up the wall. Clotilda's hair whipped in the evening air, and the tips of her ears became numb from the cold, rushing air. They shot over the top of the wall like a dolphin leaping from the sea. Clotilda spotted Acanthus jumping over the top of the wall and running down to reach the outside.

"Dive!" she commanded her steed, and Coralina instantly obeyed her and dove toward the ground outside the capital.

Coralina pulled up at the last moment as the blades of the tall grass of a field surrounding the capital skimmed under the tips of her clawed, webbed feet. Clotilda watched Acanthus as they flew closer to him. She gasped, and her eyes widened as she caught sight of the glowing, silver ring of the magical barrier as they drew closer to it.

"As long as you live here in my capital, you will never leave or cross the enchanted barrier!"

The memory of King Thierry's stern warning rang in her ears. He gave her the demand when she first came to the capital as a little girl and told her that anyone who dared to break this rule would be brutally punished. She shoved the memory of his warning to the furthest part of her mind as she glanced back at Garth, as he reached out helplessly to her.

"Clo! Help!" the faun cried out in fear.

"Hang on, Garth!" she called out to him as she snapped the reins for Coralina to fly faster.

Clotilda slowly stood on her pegasus's back and fought to steady her trembling feet. She bent her knees and drew a shaky breath.

"Keep steady, Coralina!" she said as she waited for the right moment and jumped off once she was close enough to Acanthus.

The commander flew through the air, seeing Acanthus's plated scales rolling under her like waves of water, and the air got kicked from her lungs like a gust as her chest landed roughly on his back. She glanced up momentarily to see the barrier of magic engulf her vision and shatter like a stained-glass window, opening her to the world she had not set foot in for over a century.

Clotilda firmly gripped Acanthus's wrist and pressed her thumb into his pulse until pain shot through her hand as she tried to force him to release Garth. Acanthus hissed sharply before releasing his hold on his prisoner and began to summersault to crush her. Clotilda leaped off, wrapping her arms protectively around the frightened faun to shield him before turning her back toward the rapidly approaching ground. She grunted sharply as her back hit the ground, and her body shifted to the side as the curve of her hip struck the field, then her back and shoulder. She focused on Garth, ensuring he didn't hit the ground. She shifted her legs and dug her heels into the grass, hearing her high heels crack as she speared them into the soil, slowing her down until she came to a complete stop.

Clotilda painfully groaned, and her body ached with the newly forming bruises and cracked bones. She sat up and looked to see Acanthus watching her with a malicious smirk as he ran past. She watched him until she could no longer see him as he slipped into the darkness of the neighboring forest before she dropped her gaze to the trembling Garth in her arms.

"Garth? Are you all right?" she asked him, seeing him nod to her question. "Why did you follow me?"

"I was worried about you," he said with a sob. "I heard you and Rose Hip talking about the rumors of the Battle Komodons when you were leaving, and I wanted to make sure you got home safely," he fought to say as he furiously rubbed his eyes with his trembling fists to rid them of tears. "You-you're angry at me, aren't you?"

"Of course not," she shook her head as she brushed his tears away with the pad of her gloved thumb. "I was scared. I was afraid you were going to be killed. I'm just grateful that you're all right." She gently pulled him into a loving embrace, feeling the faun's tense body relax under her touch.

She turned her gaze to the barrier where the invisible kingdom of Streng was. Stump and Rose Hip probably didn't know Garth was gone and were likely asleep by now. Her house was a good place for him to spend the night, and she could return him to the orphanage tomorrow.

"Come. Let's get you home," she said with a smile.

"You mean I can stay with you?" he asked, glancing up at her.

"For the night. I'll take you back to the orphanage tomorrow morning."

"Thank you, Clo," he said in delight.

"You're welcome . . . ah!" she sharply groaned in pain as she stood up.

"You're hurt," he said as fresh tears of guilt ran down his cheeks as he saw the red and purple bruises on her skin.

"I'll be fine," she smiled at him as she reached into one of the pockets of her waist pack and pulled out a handful of coiling vines with tiny blue flowers. "Nothing these healing blossoms can't handle," she said as she placed them on the curve of her hip, and the flowers started to glow.

The blossoms numbed her pain as the cracked bones in her hip snapped and mended back together, saving her weeks of recovery. She pulled her hand away from her hip and placed the blossoms over her shoulder and the bruises on her body, causing them to disappear as if they had never been there.

"What kind of flowers are those?" Garth asked in amazement.

"These are special blossoms called the Tears of Eir. My father and mother used to heal their troops with these flowers," she said as the blossoms she used wilted away in her grasp. She shifted Garth in her arms to secure her hold on him as she stood up and began walking toward Streng.

A wash of uneasiness ripped through Clotilda's body, and she felt as if she were walking on the taut surface of a drum. She stopped and glanced back to the forest to see if Acanthus was by the tree line watching them, but he wasn't there from what she could make out in the darkness. She knitted her eyebrows. Who was watching them? No, someone was listening to them!

Clotilda could sense the presence of any magic thanks to her intuitive nature of being half Airavata elf. This magic listening to them was powerful, ancient, and had a gravitational pull like the full moon overhead. The lunar light blanketing the ground swirled around her ankles and heels like fog, making them resonate. She glanced up at the moon, sensing magic intertwining with the celestial sphere, but this magical presence felt like it was coming from far away.

"Clo? What's wrong?" Garth asked curiously as he looked up at her.

"We should go," Clotilda said uneasily. She resumed her trek, feeling like her steps were becoming stomps to whoever was listening. She sprinted and hurried back to Coralina, who was walking toward her. "Let's go, Coralina!" she said as she jumped onto the saddle.

"What's the matter?" Garth asked, starting to sound nervous.

She dropped her gaze to him, smiling softly to mask her nervousness.

"Everything is all right," she replied as she snapped the reins, and Coralina flapped her wings and took to the air.

Clotilda held Garth securely as they flew higher in the air and reentered the barrier to see the structure of the kingdom encased inside like a snow globe. She looked over her grass-stained shoulders, watching the damaged hole in the barrier close as she looked toward the spot in the field where she was walking. She hoped it was just the stress and her tired mind playing tricks on her, but the presence of something or someone listening to her felt real. She prayed to the Father God that returning to Streng would deafen whoever was listening to her footsteps. Was that why King Thierry forbade anyone from crossing the barrier? Was it the barrier that prevented other magic from sensing them?

Clotilda drew a shaky breath. She had broken one of King Thierry's laws tonight, but if it meant saving Garth, then it was worth it. She just hoped she didn't draw the attention of something dangerous, something responsible for the genocide of her village many years ago.

CHAPTER 8

The Graffias Manticore

Clotilda gathered some of the softest and most comfortable spare pillows around her house and made a small bed for Garth to sleep in. She allowed him to sleep beside the foot of her bed and told him to wake her if he needed anything. She got some sleep last night, only having to wake up once due to Garth politely asking for some water.

The sight of Acanthus and the Graffias Assassin last night made her very uneasy. But hearing them talk about this Graffias Manticore made her curious. She had never heard of the Graffias Manticore before. Who is he? Is he a lion beast with the tail of a scorpion with the wings of a bird? Or is he a warrior? She lightly bit her bottom lip. Whatever he was, she hoped there were some books about him that she could research.

After calling for a messenger squirrel, the elven way of delivering letters, Clotilda started writing her letter for King Thierry to inform him of the Graffias Assassin and the Battle Komodon she saw last night. She guided the tip of the quill pen on the paper, hearing it lightly scratch the surface as it skated into words. As much as she didn't like the king, she hoped he would answer her letter as soon as possible so they could figure out a way to purge the capital of the threat.

The messenger squirrel chirped as he stood outside on her windowsill. She glanced up from her paper to see the little creature, smiling as she saw it cleaning its tiny paws and fluffy tail. She could tell the squirrel was anxious and ready to deliver her letter, and she wouldn't have him wait too much longer.

Clotilda read through the letter a few times before she rolled it into a scroll and melted down some pink wax from a candle. She dabbed a small circle of the wax on the hem of the paper and pressed her seal of the royal commander on it. As soon as the seal dried, Clotilda opened the window and allowed the awaiting squirrel to climb onto her open palm. She brushed the tips of her index and middle fingers on top of his head and scratched under his chin, causing him to close his eyes in contentment.

"Sweet little one," she smiled as she watched as if it were getting ready to fall asleep in her hand. The squirrel chirped softly in protest as she drew her fingers away and opened the capsule on its back attached to an enchanted harness for carrying messages and protecting the squirrels from natural predators and enemy attacks. She slipped the scroll inside the capsule and closed it.

"This message is crucial. I need you to deliver this to the king," she said, and the squirrel chirped. "I'm counting on you. Make haste!"

She smiled before raising her hand close to the nearest branches. The squirrel leaped from her palm and dashed through the treetop before vanishing into the plumage of leaves.

Clotilda changed out of her linen nightgown into yesterday's clothes and put on her waist pack. She sat down by her vanity, used a long-tooth, woodland-designed comb to slowly work through the knots in her hair, pulled it back into a half-up and half-down style, and held it together with a red feather barrette. She dabbed water lily perfume on the line of her collarbone before she heard a soft yawn and glanced over to see Garth waking up from his deep sleep.

"Good morning, sleepyhead," she said as she smiled warmly at him.

"Good morning, Clo," he smiled back as he sat up and climbed over the pillows.

"How did you sleep?"

"I slept great. But knowing what could have happened last night . . ." he paused as his smile dropped. "I'm sure I would never have had a good night's sleep again."

Clotilda's smile dropped with his as she saw the fear from last night reappear in the faun's eyes. The thought of losing him made her scared too.

She stood up from the stool and walked over toward him. She sat beside him on the edge of her bed and gently placed her gloved hand on his shoulder.

"Everything is all right. You're safe now."

"But what about Rose Hip and Stump? They're going to kill me for running away last night."

"They won't," she reassured him with a gentle squeeze on his shoulder. "You don't have to worry about explaining things when we get to the orphanage. I'll tell them you followed me home, but I'll leave out our scary encounter with Acanthus and the Graffias Assassin."

"I appreciate that," he said as he looked up at her and gave her a grateful smile.

Garth folded his ears back, and his cheeks flushed red with embarrassment when his stomach rumbled loudly in hunger. Clotilda placed her fingers over her mouth and giggled softly at the cute sound.

"Let's get you fed. I'll make some rice rolls for breakfast," she said as she stood up from the bed and held her hand to him.

"That sounds good! I'm starving," he said as he accepted her hand, rubbed his growling stomach, and followed her toward the kitchen.

With steady hands, Clotilda decorated the top of her homemade blue rice rolls with lightly cooked fish slices and shaped them into water lilies with flower petals and sea salt.

"Those look so delicious!" Garth said as he sat in one of the chairs by the table and watched her cook.

"Thank you. I hope you like them," she said with a smile.

Clotilda grabbed a couple of wooden cups and poured some nectar milk for her and Garth before placing the rice rolls and two small bowls of sauce on the plates to dip the rice rolls. She picked up the dishes and put one by Garth and the other by her place before sitting herself in the chair across from him. Before she could offer him anything else, Garth plucked one of the rolls from his plate and popped it into his mouth, chewing it quickly like a rabbit nibbling on a carrot.

"These are good," he said between chewing. "Where did you learn to make these?"

"My blood mother taught me," she replied after swallowing the first roll she had eaten from her plate. "I learned by watching her and practicing making them while growing up in the orphanage," she giggled. "I remember my first attempt at making them in Rose Hips' kitchen. I ended up destroying many rolls before I was able to make them without having them fall apart. With my mess, I feared she would forbid me from working in her kitchen again."

"Thank the Father God she didn't. Your cooking is great," he said, then he paused, smiling at her. "It's good to see that you are happy again, Clo. Yesterday, you looked miserable."

"I'm sorry about that," she said. "Yesterday was the anniversary of my blood family's deaths. I get very emotional around that time every year."

"Please don't be sad. I know you don't like it here in Streng, but seeing you happy again is good."

Clotilda smiled at him before she glanced out the window to see King Thierry's castle. She glared at the stone architecture. She always appreciated castles' ancient and fortified beauty, but this one bore her distaste. It reminded her of her thankless job working there as a guard and holding the melancholy memories that reawakened in her mind whenever she entered it.

"I may not like it here, but I serve my family and friends," she said as she turned her gaze back to Garth. "I love all of you and want to protect you, even from King Thierry and his daughter."

"What would they do?" he asked nervously.

"As long as I follow orders and do my best, I don't think we have anything to worry about. Do I like serving the king and the princess? Nope! You would be surprised how many times I've been tempted to smack them with Universeel," she said with a funny expression that caused Garth to giggle. Clotilda chuckled before clearing her throat. "Anyway, eat as much as you want. Once you're finished, I'll take you back to the orphanage."

"Will do," he chirped, eating the rest of the rolls and slurping down his drink.

After finishing their breakfast, Clotilda saddled Coralina and fed her an apple before getting her out of the stables next to her home. She lifted Garth onto Coralina's back and sat behind him. She wrapped her left arm around his waist to keep him secure and used her right hand to hold onto the reins as they galloped through town.

Citizens parted for them like waves of a charting ship as they made their way toward the orphanage. She smiled as Garth laughed in delight, petting Coralina's mane and enjoying the ride.

Clotilda's shared joy with Garth ended abruptly when the piercing sound of loud protesting shattered the morning air. She pulled on the reins, causing Coralina to break out of her gallop and slow down to a halt. Clotilda looked around, and her eyes widened as she looked toward the castle gates to see so many elven women creating chaos for the guards they were trying to get past.

"What in the . . . ?" she asked aloud, knitting her eyebrows together.

"What is it, Clo?" Garth asked.

"I need to check on something," she said as she tugged on the reins, and they made their way toward the gate.

Clotilda drew closer and saw the line of frustrated elven women and teenage girls storming past her. Looking over the heads of the female crowd, Clotilda used her sharp bird-like vision of being half Lazarus elf to look from far distance. She could see guards rounding up many women outside the capital who were close to the magical barrier. What were these women doing? Why were these girls so determined to cross the magical barrier when it was forbidden?

She looked away from the field, allowing her eyes to adjust to let her see at a close distance again as she returned her attention to the gate. She spotted Bandus and a female Dominus elf captain from one of her troops, standing beside him with her spear summoned from her hand chain.

"Captain Corinthia!" she called out as she drew near, causing the two elves to look toward her.

"Commander," Corinthia greeted her with a salute as she banished her weapon back into her hand chain. "Glad to see you here."

"Good morning, Clotilda," Bandus said with a smile.

"What's going on here?" she asked, ignoring Bandus.

"It's the Graffias Manticore," Bandus scoffed as he rolled his eyes. "He's on the hunt."

Clotilda became silent as she felt a shiver run down her spine. Was the Graffias Manticore in Streng, or was he outside the barrier?

"If that's the case, we better call forth the finest hunters and tamers we have to get ready to capture the creature," she replied, figuring to guess that the manticore was an animal instead of a warrior.

"Creature? Commander, the Graffias Manticore isn't a beast. He's an elven king," Corinthia replied.

"A king?" she asked in surprise. She expected to hear that the Graffias Manticore was a warrior or an assassin, but a king was not one of them.

"Yes, Commander. I'm afraid a beast tamer won't stop him."

"It's just some foolish story, Clo. That's all," Bandus cut in.

"Can you tell me more about him?" Clotilda asked Corinthia, feeling a little irritated by Bandus trying to interfere. He tried to cut in again but was stopped when she gave him a stern glare.

"Of course. The Graffias Manticore is a title that strikes fear, and he was once the most powerful slayer to the largest group of Seax elf assassins called the Graffias. They say he wears a suit of armor resembling a manticore. He is dangerous, has slain many warriors, and destroyed nine Seax elf assassin clans single-handedly," Corinthia spoke these words with a slight quiver.

Clotilda could sense the captain was a little afraid while telling the story of the Graffias Manticore, making it much more essential for her to learn more about him to protect her troops.

"You mentioned he is on the hunt for something. What is he looking for?" she asked.

"He's searching for a bride," the captain replied.

"A bride?" she asked. "Well, that explains why so many unmarried women and girls are out here."

"For sure. They're trying to leap over the barrier to get his attention."

"How far away is he?"

"We don't know. We've got word from the messenger squirrels from some neighboring villages that he has left his kingdom and is on the search again."

"Again?"

The captain nodded.

"It's not the first time he's searching for the finest elven woman to become his queen. The last time he went out on a quest for his bride was one hundred and thirty years ago."

"He probably killed his last wife," Bandus said rudely.

"Bandus," Clotilda warned him. "You shouldn't be quick to judge someone by rumors alone."

"But if he is that dangerous and is searching high and low for his queen, it's likely that he will come here too!"

"I don't think we have anything to worry about. The barrier makes us invisible to the outside world, and even if one of the women crosses it, the only attention she'll be drawing is King Thierry's rage."

"I'm not sure about that, Commander. From what I remember from the tales of travelers, the Graffias Manticore can hear whoever walks on the land," Corinthia replied.

Clotilda felt her blood run cold when she remembered feeling a powerful presence outside the barrier last night!

"That's what I probably sensed last night," she said softly.

"What are you mumbling about, Clo?" Bandus asked, pulling her from her thoughts.

"It's nothing. Just thinking out loud," she replied, returning her attention to the captain."So how is it that he has a power like that?" she asked, trying to hide the nervous tone in her voice.

"That's as much as I know of him. But if I have to guess, he's probably a Rune," Corinthia replied.

"A Rune . . ." she said in a whisper. Her ears rang with the memory of her pained screams when she was a little girl and the agony of her bones feeling as if they were written on by a hot metal rod. She quickly pushed the memory away to the furthest part of her mind when she felt the clawing inside her ribcage. She looked back at her two troops, trying to hide any hint of distress. "Make sure the barrier is guarded, and don't let any of these women get close to it!"

"By your orders, Commander," Corinthia said with a salute.

Clotilda dropped her gaze to Garth, who was listening to them intently. He had been so quiet throughout the conversation that she had nearly forgotten that he was there.

"I must get going. I'll see you both later." She saluted them and grabbed hold of the reins.

"Wait, Clo," Bandus said as he hurried close to them and glanced up at her. "Where are you going?"

"I'm bringing Garth back to the orphanage," she replied as she reluctantly met his gaze. "Do you have anything going on today?"

"No. But I'm waiting to hear from King Theirry."

"If you have time, I want to take you to the market. Would that be all right?"

Clotilda could see the hopefulness in the mage's eyes. It wasn't the first time he had asked her out. She knew what he wanted of her but could never give it to him. She didn't love him. Bandus has always had an obsessive crush on her since they were kids. She had refused him for years, yet he continued to pursue her. Clotilda glanced at Corinthia, noticing she was nodding and waving her hands forward as if nudging Clotilda toward the mage and mouthing the words 'go on' to her. She sighed softly before she nodded.

"Very well, Bandus. Just this once . . ." she said before she was interrupted.

"Yes!" he cheered victoriously.

"Let me finish, please," she said, and his smile dropped as he glanced back at her. "We're hanging out together as just acquaintances. Nothing more than that."

"All right," he said flatly.

"So, where would you like to meet?"

"How about the town's gardens near the market? I need to get a new staff, and we can look around there for a while and have something to eat and drink at the taverns later."

"All right. I'll meet up with you soon," she said as she tugged on Coralina's reins and got her steed into a gallop.

"I'll see you soon!" she heard Bandus call out and glanced over her shoulder to see him waving at her.

She shook her head and wrapped her arm around Garth, and they continued their trek.

CHAPTER 9

Teachings of the Fossegrim

Clotilda tugged on the reins as they approached the orphanage, slowing Coralina to a halt as they went through the entrance gate. She dismounted her steed's back and turned to help Garth, seeing his ears folded back nervously and his eyes glancing down at the pegasus's mane as if trying to count every delicate strand of hair.

"Garth?" she asked softly, causing the faun to look at her with nervousness in his eyes. "Are you all right?"

"Yes. I am," he nodded in reply, but she could tell he wasn't.

"What's bothering you? Is it about Rose Hip and Stump?"

"No, it's . . ." he began but snapped his mouth closed and shook his head. "It's nothing. Yes, it's Stump and Rose Hip."

Clotilda wasn't convinced. She knew he was worried about returning to the orphanage earlier, but he seemed calm until they spoke with Corinthia and Bandus. She decided not to push it. Garth was only six years old and had been through a lot since last night.

"Don't worry. I'll explain to my parents what we discussed this morning, okay? Just leave it to me," she said with a wink.

He nodded in reply before he held out his arms to her. Clotilda picked him up by the waist and carefully helped him down. She patted Coralina before tying the reins to the gate. She offered her hand to Garth, which he quickly accepted, and they went to the orphanage.

Clotilda could feel Garth dragging his hooves as they drew near the orphanage. She gently squeezed his hand, causing him to look up at her, and gave him a reassuring smile that made him smile back at her.

They tore their gazes from each other, and their hearts jumped to their throats when they saw the angry, soot-covered Stump standing before them on top of the stairs to the front door.

"Where have you been, young faun?" Stump demanded in an angry whisper as he stomped his long chimney brush on the ground, triggering a puff of black soot to billow from the bristles.

Stump stared down at the ground, his eyes popping in mortified shock to see a ring of soot on the top step. Clotilda looked her father over. Stump's face and clothes were caked with patches of soot. But what nearly caused her to laugh at his appearance was that his hat was gone, and his hair was sticking up wildly, perfectly matching the bristles of the chimney brush.

"Where's your hat, Dad?" she asked through giggles.

"It's stuck in the chimney. I'll have to get it," he grumbled at her before he returned his angry gaze to Garth. "Do you know how long I looked around for you this morning? I even went as far as to search up the chimney!"

"I'm sorry, Stump. You see, I . . ." Garth tried to explain but was silenced when Clotilda held her gloved hand to him.

"Don't be angry at him, Dad. Garth was worried last night and followed me home to ensure I made it safely. It was late by the time we got back, and I knew all of you would be asleep. So I decided to let him spend the night."

"Then why didn't you send a messenger squirrel to inform us?"

"Uh, the messenger squirrels don't deliver after sunset, Dad," she replied.

"Oh, that's right," he said, slapping his forehead. He looked back at the nervous faun inching behind Clotilda's legs to hide from him. "Garth, I know you are fond of Clotilda, and I understand you and the rest of the children see her as an older sister, but that doesn't mean you can sneak out of the orphanage to see her. I don't want you to repeat this little stunt ever again! Do I make myself clear?"

"Yes, Sir," he said softly with a slow nod.

"Well," the hobgoblin said more calmly, the anger in his voice fading away. "I'm glad I noticed you were not in bed this morning. The last thing I need is for my wife to stress, especially when she is with child."

"Where is Mom right now?" Clotilda asked as she looked up at the carved windows in the tree bark of the orphanage.

"She's still in bed," he replied, pointing his index finger at the top floor. "I wanted her to sleep in today. Now that she is getting closer to giving birth, she needs rest. She was shaken up last night when she told me she heard something right outside after you left."

"That was me. She must have heard me when I climbed out the window to go after Clo," Garth said shyly with his hand behind his neck.

"I'll admit, it was clever of you to wait until after Rose Hip and I tucked all of you in bed before you snuck out like that. But you could have been a little more silent with your steps! You scared my wife nearly to death, and I went out in that horrible, dark, and cold outdoors last night to ensure there wasn't some ugly Battle Komodon trying to come inside!"

"Garth said he won't do it again and is true to his words, as we both know," Clotilda said as she reached back and patted the faun on the head.

"I know. I'm just apprehensive about Rose Hip. She's the love of my life, and I want to make sure both her and our child are all right."

"I understand. We all want to ensure she is safe too," Clotilda nodded.

"Anyway. Come over here, Son," Stump gestured for Garth to come over. "Don't worry. I'm not going to punish you. However, I need your assistance cleaning up this mess I made before Rose Hip has a fit."

"All right," the faun said as he stepped out from behind Clotilda and ran up the stairs of the orphanage. Before running inside to get some wet rags, he stopped by the door to wave farewell to Clotilda, which she returned.

Stump watched as Garth disappeared before he turned his attention back to Clotilda.

"Thank you for taking care of him. Your mother worried about you last night after you left, and so did I. Promise us you'll be careful whatever orders the king gives you."

"I will. I promise." She kneeled to him and kissed his forehead. "Say good morning to Mom for me."

"You can't stay for a bit?" he asked disappointedly.

"I wish I could, but I can't right now. Bandus is waiting for me and has invited me to explore the market with him today."

"Is he the boy who was infatuated with you when you two were still here in the orphanage?"

"That would be him," she groaned as she folded her arms. "Unfortunately, he still is."

"Then why did you decide to go out with him?" he asked, raising one of his bushy eyebrows.

"I got tired of him constantly asking me out. So I figured . . . why not once," she sighed.

"That scoundrel must have joined the royal guard to stay close to you. You're a commander, Clo! Order him to leave the royal guard, for heaven's sake," he growled.

"I wish I could, but I can't. I would have kicked him out of the guard a long time ago! But the princess favored him and had ordered to keep him in the royal guard so she could see him."

"But if I remember correctly, he tried to stop you from creating your music, and he was the cause of you becoming a Hollow," he said with a protective frown.

"He doesn't want me to follow my passion for music, that's for sure. But ever since I transformed into a Hollow all those years ago, he hasn't tried to touch my music journals again. But he tries to convince me to stop composing by using my duty as a guard as an excuse."

"Well, he better not try anything stupid again! Also, make sure you control your hidden power. Because if anyone finds out about it, especially King Thierry, you could be in great trouble," he whispered.

"I'll continue to be careful," she nodded.

"Did you agree to go out with Bandus because you felt guilty?" he asked, causing her to flinch slightly from the sudden subject change.

"Yes, I did. But I told him this outing is nothing romantic, and I only see him as an acquaintance."

"You can't let your guilt get the better of you! But I'll say this: if he tries to push you into becoming his lady, I'll ensure he won't come near you again!"

"I appreciate you for protecting me," she smiled warmly.

"Of course. You're my daughter, and I will do anything to protect you," he replied. Clotilda smiled once more as she hugged him. Stump wrapped his arms around her, careful not to get soot on her as he returned the hug. "Take care of yourself. You'll find the right fellow to be your husband someday. But he'll have to deal with me if he doesn't treat you with respect and love," he said as he broke the hug and cracked his knuckles.

"I'm still waiting for him. I'll wait another one hundred and thirty years if I have to," she said as she slowly stood up. "I'll see you later, Dad, and I'll visit you and Mom as soon as possible," she said as she planted another kiss on his forehead and returned to her awaiting steed.

Stump chuckled softly as he brushed his fingers over his forehead where Clotilda kissed him, waved goodbye to her, and watched as she saddled her steed and galloped back into town.

Clotilda reached the town's gardens and allowed Coralina to rest under the shade of the trees before sitting on the edge of a stone fountain as she waited for Bandus. She looked around for him but couldn't see the young mage anywhere. She looked at the clear waters churning in the fountain and started to feel sleepy and relaxed as she listened to the soothing sound of the droplets drizzling down. She hummed softly, mirroring the music she was hearing in her mind as she waited.

Excited energy surged through her fingers, screaming at her to play this new song humming in her veins. She looked over at the string instruments in the display window at the music shop nearby. One of them catching her eye was an elegant violin that sparked a sentimental attachment.

She turned her gaze back to the fountain, drawing her gloved fingertips on the water's glassy surface, watching as ripples grew from her fingers' path as she painted shapes. Her ears twitched like dragonfly wings as the memories of a violin bloomed in her mind's ear. She remembered when she was a little girl exploring the lagoon near her village when she met the spirit of the water.

Being drawn to the beauty of a mysterious melody, the four-year-old Clotilda's musical ears and innocent curiosity drew her to the serene lagoon near Cygnus. She neared the waters and spotted a handsome, naked man standing waist-deep in the shallows.

His toned body was sculpted of both flesh and water. His copper-brown hair was mid-back length and cascaded over his broad shoulders and lean chest like a stallion's mane. His eyes were peacefully closed, and his body slowly swayed to the song he played on his violin. Clotilda sat down on a large rock near the shoreline as she listened to his song, holding still so as not to make a sound. Despite his youthful appearance, his music was sorrowful but beautiful, and he played with many years of disciplined skills.

The man weaved his song to a slow coda before he lowered his bow and fiddle from under his strong chin. He slowly opened his eyes as if waking from a deep, blissful sleep. His pale, teal eyes greeted her orange pupils swimming in tears. Clotilda sniffled as she rubbed her small hands over her eyes to clear them of her tears before she smiled and softly clapped at him. The man bowed his head before giving her a charming smile.

"It's not often that I encounter a child drawn to the Fossegrim's song," he spoke with a deep but gentle voice that reflected the soothing waters of a flowing creek.

Clotilda was in awe. She remembered stories from the female musicians in her village about male spirits called Fossegrims, who were the embodiment of music and lived in water. Seeing this man before her as one of the legendary musical spirits was exciting!

"Your music is wonderful," she said as she smiled at him.

"Are you a musician yourself?" he asked curiously.

"No. But I always wanted to learn to play music," she said sincerely.

"I can teach you if that is what you wish."

"You mean it?" she asked as she felt excitement bursting like a geyser.

"Of course. In payment, I wish for you to bring me food."

"Food?" she echoed. "Are you sure?"

"Yes. Food is my only payment," he politely nodded to her.

Clotilda excitedly rushed back home, as fast as her short legs could carry her, to find food to give the handsome Fossegrim in exchange for his musical teachings. She didn't know what food he would like, and he didn't say his favorite meals either. She didn't know how to cook yet and decided to give him something simple.

Clotilda returned to him with a small basket of berries and freshly cooked bread from her house. She hoped he would like it and it would be enough for him to teach her the art of music.

Clotilda kept her fingers crossed and watched nervously as the Fossegrim plucked each berry with his nimble fingers and popped them into his mouth before biting into the warm bread roll. She held her breath as she watched him eat, dreading that he would vomit the food in disgust. Would he get angry and never return if she gave him food he didn't like?

"Your offering will do," he said with a smile, wiping the juice and crumbs from his lips with the back of his hand. "I'll start teaching you the basic lessons on reading and writing melodies. Also, I'll teach you how to play the harp or the violin. It's your choice."

"Well . . . I have always wanted to play the piano, but I would also like to learn how to play the harp. But I need to get one first," she said as she glanced back at her village.

"You may use mine until you acquire your harp," he said as he waved his hand over the crystal surface of the water. Ripples and waves gently morphed up to form the transparent silhouette of a lyre. Clotilda looked in amazement at the aquatic musical instrument. The lyre's shape was smooth and graceful, like a rolling wave, and looked as if it were skillfully carved from ice. She hesitantly reached for the lyre only to recoil her hands back, fearing the thought of breaking it. The Fossegrim smiled before he gently gripped the small harp and brought it to her. "It's all right. It won't reject you," he reassured her.

She timidly reached for the lyre again and gently gripped it.

"It's beautiful," she said as she marveled at it.

"It will serve you well, as it did for me. Play this until you have one of your own," he smiled at her as he transformed his violin into a giant harp. "Now, let's begin your first lesson."

Clotilda's musical skills grew over the six years of her teachings with the Fossegrim. Music called out to her, she learned how to write notes, and her ears became acute to sounds of good and bad pitches.

She was gifted a piano and standing harp by her mother and father for one of her birthdays, and she practiced playing music after every lesson. Finally, she was learning to become a musician—one of her dreams, along with becoming a guard when she grew up.

Clotilda hurried to the lagoon to bring a basket of rice rolls her mother had made to her teacher. Her chest bubbled with excitement as she looked forward to learning something new from him, but she was sad, for it was her final music lesson with him!

She greeted the Fossegrim as she reached the lagoon and placed the basket on the shore as an offering. He ate the rolls, humming in contentment for the tasty meal, before turning his attention back to her.

"You are very passionate about the art of music despite your young age," he said as he placed the empty basket on the ground. "You are my finest student, and I have an offer for you."

"An offer?" she asked.

"Normally, I wouldn't offer anyone this unless they brought me food that suited my standards. But you, Clotilda, I admire your musical devotion, and I think you deserve it." He carefully held his cherished violin to her as if he were holding a newborn child. "Play your best on my violin and continue playing even when your fingertips begin to bleed. Once your blood cloaks the taut strings of the violin, your soul and my musical talents will be intertwined. You'll become one of the best musicians of Nortamia."

Clotilda felt her heartbeat rapidly like a hummingbird's wings and the temptation of instantly becoming a master musician called to her like a toy she had always wanted. But as much as she was intrigued by his offer, she politely shook her head.

"Thank you for your offer, but I want to find my fingerprint in music," she said as she placed both hands over her chest. "I think it's in here somewhere, and I want to incorporate what you taught me and use it to excel."

A proud, fatherly smile spread on his lips.

"You are a true musician. You have faith in your natural gift for music, which will take you far," he said, gently placing his hand on her shoulder. She could feel the fabric of her brown-sleeved shirt become wet from his touch, but she paid no heed to it, smiling up at him, hopeful by his words. "Continue to create music, and don't hesitate to share your gift. Your music is a hum, but soon it will grow into an orchestra."

Clotilda's smile beamed as she heard his inspiring words. She tearfully watched as her faithful music teacher finished with a farewell bow before sinking into the lagoon's waters.

Clotilda felt the memories of that day vanish from her sight, and she looked back at the water in the fountain. A smile spread on her face as she watched the ripples as if she could sense her teacher's presence in them. She suddenly felt a deep desire to play some music now.

She looked around the garden, seeing people walking through the market behind the trees. Coralina was still grazing on the delicate blades of grass, and messenger squirrels were nibbling on fallen berries from the food stands. She wanted to play her music, but the thought of strangers hearing her caused her to pause. She had never played out of her house before and made sure the windows and doors were closed and shut to prevent the melodies from escaping.Yet as much as she was shy about sharing her music, she couldn't wait to return to her house to play. Her veins sang, her fingers longed to touch the piano keys, and her heart beat with her inner melody.

Mustering her courage, she waved her right hand, summoning Universeel from the confines of her hand chain. She sat up straight as she positioned Universeel beside her like a giant harp, and the gems morphed into piano keys. She timidly glanced at the market, knowing that some people would hear her, but she pushed her worries away, firmly held Universeel with her left hand, and placed her right hand over the piano keys. Her fingers hovered over the transparent, purple, and pink jeweled keys before taking deep breaths to soothe her nervousness.

She smelled the scent of flowers from the garden and heard the harmonious melody in her mind, and her love for music coursed through her like her own blood. She allowed her fingers to land on the keys tenderly, resonating with the singing melody of the instrument. Clotilda's fingers moved independently, plucking her weapon's harp strings and her hands dancing over the keys like moonlight over the ocean surface. Her body swayed side to side, her hair waving like kelp ribbons. She closed her eyes as she lost herself to her creative sanctuary, playing a song about the Fossegrim and his teachings—a tribute to him.

People of different species, young and old, mortal and immortal, came toward Clotilda as if under a siren's song. She felt one with nature and her music, unaware of the people around her. She finished the song about her teacher, and a new piece bloomed in her heart and mind as soon as she thought of Cyril.

A new melody stemmed through her dancing fingers. She was lacing a new song that resembled what she thought of Cyril. Her fingertips felt like they had transformed into claws as she tapped over the deeper tunes of the bottom keys. She was mirroring the heavy steps of a lion, causing the bottom of her palms to tap against her weapon's smooth surface, and her fingers rolled over the keys, resembling a lion's deep roar.

"Wasting time with music again," Bandus said as he sat beside her, ripping Clotilda from her musical trance.

Clotilda gasped from being startled. Her dancing fingers recoiled from the keys as if they bit her, and the strings threatened to snap as her fingers ripped sharply through them, causing them to yelp. She regained herself and quickly clenched Universeel to stop it from falling to the ground. She gave the mage a powerful glare as she felt her racing heart return to its average pace.

"Bandus, I've asked you often not to bother me while I'm playing music."

"It's just some annoying noises," he said with a shrug, void of remorse.

Clotilda saw red. Her veins roared with anger at the insult, and she wanted to punch him in the nose or kick him between the legs. But as much as she wanted to, she restrained herself.

Her anger faded when she looked around at the people she didn't know were there glaring at him. She saw how Bandus cringed and rubbed the back of his neck as the air filled with whispers of how he rudely interrupted her.

Clotilda shyly sank her head to her shoulders, and a blush spread to her ears when she realized how large the group was. Children clapped at her, leading the rest of the people to follow suit.

"Your music is quite exquisite, my lady," a male Lazarus elf bard said as he held his lute and music books.

"Thank you," Clotilda said politely as she stood up and smiled.

Bandus didn't make eye contact with the crowd and placed his hand on her shoulder to draw her attention from her audience.

"Shall we go or not?" he asked sternly.

"Sure . . . let's go," she said as she reluctantly banished Universeel into her hand chain and followed him, waving farewell to her listeners as they made their way out of the gardens.

CHAPTER 10

The Jewelry Store

Collections of clothing, jewelry, musical instruments, and potion bottles were in the shops' display windows as Clotilda and Bandus walked along the market. She stopped as they walked past the large window of a toy shop with a display of hand-carved dolls and plush animals looking back at her. She smiled as she looked at the elf dolls, especially the male one sitting on a wooden throne with a sword and shield in his hands—a warrior king who resembled the doll companion from her childhood, Anstice.

"Stop acting like a child, Clo! You are far too old for dolls," Bandus scolded her as he stopped and looked back at her disapprovingly.

"I'm just looking at them," she glared.

"Sure," he said in a sarcastic tone. Then, he turned around and pointed to a shop across from the jewelry store near them. "Let's go into the blacksmith's shop. I need a new staff since my old one is getting worn down."

Clotilda followed his finger to the shop he was pointing at and then looked at him with one of her eyebrows arched.

"Don't they usually have a wide selection at the Airavata's sorcerer academy? Blacksmiths usually have swords and maces but not very many staffs. Besides, you know as well as I that we elves can't touch anything made of iron," she replied, feeling the scar on her cheek starting to burn from phantom pains.

"I know that!" he snapped at her. "I don't want to walk to the other side of the capital to the academy! Unlike you, I don't have a weapon hand chain, and I struggled to use one before, remember?"

Clotilda let out a frustrated sigh at his outburst. Of course she remembered.

Despite Bandus wanting to become a mage, he struggled with specific spells and magical items even as a child. When she tried to help and teach him how to use a hand chain, he would snap at her and blame her for his struggles. In spite, he attempted to steal her hand chain, but she was able to stop him. Her hand chain was too important to her since it bore the gem that Cyril gave her.

Bandus's rude stubbornness hadn't changed since they were children, and if he wanted something, he wouldn't change his mind—a trait of his that she was never fond of.

"All right, let's check it out for a while," she replied flatly.

The stubborn mage smiled triumphantly and placed his hand on her back, and they made their way across the street toward the blacksmith's shop.

Walking through the shop entrance, Clotilda was greeted by the potent smell of ash, steam, and smoke from the giant forge. The shop's dome-shaped walls were decorated with displays of iron maces, shields, swords, and battle axes. Each one was well-cared for and made with the finest craftsmanship. She was fascinated by the artistry of each weapon, but she kept her hands and arms close to herself. Even with the protection of her gloves, her skin itched uncomfortably, knowing that one touch from any of the iron pieces would cause severe pain.

Bandus made a beeline to a small selection of wooden staffs on display and held one up for inspection.

"This is a surprise," a feminine voice spoke up behind the counter, causing both the elves to turn to see a female Fire Jotnar. The Jotnar blacksmith stood fourteen feet tall, the same height as Ignis. She was strongly built and had a slender hourglass figure. She wore a heavily armored chest guard, matching gloves, and boots decorated with golden scales tarnished from her hard work in the forge. Her long, red hair was pulled back in a low ponytail that grew to her feet and pooled on the ground like a magma waterfall. She had glowing yellow eyes, and a constellation of freckles dotted her cheekbones. "I don't normally have elves here in my shop. My name is Eltana. What can I help you with?" she asked politely.

"I'm looking for a new staff, and I saw that you have some in your shop," he said.

"Pardon my observation, but don't you elves wear hand chains? I notice you're not wearing one," Eltana said as she looked at his wrists.

"Yes, that. I can't use one. So you can thank her for that," he nodded his head at Clotilda, which caused her to glare back at him.

"What kind of staff are you looking for, sorcerer?" Eltana asked, almost displeased by his rudeness.

"Well, I need a sturdy staff for when I go into battle," he said flirtatiously.

Clotilda arched one of her eyebrows at him as he stared back at her as if observing her reaction. She could tell he was seeing if she would get jealous of his flirting with Eltana. She didn't feel anything of the sort. Why should she be jealous of someone as if they were property? She shook her head and returned to looking at the weapons.

"Ah, a battle mage, huh? Well, I have some staffs that I've made recently from some of the strongest wood from the timber foragers," the blacksmith said as she walked over to her selection of staffs and held one up for him to see. "This one I made specifically for battle mages such as yourself. It's easy to channel your magic through and can defend against a sword."

Clotilda broke her gaze from Bandus and Eltana, allowing them to continue their conversation, and glanced at the racks of daggers on the wall beside her. She studied the iron blades, making sure to stand a far enough distance from them. She saw her reflections in the blades, seeing the scar on her left cheek. She felt like she was swallowing a knot in her throat, and her eyes shakily looked at one of the daggers, whose design looked terrifyingly familiar. Memories clouded her vision, taking her back to that day of the destruction of Cygnus.

The village was engulfed in fire, and a thick plume of smoke blotted out the morning sun. The young Clotilda's body was in anguish. Her throat was raw from coughing, and her skeleton groaned from the newly written rune markings imprinted on her bones.

She felt the air rush out of her lungs like a gust, and the cold, jagged shards of rocks prickled her back and crown as she was pinned to the ground. A deformed silhouette of a being hidden in the smoke, who smelled of rotten flesh, towered over her, pinning her down with the blade of an iron dagger pressed against her throat.

"Wretched child," he yelled scornfully with booming anger. "Give me the Deity of Lazarus!"

"I can't," she screamed as tears spilled down her cheeks. "I can't let you have the Deity of Lazarus! It's important to my people . . . !"

"Silence!" he roared with rage, pressing the dagger into her neck. She shrieked from the pain of the iron, its touch burning her throat, and her blood dripping down her neck and pooling to her collarbone. "You made a big mistake by taking it away from me! Now I will steal it from you by peeling the flesh from your bones!" He removed the dagger from her throat and pointed it to her temple.

Clotilda screwed her eyes tightly shut. She was going to die! At age ten, her life would be over, stolen by an unknown enemy who desired the power within her. She wanted to protect the Deity of Lazarus from this monster, but she failed! She thought of Cyril, and tears spilled down her cheeks as she realized she would never see him again. She would die with her people. But if she were resurrected by her natural ability of being half Lazarus, she and the rest of the Lazarus elves, including her father, would decay from the guilt of not being able to protect their loved ones and see the bodies of the Airavata elves around their ruined village, one of the bodies being her mother.

"No! Get away from her!" a deep male voice roared through the inferno.

An adult male elf grabbed her attacker's wrist, trying to pull the dagger away from her. Clotilda couldn't see her savior through the smoke, but something about his voice sounded familiar.

"Stop getting in my way," her attacker hissed as both men struggled, the dagger lowering to her supple, tear-stained cheek. She saw a flash of malice in her attacker's gaze as he jerked his wrist free from her protector and stabbed the dagger through her left cheek.

Clotilda screamed in agony, feeling the dagger barely grazing the top of her molars and nearly slicing her tongue. Iron and copper tainted her taste buds, and she almost choked on her blood.

"How dare you!" her savior roared as he ripped her attacker off, and the two men brawled.

Clotilda whimpered as she pulled the dagger out of her cheek and coughed out blood as she sat up. The world around her was numb and she could barely hear and see, only feeling the blood spilling from her mouth and the opening in her stinging cheek. She reached for the gem in her waist pack, clenching it in her small, trembling palm, picturing a weapon in her mind—a weapon of a harp, a piano, a staff, and an axe, sharing the same color as the gem and decorated with purple and pink jewels that resembled the beads of her bracelets and necklace. The name she would give her weapon was Universeel—a gift from Cyril so she could protect those around her.

She hurried to the fighting men, hearing her hero cry out in pain as her attacker bit into the junction of his neck. She held her weapon as steady as possible and swung it, striking her enemy's face. Universeel's blade sliced through the flesh of his rotten cheek and mouth and tore through the bottom of his earlobe until it hung as it threatened to fall off . . .

Clotilda snapped awake from the painful memory, throwing her hand over her scarred cheek. She couldn't remember all that happened next, but it was too painful to dig deeper into her thoughts, for it would lead to the memory of her mother and father's deaths. She exhaled shakily, looking over to see Bandus and Eltana still conversing. She glanced at the iron daggers again with a tremble before turning around and hastily leaving the shop.

Relief bloomed in her chest when she stepped outside and looked around to see where she could go. Her gaze rested on the music shop she had seen earlier. A smile spread on her face as she wondered if she could get new journals and music sheets.

"Excuse me, my lady," Clotilda heard a male voice call out, preventing her from taking another step toward the music shop. She looked in the direction of the voice until she saw a brown-cloaked, hooded male elf standing at the front entrance of the jewelry store. "May I interest you in some of my wares? I have the finest jewelry you will not find in any other store here."

Clotilda narrowed her eyes as she noticed the teal skin under his hood and his red hair, the color of wine framing his lower face and neck—a Seax elf. The thought of seeing the Graffias Assassin last night made her wary. He wasn't wearing a gray cloak but could be a Graffias in disguise. If he was, she needed to find out.

"I don't see why not," she replied politely with a shrug as she approached the jewelry shop.

"Ladies first," he said as he bowed graciously to welcome her inside as she stood before the door.

Clotilda thanked him as she walked inside and acted as relaxed as possible. Her body tensed up as she heard him follow her into the shop, getting ready to call Universeel in defense. But luckily, he didn't shut the door, and he didn't attack her.

Clotilda explored the jewelry display, occasionally holding a necklace to her neck, pretending to be shopping, and using the mirror to watch the shopkeeper sitting behind the counter. There were no traps in the shop, hidden assassins, or the Graffias Manticore. The shopkeeper seemed innocent enough, but there was an aura of mischief radiating from him.

"You have fine taste in jewelry, my lady," he broke the silence, and she noticed he was eyeing her hand chain. "Where did you buy that bracelet?"

"I made this," she said as she held up her wrist to show him.

"You made it?" he asked in surprise.

"Yes, I did," she said bashfully. "I usually make my jewelry, but I like coming to stores like this one to get inspiration and buy something if it catches my eye."

"I'm impressed with your craftsmanship. You did a beautiful job with it."

"Thank you," she smiled at him.

"You're very polite, my lady," he said with a smile beaming under the hem of his hood. "May I ask what your name is?"

"Sure. My name is Clotilda, but you can call me Clo for short."

"Clotilda, you say? Lovely name," his smile widened. He reached under the counter, causing the muscles in her body to tense as she readied herself to summon her weapon. He rose from behind the counter, holding a porcelain treasure chest-shaped box, and opened it carefully. "Since you've been a polite and kind customer, I want to show you this special jewelry that has arrived in my shop."

With curious caution, the commander slowly walked over. She stood across from the counter and leaned forward slightly to see what the shopkeeper had to show her. He slid the box to her. Inside was an elegant hand chain with lion heads carved from the purest rose gold and holding a pink gem that resembled the one she had.

Her gaze froze abruptly as she saw something that demanded her immediate attention. The links and the loop to wrap around the finger were rows of pink and purple beads. She gently brushed her gloved fingertips over the beads, recognizing them as the same ones she used to have on her jewelry when she was a little girl.

"It . . . can't be," she said softly.

"So what do you think?" he asked.

She looked up from the bracelet at him. She was still a little shocked at the sight of the beads. Could Cyril be here in Streng?

"I think . . . I think it's stunning. Whoever created it did amazing work," she replied as she regained her voice.

"Would you like to try it on?"

"Um, sure. Why not," she said as she carefully grabbed the bracelet from him, put it on her left hand, and slipped the loop around her index finger. She twisted her hand around to see what it looked like before she stared at the lions with their swirling manes and purple gemstone eyes. "I think the lions are my favorite part of this entire bracelet," she smiled as she brushed her finger over them. "It kind of reminds me of a boy I once knew."

"You don't say?"

"I'm sorry," she said embarrassingly, placing the hand chain back into the box. "I didn't mean to chatter like that."

"Don't be. You're a delight to talk to. However, I have a question for you, if you don't mind?"

"What's the question?" she asked hesitantly as she prepared herself for whatever he would ask.

"It's nothing too personal. But . . . are you married?"

The question took her a little by surprise. It wasn't new to her since some of the men she had previously met over the years had asked her the same question when they were interested in her. She would answer this one personal question but wouldn't go any further. She still needed to be careful.

"No, I'm not," she shook her head. "I haven't found the right man to be my husband. I'm still waiting for him."

"Oh, I see. I saw you with that mage earlier, and I wasn't sure if he was your husband or lover."

"Ew, no," she cringed, making him laugh. "He wants to be romantically involved with me, but I don't want to."

"Does he know that?" he asked after he stopped laughing.

"I told him many times, but he never listened," she said with a deep sigh. "Anyway, are you married?"

"I almost was," he said softly. "But she died before we could make our vows."

"I'm sorry," she said sadly. "Um . . . how much for the bracelet?" she smiled once more as she tried to change the subject.

"It's a gift from the artist who made it," he said as he returned the smile and held the box to her. "He told me to give it to someone special, and that would be you."

"What?" she asked as she stared back at him like an owl. She had never been given a gift from a shop before, especially from a jeweler. Something seemed off, and she started feeling very uncertain. "Are you sure?"

"Sincerely!" he nodded.

Clotilda glanced down at the hand chain once more. The deity within her brushed against the inside of her ribs, drawn to it just as much as she was. Clotilda couldn't think of leaving the bracelet here. She needed to make sure Cyril was indeed the one who made it.

"I'll take good care of it," she said with a smile as she accepted the gift.

"I'm sure he will appreciate that. I hope to see you soon."

"Likewise. May I ask what your name is?" she asked as she carefully picked up the box.

“My name is Doric,” he said with a bow, not hesitating to give her his name, and Clotilda could sense he wasn’t lying.

“Doric,” she echoed. “I’ll see you next time, and thanks again,” she said as she headed toward the door.

“Take care,” he said with a wave.

Clotilda stopped by the shop’s entrance as she carefully held the box. The sight of the beads made hope swell in her veins. She opened the box and saw the gem and the beads blinking at her in the sunlight. Her fingers tenderly gripped the jewelry, debating whether to slip it on or wait until she returned home.

“Fun to browse around, isn’t it,” a male voice spoke.

“For sure . . . ah!” Clotilda cried out in surprise and jumped when she saw Bandus leaning against the doorframe of the jewelry shop with his new staff in hand. She slipped the box into her pack and planted her hand on her chest to ease her startled heart. She turned to see Bandus with an annoying wide grin on his face. “Don’t do that,” she scolded him. “That’s twice already that you gave me a scare! Give me a reason why I shouldn’t hit you with Universeel.”

“Nah, you wouldn’t do that to me.”

“I probably would,” she muttered through her clenched teeth.

“So why did you walk out on me?” he asked, pushing himself away from the door.

“You looked like you were having a great time exploring and talking to the Eltana, so I decided to head out,” she said with a shrug.

“Were you jealous back there?” he asked with a smirk.

“No, I wasn’t,” she said as she crossed her arms.

Bandus’s grin dropped, and he went silent as he stared at her. She raised one of her eyebrows at his sudden silence. She was ready to ask him what it was when he spoke again. This time he was stern, with no trace of an annoying joking tone.

"Do you just see me as an acquaintance?"

Clotilda's eyes widened at the sudden question before she frowned. She sighed softly and tried to tell him the same answer she had given him for years.

"Yes," she replied honestly.

"What's holding you back?" he asked, his brows knitting together into a frown.

"What do you mean?"

"Just tell me!" he said more sharply.

"I haven't found the right man yet."

"So I'm not the right man for you," he said as he threw his arms open in frustration.

"Can we please not talk about this?" she asked as calmly as she could.

Afraid that someone would hear them, she walked around to the back of the jewelry shop with Bandus following close behind her.

"No! I want to know why you don't see me as more than an acquaintance!"

Clotilda balled her hands into fists. She wanted him to calm down but knew he wouldn't listen to her even if she asked him to. His yelling radiated in her chest, irritating the Deity of Lazarus within her. It hissed and pushed against her ribcage until it felt like her bones were about to splinter. She pressed her hands to her chest, hoping to keep it at bay. She must keep the deity hidden!

"I like you, Clo! Why can't you see that?" Bandus yelled.

"I can't return your feelings," she said through clenched teeth.

"Is it because of some boy you met years ago?" he asked sharply, causing rage to boil inside her for how rudely he mentioned Cyril. "Well, you need to grow up! You're one hundred and forty years old! He's not coming, and he never will! He's just a stupid figment of your foolish imagination drunk with music!"

"How dare you say that about him," she snarled.

"Listen! You need . . . Clo," he paused when he heard her groan in pain. "What's wrong?" he asked as he tried to get near her.

Clotilda stepped away from him so he couldn't touch her.

"Stay away from me," she growled, her body trembling.

She wrapped her arms around herself, her bones burning like timber in a forest fire as glowing orange runes appeared on them. Bandus's eyes widened in horror. Rune markings spread over the curves of her shoulders, arms, jawline, fingers, ribs, legs, and hair strands. Her entire skeleton was a manuscript of glowing runes.

"Clo," he tried to reach out to her, but she turned away.

"I said stay away!" she warned.

Bandus roughly gripped her shoulder, ignoring her. Clotilda snapped her head toward him, her eyes glowing like a pair of suns, and an angry birdlike shrill escaped her throat. She spun around and threw a punch on the mage's cheek. Bandus grunted and stumbled back. Clotilda snarled as a glowing crack that looked like a fissure of lava framed with soft bristles of sprouting feathers opened on her chest.

"No," she hissed through her clenched teeth as she regained control. "Please . . . calm down! We can't let anyone know of you!"

Clotilda tried to fight it. She pushed her hands against her ribcage as if trying to shut it closed before the determined beast could escape.

To her relief, the growing fissure on her chest closed. The sprouting feathers molted from her body and transformed into ash as they touched the ground. The glow of her eyes and the rune markings faded away.

"You're a Rune," Bandus said as he stared at her.

"I am," she said, narrowing her brows at him. "I became a Rune to protect the deity of my people from the one who killed them." She paused as she brushed her hand over the scar on her left cheek.

"Why didn't you tell me?"

"Because I don't trust you," she said, causing him to look at her as if he had been punched again. "I tried to keep it hidden from you, my troops, the royal family, everyone here. All except for Rose Hip and Stump. They are the only ones I trust with this secret."

She allowed her hands to fall from her chest, her right palm glowing as gentle blue magic pulsed within it as she cast a spell.

"This isn't the first time I explained this to you, and it won't be the first time I had to erase your memory!" Clotilda growled.

"You what . . . !" he was cut off by Clotilda's hand that gripped his forehead, and her palm pressed roughly to his lips, gagging him.

"It's safer that no one else knows I'm a Rune. If word spreads . . ." she hesitated for a moment. ". . . he might come and destroy the lives here, just like he did to my village all those years ago. I can't let that happen again!"

Bandus's tense body relaxed as his memory of the discovery was erased. This was for the best. Not even a selfish fool like Bandus must know. Clotilda pulled her hand from his face. Bandus opened his eyes, looking like he had awoken from a daydream, and glanced at her with a mischievous smirk.

Clotilda knew the memory of her being a Rune would be lost in his mind, but his infatuation with her wouldn't. She tried to erase his memory for years to stop him from having this unhealthy crush on her, but it didn't work.

"Ran off on me, huh?" he spoke disrespectfully.

"I have to go," she said plainly as she turned to leave.

"Go?" he quickly ensnared her elbow, which made her anger spike. "But we just started! Now that I have my staff, how about you and I go to the taverns."

"Going out with you was a big mistake, and I've had enough!"

Clotilda noticed how the shopkeeper, Doric, was watching them. She hoped Doric couldn't hear what they were saying, but she feared he saw her Rune powers. She needed to erase his memories too. She hated the thought of doing it, but she didn't want anyone to be in danger because of her.

The commander ripped her arm from Bandus's grip. He tried to reach for her again, but she got away and sprinted toward the jewelry store. Clotilda walked inside the store and felt a chill when she saw that the shopkeeper was gone.

CHAPTER 11

The Princess's Desires

Clotilda hurried through the garden to escape Bandus and found Coralina curled up in a cluster of moss, with her head tucked under her left wing like a slumbering swan.

"Coralina," she whispered as she kneeled to the sleeping pegasus and gently patted her folded wing. Coralina stirred from her sleep before lifting her head from behind her wing and looking at Clotilda. "I'm sorry to wake you, my friend. It's time for us to return home."

Coralina snorted softly at her as she stood up and pressed her muzzle worriedly against Clotilda's cheek. Clotilda could see her steed sensing her anger and stress like a shark smelling blood in the water. She smiled and gently patted Coralina reassuringly before climbing onto the saddle.

Her reach for the reins halted when something landed on her shoulder. Clotilda recoiled her fingers and jerked her head to the side to see a messenger squirrel perched on her shoulder. The squirrel wore a golden bridle with purple and red diamonds with the royal family's crest on his chest strap. Anxiousness slithered through her blood like serpents as she opened the capsule of the squirrel's bridle and unrolled the scroll to reveal the king's bold but elegant handwriting.

> *I know the rumors of Battle Komodons, but I wasn't aware that the Graffias Assassins are here too. Come to my castle right now! There are some things I need to discuss with you about the Graffias Manticore and the safety of my daughter. Be here soon!*
>
> *King Thierry*

Clotilda rolled the scroll and slipped it into her waist pack before helping the squirrel back into the trees and grabbing the reins.

"We have a change of plan. Let's make our way to the castle!" Clotilda snapped the reins. Coralina neighed in response as she galloped out of the gardens and opened her wings as she took flight.

The cool air blew through the commander's long hair, whipping the locks against her ears as she and Coralina flew. She looked down to the ground, seeing the ant-size citizens and the village rooftops of the market below. Clotilda guided her steed toward the castle, and they gracefully glided down to the courtyard. Coralina galloped as soon as her feet touched the ground and slowed to a halt.

"I'll be back soon," Clotilda said as she dismounted from the saddle and ran up the grand staircase, feeling Coralina's gaze on her before she opened one of the giant double doors of the castle and entered.

Clotilda walked down the large, marble hallways, seeing the rows of tapestries hung evenly on the walls as she made her way to the throne room. She charted her way through the crowd of busy servants and scaled the purple carpet as it guided her up the stairs to the majestic thrones.

Pacing back and forth was King Thierry with his long, golden cape dragging behind him. He turned his stern gaze to her as she approached.

Clotilda kneeled before him and lowered her head so she wouldn't make eye contact with him.

King Thierry always found it insulting whenever she looked him in the eye, and he scolded her whenever she did—telling her that a lowborn like her should never make eye contact with him. She hated his ego but drew a quiet breath as she restrained her irritation. She didn't come here to pick a fight or start an argument. The safety of her family and friends was more important.

"I came as soon as possible, Your Majesty," she said.

"I can see that," he said flatly. "I have something important for you to do. I'm worried for my daughter's safety and believe the Graffias Manticore is coming to collect her. This is why I need you to be her bodyguard."

Clotilda tried to mask her distaste. Being a babysitter to the spoiled princess would be a challenging task. The realization that it was her new orders irritated her.

Princess Malvolia was never easy to be around and was not the kindest. But what else could she do? Orders were orders. Clotilda could not refuse King Thierry's orders without getting executed for treason. And if she were to be put to death, then the Deity of Lazarus would be revealed. As much as she didn't want to be the bodyguard to the princess, she took the higher road, hiding any signs of refusal on her face.

"As you wish, Your Majesty," she replied.

"Good. I can't trust my daughter with any of my male knights because she will distract them. As much as it bothers me to say this, you're one of the finest female guards I have, and you are quite good at obeying orders, I'll give you that." Clotilda kept her gaze locked down to the violet carpet, fighting the urge to lift her head to the king as she heard him approaching.

She flinched slightly as she felt his index finger under her chin. The cold golden metal of his gauntlet caused an unpleasant shiver to slither down her spine. He tilted her head, forcing her to make eye contact with him. Clotilda fought the urge to twist her chin from his grasp, hating that she could feel his piercing eyes burning through her gaze and probing her soul.

"But I warn you. If you fail to protect my precious daughter, your punishment will be death," he said lowly.

"I understand, Your Grace," she said calmly, trying to hide her anger.

"Good. You may have died when I first met you. But a Lazarus elf, even a hybrid like you, can't come back to life a second time." The king pulled his hand away from under her chin and straightened his posture. "There will be a masquerade ball to celebrate my daughter's birthday tonight. Keep your guard up and your eyes open for the Manticore. Do you have an animal mask?"

"I do," she said with a nod. "It's a wolf mask."

"Good. The masquerade ball is animal-themed. Don't be late!"

"I'll make sure I'm not," she replied before standing up.

Clotilda was relieved to be away from King Thierry's presence after he dismissed her, but she dragged her feet as she made her way to the princess to inform her of the task of being her bodyguard.

After traversing through the labyrinth of halls, Clotilda finally came to Malvolia's bed chamber, lifting her closed hand to the wooden door and softly knocking on it.

"Who is it?" the princess snootily called from behind the door.

"It's the commander. May I have a word with you?" she politely asked.

"You may," she granted her permission in a flat tone.

Clotilda softly shook her head before grabbing the golden door handle and opening it. She walked in to see the princess sitting at her vanity and combing through her hair. She stared at the princess's hair that perfectly matched hers. It had grown long from the shoulder-length hair back when they were children.

The scissors on the princess's vanity table caused Clotilda to reach behind her back and grasp her hair. The thought of them near her locks again made her feel nauseous.

Clotilda grew her hair to match the same length as her blood mother's ankle-length hair, and it was a tradition for Airavata elves to have long hair to represent the slithering tentacles of the Kraken. Growing her hair took a long time, and she didn't want it to be short again!

The royal gardens outside the castle and the calls of swans drew Clotilda from the orphanage. Despite her fever and the leaf bandage over her left cheek to hide the healing stab wound, she wanted to see and feed the swans. She missed seeing swans and the golden peacocks that used to live in Cygnus before they fled during its destruction. She grabbed a roll of bread from the kitchen, made sure no one saw her before leaving the orphanage, made her way toward the castle, and climbed over the garden wall.

Clotilda was mesmerized by the beauty of the royal garden. She walked along the jeweled mosaic paths, enjoying the rich fragrance of the flowers and berries and ducking behind the bushes whenever she heard guards walking by. She approached the swans as they swam in the pond, ripped small crumbs from the bread she brought, and began feeding the elegant birds.

Bushes suddenly rustled loudly from the other side of the pond. The flowering branches snapped open as three small trolls appeared, one female and two males, lean and spindly like giant spiders. Their skin was gray like stone, and they had piercing red eyes. They stood five feet tall, the same height as Clotilda, and they charged toward the pond, armed with rocks and sticks, and started throwing them at the swans.

"Castle trolls!" Clotilda shrieked as she threw her hands on her head and frantically looked around for something to use as a weapon, mentally scolding herself for forgetting to bring her hand chain before she left. She grabbed a long stick from the ground and charged toward them. "I'm going to get you for hurting them!" she called out angrily as she fought them off.

Clotilda held the branch like a sword, swatting the trolls with it, and struck them on the heads to stop the fiends from hurting the frightened birds. The trolls retaliated by charging at her. She barely dodged their attacks before one of the trolls kicked her in the stomach, tossing her behind one of the flowering bushes.

Clotilda landed back-first into the ground. The soft soil cushioned her fall. A sharp gasp escaped her lips as the pain in her lower right torso intensified from the troll's kick. She eased the spot with her hands gently pressed against it, cringing as she saw the capped hoods of the trolls over the green plumages of the bushes as they began searching for her.

"Bah! Where did that little brat go?" one of the male trolls grunted as he and his comrades looked around.

Clotilda fearfully crawled back, hoping to hide from the trolls, until she felt her back bump into something. She clasped her hands over her mouth to muffle her gasp before slowly turning her head around to see an old, elven shield protruding halfway out of the ground like a tombstone. She marveled at the beauty of the golden shield that had a crown of moss on top of it. She guessed it had been there for centuries before the elves created the weapon hand chains.

Glancing up at the gray-and-purple plumage of clouds overhead, Clotilda grinned as she thought of a plan.

"Trolls are afraid of thunder," she muttered as she crawled behind the shield and positioned her legs behind it. She bent her knees until they pressed against her chest and pulled down the shield to bend it slightly like a bow. Then, with solid kicks, the shield billowed deep rumbling sounds like thunder. The castle trolls froze in place, their ears perking to the clashing sound, and they looked up to the sky in panic. Clotilda kicked the shield again, causing it to rumble louder. She smiled as she watched the trolls panic, scurry back into the bushes, and disappear.

With the threat gone, Clotilda emerged from the bushes, watching with a smile as the swans returned, and she resumed feeding the last of the bread to them in peace.

"You there!" a girl's voice called out. Clotilda panicked. She knew she wasn't supposed to be here! If the guards saw her, she would be in big trouble! She spotted a nearby marble bench and ducked underneath it. "It's okay! You

can come out from under there! I'm not going to call the guards," she heard the voice again.

Clotilda peeked from beneath the bench and saw an elf girl looking down at her from the balcony leading to a ballroom. The girl was a Dominus elf who looked like she was around nine or ten years old and had short, rose-gold, blonde hair.

"I'm sorry I trespassed," Clotilda called out. "I just wanted to see the swans!"

"Don't be! I can see that they like you, and thank you for saving them from those horrible trolls! Besides, my name is Princess Malvolia! What's your name?"

The princess's polite words and kind smile put Clotilda at ease, and she emerged from under the bench.

"My name is Clotilda! Are you mad about me being here?"

"Not at all! I've wanted to have another elf girl around my age to play with."

"To play with? You want to be friends?"

"Of course! I don't have siblings, and it gets lonely here in the castle."

"But I'm a commoner. Are you okay with being my friend?"

"It doesn't matter to me! Come in! I have a fun game for us to play!"

"Really? Great!" Clotilda cheered as she walked over to the staircase and climbed the steps.

Clotilda followed the princess happily down the hallways and up the spiral stairs to the castle's tallest tower, excited about the possibility of making a new friend.

"Right this way," Malvolia said as she welcomed Clotilda inside her bed chambers.

Clotilda's eyes widened in awe as she looked at the princess's collection of dolls and toys. Her room was beautiful! It had a giant bed with fluffy white blankets that looked soft and fun to jump on. A large wooden wardrobe was next to the bed, and a vanity with a huge mirror stood across from the door. Clotilda smiled excitedly but quickly groaned softly as the skin of her sore cheek stretched. She gently patted her hand on the bandage, wondering with dread if the wound started bleeding, but it didn't.

"Your room is gorgeous," Clotilda said as she dropped her hand from her cheek.

"Yes, it is! Now for our game! Let's you and I play dress up," the princess said with a smirk as she made her way to the wardrobe. Clotilda watched as she pushed various delicate gowns out of the way before pulling out a full, wide dress that was engulfed from head to toe with draping pink ribbons, blue flowers resembling giant pitcher plants, and purple gems the size of horse hooves. "This dress is my least favorite. So you wear this dress and these to hide your bird hands," the princess said as she handed her a pair of long, silk gloves.

"Um . . ." Clotilda said as she stared at the dress. The top part of the gown had oversized puffy sleeves with ribbons on them, and the bottom of the dress was so vast and round that she wondered how heavy it was. The thought of falling over to the side and being unable to get up worried her. How would she play with the princess wearing . . . this hideous abomination?"How am I going to get through a door?"

"You'll have to find a way. Try it on," Malvolia demanded as she handed the dress to her.

"Okay," Clotilda timidly grabbed the dress, shocked by the princess suddenly raising her voice.

Clotilda went behind the divider to put the dress on. She managed to slip it on and shuffled out, feeling ridiculous.

"It suits you," the princess snickered.

Clotilda felt her cheeks fume hot in embarrassment as she stared at the gown.

"It's too puffy," she said, patting her hands down on the sides of the dress.

"Oh, don't be silly. You look fine. Now let's get you finished," she said as she firmly grasped Clotilda's wrist, which caused the poor girl to wince, and

sat her down on the stool before the vanity. The princess stood beside her and removed the leaf bandage from Clotilda's cheek, her face morphing into disgust as soon as she saw the stab wound. "What an ugly scar!"

"It's ugly?" Clotilda asked in puzzled confusion as she looked at her reflection in the mirror. "I never thought of scars as being ugly."

"Yes, it is! But my magic should be able to hide it for a while." She punctuated her words as she cast her magic over the scar, which made it disappear.

Clotilda's eyes widened as she reached up to her cheek to feel the unmarked skin but recoiled it back as soon as she felt pain. "It's only temporary, but it should hide that hideous mark," the princess said behind her, grabbing Clotilda's long locks. "I'm impressed. You have the same hair color as mine."

"You're right. Our hairs almost look the same," Clotilda said happily as she glanced over her shoulder to the princess.

"Just like sisters," she replied, reaching into her drawer. "But I think it's a little too . . . long compared to mine," she said as she pointed at her shoulder-length hair. "We can make some adjustments."

"What do you mean . . ." her words turned into a sharp gasp when she heard a snip.

Clotilda looked into the mirror to see that her hip-length hair had been trimmed to her shoulders and saw the princess holding a pair of scissors while holding the severed locks.

"What are you doing?" she asked, mortified, as she stood abruptly, tipping the stool over and wrapping her hands around her now shortened hair.

"I cut your hair—so what? How can you pretend to be me if your hair isn't the same length as mine?"

"What are you talking about? I thought you wanted to be my friend."

"Ha! Did you honestly think I want to be friends with a peasant like you? I only needed a look-alike to take my place for today."

"Take your place for what?" Clotilda asked, feeling her eyes begin to well with tears.

"After taking these boring lessons daily, I'm quite sick of them! So I needed someone to fill in for me, and you will take my place."

"But . . ." she tried to say but was cut off.

"If you don't do it, I will tell the guards to throw you in the dungeon!"

Clotilda narrowed her brows and wanted to stand up to the royal brat's rudeness, but she held back her protesting words. Knowing she would invite trouble, she had no choice. She had to if she wanted to see her hobgoblin family and the orphans again.

"Okay. I'll do it," she said in defeat, regretting her decision to come here.

"Good. Now, go to the library and meet with the tutor."

Clotilda groaned painfully as she hunched over and pressed her hand under her stomach.

"Now what's wrong with you?" the princess snapped as she finished packing her purse.

"It's nothing," Clotilda pulled her hand away, trying to ignore the prickling pain.

"If you're so sad about your hair, it will grow back. Now be off with you, and don't let anyone know you are not me, or you'll regret it!"

"But where are you going?"

"I'm going out. You had your chance with trespassing in the garden, so it's my turn. Remember, if you tell anyone I'm gone, I'll ensure you'll be locked away forever!"

Clotilda bit her bottom lip until it almost bled as she opened the door to the bed chamber, glancing over her shoulder to see the princess sneaking out through the window and climbing down the prowling vines before she was out of sight. Clotilda sniffled sadly, walked out of the chamber, and closed the door behind her.

Even though the princess knew the commander had entered the room, she didn't bother turning to face her and only paid attention to her reflection.

"I've overheard my father asking you to protect me," Malvolia said flatly.

"Yes, he did. He wants to make sure you're safe," Clotilda replied.

"I don't need protection," the princess snapped. "I want the Graffias Manticore to come for me and take me away from here and my father," she said as she slammed her comb onto the vanity, causing the cosmetics and perfumes to topple over.

Clotilda watched as some of the perfume bottles fell to the ground and rolled toward her before bumping into the toes of her boots.

"If I may? Your father loves you. Why would you sacrifice that?"

"I shouldn't tell you what I want," she said as she finally turned to face her. "I'm not going to let anyone get in the way of my dream, including you! I know the Graffias Manticore will come for me! Wait, are you one of those crazed women who honestly believes the Manticore will come for you and make you his bride?" her words turned heavy with jealousy.

"It didn't cross my mind," Clotilda replied as she shook her head.

"That's good. I don't see any reason a king would be drawn to a lowly peasant like you with a revolting scar on her face!"

"You may think that, but I believe scars tell stories. They don't make someone ugly," she replied, knitting her brows into a glare.

"I'm through with talking to you!" she scoffed as she rolled her eyes. "Now go! I have to finish getting ready for the masquerade ball," she said as she returned to the mirror.

Clotilda sighed softly before she made her way back toward the door.

"Don't sacrifice what you have," she said, grasping the door handle. "You have everything from a home to a father who loves you. Don't take that for granted." She ended her speech before opening the door and leaving the princess's chambers.

CHAPTER 12

The Royal Disguise

Clotilda felt her temper cool as she walked away from the king and his daughter. However, she knew she would have to do her duty to protect the princess and be more patient than she had ever been before with the royal family.

She walked down the hallways, slowing down when she saw the giant double doors of the library. An excited smile spread on her lips as she gently pushed one of the doors open to see the six colossal bookshelves that reached the high ceiling, bloated with books and scrolls.

She walked toward the shelves, brushing her fingers on the engraved titles on the spines of the novels as she recognized some of her favorite books. One of the novels about the history of Nortamia attracted her attention and caused her to stop exploring. She hooked her fingertips over the novel's top and carefully pulled it off the shelf. She traced the book's title with her fingertips, remembering the first time she looked at it while masquerading as the princess.

Clotilda timidly opened one of the library doors with trembling hands. Her mouth fell agape to the towers of bookshelves, and her small chest fluttered excitedly at the numerous novels waiting to be read. Books were one of her favorite things in the world, and she remembered how her love for reading was born when she was learning to read music when the Fossegrim was teaching her. She wanted to run over to those shelves, take a bunch of books, and start reading them immediately!

"There you are, Your Highness."

Clotilda jolted in surprise and jerked her head toward where the high-pitched female voice was coming from. A small fairy the size of a pinkie finger stood on top of one of the wooden study desks. Her butterfly and beetle-shaped wings fluttered, causing the colors of her turquoise wings to be illuminated in the sunlight behind her like a stained-glass window. She had hip-length, teal hair that flowed behind her like waves of water, and she wore a knee-length veil dress resembling a fish's delicate fins.

The fairy was beautiful, with her soft face, fairy wing–shaped ears, and fair skin the color of seafoam, but Clotilda felt a wave of worry hit her when she saw that she had large purple bruises on her left leg and arm. Dread hit her. Who would hurt her like that?

"Come, Princess. We need to get started on your teachings," the fairy called out again, her voice dripping with hesitation.

At first, Clotilda didn't realize she was calling out to her until she remembered she was in disguise.

"Oh, coming," she replied timidly.

Clotilda quickly slipped sideways through the slightly open door with her wide gown and hurried to the study desk. She struggled to sit on the chair, roughly patting the dress flat to pull her chair closer to the table.

"Princess, what are you doing?" the fairy asked frustratedly as she flew over to Clotilda with her hands planted on the sides of her hips.

"I'm sorry. I'm not used to a puffy dress like this," she apologized as she pulled herself closer to the desk and rested her hands on the smooth wooden surface.

"By all means, Your Highness, wear a more appropriate dress that doesn't make you look like a mushroom. Besides, didn't you say you despise that dress?"

"I did?" she asked, her mind returning to the princess's warning. She had to ensure no one knew she was an imposter, or she would be thrown into the dungeon! But did that mean she had to act like the princess, too? To act mean? The thought of it made her feel like she was going to vomit. She was raised to treat others with respect and compassion. Kindness was a part of who she was. Being rude and mean was not one of them!

"Um . . . yes, but I guess it has some nice elements. I mean, the ribbons look pretty," she replied, trying to hide her nervousness and making her voice sound as princess-like as possible without losing politeness.

"I guess," the fairy said as she looked at her with an arched, teal eyebrow. "But let's not talk about it anymore. We should get started on your teachings," she insisted before flying to the other side of the study desk and standing on a stack of books. Clotilda looked worriedly at the fairy's bruises, her mind storming with questions as to what she went through to get such painful marks. "What is it, princess? You're staring."

"Mind my asking, but where did you get those bruises?" Clotilda asked, forgetting all about pretending to be someone she was not.

The fairy looked at her in confusion before hesitantly answering.

"You got angry with me yesterday during your lesson and swatted me with one of your books."

Clotilda felt sick, and a wave of emotional rage hit her like one of the castle trolls who kicked her earlier.

"That's horrible! Why would she . . . I mean, why would I do that? It's mean!"

"That bothers you?" the fairy asked, her eyes widening at the girl's emotional burst.

"Of course it does," she said as her voice broke, her eyes beginning to burn as a thin layer of tears welled in them.

Clotilda threw her hands over her eyes, unable to hold back the tears, not caring if anyone knew she wasn't Malvolia. The princess was crueler than she thought!

She felt a gentle, tiny hand on her fingers. She pulled her hands away to see the fairy smiling warmly at her, no longer nervous and frustrated.

"It's unlike Princess Malvolia to cry for one of her servant's injuries. But you needn't worry about me, sweet child. I may be small, but that doesn't mean I'm not strong. Now then, let us begin 'your' lesson for today."

"Sounds good . . . ah," she gasped in pain.

"Are you all right?" the fairy asked with worry.

"Yes, I am," she said as she bit her lip and gave the fairy a reassuring smile. "Sorry about that. I'm ready to begin, please," she said as she grabbed a quill pen and a stack of paper to take notes and gave her delighted teacher her full attention. "One more thing, is it all right if I ask what your name is?"

"My name is Turquoise," the fairy replied before she opened one of the history books and began the lesson.

Clotilda smiled as she looked at the book, remembering her first and last lesson at the castle.

"It's been so long since I last saw you here, Clotilda," a familiar voice pulled her from her thoughts.

The commander turned to see her fairy teacher flying behind her. Her beauty remained unfazed by time, and her teal hair flowed gracefully behind her.

"It has been a long time since we last met, Turquoise. It's good to see you again."

"You as well. Congratulations on your promotion to Commander of the Royal Guard."

"Thank you," she said with a grateful smile.

"So what brings you back to the royal library? Can I help you with anything, or are you exploring?"

"You know me, I love books, but I'm here because of an order from King Thierry. He's asked me to be his daughter's bodyguard," she said the last words as if she were going to swallow a worm.

"Uh, splendid . . ." Turquoise cringed.

"If I may, do you mind if I ask you something?"

"Of course not. What can I help you with?"

"I have questions about a warrior known as the Graffias Manticore. Can you tell me anything about him, or are there any books here that might have information about him?"

"Are you romantically fascinated by him as well? I don't blame you. He is quite intriguing," Turquoise asked with a smirk.

"I'm curious about him, but I still have feelings for someone else, and I've been waiting for him. Anyway, back to my question, how much do you know about the Graffias Manticore?"

"I'm afraid I have little knowledge of him."

"I see," Clotilda said softly, remembering the conversation between the Graffias Assassin and Acanthus last night. They mentioned that he was a gladiator who escaped from the Slachten Arena, and she couldn't help but wonder if he had something to do with a king dethroned one hundred and forty years ago.

"I'm sorry I couldn't tell you more about him," Turquoise said.

"No, it's all right. I'll go through my library when I return home," she said politely.

"That's a good idea. Hopefully, you can find the answers you are looking for."

"I hope so too," she said as she returned the book to the shelf. "Well, I better be on my way before the king gets angry at me for looking through his books again."

"All right. It was good seeing you again, Clotilda. Don't be a stranger," she said with a smile.

"You too," Clotilda said, turning toward the door but stopping midway. "Even though it was a brief time that you were my teacher, I learned a lot from you that day, and I thank you for sharing what you know with me," she glanced over her shoulder to the fairy and smiled at her.

"You're welcome, sweet child," Turquoise said warmly as she waved farewell.

Clotilda waved back before leaving the library.

Her high heels clicked against the smooth marble floor as she entered the ballroom.Clotilda politely excused herself as she walked past scrambling servants preparing for the ball and looked up at the glowing crystal overhead. She had long since memorized the fine details of the crystals, but back then, she could barely see it through her blurry vision and the intense pain when she was a child. She pressed her fingers to her lower torso and felt the scar through the fabric of her jumpsuit as she remembered that day—the day of her first death.

Clotilda stood on the open ballroom floor that looked like the calm surface of the ocean horizon. She sat on one of the benches, trying to push down her full gown as she tried to sit comfortably.

The tutoring with Turquoise was relaxing. She had a great time learning so much about the history and geography of Nortamia. But she didn't understand why the princess would find a class like that boring.

Clotilda met many tutors who taught her the peaceful art of flower arrangement, preparation for horseback riding when she reached her teenage years, and calligraphy writing.

Clotilda could sense that the tutors noticed her politeness and knew who she wasn't. She was surprised that no one called the guards on her, but after learning how they were either yelled at or hurt by Malvolia, it was pretty clear they didn't mind that they were teaching someone willing to learn, and they didn't seem to care where the princess was.

The lessons were fun for Clotilda. But her hunger for learning grew with the pain in her right side. It just wasn't stopping, and it was beginning to worry her.

Pearls of sweat rolled down Clotilda's cheeks. Her soaked bangs stuck to her forehead, which was on fire from the fever, and she feared she would vomit at any moment. But she had to hang in there! The last lesson for the day was ballroom dancing. A little time to sit down while waiting for the teachers gave her some relief, but the pain was steadily growing. She hoped to return to the orphanage soon and get help from Stump and Rose Hip.

The head royal chef, a male Eclipse dwarf named Duril, brought a tray of food from the kitchen and placed it on the table. Clotilda weakly glanced over at him curiously. He stood around four feet tall and was very handsome, clean-shaven, wore tribal-like clothing, and had crow's feet on the corners of his black and gold eyes that resembled a solar eclipse, showing cheerful years of smiling.

"My, it's a surprise to see the princess here on time for her dancing lessons," he said and then paused when he looked at Clotilda's face. "Are you all right there, Princess?" he asked, his teasing tone becoming concerned. "You look a little pale."

"I'm all right. Thank you," she smiled at him, causing the dwarf to nearly stumble from her polite and gentle words.

"Are you hungry?" he asked, regaining himself from shock. He plucked one of the cakes from the tray and held it to her. "It's freshly baked and made with a special recipe that my wife and I made."

The cakes looked so good and elegantly decorated with dripping chocolate and laced with tiny flower petals. But as much as Clotilda wanted to try one, she couldn't.

"I appreciate your offer, but no, thank you. I'm not feeling hungry right now."

"Okay. If you change your mind, please take one," he said as he returned the cake to the tray.

"Thank you . . ." she smiled, hoping her nausea would subside soon to try one of those delicious treats.

Three female elven tutors approached her with dragging feet, not looking forward to another struggle with teaching the princess how to dance. Clotilda slowly lifted her head and smiled as she saw the approaching teachers. The tutors narrowed their brows as they looked at her. They didn't look angry or bothered by her, but she could tell they probably noticed she wasn't feeling well.

"Princess? Are you all right," the lead teacher asked her as she kneeled to her.

"I'm fine. Thank you," Clotilda tried to reassure them.

"Are you sure?" the teacher wasn't convinced.

"Yes," she nodded as she stood up. "I'm ready to learn how to dance."

Clotilda fought the pain as she made her way to the dance floor. She listened carefully to their instructions, learning step by step. Even Duril came over to be her dance partner. She had fun dancing with him but apologized profusely when she stepped on his feet a few times. Despite having no experience with dancing, she loved it, and Duril was a great and patient dancer!

The joyful dancing stopped when she felt like the bones in her legs had transformed into water. Weakness overcame her, and pain shot through every root of her nerves. Her hold on the dwarf's strong but soft hands loosened, and her fingers slipped from his. Panicked voices surrounding her sounded like they were coming from underwater as she felt her strength leave her. Her legs and back met the marble floor, but her crown never touched it. Duril cradled her head with his large hands and kneeled beside her.

"Child, what's wrong?" he called out as he combed his fingers through her hair.

"It hurts . . ." she sobbed weakly as tears rolled down her cheeks.

Malvolia's spell hiding her scar faded to reveal the wound on her cheek.

"What hurts?" one of the worried tutors asked her.

"Down here," she replied, pressing her hand on her aching right side.

Duril placed his palm on her forehead, her skin cooling slightly from the contact of his touch.

"She has a terrible fever," he said as he glanced down at her lower body. His face morphed into horror at the sudden realization. "It must be her appendix!"

"Get her to a healer! Quickly!" the second female tutor said.

Duril quickly scooped up Clotilda, and he and the tutors hurried down the ballroom toward the healer's chambers.

Clotilda blacked out off and on. She woke up to find herself in the healing chamber of the castle, with the royal, Dominus elf healer, working quickly to apply herbs to numb the pain. He used his dagger summoned from his hand chain to cut open her skin to the infected appendix. His expression was horrified as her appendix ruptured.

Her breath became shallow, each one becoming challenging to draw. The life slipped away from her body. She could hear the voices of Turquoise, Duril, and each of the tutors calling to her, begging her to stay strong before she slipped away.

Clotilda's lifeless form lay sprawled on the bed, similar to how her blood mother lay when she died. The people she encountered sobbed beside her, and the healer shut his eyes sadly before slowly putting his healing remedies away.

King Thierry overheard the traumatic event. He initially believed it to be his daughter but realized she wasn't when he saw it was Clotilda, not Malvolia.

The people slowly walked out of the chamber with deep grief for Clotilda's death while the king called for the guards to set up a search for his missing daughter.

Once the room was empty, orange rune markings, the color of fire, shone through Clotilda's skin, glowing as they spread under her flesh and covered the bones of her skeleton. Her open torso, where the healer attempted to remove her burst appendix, closed up instantly, only leaving behind a scar. Clotilda's eyes shot open as they glowed like suns, and she drew a sharp breath as she did on the day of her birth.

Clotilda's chest heaved as she panted to catch her breath. She held her hands up, seeing the runes under her skin disappear. Her mind was a vortex of questions. How is it that she was resurrected? How was she alive? This isn't the natural magic she had for being half Lazarus elf to resurrect. But it soon dawned on her that her resurrection was a gift from the deity within her, a power for being the Rune of Lazarus.

Feeling her strength rekindle, Clotilda slowly sat up, threw her legs over the bed, and pushed herself off it. She saw the princess's dress draped over the high seat of the chair and looked down at herself to see she was wearing a linen shirt and pants.

A sudden, high-pitched gasp caused Clotilda to jerk her head toward the door of the healing chambers to see Turquoise holding her hands to her mouth and her eyes wide in disbelief. Her fluttering wings gave out, slowly causing her to fall toward the ground. Clotilda cupped her hands together and caught the fairy before she landed on the floor.

"It's all right. I'm okay. See," she smiled as she looked at the puzzled fairy.

"But, you died," Turquoise said hesitantly, her eyes swollen and red from crying.

"I died? I guess I did. But I'm back now," she smiled.

"How?" Turquoise asked.

"Because she is a Lazarus elf," Duril said as he walked into the chamber with surprise in his eyes. "They can resurrect once after they die. I thought she was an Airavata elf, but with her coming back to life, she must be half Lazarus."

Clotilda smiled as she opened her mouth, ready to tell them she was a Rune, but quickly snapped her mouth closed, remembering that her being a Rune must be kept a secret. "So what is your name? We know it's not Malvolia," Duril asked as he kneeled to her.

A cold wash of dread engulfed Clotilda.

"I'm going to be thrown into the dungeon, right?" she asked sadly.

"Of course not. Who told you that?" Turquoise asked as she flew off Clotilda's cupped palms and fluttered until she was at eye level with her.

"The princess did," Clotilda replied hesitantly.

"But why didn't you say anything about being sick?"

"I didn't want to trouble you. I was thinking of hanging in there until I could return to the orphanage."

"You could have died permanently. A sickness like the one you experienced is not one to ignore," Turquoise softly scolded her.

"I'm sorry."

"You're an adorable little girl, but don't neglect yourself like that again! Ever!" Duril said as he placed his hand on her shoulder.

"My blood parents used to tell me the same thing before. I understand how important it is now."

"Good. We better get you back to your family, miss . . . ?" Duril paused as he waited for her to tell him her name.

"My name is Clotilda. It was very nice to meet all of you," she gave everyone a warm and beaming smile.

Clotilda made her way toward the cremation grounds. She respectfully and carefully walked around the sacred urns, holding the ashes of elves and other species that had died from battle, illness, or old age.

She kneeled before one of the slabs and placed a small bouquet of lilies she had gathered from the royal garden. She smiled softly as she looked down at the urn, resting her right hand over the engraved words.

"Thank you for your kindness, Duril," she said softly.

Duril had reached the age of eighty-eight years old, around the time she had finished her training when she was in her early twenties. He lived a long and happy life cooking food and sharing his recipes and kindness with others and was later cremated with his wife when she passed. Clotilda missed him and made it a ritual to visit his grave whenever possible. She remembered how he and Turquoise walked with her back to the orphanage after she was resurrected, and he gifted her one of those chocolate treats he had made that day.

CHAPTER 13

The Masked Gentleman

Clotilda returned home shortly after visiting Duril's grave, collapsing onto her bed as she allowed the day's events to melt away. She lay on her chest as she rested on the soft blankets, looking at her piano and harp standing by the arched window of her bedroom.

She sighed as she nuzzled her left cheek in the fabric, smelling the light fragrances of honey and wild berries from her bedding. Her mind began to rattle with questions like leaves in a windstorm as she thought about the Graffias Manticore and how Corinthia told her he might be a Rune. She looked over at the bookshelf near her writing desk. She had some free time to research, so she should start.

Clotilda pushed herself up, swinging her legs over the edge of the bed, and made her way over to the bookshelf. She ran her index finger down the spines of the leather-bound books, pulling out many volumes of elves, legends of warriors, and the rare book of the Slachten Arena she could stack in her arm before carrying them to her writing desk. She picked the top book from the tower of novels she had gathered and sat down in her chair as she began to read.

Clotilda flipped through the pages of each book and carefully scanned the beautiful illustrations. Hand-drawn, slitted pupils caused Clotilda to halt her search and quickly turn a few pages back. She studied the pictures, marveling at the long, regal beards of the male elves that were neatly styled and wrapped around their muscular bodies. The females were adorned with hairstyles decorated with braids and held together with beast claws and fangs from numerous hunts.

Clotilda studied the male and female armor sets, seeing the designs and symbols of lions on them. She gently placed her fingers on the page, the paper crinkling as she started reading.

This species of elf was known for their military skills, their honor of the hunt, and were the inventors of the weapon hand chains. They were the tallest of all the elves, the strongest, and the fastest, and she remembered her father telling her in the past that they were close allies to Lazarus elves before a tyrant elf king turned them against them. Clotilda ran her hand to the elf species title on the page's top left corner.

"Regulus elf," she read out loud.

Clotilda remembered the memory of the hooded male elf who towered over the Graffias Assassins and how he outran them with ease, and the shield he summoned from his hand chain had a lion's head design on it. He had to have been a Regulus elf!

She looked at the stunning images of the male elves, seeing their long beards wrap majestically around their strong necks, shoulders, thighs, and broad torsos in intricate styles. She pictured the hooded warrior, remembering he was clean-shaven. She matched her memory of Cyril with the illustrations, knitting her eyebrows together when she saw that, unlike him, the male and female Regulus elves had either golden blond, deep rose red, ebony, or brown hair colors. Their eyes were green, blue, yellow, or brown. Cyril's hair was white, and he had celestial blue eyes. She remembered him telling her he was a Regulus elf, but he seemed more than that.

Clotilda flipped through the pages, stopping at a chapter about silver-haired elves. She studied the illustrations, seeing the images of all the species of elves—Regulus, Lazarus, Airavata, Beetje, Seax, Dominus, and Fairy—each with silver hair, pale skin, and celestial blue eyes. She glanced up at the title of the chapter on the top page.

"Celestial Born," she said softly.

A knock caused her to jolt from her reading. Clotilda turned toward the front door, noticing someone standing just outside. Annoyed that she had to stop her research, she tucked the ribbon bookmark of the novel between the pages before carefully closing it and standing up from her chair. She dragged her feet a little as she approached the door, worried it was Bandus.

She thought of her options, wondering if it was Bandus. She could pretend she wasn't home or open the door and punch him in the nose, and she was leaning toward the latter of the options. She opened the door once she had rolled her hand into a fist but firmly held her punch when she saw it wasn't Bandus. Standing before her were Rose Hip, Stump, and Garth.

"Hi, Clotilda," Garth said as he waved at her.

"This is a pleasant surprise," she said as she internally let out a sigh of relief. "What brings all of you here?"

"Garth was worried about you," Stump said as he firmly patted the faun on the back, causing him to stumble slightly from the impact. "He kept pacing around the rooms and hardly ate anything after you left."

"I wasn't that bad! I did eat a little bit," Garth defended.

"Barely enough to feed a moth," Rose Hip said as she adjusted her grip around her husband's arm. "We decided to come over together to check on you. Are you doing well, Clo? Your father told me you went out with Bandus today."

"I'm doing okay," she said politely, welcoming them in. "I did go out with Bandus for a while, and it was anything but pleasant."

"Did he hurt you?" Stump asked, his words dripping with protectiveness.

“He said some things that hurt, but that is the first and last time I will go out with him! Anyway, enough about him. Let’s hang out before I go to the masquerade ball tonight.”

“A masquerade ball?” Rose Hip asked with intrigue.

“A masquerade ball is being held at the castle for Princess Malvolia’s birthday. I will be on duty and disguised as a masked guest to watch for any signs of danger.”

“You should be celebrating and having a great time, not on duty!” Rose Hip growled.

“I’ll make the most out of it,” she sighed as she closed the front door and led her family into the kitchen. “Let’s get you something to drink.”

“Do you have time?” Garth asked.

“Of course,” she replied with a nod. “The ball won’t start for a couple of hours. I have plenty of time to visit with you for a while, and then I can get ready.”

Clotilda set three wooden cups and poured nectar milk for her mom and Garth and water for her father, who didn’t like eating sweet foods and drinks. Garth walked over to her as she handed him a cup.

“I’m sorry to trouble you, Clo. I just wanted to make sure you were all right since . . .” he went silent as Clotilda softly shushed him.

“I’m all good. I’m glad you didn’t sneak off on your own again,” she gently patted his shoulder before whispering. “So, what’s been bothering you? Is it from what happened last night?”

“That too, but . . .” he paused as he and Clotilda overheard Rose Hip and Stump talking.

“I’ll be fine, my love,” Rose Hip said sweetly, patting her husband’s arm as they sat together by the table. “Our baby won’t be here until two months from now. A little walk from the orphanage to our daughter's home will not hurt me."

"I want to make sure. You're too special to me, Rose," he said lovingly as he kissed her lips.

Clotilda smiled at her mother and father before returning her gaze to Garth.

"Now, as you were saying," she whispered.

"Oh yes, I was thinking about those monsters last night too. But my mind has been whirling since you spoke to the captain and the mage today about the Graffias Manticore. Talking about how he is hunting for a bride and . . . well . . . I'm worried that he might come after you," Garth replied, becoming more nervous with each word he spoke.

"I don't think you have anything to worry about. The Graffias Manticore is probably seeking a princess or a queen for his bride, not a guard like me," she said with a smile.

"Are you sure about that?"

"I'm sure," she nodded. "Customarily, a king usually chooses a woman of royal blood for his queen. I don't have royal blood in my family. So it would be a lost cause for him. If he does find this capital, he'll probably come after Princess Malvolia. If he does, I'll be ready as much as I can to protect her."

"But didn't you say you don't like the king and the princess?"

"I certainly don't," she grumbled. "But as a guard, I have to protect them. So even though I'm not fond of them, it's not my nature to stand back and do nothing. I am protective, always have been, and always will be."

"Just be careful out there, and don't let the Manticore catch you, okay?"

"I will," she said as she gently patted his head.

The family's visit was brief as Garth and Clotilda's mother and father finished their drinks and bid her farewell. Clotilda gave them a ride on Coralina's back to the orphanage to make things easy for her mother, despite Rose Hip's and Stump's reluctance to be on top of a horse. She quickly returned to her house and got herself ready for the ball.

Clotilda got dressed in a ballroom gown made from woven green vines knitted together into a pink, mermaid tail–shaped dress with a red gem attached to the collar. She combed her hair back into a ponytail and applied light makeup on her eyes, cheeks, and lips. She picked up the wolf mask on her vanity and carefully slipped it over her face to avoid smearing her makeup.

The mask was covered with alabaster fur, a pointed snout, and a black triangle gem resembling a nose. The eye openings were decorated with clusters of black gems that framed Clotilda's eyes and had bristles on the tops of them that resembled eyelashes, giving the illusion of eyelids.

Clotilda looked down at the jewelry she had set out on her vanity table, instinctively putting on her hand chain. She glanced down at the new hand chain she received from the shopkeeper, Doric. She inspected it, making sure there were no dangerous enchantments upon it. She could sense magic radiating from it, but it was the same as the one she had been wearing for years. It didn't seem dangerous, and it looked safe enough to wear. She picked up the hand chain and slipped it on her left wrist.

Finishing up by grabbing a clutch and packing it with an enchanted comb, some makeup, and a handkerchief, she was ready. Clotilda stepped out of her house, locking the door behind her as she saddled Coralina and made her way to the castle.

Clotilda held the bottom hem of her dress so she wouldn't step on it and allowed the train of the pink fabric of her dress to drag behind her as she made her way toward the ballroom filled with animal-masked guests. She glanced at the grand staircase to see the king and his daughter sitting on their thrones, with a group of elven men surrounding the princess and asking her to dance with one of them. Clotilda wasn't close enough to hear them, but she could tell by the princess's gestures that she was rejecting them.

The hidden commander tore her gaze from the royal family and scanned the ballroom for any of her troops. Clotilda studied familiar gestures and pinpointed some of her troops who blended well with the guests.

Captain Corinthia wore a scarlet ballroom gown that reminded Clotilda of a bleeding-heart flower. She had her brown hair pulled back in a low bun and wore a green and purple hummingbird mask that enhanced the red of her dress. Clotilda spotted a couple more hidden troops by the banquet table. Ivan wore a falcon mask and dressed in his fine green tunic and black dress pants, while his female companion, one of the archers in Clotilda's troops, was wearing a delicate silver gown. The archer's mid-back hair was curled, and she wore a fish mask as she and Ivan conversed.

Relieved that she could spot three of her troops, Clotilda adjusted her wolf mask, approached one of the columns, and stood against it as she looked around. She carefully scanned the conversing guests, keeping her eyes sharp for any hidden danger and the slightest hint of a weapon being summoned.

"You look lovely tonight, Clo," Bandus's voice pulled her from her concentration. She reluctantly turned her head toward him, only to be met with a lion's face made of rich, brass paint, stern eyebrows that gave the mask a frown, and gold feathers attached from the forehead that spiraled down underneath the mask's open mouth that emanated a silent roar. "What do you think of my mask?"

"You chose a lion mask?" she asked flatly.

"Of course, I thought you'd like it," he grinned, oblivious to her anger. "You do like it, don't you?"

"What gave you the thought I would?"

"Well, I heard you telling that jewelry shopkeeper you like lions, and I thought this would impress you."

"I don't like it when you eavesdrop. It makes me uncomfortable," she said, then pushed herself away from the column and began walking away.

Clotilda wasn't happy with how Bandus acted today at the market, and his rude words still rang in her ears. She thought of erasing his memory of him knowing about her connection with the lion, but she knew she couldn't do it here. Not in the castle with a sea of guests.

"Why do you have to be so secretive with me? Stop acting so cold, and tell me more about yourself!"

"If I don't feel comfortable being around someone, I don't talk to them," she glared at him through her mask. "I'm going to higher ground," she said as she glanced at the stairs.

"I'll go with you," he insisted but was quickly stopped by her hand to prevent him from coming any closer to her.

"I want to be alone right now."

Clotilda politely excused herself as she walked through the crowd of guests toward the stairs. She bent down to grab the bottom hem of her dress and lifted it as she climbed the stairs.

Reaching the top of the staircase, she walked toward the balcony and folded her arms as she rested them on the marble railing. From a bird's eye view, the commander scanned the ballroom. The orchestra had begun to play its music, and the guests paired up for their dances. Clotilda looked at the faces of the paired men and women twirling together, lost in their world of dance and music. She let out a soft sigh as she listened to the music, the melodies soothing her anger for Bandus, and her body swayed slowly to the rhythm the musical instruments made. The harp and piano called her to play on them, but she couldn't. Not in front of Bandus and the royal family.

"May I join you?" A deep male voice pulled her from her thoughts. She glanced to the side to see a male elf standing behind her, wearing a grizzly bear mask.

Clotilda forgot to breathe. Beneath the pointed snout of the brown-furred mask he wore, she could see the hint of his handsome face. He had a strong, clean-shaven chin and jawline and nicely shaped lips. His skin was pale and warm like moonlight. She guessed he was around seven feet tall, and he wore a dark-navy, formal suit that embraced his toned, muscular body and was decorated with gold markings resembling claws. A white, elegant cape spilled over his broad shoulders. It was wrapped neatly around his neck, revealing a turtleneck that hugged him comfortably and was open in the middle that ran down to show the skin of his throat and Adam's apple and stopped at the base of his collarbone.

Clotilda tried to look at his eyes, but his mask's visors were darkened as if trying to hide them from everyone around him. His hair was dark brown, almost matching the fur on his mask. But it looked unnatural.

Realizing she was staring at him, Clotilda quickly but politely answered his question to avoid being rude.

"Please. I don't mind at all," she said and gestured with her hand for him to stand beside her.

He smiled at her before he stood beside her. He folded his arms and rested them on the railing, mirroring her position.

"Are you waiting for someone?" he asked, causing her to look back at him. "I noticed you were alone up here. I wasn't sure if you were waiting for someone."

"No, I'm not. I decided to stay up here and watch," she said, not wanting to tell him she was a guard for the royal family.

"Are you sure you're all right with staying up here? You're going to miss out on the celebration."

"I know. But it's not fun celebrating alone," she said with a shrug.

She noticed how he glanced back at her, a closed smile spreading on his lips.

"Why don't we go down and join them," he suggested as he pushed himself from the railing. She glanced back at him shyly as he fixed his cape. "I came here alone myself. If it's all right, it would be an honor to spend some time with you."

Clotilda tucked some of the loose hair behind her ear. She knew she needed to keep watch during the ball, but she would blend in with the guests if she were with someone instead of standing alone in a corner or atop a staircase. This gentleman seemed very kind and charming. It wouldn't hurt to spend some time with him.

She pushed herself from the railing and smiled at him.

"I don't see why not."

His smile widened before he offered his arm, and she timidly slipped her fingers into the crook of his elbow, blushing a little when she felt his firm muscles . . . a warrior's arm. Disciplined and very strong. She grabbed the hem of her gown and followed him down the stairs to the awaiting crowd below. She would allow herself a chance to have a little fun for once, as Rose Hip suggested. Besides, how could she resist a polite gentleman?

CHAPTER 14

Dance of the Bear and the Wolf

Orchestra music began to fill the air, and the fluttering fabric of the vibrant gowns of the women billowed over the grand ballroom floor like an aurora as they danced with their male companions.

Clotilda stood with the handsome, bear-masked gentleman as they piled their small plates with food from the banquet tables. She was famished, having not eaten since this morning. She plucked up one of the berry-glazed fish fillets, a salad of fresh vegetables, and a fruit tart. She saw that her companion had nearly every sliver of medium-rare meat on his plate. Each was glazed with gravy and smelled of fresh herbs and salt. There were no vegetables on his plate only a small portion of red berries.

"My goodness, you have quite the feast there," she said in awe.

"Yours look good as well. You like aquatic food?"

"Yes, I do. Meat from the waters has always been my favorite, especially fish," she said as she stabbed her fork through a piece of the fish fillets on her plate and placed it into her mouth.

Clotilda slowly chewed her food, nearly choking as she swallowed when she heard a loud crunch. She jolted in surprise and looked over at the gentleman to see he had bitten into a piece of bone from one of the ribs of his food. However, he seemed unfazed as he chewed on the bone calmly as if eating an apple.

"Are you all right?" she asked, concerned about whether he hurt his teeth or jaw.

He gave her a reassuring, closed smile as he chewed his food and held his plate with the rib he had bitten into. Clotilda glanced down at the bone for blood, but it was void of any red stains from the male elf, and he was chewing it with minimal effort.

"I'm fine, thank you," he replied after he swallowed.

Clotilda's eyes widened as her gaze was transfixed on his slightly parted lips, seeing rows of something sharp peaking behind them. Her heart rate spiked a little when she realized that he had fangs! She could tell they looked strong and pointed, quickly identifying him as a carnivore. But his fangs were white like dove down and well taken care of.

"Is something wrong?" he asked, pulling her from her concentration.

"Oh, I just wanted to make sure you were okay," she said bashfully.

"I appreciate it. You're a caring woman," he said with a smile.

"Thank you," she said shyly.

"Is it possible that the Graffias Manticore will come to the ball?"

Clotilda glanced over her shoulders as she heard a woman's voice and saw two elven women conversing, a Dominus and an Airavata.

"I hope so! I tried crossing the barrier earlier until the guards stopped me," the Airavata woman replied.

"I wouldn't mind if he spirited me away from here. I mean, I always wanted to have a king as a husband. And I've heard that the Graffias Manticore is very wealthy," the second woman said in intrigue.

"He better be if he's a king! Although, I'm sure he'll take me away instead," the other woman said.

Clotilda shook her head in disapproval as she listened to the women beginning to bicker. Was this really what it was all about? Power? Wealth? There was no love in any of those. She felt a ping of sympathy for the Graffias Manticore. He must be very lonely. She prayed for him that he found a loving woman to be his wife and hoped he didn't come for Princess Malvolia, for his sake!

Clotilda heard her companion sigh through his nose in equal disapproval as he listened to the conversation between the two women.

"Don't mind them. There's been a lot of chaos this morning," she said as she glanced back at him.

"I see," he said flatly before he glanced back at her. "Is that . . . the kind of man you're looking for too?"

"No. As long as he's a nice man with a good heart, kind, honest, and loyal, that's all that matters to me," she replied.

"That's . . . very refreshing to hear you say that. There should be more people like you in this world."

Clotilda felt her heart race. Her companion is a wonderful gentleman, and she was glad to hang out with him tonight.

The orchestra ended their current song. The musicians rested briefly as the composer prepared to play the next piece.

"Would you like to dance with me?" he asked.

"I'm not so sure that's a good idea," she softly chuckled.

"Why's that?" He tilted his head to her. Even with his mask on, she could sense that he was curiously arching one of his eyebrows.

"I'm a very clumsy dancer. The last time I tried dancing with a gentleman named Duril, I kept stepping on his feet," she said embarrassingly as she brushed her hand behind her neck. "In short, I can't dance and might end up stepping on your feet too."

He chuckled softly, but he wasn't laughing at her. Instead, his laugh was so light-hearted and pleasant that she felt at ease. It was nice to have someone laugh with you, not at you.

"I'll take my chances," he replied, putting his plate on the table.

"I couldn't. I will end up stepping on your feet if I try to," she nervously giggled, holding her free hand up in warning.

"So? It has been a while since I've danced, so I think this is a great opportunity."

Clotilda gently bit her bottom lip as she glanced back and forth between him and the dance floor. She was very self-conscious about dancing and still felt the sting of embarrassment from when she stepped on Duril's feet.

How bad could it be? One dance couldn't hurt, could it? After a short pause, Clotilda nodded shyly and placed her plate on the table beside his.

"If you're willing to take the risk, so am I," she said with a shrug.

"May I have this dance?" he smiled as he offered his left hand to her.

"Sure thing," she said as she nervously grasped his offered hand. He curled his strong fingers over her hand and gently guided her toward the dance floor.

Clotilda walked by his side as they made their way to the large dance floor, and they turned to face each other. She felt him slip his hand around her waist until it pressed against her lower back, and he tenderly pulled her closer to him.

"Now your feet are in danger," she said as she glanced down.

"Don't worry. Forget your worries and follow my lead," he reassured her.

"Okay," she said and blushed as she gently grasped his shoulder.

The orchestra began to play their next piece, and the guests paired up to start their dances to the new music. The masked gentleman began to lead Clotilda into the dance. She clumsily moved her feet, the toe of her slipper lightly resting on his shoe.

"I'm so sorry! I didn't mean to," she apologized, quickly recoiling her foot back. Embarrassment swelled in her as if she were stung by a swarm of wasps. She tried to slip her hand away, but he gently held her, stopping her from parting from him.

"Don't be. It's perfectly fine," he smiled reassuringly, making her heart leap like a frolicking fawn. "Silent those worries in your mind and enjoy the music around us."

She exhaled slowly to clear her mind of concern and embarrassment before following his lead and feeling the music resonate.

The world around her disappeared, leaving only her and her masked companion. Her body instinctively swayed with the rhythm of the music, and her gown fluttered over the ground as they spun around. He lowered her into a graceful dip before pulling her up with ease.

The music slowed to a coda, and she felt pulled back into the real world. Dancers parted away to bow to each other, and some clapped at the end of the music piece, but Clotilda couldn't and wouldn't part from her dance partner. Something about him seemed familiar, and she tightened her hold on his shoulder and hand, afraid he would let go. Much to her surprise, she sensed he didn't want to part either. His fingers interlaced with hers, and his arm tightened around her waist like holding someone in a stormy sea so they wouldn't sink beneath the waves. She glanced at him through her mask, wishing to see his eyes.

Clotilda jolted when she felt a tap on her shoulder. She jerked her head back to see Bandus standing behind her with a scowl.

"What is it?" she asked him.

"There's something I need to tell you, Clo. Can I have a moment with you?" he asked.

"Can it wait?" she asked reluctantly.

"No, it can't. It's about the rumors," he said sternly.

"Very well," she said hesitantly as she parted from the masked gentleman. She didn't want to leave him and gestured with her hand for him to follow. "You're welcome to come if you want to."

Bandus looked at her companion and gave him a frown before he grabbed her shoulder firmly.

"Don't bring him along," Bandus sneered.

"He can come too," she said sternly before she jerked her shoulder free from his tight grasp and walked past him.

Clotilda glanced back as she looked at the gentleman, feeling him giving Bandus a piercing, deadly glare. She was afraid they were going to start fighting. But after a tense pause, she felt the gentleman restrain himself and walk past the mage.

Clotilda returned to the banquet table to retrieve their plates. She looked at the fountain with rippling purple fruit juice in it. After such an intimate dance, a refreshing drink and a pause sounded like a good idea to catch her breath.

"I'm starting to get a little thirsty. Do you want something to drink too?" She asked him.

"I would appreciate it," he replied to her.

Clotilda smiled at him before she made her way over to the fountain. He seemed to calm down, and she hoped that Bandus wouldn't do anything else to provoke him. A fight was the last thing she needed to have happen at the ball. She grabbed a couple of drinking glasses and held them over the thin, pouring stream of juice from the fountain. Bandus walked over to her as she filled the glasses, speaking quietly.

"Why were you dancing with him? I thought you said you were going to keep watch!"

"I am," she said as she pulled the first full drinking glass away and filled the second one. "He asked politely if I would dance with him, and I wanted to. Besides, it allowed me to look around without being too obvious."

"It didn't look like you were keeping watch. It looked like you were paying more attention to him," he growled, which made her skin bristle.

Clotilda sighed before pulling the full drinking glass away from the streaming fountain and returning to the gentleman waiting patiently for her.

"So what about the rumors you wanted to talk about, Bandus?" she asked as she gave the gentleman one of the drinking glasses while she held the other one.

"The rumors about the Battle Komodons in the capital are true," Bandus said.

"Go on," she urged him to continue before she turned to the gentleman to see that he was listening intently to the conversation.

Her eyebrows knitted slightly when she noticed his hand trembling, almost like he was in pain. Clotilda was about to ask him if he was all right when she heard Bandus speak up.

"There's more. There are also assassins from the Graffias here as well. . . ."

The sound of shattering glass cut off Bandus's words.

Clotilda spun around to see broken pieces of the chalice and juice on the ground around their feet and the fractured drinking glass clenched in the gentleman's bleeding hand.

"My apologies," he said.

Clotilda swiftly opened her clutch and fished out her handkerchief.

"Let me see your hand," she said as she gently cupped his hand, dabbed her handkerchief over it, and carefully removed some of the shards of glass.

"You don't have to do that. Your handkerchief will get ruined," he said.

"I can always get another one," she smiled at him as she carefully wrapped it around his palm and tied it securely like a bandage. "There. That should help stop the bleeding," she said, feeling bad that she didn't bring the Tears of Eir flowers with her. "Let's bring you to the royal healer."

"That won't be necessary. I'd best be going," he said.

"Are you sure?"

"I'm sure," he said with a nod.

"All right," she said softly, sad to hear that he had to go so soon. "This has been the most fun I had in a long time. Thank you for tonight."

"As have I," he said before gently grabbing her right hand and holding it to his lips. "This is farewell for now, but I look forward to seeing you again."

Clotilda's heart skipped a beat as she felt his warm lips press against her knuckles, and he turned her hand to kiss the inside of her palm. She looked at him with flushed cheeks before her eyes widened to see his mask slip down a little to reveal a pair of celestial blue eyes and slitted pupils staring back at her. He quickly pulled away, pressing his mask to his face, and spun into the crowd.

"Wait," she called out to him before she chased after him. "Please wait!"

Clotilda excused herself as she hurried past the guests until she reached the balcony from where he ran. She grabbed the railing, looking at the staircase, the gardens, and the still pond below to see if he was down there. Her heart sank as she untied her wolf mask from her face and dropped her gaze down, resting her trembling hands and mask on the railing. She swallowed thickly as her throat began to swell. She had waited so long for Cyril and worried for him. At long last, he was here. She had so many questions. She wanted to know how he was doing, if he had reclaimed his home, and how he found her.

"Cyril . . . you're alive. It was good to be with you again and dance with you. I miss you so much," she said softly as tears rolled down her cheeks.

Fluttering caused her pointed ears to perk, and she saw pulsing, delicate wings flying near her cheek. A butterfly with white wings like moonlight flew up to her. It nuzzled close to her scarred cheek as if it were planting a kiss. It flew up to her until it was at eye level with her for a few moments before it spun around and flew down toward the gardens.

Clotilda watched the butterfly until it disappeared, her heart fluttering with bittersweet joy, wondering when she would see Cyril again.

CHAPTER 15

The White Lion

Clotilda found herself reminiscing about the gentleman kissing her knuckles and palm last night. She leaned against the column of the ballroom balcony, brushing her gloved fingertips over her hand. She wondered if the grizzly bear–masked gentleman was genuinely Cyril or if she was simply hopeful. Her gaze shifted to the two rose-gold lions with the pink gem between them, attached to the second-hand chain around her left hand.

Clotilda shook her head to clear her mind. Now was not the time to be daydreaming. She was beginning her duty of watching over the princess today, and she needed to focus.

Clotilda hurried to get dressed into her armor early this morning, quickly packing a small bundle of food if she got hungry and the whistle to call for Coralina if she needed her. Clotilda didn't tie her steed to a hitching post as they arrived at the castle. She needed to have Coralina accessible so she could come when needed.

Aside from Princess Malvolia arguing with her father about not wanting to have a bodyguard, the rest of the morning was calm and quiet. There were no signs of Battle Komodons, assassins, or the Graffias Manticore. But Clotilda didn't want to take any chances. She had her troops patrol the castle from the inside out and had some of them up on the sentinel tower to keep watch from a bird's eye view and to sound the horn as soon as they spotted any danger. Everything was ready!

Clotilda scooped up her helmet on the ground next to her feet, fished out an enchanted comb from her pack, and ran it through her hair. The magic of the comb allowed her to tuck her hair back and the bun of her half-up and half-down hairstyle into the helmet, slipping it comfortably over her head and covering her entire face without constricting her head with the locks.

Looking through her crystal eye visors, she went down the stairs to the royal gardens, hoping that the fragrant scent of flowers and the company of the swans down by the pond would help clear her mind. Clotilda was nervous. She didn't know much about the Graffias Manticore and hoped to hold him back with her troops' aid.

As she approached the pond, the sunlight reflected off her armor and helmet, causing it to glimmer like shattered shards of a broken mirror. Clotilda kneeled by the pond's edge, watching the swans gracefully swim around the water like dancing ballerinas. She looked toward the fountain in the heart of the garden to see Princess Malvolia sitting on a bench, boredom prominent on her face.

The soft water rippling caused Clotilda to turn her attention back to the pond to see the swans watching her with interest and hope in their eyes for food. She reached into her pack and pulled out a roll of bread she had brought before hurrying to the castle. She tore small pieces from the bread and threw them into the water to feed her feathery companions. The birds dipped their bills into the water to pluck the bread and raised their heads, allowing water drips to roll down their long, slender necks. They drew closer to her like clusters of clouds, nearly climbing onto the shore.

A small cygnet neared her, drawing closer so he could have a piece of bread without worrying about the other swans trying to take it. Clotilda took the last bit of her bread and held it out to the cygnet so that he could eat from her hand. He cautiously outstretched his neck toward her, plucked the bread from her fingers, and ate it. The swans looked up at her for more food, but she held up her empty hands, her voice muffled by the helmet as she spoke.

"I'm sorry, my friends; it was all I had."

The cygnet swam closer to her, outstretching his neck to her and brushing his head over her high-heeled boot. She smiled warmly at his grateful gesture and gently traced her thumb over his forehead.

She glanced back to the fountain to see that the princess was no longer there.

"Now, where did she go," Clotilda said before standing up to search for the princess.

Her eyes darted around until she saw Malvolia sitting at the foot of the flowering hedges. She was kneeling with her yellow dress rippling on the grass like a waterfall of melting gold, and her shoulders were shifting as if she were moving something around. Curiosity and suspicion swelled in Clotilda's mind, and she slowly crept over to Malvolia.

"Princess," the princess flinched at the sound of Clotilda's voice, but she kept her back to her. "May I ask what you are doing?"

"It's none of your concern," she sneered at the commander. "Can't I enjoy being outside in the gardens?"

"Suit yourself," Clotilda said as she tried to peer around the princess to see what she was doing. The flicker of a fluffy tail waved back and forth before the princess shifted to the side and blocked Clotilda's sight. "But your father has given me orders to protect you and . . ."

"I don't need protection!" Malvolia cut Clotilda off as she glanced over her shoulders. "What part of that don't you understand, you stupid peasant?"

"I understand that it is important to follow orders," she replied evenly.

Clotilda's eardrums throbbed as the mighty surge of the giant sentinel horn sounded off, signaling that her troops saw danger! Both she and the princess threw their hands over their ears. She turned to see the tip of a fluffy tail disappearing into the treetops above, and the princess quickly made her way up the stairs and into the castle. Clotilda sprinted after her.

Clotilda followed Malvolia until her troops spilled out from the hallways, cutting her off from the princess. She tried maneuvering through them, their charge ceasing when they saw their commander. Clotilda quickly caught up to the princess and firmly grasped her forearm before dragging her back to her troops.

"Let go of me!" she ordered, but Clotilda paid her no heed.

"Commander," Captain Corinthia spoke as she saluted her. "Thank the Father God we've found you."

"What's going on? Who sounded the warning call?" Clotilda asked.

"I did. I was on patrol when I spotted an intruder," the captain replied.

Clotilda felt her stomach churn.

"What did the intruder look like?" she asked.

"Manticore!" Ivan called out as he ran toward them. "The Graffias Manticore is coming! He's coming straight to the palace!"

"Fortify all of the doors and gates to the castle!" Clotilda ordered her troops. "Make sure every one of them is guarded! Don't let him in!"

"Yes, Commander," her troops said in unison.

"No!" the Princess snarled as she ripped her arm from Clotilda's grasp and fled.

"Princess! Come back here!" Clotilda called out.

Clotilda hurried past her troops and went after Malvolia. She needed to stay close to the princess, or the Graffias Manticore would capture her. King Thierry had given strict orders not to let anyone leave his capital. However, if the Graffias Manticore had taken his daughter, there was a high likelihood that the king would send Clotilda and her troops to retrieve her. With the Graffias Manticore coming to the castle, it was clear to Clotilda that he was after the princess!

Clotilda stopped at the cross of the hallway, catching her breath and scanning the three long hallways after Malvolia had disappeared like a sunbeam. Her mind was racing with questions about which hallway the princess had taken, and her breath filled her helmet, causing the crystal visors to fog over.

Clotilda was drawn to a loud tapping sound reverberating down one of the hallways. She perked her ears through the holes of her helmet and looked around, trying to locate the source of the sound. As the tapping grew louder, she realized that something was approaching her position. She listened carefully and identified the sound from the west hallway on her right. Acting quickly, she ran toward the wall and pressed her back against it, watching intently as the source of the noise came into view. To her surprise, a giant lion emerged from the right hallway and stopped abruptly.

The lion was beautiful. His coat was white, like the first day of winter, and his mane was full and long, glistening in the light of the row of chandeliers overhead. Clotilda stared at the lion, seeing that he was looking around as if contemplating which way to go. She held her breath, her pulse ringing in her ears and helmet like a bell as she braced for the majestic but dangerous beast to turn around and look straight at her. She held her right hand across her chest, readying herself to summon Universeel.

A startled scream echoed in the hallways, causing Clotilda and the lion to jerk their heads toward the feminine figure standing in the north hallway. The princess looked like the size of a pomegranate seed from where she stood. Clotilda could tell from afar that she was looking at the lion fearfully before she turned around and fled. She could see the lion staring at the princess as she ran away from him, his eyes locked on her long hair fluttering, and he sprinted after her.

"Oh no . . ." Clotilda said to herself as she quickly ran after them.

Her high heels echoed off the hallways, but the lion didn't pay any heed. His focus was locked on the princess. Clotilda pumped her arms and moved her legs as fast as possible, but the lion was faster. He stormed down the hallway and turned sharply to the next one as he followed the princess. Clotilda slowed down to make her turn without running into the marble wall and continued the chase.

CHAPTER 16

The Manticore Hunts

Clotilda hurried down the hallway and skipped over a couple of steps of the spiral stairs that led up to the towers as she followed the lion and Malvolia to the princess's bed chamber. The princess was going to be trapped! The commander knew she needed to get to them as soon as possible before the lion harmed her.

The loud clanking of a giant door echoed in the air, signaling to her that Malvolia had locked herself inside her room. Clotilda stopped running when she saw the lion stopped by the closed door. Her eyes widened in disbelief when she saw that the lion was changing. The lion stood upright on his powerful hind legs. His white fur dissolved into navy-blue armor, a long flowing cape that was the color of blackberries cascaded from his broad shoulders, and his head was covered with a helmet shaped like a lion billowing a silent roar.

"The Graffias Manticore . . . is a Regulus elf?" she asked as she felt a cold shiver run up her spine, remembering her family telling her about them.

"Have you and Mother ever met a Regulus elf, Dad?" the young Clotilda asked as she held a book open to show her blood father, Cadmar, the illustration of male and female Regulus elves.

Cadmar's rough beauty was untouched by the one hundred and seventy-six years of his life, with a strongly built body from years of many battles. His face was very handsome, his bangs framed his cheekbones, and his skin was smooth and sun-kissed. He was dressed in red and dark-blue armor, with golden feathers decorating the shoulder guards, chest guard, the top hem of his knee-high boots, and a brown leather belt with the swirling Phoenix insignia of the Lazarus culture, only given to the highest-ranking commanders. He wore a pair of brown leather gloves with his two phoenix-designed hand chains on each hand, with the loops around his index fingers to show his rank as a military leader and that he was skilled in dual-wielded weapons. His long, hip-length red hair was pulled back in a braid and was the color of a vibrant sunset. His eyes were fiery orange like his daughter's and shimmered like dragon scales in the sunlight.

Cadmar's smile dropped as soon as he laid eyes on the illustrations in the book, and his brows knitted together.

"Your mother and I have encountered Regulus elves in the past," he said with concern in his deep voice.

Clotilda felt a chill run up her spine when she saw her father's mood darken like a cloud blocking the sun.

"What were the Regulus elves you encountered like?" she asked hesitantly.

"They attacked us," he replied.

"What?" she asked, her eyes widening like medallions. "Attack? Why would they do that? I thought Lazarus and Regulus elves were allies."

"I'm not sure what we did that provoked them to attack us, but they are very aggressive right now because of the tyrant sitting on the throne of the Regulus elf kingdom."

He punctuated his sentence by slipping off his shoulder guard and tugging the collar of his shirt down the curve of his shoulder to reveal a large scar.

Clotilda couldn't hold back the gasp when she saw the scar. The skin on Cadmar's shoulder was mangled and littered with deep, pale lacerations that she could quickly identify as claw marks.

"A Regulus elf did that?"

"Clotilda . . ." Cadmar said as he tugged the fabric of his shirt up to the junction of his neck to conceal the mark. "Do you remember the warning your mother and I gave you about staying away from lions?" Clotilda bit her bottom lip before nodding in reply. "The reason is that Regulus elves are not only the tallest and the strongest of the elf species, they also can shapeshift."

"They can shapeshift? Into what forms?"

"Any form. But their favorite form is a lion. So, when you see a lion, you are not only to stay away from them because they are a large carnivore, but they might be a Regulus elf in disguise."

The rattling of a door handle instantly ripped Clotilda from her memory. Then the door splintered as the Graffias Manticore began to kick his knee against the wooden door. Clotilda watched him punch a hole in the door, and he slipped his arm through the opening and reached for the handle on the other side.

Clotilda quickly pulled the whistle from her pack. She tilted her helmet until her lips peeked beneath the rim and blew into it. She couldn't hear the whistle, but she knew that any aquatic pegasus nearby would, and since Coralina was one of the few in the capital, she would come.

"Please hurry, Coralina," she prayed before she tucked the whistle into her pack and summoned Universeel.

The Graffias Manticore swung open the door and quickly slipped inside the princess's bed chambers. Clotilda could see him looking around until his head turned toward the princess hiding behind the tall head frame of the master bed, with her back facing them and her hair draped over her spine. He stood there a few moments before slowly walking to the hiding princess.

"Stop!" Clotilda demanded as she charged into the bed chambers.

The Graffias Manticore paused mid-step and calmly turned his head toward her. His feral lion armor glared in hunger and gleamed like swirling ghosts in the sunlight flooding the chamber through the large arch windows. Clotilda tried to meet his gaze, but his eyes were hidden as if she were looking into a skull's hollow sockets. She could see the outline of the chiseled arms and chest muscles beneath the navy fabric of his long-sleeved tunic, and his pants hugged his powerfully muscled legs that looked long and steady, showing that he was a formidable fighter and a fast sprinter. His cape hung from his broad, armored shoulders and dragged behind him like a ribbon of a starless night sky. He wore clawed gauntlets with two lion-clawed hand chains, and the loops were around his middle fingers, a traditional elven sign of his rank as a regal leader.

Clotilda felt his glare, not anger or bloodthirst, but a glimmer of determination and a dominating presence. She was grateful for her helmet that completely concealed her face, knowing it would shield it from him looking at her hesitant eyes. She hoped to research more about the Graffias Manticore so she could be ready to fight him just like she had done with Acanthus and other dangers that threatened the safety of her troops and the citizens of Streng. Still, she knew hardly anything about him, and there was a chance that she might not survive. Yet despite her nervousness, she held firm.

"I know who you are, Graffias Manticore, and I ask you to leave her be! I will let you escape if you obey and promise not to come near her!" Clotilda demanded.

He slowly spun completely around until he was facing her.

"You're brave," he spoke through his helmet. Much to Clotilda's surprise, his voice didn't sound menacing and rasping. Instead, it was deep and gentle—something she wasn't expecting to hear from a former assassin of the Graffias clan. "But I am not going to accept your offer. I have waited four hundred years of my life for someone like her, and I will not lose her again." He waved his right hand, and the blue magic from his hand chain wove together to form a large two-handed sword.

The sword had a thick, slightly curved blade with runes and claw marks decorating it. It looked heavy for even her to carry with two hands, but the Graffias Manticore could wield it easily with one hand. Clotilda swallowed thickly. She wasn't as strong as him, but she would have to try. But his sword was not her only concern. It was his second hand chain. If he were to summon a shield, or worse, a second sword, it would be a struggle even with Universeel.

"Again? What are you talking about? Have you and the princess been seeing each other?" she asked.

"Now it's my turn to warn you," he said, ignoring her question. "Don't get in my way. I don't wish to hurt you, but I'm not leaving without her."

"I can't let you do that. As a guard, I have orders to protect the royal family," she declared as she stood in a battle stance. "If you want to get to her, you must go through me first."

"I've been searching for her for the past one hundred and thirty years. I won't let anyone get in my way, not even you," he said with a snarl.

"Wha . . . ?" she tried to ask but was cut off when he charged toward her.

Clotilda stood her ground as he swung his sword toward her. Clotilda retaliated with Universeel, clashing it with his sword, the impact causing the delicate harp strings of her weapon to vibrate to the point that they threatened to snap apart. They pushed against each other. Clotilda ground her teeth together until her gums hurt as she struggled to keep his sword back. She felt herself sliding backward. She locked her knees and dug her heels into the marble floor as if trying to root them in place, pushing forward and breaking their weapons apart. Clotilda and the Manticore recoiled from each other, creating a pregnant distance between them as they faced each other. They charged again, the air shattering with the piercing sound of their weapons clashing.

They fought and dodged their attacks like dancers. Clotilda swung Universeel toward him, but he was faster, defending himself with his sword and pushing her weapon away as he shot his free hand toward her.

The Graffias Manticore grabbed her wrist—not too rough, but causing Clotilda to gasp in surprise, and he pushed her back. She grunted as her back met the marble wall, her helmet rang, and her heart rate spiked when she saw him bring the blade of his sword to her throat and press it to her neck. She growled as she bent her knees, readying herself to kick him away before he could slit her throat open. She paused as he drew closer and leaned his concealed face toward her.

"You fought well. But I wish to continue my quest without spilling blood," he said as blue rune markings appeared on his arms and ran down to his fingers. Clotilda's eyes widened as three halos of pale-blue light glided over the ground like wisps. Ghostly lions emerged from the orbs of light and crept around them. "Keep a watch on this guard. Don't harm her, but don't let her get near us," he ordered them before he drew his sword away from her neck and hurried over to the princess.

Clotilda stared at the lions surrounding her as they snarled and bore their sharp fangs before she looked at the Graffias Manticore. She watched as he slowly approached the princess, his sword pointing to the ground and his gloved hand slowly reaching her shoulder. The princess turned around, revealing her face to him. To Clotilda's surprise, the Graffias Manticore recoiled his hand and stepped back, puzzled.

"I knew you would come for me, Graffias Manticore!" Malvolia chirped as she stood up. She opened her arms and leaped over to him for an embrace, but he stepped out of her way as if dodging an enemy attack. The princess stumbled and turned to him, giving him a confused and angry stare. "What was that for?"

"Deceiving imposter! You're not her!" he growled, causing Malvolia to flinch and step back from him.

Clotilda stood frozen as she watched the Graffias Manticore and the princess. Deep growls caused her to return her gaze to the ghostly lions at the corner of her eyes. She didn't know what the Graffias Manticore wanted and why was it that he had avoided the princess's hug, but she had a duty to fulfill. She tightened her hold around her weapon before she swung it toward the lions. Orange runes glowed down her arms, sipping into Universeel and causing rippling waves of fire to flutter over the crescent blades. These lions were made of ancient magic from the deity within the Graffias Manticore. His Rune powers must be mighty if he is four hundred years old, as he told her, and she needed to use some of her Rune powers to aid her.

She slashed the blade into the first ghost lion's head, causing it to flinch and fire runes to litter its body before it evaporated into mist. The last two lions roared as they charged toward her. Clotilda dodged the beasts, swung her weapon to the second lion, and slayed it like the first. She turned to face the last lion, but her gaze became engulfed by its large paw as it swiped at her.

Her head was forced to the side when the lion's paw struck her helmet. The sharp, hook-like claws scratched along the decorative engravings of the helmet and caused her to cringe at the piercing sound. Her sight blacked out for a moment before she opened her eyes to see that the crystal sheet of her visor was littered with a spiderweb of cracks. Blinded, she grabbed her helmet and ripped it off, causing her long hair to spill over her shoulders. Then she tossed her helmet and turned her angry gaze to the lion, who returned for another attack. She blocked one of its giant paws with her weapon, transformed it into a dagger, and pierced it through the lion's skull, causing it to disappear into stardust.

Clotilda panted as she turned her attention back to the Graffias Manticore. She transformed Universeel back into its original form and charged toward him.

The princess tore her glare from him and shot her attention to the charging commander.

"Stay away, Clotilda!" she ordered.

"Clotilda . . ." he echoed, jerking his head to her.

Clotilda's long hair flowed behind her like a war banner, her face wrinkled into a snarl, and she bore her teeth like an attacking jaguar. She readied for him to lift his sword and collide it with hers as they had done earlier.

As Clotilda neared him, ready to fight him again, he banished his sword back into the confines of his hand chain. Clotilda gasped and stopped abruptly in surprise, holding her weapon over her shoulder, frozen in a battle position. The Graffias Manticore stood still as if he had been turned to stone. She could feel his gaze on her as if he were studying a painting.

"What's wrong? Why did you banish your weapon?" Clotilda asked him.

"I can't fight you," he spoke to her softly, anger and desperation no longer lacing his voice.

He slowly reached his hand toward her, but Clotilda flinched nervously and quickly stepped back.

"What do you mean by that?"

Coralina's neighs echoed outside as she flew around the tower. Clotilda broke her stare with the Graffias Manticore before she banished her weapon and hurriedly slipped past him. She heard him gasp from her sudden escape from him, feeling his gloved fingertips comb through some of the stray locks of her hair as she sensed him trying to reach for her again. Clotilda grabbed the princess's forearm and dragged her toward one of the large windows.

"Let go of me! How dare you take me away from my king!"

"Hold on," Clotilda said as she gripped the princess's shoulder and leaped out of the window.

The princess screamed as they fell toward the ground below. Coralina swooped toward them, hovering midair like a hummingbird as she caught her master and the princess on her back.

CHAPTER 17

The Chase

Clotilda grabbed the reins, ensuring she had a firm hold on Malvolia as Coralina flew them toward the sentinel tower. She glanced over her shoulder to the princess's tower to see the Graffias Manticore standing by the windows watching them.

"Take me back to the Graffias Manticore right now!" Malvolia yelled as she slapped her hand repeatedly on Clotilda's forearm.

"You can't go with him! You're already betrothed to the prince of a neighboring kingdom," she answered sternly before she looked back to see that the Graffias Manticore was gone. "Where did he go?"

"But the prince means nothing to me! I want the Manticore . . . ah!"

Clotilda growled as she grabbed the princess's wrist and yanked her off the saddle. She held the squirming royal in her outstretched arm like an angler catching a fighting fish as Coralina lowered them down to the sentinel tower, where the guards watched with worry and amusement. Bandus pushed himself to the front of the guards with his new staff and looked up as Clotilda and Coralina lowered the princess down to them.

"Let go of me at once!" the princess shrieked.

"As you wish," Clotilda replied with a smirk and swung the princess toward Bandus, who reluctantly caught her and wrapped his arms around her waist to prevent her from slipping away. "Where's the king?"

"We escorted His Highness to the tunnels that lead to the hidden safety chambers, and he ordered us to bring his daughter to him as soon as we found her," Ivan answered.

"We better not keep him waiting then. Please bring her back to the king. I'll stay out here and keep watch for the Graffias Manticore."

"Where is he?" Corinthia asked.

"He's gone. I'll head out and search for him. Protect the princess and the king while I'm gone."

"Be careful out there, Commander," Ivan said before he saluted her.

Clotilda flew overhead, watching her troops race down the tower with the princess. Malvolia struggled against them to break free, demanding they let her go. Clotilda scanned the empty capital below that had been cleared of citizens once the warning horn went off, keeping her eyes open for any signs of the Graffias Manticore.

Clotilda knitted her eyebrows together as she thought of how the princess tried to run to the Graffias Manticore and how he quickly moved away from her. But what puzzled her the most was how his actions changed when they fought.

Earlier, he fought her like an opponent, but he didn't try to hurt or kill her, which she was grateful about. But when she tried to fight him again after she lost her helmet, he didn't raise his sword at her and left himself completely open for an attack. His actions today didn't match the rumors about him being a bloodthirsty murderer, and she wondered why he hesitated.

Clotilda glanced down to see her troops opening the barred gate to the underground tunnels, reuniting the princess with her father before having a group of guards protecting the entrance.

"It's strange, Coralina," she said, gently petting her steed. "I don't know whether I am protecting the princess from the Manticore or the Manticore from the princess." She giggled at the last words, causing Coralina to neigh gleefully as if laughing with her.

Coralina snorted loudly as she picked up a troubling scent and threw her head back. She flapped her wings erratically and neighed loudly, bearing her fangs in a snarl. Clotilda tugged back on the reins, trying to calm down her steed with gentle pats on the neck.

"Shh, what's wrong? What do you smell?" she asked as she tried to soothe her.

Clotilda's ears perked when she heard the drumming of charging footsteps. She looked around, only to realize that the footsteps were not coming from the streets below but from the rooftops, and they were getting closer! The quick steps ended with the toe of a boot scraping against the roofing, indicating that whoever was running toward her had just jumped!

A startled gasp escaped from Clotilda's lips as she felt a muscular arm wrap around her waist and pull her backward until her back pressed against a firm chest guard. Unprepared for the ambush, Clotilda's legs slipped off Coralina's back, and she lost grip of the reins. She jerked her head over her shoulders, pushing her hair out of the way to see her captor. Her eyes widened when she saw the lion helmet of the Graffias Manticore staring back at her.

"Let go!" Clotilda demanded as she tried to break free from his grasp, but he held her close, his body acting like a shield as they fell toward the rooftops.

They grunted as they hit the rough surface of the roof and tumbled over toward the edge. She watched as he held out his arm, grabbing the rain gutters, and they hung over the market and the town's gardens two stories below. The Graffias Manticore swung his powerful legs toward the shaded balcony and let go. They landed safely, the mushroom surface of the patio straining as it supported the two elven warriors. Clotilda heard Coralina's panicked neigh and the flapping of her wings overhead.

"Cora . . . mph!" She tried to call out to her steed but was silenced by the Graffias Manticore's hand pressing over her lips. She grunted as she shot her hands up to his wrist to pry his hand off, but he held firm and pulled her back under the balcony, hiding them in the shadows. Coralina neighed loudly as she flew over the homes, her head jerking side to side in a frantic search for her master before disappearing out of sight.

Clotilda swiftly reached back, planting her hands on her captor's chest, and pushed away, breaking free from his grasp. She distanced herself from him, sprinting toward the vine railing of the balcony before she spun around to face him.

"If you're looking for the princess, I'm afraid you won't find her here," she said as she glared at him.

"I'm not after the princess. I never was," he said as he walked closer to her. Clotilda took a step back and grabbed the railing behind her. "There's someone else I've come for."

The commander's eyes widened in disbelief. If he wasn't after the princess, then who? The queen was dead, and the only princess here was Malvolia. Was he after a noblewoman from the court? Was he after a commoner woman? She felt a chill. His approaching and reaching out to her made it uncomfortably clear who he had in mind. He couldn't! She was a peasant, not a royal! Besides, Cyril was somewhere in this capital, and she wouldn't let the Graffias Manticore take her when she had waited for Cyril after all these years!

"Stay away," she glared as she summoned Universeel.

"It's all right. I'm not trying to hurt you, Clotilda," he said as he slowed his steps.

"Why me?" she barely spoke as her breath hitched.

"How can I choose anyone else? I went after the princess because I thought she was you. She has the same hair color, but when I saw her face, I knew she wasn't you."

Clotilda tightened her grip on her weapon, and her transfixed gaze was locked on the Graffias Manticore as she tried to draw further away from him. Her legs and the lower half of her spine were pressed against the railing, her upper half nearly hung over the gardens below, and her hair flowed over her shoulders like a flag. As her fear grew, she noticed that he had stopped his approach.

"Clotilda. Please. Don't be scared," he said as he slowly reached up and pressed his hands on the side of his helmet, beginning to take it off.

The tense air between them erupted as a burst of white light from an orb of magic shot out from the doorway of the building and struck the Graffias Manticore on the back. He grunted from the impact, but his feet remained rooted to the ground as if the attack was a slap. Clotilda looked toward the door to see Bandus standing at the frame with his staff aimed at the Graffias Manticore, smoke emanating from the enchanted gem on top of it.

"Come here, Clo!" Bandus demanded.

Clotilda shook her head at him. Of all the people she didn't want to be near and didn't trust, Bandus was one of them. She glanced down at the gardens. It was high, but she knew she could land at the bottom safely and figure out a way to escape.

"I'll meet up with you and the rest of the troops later," she said before she banished her weapon and climbed over the railing.

"Clo!" Bandus called out as he rushed toward her, only to freeze when the Graffias Manticore growled at him.

"Bandus, get out of there!" Clotilda ordered.

The Graffias Manticore grabbed Bandus by the collar of his cloak and held him up until the mage's feet were a foot off the ground. Bandus gasped for air and grabbed the Manticore's arm to free himself.

"Don't interfere again!" he snarled before punching Bandus in the face.

The mage grunted as he slammed back-first into the wall and slumped to the ground. Clotilda was ready to climb back over the railing to help, but her eyes caught the approaching Graffias Manticore coming toward her. She quickly turned around, leaped off the balcony, landed safely on the mossy ground, and fled into the gardens.

Flowering branches whipped against Clotilda as she pushed them out of her way as she ran. Witnessing the Graffias Manticore shapeshifting earlier, she knew he was a Regulus elf, and they were known for being swift runners. She wasn't sure how fast he could run in person, but she didn't want to find out. He was after her, and she needed to get far away!

She studied her surroundings, drawing a map in her mind of possible routes she could use to help give her an advantage. From her past experiences of playing with Cyril, she needed to avoid running down open trails of the garden, knowing it would provide the Manticore with an easy opportunity to catch her.

Clotilda pumped her arms to gain speed, glancing over her shoulder to hear his loud footsteps approaching her. Her muscles grew taut, ready to turn. She took a deep breath and quickly shifted her feet to the right, turning around one of the trees and hearing the Manticore's footsteps running past her.

Clotilda gasped as low-hanging branches threatened to snag her hair as she ducked underneath them. She glanced over her shoulder to see that he was in close pursuit again. She panted heavily as she scanned her surroundings, her eyes locking on a fast-approaching tree whose trunk was split slightly like a fork in a road. Quickening her pace and planting her feet firmly on the sloped tree trunk, she slipped sideways through the narrow opening. She swung her legs as if trying to run in the air before she landed on the grass and continued her sprint. She heard his boots clunking on the tree trunk before the muffled crunch of grass. He was catching up to her fast!

Clotilda navigated through the labyrinth of flowers until she exited the maze. Her chest heaved as she stopped, her feet throbbed, and every muscle in her legs burned. She dreadfully knew she couldn't run from the Graffias Manticore any longer and looked around for a place to hide. She perked her ears as she heard his footsteps getting louder as he neared the maze exit. There was no place to hide in the garden. She desperately turned her attention to the shops and hurried toward them.

Forcing her exhausted body to keep moving, she sprinted down the empty street of the market. Clotilda looked at the buildings around her, figuring she could hide in one of them until the Graffias Manticore lost interest in her. Much to her luck, she spotted a pottery shop and hurried over to it.

Entering the workshop, Clotilda was greeted by an army of planting pots of various shapes and sizes. The rows of enormous jars drew her interest, knowing she could easily hide entirely inside one of them. She approached the pot next to the last two at the end of the line and hopped inside.

Clotilda crouched down, the smell of clay and varnish invading her nostrils as she hid. She forced herself to breathe through her nose, not wanting to relinquish her position with her heavy panting. She stared at the inner walls of the pot, gently brushing her gloved fingers over it as she remembered hiding inside her blood mother's ceremonial pots of water when she was a little girl. Her mother didn't realize she was there and filled it with water, forcing the surprised but laughing Clotilda to spring from her hiding place.

Her smile dropped, and her alertness peaked when she heard the rapid, heavy steps of boots coming toward her. She held her breath as she listened. Then she heard the Graffias Manticore's footsteps echoing loudly as he entered the ceramic shop.

"Oh great . . ." she whispered as she heard the footsteps abruptly halt.

The air was intensely quiet for a moment, all except for her pulse drumming against her eardrums. The scratching of a heel scraped against the floor, and the boots clunking resonated through the clay walls of her hiding place. Clotilda closed her eyes tightly and remained completely still, anticipating that he would approach and peek into the pot where she was hiding. She cautiously opened her eyes halfway and raised her head to find no one was looking down at her.

Gathering her courage, Clotilda slowly peeked over the lip of the jar, seeing the Graffias Manticore walking along the rows of large pots and jars, peeking inside each one. She looked down the row, knowing it was only a matter of time before he came to the one she was hiding in!

She swallowed thickly as she drew a shaky breath before slowly standing up and planting her hands on the mouth of the pottery. Not taking her eyes off him, she slowly swung her first leg out of the pot, stepping on the tips of her toes to prevent her heel from tapping on the stone ground. She felt beads of sweat roll down her jawline, and her heart raced as he drew closer, hoping and praying that he didn't raise his head and look toward her. Clotilda rooted her weight into her standing leg and held onto the jar for balance as she lifted her second leg out of it. Her heart dropped to her stomach, and her blood went cold when he turned his head toward her.

He leaped over the rows of pottery toward the alley where she stood, knocking down and breaking pots with the heels of his boots and the fabric of his cape. Clotilda stumbled back as she faced him, summoning Universeel and holding it across her like a shield. They stood face to face, unmoving.

"I can't be your choice for a bride! I'm not from a royal family," Clotilda said as she glared at him.

"It doesn't matter to me," he said softly.

"It should. You're a king, and I'm only a guard," she replied as she glanced down at the reflection of the exit behind her on Universeel's blades and took slow steps back toward it.

"Only?" he questioned as if the word offended him before he charged toward her. Clotilda gasped as her eyes popped wide in startlement, and she spun around toward the exit, but the Graffias Manticore slipped past her and blocked her escape. "You're more than that! You're more to me!"

"What are you talking about?" She stepped back.

"I wouldn't be alive now if it weren't for your intervention that day when you woke me up," he said as he fished his hand into the pocket of his waist pack and pulled out his closed fist.

He opened his hand to reveal a pink bead rocking back and forth on his palm. Clotilda felt her breath hitch, recognizing the small bead as the one she had fired when she had torn apart her bracelet and used it as a slingshot to help wake a stranger from death. She looked at the hand chain around her left wrist, seeing the remaining beads of her broken bracelet.

"I thought I lost that bracelet while fleeing home that day," she said softly.

"I found it on the forest floor on top of a slope, along with the ones you used to exploit the group of Graffias Assassins when they were hunting for me. I originally wanted to return it to you, but I decided to reassemble your bracelet into a new piece of jewelry for you as a gift."

"But I don't see why a rescue like that would convince you to come for me," she said and paused as she glanced up at him. Then, as pieces began to come together in her mind, she felt her eyes starting to burn from oncoming tears. "Unless you're . . ."

"You did more for me than save my life," he replied, slowly pushing his helmet up.

A handsome face framed by blades of silver-split bangs and short neck-length hair appeared beneath the beastly helmet. The light outside the shop revealed his strong but handsome features and lit his piercing blue eyes as they locked on hers. The shy Regulus elf boy she befriended all those years ago was now before her as a grown man.

"Cyril . . ." she sobbed as tears spilled down her cheeks, and she banished her weapon.

Clotilda felt her legs become weak. She snapped her hand on one of the giant pots to prevent herself from collapsing. Her cheeks flushed as she bit her lips and swallowed her sobs.

Clotilda heard Cyril approaching her with hesitant steps. She turned to face him, felt his strong thumb trace her cheek, and rubbed the tears away.

She glanced up at him, seeing guilt and remorse heavy in his slitted pupils as he stared at her.

"I'm sorry it took me so long to find you," he said softly.

"I've been . . . wanting to see you again for so long. I thought I lost you." She fought to speak the words through her swelling throat.

"I thought I lost you too," he said, brushing his fingers through her hair.

"Get away from her!" Bandus's voice roared like thunder.

Clotilda quickly rubbed the tears from her eyes and looked around Cyril's shoulder to see the mage standing at the shop exit with his staff pointing at Cyril's back like a sword.

"Stand down, Bandus!" she commanded sternly at the mage as she glared at him.

"What are you saying? Get out of the way so I can fight him!"

"I order you to stand down!" she said as she attempted to walk around Cyril, but his protective arm kept her from proceeding further.

Clotilda froze when Cyril held his arm in front of her like a shield and watched as his expression morphed into anger as he put his helmet back on and approached the mage.

"Don't get any closer or I will attack!" Bandus said sharply, but Clotilda could sense the nervousness in his voice.

"I made it clear to you not to interfere," Cyril growled deeply like a lion.

"I don't listen to murderers like you," the mage sneered.

"Bandus . . ." Clotilda warned him, but he didn't listen.

Bandus cast his magic through the staff, only to backfire as it burst into splinters. Both Clotilda and Bandus stared at the cleanly sliced stump of what was once a finely crafted staff. She looked over to see Cyril had his sword summoned from his right-hand chain and held it in his outstretched arm.

"He's fast . . ." Clotilda whispered as she barely saw him summon his sword, let alone slice it through the wooden staff. Apparently, the staff couldn't defend against a sword, as Eltana said it would.

"That was my newest staff!" Bandus yelled.

"You should be grateful that your weapon got severed in half and not your body," Cyril said before he rotated his sword around and struck Bandus hard in the temple with the handle, and the mage collapsed to the ground unconscious. Cyril turned to Clotilda before dismissing his sword. "He'll wake up with a migraine, but he'll be fine," he reassured her.

Clotilda watched as Cyril lifted his helmet and placed his thumb and index finger between his mouth, and a powerful whistle escaped his lips.

"Let's get out of here," he said as he walked toward her.

"What? No, I can't. I have . . ." Her words got caught in her throat as one of his strong hands gently grasped her waist, the other slipped behind her knees, and he scooped her up in his arms.

"I'm sorry to do this, but we must go now," he said as he held her with care.

"But why? What's going to happen?" she asked in concern.

"With my old enemies here, I don't want you in harm's way, not again," he said as he turned around and walked toward the exit.

Clotilda flinched in surprise when she saw a giant horse-like beast standing on the street. The beast was streamlined like a cheetah and had sharp tusks like a wild boar. Its mane encircled its neck and spread into a trail down its stomach, and it had scaly plates on its back and claws like a dragon. The beast looked at her and Cyril with its orange, slitted eyes and snarled with a grunt.

"A dracstal," she said softly as she recognized the beast.

"A friend of mine is letting me use his steed for now. Xavier here is not as fast as Sleipnir, but he is a good steed all the same," Cyril replied as he stepped on the saddle stirrup with his left foot and swung his right leg over Xavier's back. He carefully sat Clotilda on the front of the saddle and held her waist with one hand and the other on the reins. "Let's go, Xavier!" he said as he snapped the reins, and the creature roared as it raced down the empty streets.

CHAPTER 18

Iron Arrow

Clotilda's hair whirled around her face and coiled around her armored shoulders in the fast-moving winds. She shifted slightly on the saddle to see the orphanage quickly approaching them. She jerked her head and watched as they rode past it, and her eyes followed it as it disappeared. Clotilda felt her heart tug painfully. Stump, Rose Hip, Ignis, Garth, and the rest of the orphans—was she ever going to see them again?

She felt Cyril's arm protectively snake around her waist as if keeping her from leaping off the saddle. She dropped her head down sorrowfully, her mind racing with conflicting thoughts. Pain struck her at the idea that she would never see her family and friends again, and she worried what would happen once they found out she was gone. Her loved ones would be worried sick about her. They might fear that she was thrown into the dungeon or that the Graffias Manticore had taken her, just as Garth had feared. She recalled Ignis's words, expressing his concern that he didn't want anything terrible to happen to her and the protectiveness evident in his eyes. Ignis was a gentle Jotnar, but he was fiercely protective. She hoped Ignis wouldn't do anything that would endanger him or anyone else.

Clotilda was lost in her thoughts when she felt a gentle caress on her waist. She looked down and saw Cyril's hand and thumb rubbing her side, trying to comfort her as if he could sense her distressing thoughts. Raising her gaze to his helmeted face, she tried to peer into the pitch-dark sockets of his visors. Though she couldn't see his eyes, she could feel his empathy radiating from them.

A faint glimmer on the rooftops caught the corner of Clotilda's eye. She jerked her head up, seeing an oversized silhouette on the roof's edge over one of the village homes. She studied the shape carefully, realizing with horror that it was a Battle Komodon and how he was positioned. He was drawing a bow and aiming it right at them! Her eyes shot wide, and she jerked forward protectively toward Cyril.

"Look out!" she tried to warn him, but she watched helplessly as the reptilian archer released his hold on the arrow, and it speared through the air toward them, puncturing Cyril's lower back.

Cyril cried out in pain and his spine arched sharply, looking like it was about to snap in two. He quickly unwound his arm from around her as he slipped backward off the saddle and plummeted toward the market street. Clotilda pushed herself off the saddle toward him. Wrapping her arm around him, she quickly attempted to pry the arrow from his back. The wooden stick of the arrow snapped in half, and they both grunted as their bodies struck the ground.

Their tumbling came to a halt, and Clotilda pushed herself up with trembling arms. She glanced over at Cyril to see him lying face down on the ground. His helmet had a deep crack with a chunk of the lion's face missing. He planted his violently trembling hands on the ground as he attempted to push himself up. He tried moving his legs, but they didn't respond, and he collapsed back to the ground.

"Cyril!" She called out in panic as she got to her feet and dashed over to him.

Clotilda looked down at the broken stub of the arrow, seeing that Cyril's skin was swollen around the spine. She quickly realized in terror that his spine was damaged, and watching him struggling to move his legs meant he was paralyzed.

She glanced up at the rooftops, sensing that the archer was still up there, reloading and readying to fire another shot. Clotilda hurried behind Cyril, looped her arms under his, and securely hooked her hands around his shoulders.

"No, Clotilda. Leave me," Cyril said, strained in pain.

"I'm not leaving you like this," she said as she stood up. She grunted as she walked backward and dragged him toward one of the shops. "We need to find cover!"

Clotilda glanced up at the rooftops and made haste as she hurried to get Cyril into a nearby flower shop. She carefully laid him down on his side and kneeled beside him. She hesitated a little before grabbing the snapped wooden rod of the arrow.

"I'm sorry this will hurt you, but I must remove the arrow," she replied.

"Go ahead." He gave her his consent.

Clotilda nodded slowly before pressing her other hand on his back. Her gloved index finger and thumb pinched the arrow before carefully and swiftly pulling it out of his back, feeling it pry out of the links of bones in his spine. Cyril groaned loudly but relaxed as she rubbed her hand on his back to comfort him from the intense pain. She held the arrow up, seeing it had a dark, sharp iron point.

Casting her fire magic to ignite from her fingertips, Clotilda burned the arrow like a match. Iron was harmful to many elves and fairies. The last thing she needed was someone else to find it and get hurt.

Clotilda slipped her hand into her waist pack and fished out a handful of the Tears of Eir blossoms. She carefully placed the flowers over Cyril's injury and pressed them down gently to encourage them to heal him faster. She heard him hiss through his fangs from the pain, but his breathing soon stabilized, and his trembling slowly subsided.

"It will take a little while for the blossoms to heal you, but you should be able to walk again soon," she reassured him.

The tapping of claws above them caused her to tilt her head back. She looked up at the ceiling as she heard the Battle Komodon prowling the rooftop. She switched her right hand and pressed it against Cyril's back with her left to keep pressure on the blossoms and summon Universeel. She narrowed her brows together and held her weapon secure, waiting for their attacker to come down.

"Come out," she heard the Battle Komodon hiss, and she recognized his voice as Acanthus. "I know you're down there, my dear Clotilda. You have something that belongs to me."

"He belongs to no one," she whispered as she braced herself for the beast to show himself.

"I have an offer for you, my dear." She listened as she heard him scaling the roof with his long, armored tail dragging behind him. "Give the Graffias Manticore to me, and in return, I will call off my followers from your capital and never bother you and your people again. Deal?"

Clotilda clenched her teeth in disgust as she heard Acanthus's words. She felt Cyril's gaze and his strong hand grasping her left forearm. She placed her hand over his. She would never surrender Cyril to these evil creatures!

"I need an answer! My patience is growing thin," Acanthus said mockingly.

"There is no deal," she called up through the confines of the shop's ceiling. "He's not a bargaining chip, and I won't treat him like one!"

"It's such a shame to hear you say that," he said and clicked his forked tongue in disappointment. "Oh well. He would be useless to us with a damaged spine, let alone fight in the Slachten Arena again. Poor Delilah will be so disheartened that she lost her favorite pet."

Clotilda felt uneasy. She protectively swung her weapon over Cyril. "Well, farewell, my sweet Clotilda!" Acanthus hissed sinisterly as she heard his powerful arm swing, followed by a loud, metallic clanking of something bouncing off the ground.

A metal sphere with a swirling cloud of indigo inside it bouncing toward them caused her to recoil. An explosion orb! A dangerous invention of the Battle Komodons. Time slowed as she attempted to reach for the sphere to throw it away from them, but her heart sank and nausea fountained in her stomach as the orb shattered open.

A pale blue light engulfed the shattering orb and transformed into a ghostly lion cub before her. The explosion orb froze as if time had stopped, and the cub glanced up at her with glowing eyes as if waiting for a command. She turned to Cyril to see his rune markings along his arms and the gap of his broken helmet that exposed his handsome face and glowing eyes. Cyril grunted as he pushed himself into a sitting position, his paralyzed legs beginning to move.

"Bring that back to our attacker!" he commanded as he looked at the cub.

The cub growled softly, answering his command, before rushing toward the shop wall and climbing up the stacks of boxes toward the rooftop.

Acanthus gasped, and the ground shook as he leaped off and ran away from the little cub chasing him. The cub coughed up the explosive orb and spat it toward Acanthus before it faded away into a shower of stardust. The sphere exploded on impact, and tongues of lapping flames spread throughout Acanthus's armored body. He shrieked as the heat intensified as he climbed back on top of the rooftops and fled.

CHAPTER 19

Apple Blossom

Yelling could be heard nearby, and the clunking of armored boots grew louder like rumbling thunder. Clotilda perked her ears, recognizing the approaching steps.

"My troops are coming," she said as she planted her left hand on her thigh. "I'll distract them long enough for you to heal completely, and then you can escape."

Clotilda attempted to push herself upright, but Cyril's hand gently grasped hers.

"Come with me," he said softly, his slitted pupils gleaming with a hopefulness that made her heart melt.

She stared deeply into his eyes through his broken helmet, her mind whirling. Torn like the split faces of a canyon, she didn't know what to do! Should she stay with her adopted family and friends in the capital or go with Cyril?

"Commander!" her troops called out to her.

Panic prickled inside her chest as she glanced toward the direction of her approaching troops before returning her gaze to Cyril.

"I can't. Not yet," she said softly. She lowered her head, her hair cascading down and blanketing her face. "If they find you, they will send you to the dungeon. I don't want that to happen to you! I can't lose you again!"

Cyril strained as he reached up to her and tenderly combed his fingers through her hair, causing her scalp to shiver and her breath to hitch.

"Half-moon," he said. "On the night of the half-moon, I will come for you," he ended his sentence as he slipped off her left glove and the hand chain he made for her, planted his lips on her knuckles and turned her hand around to kiss her palm.

The nerves in her hand beat wildly like dragonfly wings. Clotilda felt slightly self-conscious that her hands and fingers were sweaty from fighting and running when he first took off her glove, but her worries soon vanished once she felt his lips. He pulled away before gently tightening his hold around her hand, a silent promise of returning to her, before reluctantly releasing it.

Clotilda hesitated before forcefully pushing herself onto her feet and sprinting toward her approaching troops, hoping she could devise a plan to lead them away from Cyril.

Captain Corinthia led the troops down the alleyways, ceasing their charge as Clotilda ran toward them.

"Commander! What happened?" she asked as she quickly saluted her. "We heard a loud explosion!"

"It was from a Battle Komodon's explosion orb," Clotilda replied.

"Battle Komodons are attacking? At a time like this?" Ivan growled.

"I'm afraid so," Clotilda nodded.

"What about the Graffias Manticore? Where did he go?" Corinthia asked.

"I don't know," Clotilda fibbed. The sickening feeling of the lie she spoke burned her tongue and made her nauseous. She always hated lying and knew she was horrible at it. But she needed to protect Cyril and hoped her lie convinced her troops to believe her when she wove some truth into it. "I lost him after being separated from Coralina, and Acanthus ambushed me."

"Where did Acanthus go?" Ivan asked.

"He fled on top of the roofs. I don't know exactly where he is and don't want to take any chances with leaving him roaming free in the kingdom. We need to begin our search! I want each of you to form groups and search the roofs and the slums. We need to make sure he doesn't get to the castle!"

"Yes, Commander," the troops said as they divided into smaller groups and split off into different directions.

"We'll stay with you and search this block, Commander," Ivan said as he tightly held his shield and spear.

Clotilda felt her blood freeze and dared not look toward the shop where Cyril was hiding. But she saw an advantage with some of her troops being here. She didn't want to leave Cyril alone in the proximity of Acanthus if he returned to finish where he had left off. Having two of her forces as extra reinforcement gave her a sense of comfort and confidence in fending off Acanthus if he were to return. But she had to be watchful not to provoke any suspicions from her troops.

"Very well then. Don't let your guard down, and stay close to each other!" She saluted them before turning and marching down the alleyway.

The royal guard searched the town square. Clotilda glanced at the shop where she had left Cyril. Concern for him constricted her heart like a serpent's coils, and she wondered if he had completely healed yet. She tore her gaze away from the shop and pretended to search as she eyed her troops, seeing them searching the street and market stands with their weapons summoned.

Clotilda turned her gaze back to the shop, only to feel her heart drop when she saw the captain making her way over there.

"Captain!" she called out as she hurried to the shop.

Relief bloomed inside when she looked at the empty spot where she and Cyril hid.

"What is it, Commander?" Corinthia asked as she looked back at her.

Clotilda quickly looked up from the ground to the captain.

"Uh . . . I don't think it's wise to search the shops alone. We need to stick together as a group."

"That's true," the captain agreed flatly. Clotilda worriedly sensed that Corinthia suspected she was hiding something from them. "We'll continue our search."

"Yes, good," she said as she looked around, wondering where Cyril had gone.

Soft humming like a bee caused Clotilda to perk her ears and look around the shop. The humming sounded again as if guiding her where to look. She tilted her head back, her eyes searching the wooden rafters overhead until a small plumage of white caught her eye.

A hummingbird was perched on top of one of the wooden beams. Its feathers were white and silver like a snowflake, looking down at her with familiar blue eyes. A smile slowly spread on her lips as she looked at him, relief blooming inside her like a garden of awakening flowers in the spring.

"What do you see?" the captain asked as she glanced up to see what Clotilda was looking at.

"A hummingbird," Clotilda replied as she kept her gaze on the tiny bird, fully knowing who he was.

"Adorable little thing. It's not often we see one inside the market shops like that," the captain said before returning her gaze to her leader. "Well, we better return to searching."

"Right," Clotilda agreed with a nod as she followed the captain, her gaze not leaving the hummingbird as she walked away, feeling Cyril's protective gaze on her, and he flew above as she continued her search.

The royal guard searched every corner of the capital, from the winding veins of streets to the tiniest alleyways, searching behind stacks of crates and in every shop for hidden Battle Komodons. Clotilda volunteered to venture into the more ominous areas, not wanting to risk her troops' lives when her Rune power could resurrect her. But she wasn't alone. She could sense her hidden protector following her everywhere she went. From a hummingbird to a mouse and a lizard, she could see Cyril shapeshift into each animal as he followed her, watching out for her.

Much to her relief, Clotilda and her troops didn't find Acanthus or any more Battle Komodons. She hoped he was the only one here, but she couldn't shake the creeping feeling that more of them were hidden in the kingdom. If there was one Battle Komodon, there was a big possibility that there were more nearby.

Clotilda dragged her feet as she went home, feeling utterly exhausted from the day's events. Her body was sore, her muscles burned, and her joints felt stiff and rigid. Her mental fortitude was also dwindling, along with her physical strength.

After the emotional revelation of the Graffias Manticore's identity, she felt like her strength had melted away with her tears. She still couldn't believe that Cyril was the Graffias Manticore.

Finishing their search, Clotilda and her troops learned that King Thierry and Princess Malvolia were escorted back into the castle after it was searched, and the capital was pulsing with the bustle of citizens resuming their daily lives.

Clotilda called the worried-sick Coralina back home with her whistle and helped settle her down in the stable to rest up from the long day. She reached the door of her house, looking around for any signs of her stealthy guardian before she unlocked and opened the door. She locked the door behind her and went to her room. She breathed a drawn-out sigh as she removed her heavy armor and put it inside her dresser, ready to be worn again for her next guard duty.

She took off her glove and right-hand chain and instinctively reached for her left arm but realized that Cyril had taken the glove and the second-hand chain off earlier to kiss her hand. Clotilda sighed softly, grateful that she didn't lose the hand chain Cyril made for her, but a part of her felt connected to it. It was a gift from him, and she wanted to protect it.

Wearing only her brown jumpsuit, Clotilda sat down on the edge of the bed to get the thigh-high boots off her sore feet. Her legs and feet bloomed with relief as soon as they were released from their leather confines. She took them off, let them slip from her grasp, and heard them fall to the wooden floor by her bed. The commander laid down on top of the soft blankets, her hair cascading over her form as she rested her left cheek on the pillow. Clotilda's exhausted mind wandered, wondering where Cyril could be. She was grateful for his protection, but her thoughts turned to worry as she recalled his earlier words. He had come for her as promised, but could she leave Streng with him? Could she leave behind her family and friends? She felt her heart twist painfully at the thought. What was she going to do? She wasn't prepared to go, let alone be chosen by the Graffias Manticore.

Clotilda jolted up in awareness when she saw the setting sunlight spilling out her window flicker as if something had walked past it. She glanced at it, focusing on something on top of the windowsill. Clotilda walked over and peeked through the crystal glass to see that it was her missing glove and hand chain, with an apple blossom resting on top of them. She opened the window, scooped up her glove and hand chain, and plucked the flower by its wooden branch. A smile spread as it reminded her of the apple tree orchard in Cygnus. This one must have come from the royal gardens when Cyril followed her. She smiled as she brought the humble blossom to her nose and smelled the sweet scent.

Clotilda noticed a white butterfly standing on the windowsill, the same one she had seen last night at the masquerade ball. She realized it was Cyril again, looking up at her. They locked eyes as she smiled at him.

"Welcome back, Cyril," she whispered as he fluttered his wings in response.

CHAPTER 20

Scars and Love Letters

Dreamless sleep came once Clotilda forced her racing mind to block out all thoughts and worries. The energetic duets of birds and messenger squirrels chirping outside her home woke her from her deep sleep. She stared at the apple blossom that Cyril had given her last night, putting it in a crystal vase and placing it on her nightstand before getting dressed in her white nightgown and falling asleep.

Feeling the heavy haze of sleep lift from her gaze, she gathered her rekindled strength and sat up. She pushed the blankets off and sat up from her bed to get dressed, ready to face whatever challenges awaited her.

She slipped out of her nightgown and pulled on a brown peasant top and a pair of slim, black pants. She opened her jewelry box and put on a simple black choker with a pink pendant. She sat by her vanity and held her long hair as she carefully combed through the locks.

Clotilda stopped her wooden comb midway down her hair when she saw a feline silhouette in front of her window through her vanity mirror. She glanced over her shoulder to see a lion cub sitting on her windowsill.

Recognizing the white fur and the blue eyes looking back at her, Clotilda put the comb on the vanity table and got up from the stool. She walked over to the window, seeing Cyril tilting his head back to look up at her as she neared him. She hesitated momentarily as she stared at the lock of her window. Then, gathering her courage, she unlatched it and slowly pushed it open. She expected Cyril to make his way in as soon as she opened the window or leap off and run away, but he remained sitting patiently and looking up at her. She couldn't stop the smile from spreading on her lips. Cyril is undoubtedly a gentleman.

Clotilda slowly approached him, watching his ears fold back shyly as her fingers stroked his forehead. She slipped her hands under his stomach and chest and carefully scooped him up in her arms. She stepped back into her room and held Cyril up to see him looking back at her, his body limp in her hands.

"I'm glad to see you're doing better after what happened yesterday," she said as she gave him a soft smile and sat on the bed. She laid him on her lap and stroked her hand over his furry back. She paused when her fingers grazed over patches of bare skin. She focused her attention on his body, her eyes immediately drawn to one of the scars on his back. She studied the circular-shaped scar between his shoulder bones, seeing old puncture marks that looked to be made from fangs. Clotilda felt him tense under her touch and shift as if ready to leap off her lap.

"It's all right. I won't hurt you," she reassured and continued petting him.

She saw another old scar on his lower back from the bite marks that looked like he had been sliced with a large blade.

From his spine, her curious gaze locked onto chalk-colored rings around his wrists. She carefully picked him up and pressed him against her chest for support, noticing how his ears perked with interest.

"I'm sorry," she shyly said before petting his arms and feeling the deep scars on his wrists. She looked at them with concern before a chilling realization caused her to shiver when she identified them. The wounds were from shackles, and the deeper rings under the junction of his paws told her that he had been hanging from where his binding had been holding him up . . . like a prisoner.

Clotilda remembered seeing prisoners and criminals wearing shackles when she had to go down to the dungeon on King Thierry's orders. The bindings they used were made of magic instead of iron. But feeling the texture of the damaged skin on his wrists to the same texture as the scar on her cheek, Clotilda felt her heart drop when she realized that Cyril had worn iron shackles.

She released her hold on his paws and stroked her fingers along his jawline and ears, hearing him purr in contentment to her comforting touch and leaning his head against her collarbone.

"What have you gone through, Cyril?" she asked as she looked down at him with concern.

Loud knocking on the front door caused Cyril to perk his ears and jerk in Clotilda's embrace. She looked at the door and then back down to see Cyril slip out of her arms and run out of the bedroom.

"Cyril!" she called out to him in a whisper as she stood up and followed him.

She went to the kitchen, looking around for him as she walked to the door. She slowly opened the door and was greeted by the captain.

"Corinthia? What are you doing here?" she asked, surprised.

It was unusual for Corinthia to come to her house, but from the urgent look on her face, Clotilda could tell it was an emergency.

"I'm sorry to bother you, Commander, but I'm here because of orders from the king," Corinthia said with a salute.

"What are his orders?" Clotilda asked as she glanced at the small mirror on the right side of the door frame. She used the mirror to look around for Cyril until she saw him hiding underneath the dining table, lying on the floor like a sphinx as he watched them. Clotilda felt at ease knowing where he was and returned her gaze to Corinthia.

"He's asked for you to come to the castle. He wants you to guard his daughter again like you did yesterday and make sure the Graffias Manticore doesn't try to kidnap her. . . ." Clotilda glanced into the mirror to see Cyril. She bit the inside of her cheeks to prevent them from curving up into a smirk and swallowing a giggle when she noticed Cyril rolling his eyes at the captain's words. "What are you looking at, Commander?" Corinthia asked as she tried to peek into the house.

"It's nothing," Clotilda replied as she leaned against the door frame in front of the captain to block her prying sight, not wanting to take the chance of her seeing Cyril. "I'll get my armor on and report to the castle as soon as possible."

"Make sure you're quick. The king has been impatient since his daughter argued with him yesterday in the tunnels."

"I will," she sighed before closing the door and turning her attention to Cyril, but he wasn't there. "Cyril," she called out, keeping her voice down as she looked around for him and returned to her bedroom.

Once she realized Cyril wasn't inside her bedroom, she quickly changed into her jumpsuit and armor and put on her hand chains. She hurried to get her thigh-high boots and waist pack on before racing out of the house and saddled Coralina before galloping back to the castle with the captain following close behind.

She urged her pegasus towards the castle and glanced back at her home as it began to shrink away in the distance until it was barely a speck. Clotilda couldn't help but worry about Cyril. She prayed to the Father God that he would wait for her to return. The last thing she needed was for him to be in danger if he followed her to the castle.

The commander and captain arrived at the castle, only to be greeted by the furious king. Clotilda didn't say much to him but greeted him with a bow and went to the princess once the king told her where she was. She went to the royal gardens to see the princess looking up at the trees, appearing to be waiting for something. She approached the princess and kneeled behind her.

"Good morning, Your Highness," she said politely, but the princess silently ignored her and kept her eyes on the treetops.

Clotilda sighed softly in frustration, knowing she should have expected no response, but a part of her was relieved that she was ignored. It gave her some reprieve from the princess's rudeness.

The soft tapping of tiny, nimble fingers caused her ears to perk, and she looked up to see a messenger squirrel wearing a royal bridle with a message inside the capsule on its back. The squirrel quirked its head to the side as it looked at Clotilda and Malvolia, appearing to need clarification on whom to deliver the message. After a pause, it turned its gaze to Clotilda and walked over to her.

Clotilda held her palm to the squirrel, allowing the little creature to climb onto her hand. She turned to the princess to see her still gazing at the treetops. She wondered if she was waiting for this messenger squirrel. The princess tried to hide a messenger squirrel from her yesterday, and a ripple of suspicion grew in Clotilda's veins. What was the princess up to?

The princess had committed reckless and selfish actions in the past that nearly endangered the people in the capital. Clotilda usually didn't pry, but something about this message demanded her to read it! The last time she tried respecting the princess's private letters with a wicked nobleman from the court, it almost cost the lives of innocent people! Was Malvolia doing it again? She had to find out!

Clotilda patted the squirrel as she opened the capsule on its back. Inside was a purple pendant and a small scroll decorated with stairs of beautiful handwriting. The pendant was the shape of a monkshood flower with a small cluster of round, black gems that resembled seeds inside it. She fully opened the scroll and began reading it.

My beloved princess,

I have received your letter and map to the kingdom, and I will come for you tonight. I'm afraid you're mistaken when you wrote to me last night, asking me why I was chasing after another woman. I assure you that the mage you speak of who told you that is wrong. You're the only one for me, and I shall prove it to you tonight. Meet me outside in the castle gardens near the pond and read the writing aloud on the back of this pendant to call for me.

Your husband-to-be,

The Graffias Manticore.

Nausea erupted inside Clotilda's stomach, and pain seized her as if her organs shattered like glass and studded the inner walls of her body. Did Cyril write this letter? It couldn't be . . .

"My letter!" the princess shrieked before running over to Clotilda and ripping the scroll and pendant from her grasp. "How dare you read one of my love letters!" she sneered at her with a glare.

"One of them? How long have you been sending him letters?" Clotilda asked, her hands trembling.

"It's none of your concern!"

"It may as well be," Clotilda replied sharply. "How long have you been writing letters to him?"

The princess flinched from Clotilda's growing anger before glaring back at her.

"Ever since I heard the rumors about the Graffias Manticore! I'm in love with him!"

"How did you manage to write to him?"

"I sent as many messenger squirrels as possible in different parts outside the kingdom," the princess replied nonchalantly.

"You what?" Clotilda asked as her blood roared. "It could be anyone writing back to you, pretending to be the Graffias Manticore!"

"Of course it's him! I would know if it wasn't him!"

"Is it true that you sent a map that pinpoints the kingdom's blind spots and secret passages?" Clotilda asked through her clenched teeth. "If that map gets into the wrong hands, you have endangered the lives of your people and your family again!"

"Watch your tongue," the princess said, slapping her free hand on her hip. "I think you're jealous that the Graffias Manticore loves me! Bandus told me that the Manticore was chasing after you yesterday. But I know the truth! He was going to torture you into telling him where I was!"

"Princess . . ." Clotilda sighed frustratedly as she ran her gloved hand down her face, flattening her bangs. "I'm not jealous. I'm worried sick for his safety and everyone here . . ."

"Wait! Who's 'him' you're referring to?" she sneered.

Clotilda felt her chest tighten at her mistake. She didn't say Cyril's name but knew it caught the princess's attention.

"It's nothing," she said, returning the glare, feeling the burn of the rune markings threatening to appear on her skeleton.

"You better stay away from my Graffias Manticore! You will suffer the consequences if you tell my father or anyone else about this! Now get out of my sight!" she yelled before running away with the letter and pendant.

CHAPTER 21

Graffias Assassins

Leaving the princess to daydream and read the letter over and over to herself, Clotilda wasted no time taking the opportunity to retreat to the archway under the staircase to the palace balcony and stand inside it. She needed to be alone. A storm of emotions, anger, confusion, and sadness swelled in her body as if she were stung by jellyfish. She growled frustratedly before punching her right hand against the stone wall. She ignored the pain and the blooming bruise as she shot her hands up to her forehead and raked her fingers through her scalp, fighting the tears threatening to spill.

"Come on, Clo," she breathed shakily as she tried reassuring herself as she felt the clawing of the Deity of Lazarus inside her. "Don't jump to conclusions."

Distressed thoughts vortexed in her mind like a typhoon. She tried to narrow her thoughts, gathering memories of her first encounter with Cyril since his arrival in the capital. His words echoed in her mind about how he had come for her and his attempt to escape the kingdom with her.

Clotilda let her hands drop, easing herself with the recounted memories. However, she still couldn't believe that the princess went this far with a selfish plan of sending random letters to numerous places and even a map of Streng's blueprints to an imposter. She glanced over at the frolicking princess and stared at the pendant in her hands, sensing ominous magic radiating from it.

Clotilda caught a glimpse of movements at the curve of the archway and jerked her head up, ready to summon Universeel. Feathers glistened like falling snow, and wings beat rapidly like ripples on the water's surface as a white hummingbird flew toward her. Clotilda calmed down and stepped back as the hummingbird hovered at eye level with her before he began transforming. His bird form grew and formed into the muscular build of his elven form.

Cyril stood before her, his handsome face framed by his hair and powerful body covered with his Graffias Manticore armor and the damaged helmet tucked under his left arm. Clotilda took a few more steps back, feeling her spine press against the stone wall as she stared at him. She hadn't seen him anywhere since she got dressed in her armor back at her house and rode off to the castle. She wondered where he had been hiding and hoped no one saw him.

Cyril looked at her with concern, confirming her suspicions that he had been with her all this time.

"How long were you here?" she asked him in a whisper, hoping the princess and the rest of the castle guards wouldn't hear them.

"Since I came to your windowsill this morning," he whispered.

"You were still in my house the whole time? Even when I . . . oh dear," she blushed at the thought of him being nearby when she changed into her armor.

"No, no," he quickly said, holding his hand up as if making a vow. "I went outside when I saw that you were starting to change. So I didn't peek."

"I appreciate that," she smiled at his polite actions as she brushed her hair behind her ears.

"I heard what you and the princess were talking about. I swear on my ancestors' names that I didn't write those letters to her."

"Then who did?" she asked, feeling relieved and horrified at the same time.

"It must be from one of the assassins of the Graffias clan. I recognize the pendant," he said with a frown that made her nervous.

"What does the pendant do?"

They went silent as they heard the castle guards pace overhead. Clotilda watched silently as the guards walked around the garden, greeting the princess before patrolling. She returned her gaze to Cyril after she watched the guards walk away.

"That pendant harbors dark magic. Destroy it whenever you have the chance," he said.

"I'll try, but I've never stolen before."

"If you want, I can try," he offered.

"No, it's too risky," she shook her head, not wanting to risk Cyril's safety.

They went silent as one of the castle guards walked by. She glanced back at her male companion after the guard left and continued in a whisper.

"If the princess sees you, she will cause an uproar. I'll have to wait until she puts the pendant down before I can destroy it. She'll lose it if she sees me spiriting the necklace away or holding it."

Cyril stepped closer, causing her to tilt her head back, realizing how much taller he was than her, even with her high heels. She felt her skin tingle as he reached down to her right hand with his and held it up as if he were going to kiss it again. Instead, his thumb lightly brushed over the spot where she punched it against the wall, soothing the stinging nerves in her palm with his thumb.

"I don't like seeing them mistreat you like that," he said softly, but she could sense slight anger in his voice. Although this anger wasn't directed toward her, it made her shrink back a little. "Tomorrow night is a half-moon. I'll get you out of this prison of a capital," he vowed before gently placing his other hand over hers affectionately. "Please don't hurt yourself again. An artist needs to protect their hands. Especially with how precious your music is."

Clotilda felt her heart flutter. He remembered she was a musician, even after all these years. Cyril reluctantly released her hand before shapeshifting back into a hummingbird and flying out into the garden.

Clotilda slowly pried herself from the rough, cold stone wall, her heart beating faster from Cyril's words, and she felt waves of emotions washing over her, drowning out the hurt and wrath and replacing it with a sense of hope and relief. She took a deep breath and held her right hand up, feeling Cyril's warm touch through the fabric of her glove. She felt a sense of calm at the realization that Cyril hadn't sent the letter, but she felt uneasy about his warning. Who gave Malvolia the pendant and sent the princess the fraudulent love letters?

She wished Cyril and her had more time to talk about it, but the garden was prowling with castle guards, and she had to get back to guarding the princess before anyone saw her and suspected her of loitering around. She balled her hands into fists, knowing there was only one way to find out who was writing the love letters, but she would have to wait until nightfall.

Clotilda stayed close to the royal gardens, watching every corner of the trees, flower hedges, and even the reflection of the starry night and crescent moon in the pond. The commander leaned against one of the columns of the castle, watching as the princess stood by the balcony railing, clenching the pendant in her slender fingers. Clotilda flipped through the written pages of her music journal as she waited for the princess to drop her guard and occasionally look up from it to eye the pendant.

She had been planning how to swipe the pendant all day. But the princess kept it very close to her, making it impossible for her to snatch it. She didn't want to think about what kind of powers the pendant possessed and hoped she could destroy it once she had the opportunity.

Clotilda put her music journal back into her waist pack and attempted to follow the princess heading down the stairs to the garden but stopped once the princess did. Malvolia looked back at her with a glare.

"You stay here! I want to enjoy my time with him alone," she said before she descended the stairs, grabbing a torch from the sconce as she approached the pond.

Clotilda shook her head before she leaned against one of the columns and folded her arms across her chest. She looked around, seeing the princess standing at the pond's edge and holding the pendant in the torch's light. Clotilda listened closely with her sensitive hearing to the words the princess was reading out loud:

Lost wanderer of my desires,
I call to you from my blackened heart,
Let your worries and cautions slip into the darkness of the abyss,
Come to me as my slave.

The words dripped with malice. Clotilda felt an unsettling nausea in her stomach as she sensed a powerful aura of dark magic resonating from the pendant. She wished that she had heeded Cyril's advice sooner and snatched the pendant from the princess, even if it meant prying it from Malvolia's fingers.

Clotilda glared as she looked out the corner of her eyes. Someone was standing behind her! A large hand grazed her armored shoulder, and her skin prickled as she felt his fingers brush her hair. She shot her hands up to her shoulder toward the hand, slapping it away, and turned sharply to see who was behind her.

"Bandus," she whispered sharply, seeing the mage standing behind her wearing a mischievous smirk on his lips.

"Scared you, didn't I . . . ?" he asked but was cut off as Clotilda slapped her hand onto his lips.

"Be silent," she hissed at him before she pushed him against the wall and returned her attention to the garden.

Clotilda looked around, her eyes fixed on a male silhouette framed between the trees. Her eyes went wide, and she felt her heart drop when she saw that the approaching figure was Cyril. The princess beamed as soon as she saw him and sprinted toward him.

Clotilda narrowed her eyes at how Cyril walked. It looked very . . . unnatural. Every step he took looked like his limbs were held and guided by strings. The princess collided with him, wrapping her arms around him in an embrace. Cyril didn't move out of the way like the first time the princess tried to hug him. His body was limp, and he jerked from the impact of the princess, like a slab of raw meat hanging on a hook at the butchers.

The crunching of branches ensnared Clotilda's attention toward the circle of trees surrounding the princess and Cyril. Shadowy figures emerged from the darkness and approached them. Clotilda recognized the gray cloaks of the Graffias Assassins, each stained with splatters of red, which made her stomach churn. Their armor resembled the armor plating of a scorpion's body, and their hoods were up and darkened their faces, so they were hard to identify. Clotilda felt the slit wound scar on her throat throb.

Three years ago, she was training Ivan, a trainee, before dawn when they were on guard duty. She remembered the peacefulness of that night and how her advice and calm conversations with Ivan were the only sounds in the air. Out of nowhere, a female Graffias Assassin had entered the kingdom and had made her way to the sentinel tower, where Clotilda and Ivan were patrolling. Ivan was unaware of the hidden assassin, who was creeping up on him with a dagger, ready to strike. Protecting her new friend, Clotilda slipped between him and the assassin and had her throat slit open before collapsing to the ground, drowning in her blood. The Deity of Lazarus resurrected her in time to see Ivan struggling against the skillful killer before Clotilda struck her down through the skull with the blade of Universeel. Ivan was surprised by her resurrecting, but he didn't suspect her to be a Rune and thought her natural ability to be a Lazarus elf brought her back to life. There was no need to erase Ivan's memory of that night, and he told her how grateful he was for her saving him and was gifted with a hug and years of appreciation. Clotilda was thankful that she had saved Ivan; it was a death she was willing to take, even if it meant protecting one of her friends.

A figure charted through the group of assassins. Clotilda studied the small shoulders and slender movements and could tell that the newcomer was a female elf.

"Who are you? How did you get into the castle?" the princess demanded as she looked around frantically for an escape.

"Your poor excuse for guards was of no challenge to us," the female Seax elf said as she pushed down her gray hood, her red hair spilling over her armored shoulders like fresh blood from an open wound. "They were easy to kill, like lambs."

"Who are you??" the princess demanded again in terror.

"My name is Delilah, and I am the leader of the Graffias Assassins. But, first, I must applaud you. You've followed my instructions perfectly."

"What do you mean by that?"

"It's rather amusing. One of my followers did a fine job writing those love letters to you. He always had an alluring charisma to his written words. But I must say, if you are the future queen of this kingdom, it would be in ruin in no time," Delilah said as she reached into the pocket of her cloak and pulled out a small bundle of blood-stained fur in her hand. Clotilda squinted to look closer, realizing in despair that it was a slain messenger squirrel. Delilah smirked menacingly before she threw the corpse into the pond with a splash, turning the water red with an ink of blood from the poor creature. "Now hand over the pendant and the Graffias Manticore! He belongs to me," Delilah demanded the princess like a roaring ogress.

"Why would I give him to you? He's mine!" Malvolia protested.

"I beg to differ. Now that he is under the spell of my pendant, he's mine again. Now fork over my pendant, or you will die," Delilah said as she summoned a dagger from her hand chain and pointed it to the princess.

Anxiousness roared through Clotilda's blood. She looked over at Cyril, guilt burrowing inside of her like tunneling worms.

"Hang in there, Cyril. I'll free you somehow," she whispered before looking at the princess.

"Fine! Just don't kill me," the frightened princess pleaded as she held the pendant out to Delilah.

Clotilda knitted her eyebrows in disgust at the princess's actions. She treated Cyril as she did to all the other men she flirted with before discarding them. Clotilda had enough! She didn't care what punishment she would get from the royal family. She had to save Cyril!

Clotilda held her left palm up, warmth blooming in her nerves like lava. Bandus muffled words behind her right hand that stayed firmly pressed against his lips. Fire lapped from her palm, swirling into an egg-shaped orb. Feathers grew from the orb, and fiery wings ripped from her fingertips, uncurling to reveal a small bird made of fire.

"Destroy the pendant," she commanded the firebird.

The firebird leaped from her hand and charged toward the princess and Delilah. The princess shrieked as the bird rammed into the pendant, disintegrating it into ash on the lush garden ground.

Cyril gasped as he awoke from his trance as if waking up from a nightmare. He stepped away from the princess and placed his hands on the temples of his helmet as he breathed heavily.

"No!" Delilah roared as she stared down at the pile of ash on the ground.

Clotilda pulled her hand from Bandus's mouth before summoning Universeel from her hand chain.

"Stay here!" she ordered the mage before she stepped onto the railing.

"What are you doing?" Bandus tried to stop her.

"Stay here!" she ordered again before leaping over the railing and landing safely on the garden ground below. Cyril, the princess, and the assassins turned their attention to the new arrival. "Leave the Graffias Manticore alone!" Clotilda said as fire leaped from her fingertips and encircled Universeel's blades.

"Who are you?" Delilah asked as she glared at her.

"I'm one of the guards here, and you're trespassing on castle grounds. Leave now!"

Clotilda watched as Delilah looked out the corner of her eye at Cyril, noticing the worried stare through the broken eye visor of his helmet.

Clotilda glanced back at him, her frown softening as she met his eyes. She gave him a reassuring and apologetic gaze before returning it to Delilah, along with her glare. She watched as Delilah knitted her eyebrows into a frown.

"Slave," Delilah called out as she tapped her hand against her waist pack.

A woodland sprite with rotted, twig-like fingers clawed out of her pack and cranked his head to the side as if his neck was broken. The sprite looked like an old broken puppet and a walking stick insect. His body was made of wooden twigs, his arms and legs were long like a spider's, and he had a large head with a pointed snout like a rat. He had long, withered, flying ant wings on his back that were transparent and crinkled.

"Yes, mistress?" the sprite asked with a raspy voice.

"You mentioned one hundred and thirty years ago that you witnessed an elven girl with the Graffias Manticore, right?"

"Yes, mistress. I did. I did indeed," he nodded rapidly.

"Does this woman look anything like the girl you saw?"

The sprite looked around, his beady, brown eyes locking onto Clotilda. He stared at her for a few moments before cackling as he pointed his spindly index finger at her.

"It's her! I recognize that pretty face with that scar anywhere!"

Delilah glared at Clotilda.

"So you're the wretched girl who stole him from me!"

CHAPTER 22

Healer of the Crescent Moon

"Why did you choose her over me?" Delilah snarled as she glared at Cyril. "I knew your time in the Slachten Arena would jeopardize your mental well-being, but never would I have imagined that you would fall for an elf woman who is not only two hundred and sixty years younger than you but who was also a little girl!"

"You know him?" the princess asked as she looked at Clotilda. "Why didn't you tell me you knew the Graffias Manticore?"

Clotilda kept silent, ignoring the princess's question as she held her worried gaze on Cyril.

"She's done more for me than you could ever understand, Delilah," Cyril replied as he removed his helmet and returned her glare. "I wasn't attracted to her back then because she was a child, but I treasured her for who she was and still is, and I wanted to protect her. She saved my life."

"So, you're saying that I didn't? I made you excel in your ranking when you were in the Graffias clan, and I awakened the beast within you so you could receive the title of the Graffias Manticore!"

"By controlling my will and body with the pendant's power and forcing me to murder for you?" His tone grew sharp with anger.

"She's done nothing!" Delilah yelled as she pointed at Clotilda.

"What she's done is heal me!" Cyril retaliated, making Clotilda's heart flutter at how he defended her.

Cyril turned his gaze to Clotilda's, his eyes softening as he looked at her.

"I was a broken man back then—a fallen king who failed to protect his kingdom and was dethroned by a cruel tyrant. I was forced to kill when I was a slave to both the Slachten Arena and the Graffias clan. I lost everything. That is until I met you, Clotilda. You may have been a little girl back then, but your bravery and kindness gave me the strength I needed to reclaim my kingdom, and I promised myself, after I lost you when your village was destroyed, that I would not stop searching for you," he explained.

"You've been searching for me all this time?" Clotilda asked, feeling guilt fester inside her.

"I almost gave up until I sensed you the other night. Your footsteps were the heartbeats I was waiting so long to hear," he said with a smile that ignited her heart, and she softly smiled back at him.

"I've heard enough," Delilah interrupted. "I've waited long enough to get him back, and I am not going to allow you to steal him away from me again!"

Clotilda turned her gaze to the assassin, knitting her brows together, and her smile fell.

"If you wanted Cyril so badly, why did your assassins try to kill him while he was sleeping in that cave?"

"I wasn't the one who ordered them to kill him! Our former leader wanted him dead after he escaped, but I wanted him back alive. Our leader and some of our assassins went out to hunt for him. I was relieved when I heard from my slave that Cyril killed them all," she said as she patted her waist pack, the wood sprite poking his head out from the bag, and he cackled as he waved at Clotilda. "I was next in line to be the clan's leader, so once he was slain, I took over. Since you destroyed my pendant and ruined my plans," she said as she tightened her hold on her dagger and started walking toward Clotilda, "I will take great pleasure in killing you."

Cyril swiftly stepped in Delilah's way, blocking her path toward Clotilda, and growled as he grabbed her throat with his large hand, his fingers nearly wrapped around her neck.

"Try to hurt Clotilda, and I will kill you," he snarled as he bore his fangs at Delilah.

"Seize him!" Delilah choked out her order, causing her followers to summon their daggers and charge toward him.

Cyril threw Delilah to the ground, summoned his dual swords, and charged toward the wave of assassins, plowing through them as if they were made of paper.

Clotilda sprinted, hurrying toward the princess, and grabbed her by the forearm. She dragged the princess across the garden and guided her to the stairs.

"Get her out of here, Bandus!" she said to the mage, who stopped midway down the stairs. Clotilda shoved the princess up the steps toward him before she spun around on her heels and dashed back.

"Clo! Wait!" Bandus called out, but she ignored him and hurried back toward Cyril.

Clotilda charged, wielding Universeel as she struck the blades upon the Graffias assassins surrounding Cyril, trying to help reduce their numbers for him. She wanted to protect him just like he protected her!

Her fluid fighting abruptly stopped, and pain shot through her body like acid. Copper fountained in her throat, and warm streams of blood rivered down the corners of her mouth and chin. Clotilda turned to her invisible attacker, being greeted by Delilah standing right in front of her with a murderous smirk as she appeared before her, with the dagger plunged into Clotilda's chest.

"I don't forgive those who steal from me," Delilah said before roughly ripping the dagger out of Clotilda's chest, causing her to grunt sharply from the pain.

Clotilda looked over to see that Cyril had shot his gaze toward her. His eyes were wide in horror as soon as he saw the scene. She felt like the bones in her trembling legs caved in on each other, and she collapsed to the ground with Universeel shattering into ribbons of magic and disappearing back into her hand chain.

The sound around her faded, except for Cyril's roar of rage. She placed her hands over her bleeding chest and weakly watched through her blurring vision to see blue rune markings glowing all over Cyril's skeleton, and his eyes glowed like novas.

Clotilda fought to keep her eyes open as she watched him fight through the assassins. He effortlessly swung his swords, slicing through them and their weapons as he charged toward her, thirsting to spill Delilah's blood. Delilah's transfixed gaze lingered on him as he drew closer. She took hesitant steps back before spinning on her heels and fleeing away.

Cyril banished his swords into his hand chains as he kneeled next to Clotilda, carefully slipping his hand behind her back and lifting her until she sat up.

"Stay with me," he said softly to her.

Cyril brought his gloved hand to his mouth and bit into his glove. His sharp fangs dug into the fabric, and he tugged off the glove before spatting it to the ground. He gently placed his hand tenderly on the stab wound on her chest. His eyes glowed white, and the branches of his veins shone through his skin, reminiscent of moonlight.

Clotilda felt a warmth like the light of dawn and the dancing pulse of the northern lights course through her, soothing the pain and closing her wound. Her strength rekindled like a reborn flame.

"You're a healer?" she asked, looking up at him with amazement and gratitude.

"Only during the crescent moon," he smiled as the celestial glow faded in his veins and eyes.

Was this a power that Celestial Born elves had? she wondered. Clotilda barely had time to read the chapter about them, but she remembered catching a glimpse of them having certain powers depending on the shapes of the moon. But then her mind turned to how she watched Cyril use his Rune powers when they last fought and how he fought the Graffias. How was he able to control it?

"How do you control your rune powers?" she asked curiously.

"I don't control it. I only guide it. Have you ever used your powers as a Rune?"

"Only a small portion of it. I'm afraid I might lose control and hurt others again," she said solemnly, remembering Bandus and some of his friends who were bullies at the orphanage.

Bandus and his friends used to pick on her and her music when they were children and stole her music journal before tossing it into an unlit fireplace under the logs that Stump could have accidentally burned that frigid winter evening. With the agony of losing her blood family and her inability to create her music, Clotilda decayed into a Hollow and attacked everyone in the orphanage. Despite being somewhat aware of her actions as if she were in a quasi-state of sleep, Clotilda couldn't control herself, only watching in horror as she stalked and attacked Rose Hip and Stump and the orphans trying to escape her.

Somehow she could use her Rune powers in her Hollow state as she hunted after Bandus and his friends and used her fire magic to burn the bullies alive, reducing them to ash. Clotilda remembered their agonizing screams, engulfed in the roar of the inferno as their skins melted from their scorched bones. Bandus abandoned his friends as they burned to death.

Wanting to protect the rest of the orphans and save her from the horror of the Hollow form she was trapped in, Rose Hip and Stump demanded that Bandus reveal the hiding place of her music journal. They bravely approached her and returned her music to her, and she transformed back into her Lazarus elf form as they embraced her to comfort her.

After being comforted by the loving hobgoblins, the enraged Clotilda chased after Bandus and erased his memories of her being a Rune. Rose Hip and Stump feared for her safety once she explained how she acquired the Deity of Lazarus and what had happened to her village. They reassured her that her being the Rune of Lazarus was safe with them and told her never to reveal it to King Thierry.

"You have nothing to be afraid of," Cyril's voice pulled her from her memory, causing her to look up at him. "I used to be afraid of my powers as the Rune of Regulus too. Break free from the cage you've trapped yourself in and spread your wings. You have no reason to hide this incredible woman you have grown into."

"You have a lot of faith in me, even though we hardly know each other, except for that short time when we first met," Clotilda replied with a smile.

"I do have faith in you. But I also want to learn more about you," he said as he wiped the streams of blood off her chin.

Clotilda felt a blush bloom on her cheeks as she heard his words. Quick movements caught the corner of her eyes, and she saw one of the female assassins coming up from behind him with a dagger. Clotilda jumped to her feet, surprising Cyril as she summoned Universeel.

"Stay down!" she said as she stood over his broad shoulders and swung her weapon at his attacker, piercing the assassin's chest.

The assassin drew her final breath as Clotilda pried Universeel out of her ribs before she collapsed. Clotilda took a few steps back as Cyril planted his hand on his kneeling thigh and pushed himself up as he stood before her.

Cyril glanced up at the crescent moon looking down at them as if smiling at their reunion.

"I thought I could wait for the half-moon, but it's not safe here with all that's going on." He paused as he turned his gaze back at her. "Come with me tonight. We'll travel as far as we can, and then we can make the rest of the way back to my kingdom once it is a half-moon."

"But why were you wanting to wait until the half-moon?" she asked.

"Easier travel," he said with a wink. "Come with me, please," he said as he slowly held his open palm to her.

Clotilda's heart tore into two pieces, one wanting to go with Cyril, while the other half wanted to stay with her family and friends. She bit her bottom lip, looking up at Cyril, who stood patiently, his hand still outstretched.

Clotilda had been waiting for him, and he had kept his promise. She wasn't sure what would happen once she was with Cyril, but she knew she could trust him. Aside from her family and her friends, Cyril was among the few people she could ever count on and trust. He took a significant risk by coming here for her. Now it was her turn. He deserved a chance, and she would give it to him.

Purging the hesitation from her mind and body, Clotilda inhaled before she lifted her right hand, slowly reaching it to Cyril's, seeing his eyes widening in anticipation and hopefulness.

A high-pitched scream from the princess caused Cyril and Clotilda's hands to recoil from each other. They jerked their heads toward the castle to see tall, slender shadows of the Graffias Assassins gliding over the palace walls.

"Oh no . . ." Clotilda said as she sprinted toward the castle by instinct.

"Hold on," Cyril called out, causing her to stop and look at him.

"I'm sorry, Cyril, but I can't leave with you yet," she said apologetically.

"I'm not letting you fight them on your own," he said as he ran up to her. "I'll fight alongside you, just like you did for me."

"Thank you," she said with a smile.

"I'll help you protect the royal family, but once they're safe, let's leave this place."

"Let's do it," she said with a nod.

Cyril smiled at her before he summoned his dual swords, and they ran toward the castle together.

CHAPTER 23

Awakening

Cyril and Clotilda skipped a few steps as they ran up the staircase and sprinted down the hallway once they reached the top. The princess's screams and the screeches of Bandus's magic spells being cast were their compasses to guide them down the labyrinth of hallways.

The walls opened, revealing the Graffias Assassins surrounding the princess and the mage. Bandus held his ground and used his poorly mended staff to form a dome-shaped forcefield around himself and the princess. Delilah and her assassins turned their attention from their trapped victims to the approaching Cyril and Clotilda as they stopped abruptly.

"You healed her," Delilah frowned as she glanced at the crescent moon outside. "Enough wasting my time, Cyril! Surrender yourself to us, and I promise we won't harm the princess, the mage, and her," she hissed the last words as if they were dipped in venom as she glared at Clotilda.

Clotilda and Cyril looked around to see so many assassins—forty, they guessed. They were barely able to see the princess and Bandus through them.

"Spread your wings," Cyril said to her.

"What if I can't control myself?" Clotilda said nervously.

"You will. If I can wield my Rune power, you can too."

Clotilda allowed her eyes to follow the glowing blue runes on Cyril's skeleton. His hair glowed in the light of the torches on the wall and the chandeliers overhead. She noticed that his hair was dripping as if wet. But it wasn't water drops—it was fine particles of stardust. She followed the flow of his bangs, leading to his glowing blue eyes that looked back at her.

They tore their gazes apart to see the assassins charging toward them. Cyril stood protectively in front of Clotilda like a shield and summoned his sword. He bore his fangs as he waited for the attackers to come near. Then he quickly swung his sword, knocking down the assassins and slicing through them, spilling beads of blood on his armor and face.

Moonlight spilled through the balcony window, bathing them in its glow. Clotilda instinctively stepped back when she heard Cyril snarl as if the moonlight was enraging him. He glanced over his shoulder at her, causing a shiver to run up her spine. However, this wasn't just Cyril looking back at her. The Deity of Lazarus within her chirped, responding to the Deity of Regulus inside Cyril.

Cyril turned his attention back to the assassins, his aggression returning as soon as he gazed upon them and attacked them as they drew closer. Clotilda summoned Universeel and joined Cyril in the fight. She sliced off their weapon hand chains and stabbed them with Universeel's blades.

Cyril's sharp grunts caused adrenaline to stab through her, and she jerked her gaze to him, worried that he had gotten hurt. Cyril stood around the corpses of the assassins who foolishly attacked him, and she quickly glimpsed at his body to see he wasn't fatally injured, much to her relief. Then Cyril's body began to morph; his armor and clothes dissolved into his flesh, revealing his toned, bare body. His skin split open, revealing an indigo abyss with plums of teal-blue underneath.

The rhythm of charging assassins snapped Clotilda back to the battle. She fought off the second wave of assassins and saw Bandus keeping his magic barrier around him and the panicking princess beside him. She tore through some of the assassins and glanced back at Cyril, tilting her head back to see he had transformed into a giant lion.

Cyril's lion body was made of an indigo celestial sky, painted with aqua and purple cosmos. His mane was a halo of falling stars raining down on the marble floor like snow, and his eyes glowed like a pair of albino suns.

From what she remembered from the stories told by her blood parents, Runes were said to transform into the animal deity that represented the seven elven cultures and become infused by the Rune's characteristics. One of those stories was the legend of King Fenrir, the Rune of Beetje, who can transform into a giant wolf made of a spiritual forest of animals to represent the Beetje elves' gift of talking to animals.

With Cyril being the Rune of Regulus and a Celestial Born elf, he transformed into a celestial lion. He towered over everyone, and his back pressed against the castle ceiling as if he were balancing the entire weight of the kingdom, forcing him to bend his head down, giving him a more aggressive and intimidating presence.

His breath curled like smoke plumes from a dragon's mouth before it breathed fire as he opened it. He bellowed a mighty roar that sounded unworldly and echoed as if it were the breaths of the universe. Clotilda threw her hands over her ears and stared at him in amazement. Cyril's rune form was beautiful. She was afraid he might lose control, but he was still there, in complete control of his will, and intertwined with the Deity of Regulus.

Cyril held up his paw and swiped away groups of assassins at a time as if they were clusters of mice. Clotilda tore her gaze from Cyril's eyes to the movement of another wave of assassins charging under the celestial lion with their weapons transformed into spears and polearms long enough to reach his underbelly. Fear struck her in the stomach like nausea. They were going to try to gut Cyril alive!

Clotilda spun quickly on her heels and ran toward Cyril and the assassins. She thought of how Cyril told her she had nothing to fear and could transform without losing control of herself. She had locked herself away in walls of self-doubt and worry of exposing the Deity of Lazarus in fear of endangering those around her. But Cyril was right. She had to break free and spread her wings.

The Lazarus deity within her chirped anxiously like a hungry hatchling, calling for freedom. Rune markings spread over her skeleton as she ran underneath him and fought through the Graffias Assassins. Memories flashed before her eyes, nearly blinding her as she remembered that day when she drank from the sacred waters that housed the slumbering Deity of Lazarus.

Despite the shock and terror of the invaders destroying her village and attacking her people, Clotilda hurried to the fountain of the sacred treasure of Lazarus. Her people cherished the Deity of Lazarus, and she couldn't think of letting it fall into the hands of their undead attackers!

Clotilda looked into the gold water flowing through the egg-shaped bowl of the fountain. She grabbed a seashell bowl on the offering slab. Her hands were trembling as she scooped up some of the glowing water. She forced the shell into her hesitant mouth and poured the water down her throat. She glanced down at her reflection, only to be greeted with a large pair of glowing orange and gold eyes of the Lazarus deity looking back at her.

Burning pain struck her throat as if she had drunk melted iron. She coughed aggressively, gasping for air and screaming in agony as the rune markings were written on her bones. Hunched over choking, Clotilda watched as the golden water in the fountain evaporated and the bottom cracked as if it were dry bones in a desert. She pressed her small hands against her chest, feeling the deity nuzzle inside her ribcage, intertwining with her essence and powers, becoming a part of her and ready for her to call for it!

Clotilda grunted as she sliced through one of the Graffias Assassins before she glanced up at Cyril as he moved his legs around, careful not to step on her as he tried to fight off the assassins and protect her at the same time. Clotilda's eyes softened as she looked up at him.

"You trust me with this power, Cyril," she said as she drew a shaky breath, hearing the still flames from the chandelier above flicker like a racing heartbeat. "Now . . . it's time for me to learn to trust myself," she said as her eyes glowed orange like phoenix feathers.

Her clothes, jewelry, and waist pack dissolved into her skin as if enveloped in water, leaving her long hair to cover her bare body as it transformed. Bird talons tore through her fingernails, and barbs of red and orange feathers spread down her body. A glowing crack opened on her chest and pulsed like magma. Her arms transformed into wings, and her slender legs turned into the powerful legs of a giant bird. A train of long feathers like that of a peacock sprouted on the base of her spine and ribboned over the marble floor. Fire from the torches, chandeliers, and water from the palace fountains ribboned toward her, interlocking into a chain of fire and water. Steam hissed furiously as the two elements met, circled her, and fused into her body. Clotilda was a unity of fire and water, like her mother and father, whose love had created her. The Deity of Lazarus, the bird of rebirth, was now truly a part of her.

Clotilda rose in her large phoenix form. She flapped her large wings, and the water mixed into her fiery wings enshrouded her in vapor. She opened her eagle-shaped beak, and a melodic and powerful shriek erupted from her throat. She stayed crouched under Cyril, noticing how he carefully moved away from standing over her and looked at her with amazement, just like how she looked at him. She met his gaze, noticing she was growing until she was the same height as him. She spread her wings open, barely standing as she felt her head touch the ceiling, and screeched at the Graffias Assassins before flapping her wings to summon waves of fiery water toward them, catching them in her wake and flooding them out of the castle.

The few remaining Graffias Assassins, including Delilah, retreated. Clotilda looked around with Cyril, their eyes landing on a gruesome sight.

Bandus lay injured with laceration marks on his body, no longer inside a magical barrier, and beside him was Princess Malvolia's mangled corpse.

Dread engulfed Clotilda as she realized that she had failed in her duties. The weight of her failure bore down on her, causing her wings to shake and her breath to quicken. She searched her mind for anything she could have done differently, but none came. The disappointment and fear of the consequences left her feeling paralyzed and helpless. Now that Princess Malvolia was dead, what kind of danger did she put her family and friends into?

Darkness crept around the corners of her eyes as her body began to feel weak. What was going on? Why did she feel so tired all of a sudden? Clotilda watched as her phoenix body started to transform into ash. She screeched again, hearing Cyril roar with her before his beastly body transformed into a shower of falling stars as he reverted into his elven form with his armor reappearing.

Her sight went dark momentarily as she collapsed to the ground, slipping into the blanket of cinders and ash until she found herself inside what looked like an egg. She pressed her hands against it, realizing that she had transformed back into her elven form, with her clothing and waist pack reappearing on her body. She dug her gloved fingertips into the egg, causing ash to rain down her face and chest.

Her prison cracked open as Cyril's silhouette greeted her through the chandelier's light. He pulled away the giant shards of ash and reached down with both hands as he carefully picked her up by her waist. She struggled to keep her eyes open, gripping Cyril's broad shoulders as he helped her out of the ashen egg. She wrapped her arms around his neck and lowered her head in defeat until it pressed against Cyril's collarbone.

"What happened? Why did I transform back?" she asked softly.

"The Rune transformation is overwhelming on the body the first time you use it. But soon, you'll be able to stay in the form longer and transform by your own will as you grow accustomed to it," he explained as he gently ran his gloved hand over her crown to comfort her.

"I failed . . . I failed to protect the princess. As a result, King Thierry will . . ."

"He won't touch you! I'll get you out of here before he has the chance," Cyril said protectively as he wrapped his other arm around her waist.

Clotilda raised her head to him, jolting back into alertness as she saw an arrow fired from one of the castle guards, striking Cyril in the back before she could warn him. Cyril groaned sharply before falling to the ground with her lying beside him. Clotilda grunted as her back hit the floor and she stared weakly at the unconscious Cyril. The smell of the sleeping potion coating the arrow that hit him penetrated her nostrils.

"Cyril . . ." she said as she reached out to him.

Her hand fell limply on his shoulder as she felt her strength leave her, and she slipped into unconsciousness.

CHAPTER 24

Punishment

The sound of heavy armored boots echoed off the kingdom's marble halls like weapons getting sharpened. Clotilda's eyes blurred as she stirred from unconsciousness.

"She's waking up," Clotilda heard Ivan's voice.

"Keep a firm hold on her. We're almost to the court," she heard a second male guard speak up. One she recognized was Kay, one of her troops tasked with working as a castle guard for the king.

Kay was one of the male Dominus elves she trained along with Ivan. He was fifty when he joined the royal guard ten years ago, but he surpassed many challenges and was one of Clotilda's fastest-learning students. He had dark hair like granite, and his eyes were silver like moonbeams. He had a nicely trimmed mustache and beard, and over his right cheek and forehead was a scar from a dagger wound inflicted while defending King Thierry during an attempted assassination a couple of years back. Unlike the quieter and shy Ivan, Kay was calm, serious, and always confidently carried himself. He and Ivan acted like father and son whenever she saw them hanging out, but they commonly bickered at each other in a heated feud, like two teenage brothers fighting over the same girl they had a crush on. It turned out that was the case. Ivan accidentally blurted out one day that he and Kay liked one of the women in the royal guard, but they refused to tell her who this mystery woman was. It wasn't her business, but Clotilda was curious since she was a hopeless romantic. Maybe it was the Dominus archer woman wearing the fish mask who Ivan was standing with during the masquerade ball.

Clotilda slowly opened her eyes, her blurry vision clearing, and she saw that she was facing down to the marble ground as it moved slowly below her. She felt her legs dragging behind her as Ivan and Kay walked by her sides, firmly holding her biceps. Clotilda looked down, seeing enchanted shackles pinning her wrists together, slowly draining her of her magic. Dread rotted her insides, and her blood ran cold to the point that she shivered. She craned her head over her shoulders as far as possible, realization hitting her like an axe. Where was Cyril?

"What's going on?" she asked, her voice hoarse.

"Your trial," Ivan answered her, his voice heavy with remorse. "I'm sorry, Commander."

Fear bloomed inside her, as she remembered the events that took place the previous night. The Rune transformations, the attack of the Graffias Assassins, and the death of the princess made Clotilda sick.

The doors to the royal court opened. The morning sun flooded through the arch window with its bright glow, blinding Clotilda and forcing her to shut her eyes tightly. Her pointed ears perked to the sounds of muttering and whispers of the people in the court, and she felt their eyes on her like the sunlight on her skin.

Clotilda forced her eyes to open. She saw two stands, one with a male prisoner on it and the other empty—she knew that one was for her. She quickly turned to the male prisoner beside her, wondering if he was Cyril, but he wasn't. Bandus stood upon the stand, watching her with dried, brown stains of the princess's blood on his robe, his hands bound together in enchanted shackles.

Kay and Ivan helped Clotilda onto the stand she hesitantly stepped onto. She glanced down at them, but they didn't look back at her. They hid their eyes from her under their helmets, but she could feel their solemness radiating from them.

"Ivan, Kay, it's all right. No matter what happens," she reassured the two elven men in a whisper and a smile.

They glanced at her briefly before they walked away from the stand and stood side by side at the arched entranceway from which they came.

"Order!" King Thierry demanded as he entered the court and stood atop the podium. The seated audience became silent like wildlife hiding from a hunter and looked up at him. The king faced the two defendants, anger and loss in his narrowed eyes as he looked at them scornfully.

"Lady Clotilda and Sir Bandus," he said threateningly, causing Bandus to keep his gaze on his bound hands. Clotilda didn't avoid eye contact with the king as usual but met the king's gaze. Thierry knitted his eyebrows by her boldness and gripped the lips of the marble railing of the podium. "I will make this quick! I had given you orders to protect my daughter, and you have failed! Therefore, you are stripped of your title of Commander of the Royal Guard, and as punishment, you and the mage will be executed tomorrow at first light!"

Gasps and whispers echoed in the court.

"W . . . wait, Your Majesty," the frightened Bandus called out, causing Clotilda to glance sideways at the trembling mage. "It wasn't my fault! I did everything I could to protect your daughter!"

"It wasn't enough!" Thierry sneered.

"You see . . . Clotilda knew of the Graffias Manticore," Bandus blurted out.

Clotilda shot a glare at the mage, and her throat went dry.

"She what?" Thierry asked, his voice low and dangerous.

"Yes, Your Majesty, I heard her confessing it to the Graffias Assassin leader, who was also looking for him."

Clotilda wanted to punch Bandus and set his feet on fire. But the shackles prevented her from doing so. She clenched her teeth, and her blood roared as she was forced to listen to the mage's desperate confession.

"Go on," the king encouraged him.

"Clotilda and the Graffias Manticore have known each other since she was a little girl, and it turned out he had been looking for her all this time. That's why he came here."

Bandus was making things worse than they already were. Clotilda could tell he was afraid of being executed, but she could sense the passive aggression in his voice. He figured out who she liked and took every opportunity to inflict damage with each word he spoke.

"Then how did the Graffias Manticore find the capital of Streng? The barrier hides us from the outside world," King Thierry stated.

"Unless someone were to cross the barrier. Captain Corinthia told Clotilda and me that the Graffias Manticore could hear those walking upon the land outside the barrier. He mentioned that he heard Clotilda's footsteps and . . ."

"That's enough, Bandus!" Clotilda said sternly.

"Is it true that you crossed the barrier?" the king said, turning his attention to her, and his glare deepened.

Clotilda remained quiet for a few moments but kept her gaze strong.

"It's true. I crossed the barrier to save someone who needed help when a Battle Komodon captured them."

"You disobeyed my rules! Anyone who comes to my capital is forbidden to leave!"

"If it meant saving someone's life, I would break the rule again!"

"Enough! You have become an enemy to my capital for my daughter's death and for crossing the barrier when you knew it was forbidden! Do you have anything to say?"

"Just one question," she said evenly. "Where is the Graffias Manticore?" she asked, not wanting to reveal Cyril's name to him.

"You'll be joining him in the dungeon. You, the Graffias Manticore, and the mage will be executed tomorrow at dawn! Get them out of my sight!" he ordered the Dominus elf dungeon guard standing by his side. The guard walked toward Clotilda and the protesting Bandus before escorting them out of the court.

The frigid air of the dungeon caused shivers through Clotilda's body, and the tips of her pointed ears went numb from the cold. The stench of blood, sweat, and urine struck the back of her throat, causing her gag reflexes to twitch. Her eyes scanned the cells for Cyril as they walked past each one, hoping he wasn't inside one of the torture chambers.

Nearing one of the cells, her hopeful and worried gaze fell upon a handsome male Regulus elf. His muscular arms were outstretched and chained to the cell wall, and his ankles were shackled to the ground. His head was facing down to the floor, with his silver hair hung over his eyes and cheeks. Clotilda quickly turned toward him, nearly hurting her neck, when she realized he was Cyril.

Cyril lifted his gaze from the ground and tilted his head weakly as if it were heavy as stone. His eyes shot wide once he saw her. He jerked forward, his chained arms held back as his sudden movements made the enchanted links taut. Clotilda stopped, reluctant to go any further.

"Keep moving," the dungeon guard said as he firmly pushed her on her back, nearly making her stumble.

Cyril growled, making the guard flinch. She looked over at Cyril, noticing that he was forming words in his mouth without using his voice. She carefully read his lips, seeing him form the word 'tonight.' She discreetly nodded at him before reluctantly walking down the dark dungeon. She bit her lower lip, thinking about the word Cyril silently said. Tonight was a half-moon!

The dungeon guard pushed Clotilda and Bandus into two separate cells next to each other and locked the new prisoners inside with the large key ring he had. Clotilda walked over toward the cell door and grabbed the enchanted bars. She looked toward the direction they came and watched the guard walk away. She pressed herself against the bars as she tried to look down the hallway to see if she could see Cyril's cell.

Unable to see anything past the sharp corner of the hallway, Clotilda pried herself from the bars and turned to look at the stone wall of the cell. She gently planted her palm on the wall, trying to use her elven powers to go through it. But much to her disappointment, it didn't work.

From her arrival to the kingdom of Streng, Clotilda learned that many of the walls of the buildings and the castle weren't made of stone, as it was known that elves could go through them with their natural powers. Instead, many of the walls were made of wood or, in rare cases, iron to prevent elves and fairies from sneaking into other homes. The dungeon's walls had thick blocks that looked like they were made of stone, but she could sense the presence of iron rods inside. She sighed, knowing she shouldn't have gotten her hopes too high.

Worry infested her thoughts like an infection. She hoped that whatever Cyril was planning would help him escape, and she worried about how they would protect the Deities of Regulus and Lazarus. She knew if Thierry discovered they were Runes, he would no doubt try to obtain their powers.

Clotilda looked down at her shackled hands, noticing, much to her relief, that she was still wearing her hand chains. She figured that Ivan and Kay must have left them on. She opened her waist packs, seeing that she still had everything on her—the whistle, Tears of Eir, her comb, water-resistant music journals, elven currency, and a few other items, including her homemade tea packs, salt, and some food she packed earlier. She smiled softly in gratitude, realizing that her troops still harbored loyalty to her and risked their safety to ensure she had a chance to escape. She closed her pack and began thinking of a plan and time to break out of her cell and help free Cyril. He mentioned that tonight was a half-moon, and she knew nightfall would be the best opportunity to escape.

"Clotilda," Bandus called out from the cell next to hers.

"What is it?" she asked, irritated.

"I'm sorry for what I said at the court. It wasn't like me back there."

"Really," she replied flatly as she glanced up at the window, seeing the morning sun reaching the center of the sky, signaling that it was nearly noon. "Tell me, who was it that killed the princess?"

"It was the female leader of the Graffias Assassins," he answered.

"Why did you dismiss your magic barrier?"

"I didn't! She had some magic seal on her palm. She placed it on the shield and was able to go through it. She wounded me and killed the princess before fleeing. I did everything I could to stop her."

Clotilda sighed through her nose.

The tainted air between them became silent briefly before Bandus spoke up again.

"My powers are weakening because of these shackles. But I have enough to cast one more spell, and I'll use it on you," he said. Clotilda knitted her eyebrows together in confusion before realization struck her like a whip.

"I will get you out of here, Clo, and send you back to your home in that forest before you came to the orphanage."

"Bandus . . . don't!" she said as she clenched her teeth.

"I don't want the Graffias Manticore near you again. I'll find a way to get out of here and come find you."

Clotilda leaped onto her feet. She bit into her finger to allow a drop of her blood to spill on her palm and dug the other hand into her pack to sprinkle shards of sea salt on it before she closed her hand into a fist and reopened it to reveal a red water lily growing in her palm.

This was another ancient Airavata spell she had learned from her blood mother, passed down to the ten Airavata priests and priestesses of the Kraken. In the past, Clotilda created a vast garden of these lilies to put invading enemy soldiers to sleep when they managed to invade Streng so she and her troops could take them to the dungeon before they awoke.

Inspired by the faun's ancient power of putting those to sleep when they heard their song, the Airavata elves created a spell that called forth this flower, known as the Lily of Sluimeren, that can only be made with Airavata blood and sea salt.

"Get some sleep, Bandus," she said as she blew the flower petals toward the wall that divided the mage and her. The petals danced through the air and went through the wall like water. She heard Bandus gasp in surprise before he collapsed to the hay-carpeted floor. Clotilda sighed in relief but knew the sleeping spell was temporary. The garden of lilies she created in the past was enough to make the army sleep for an hour, but one of these flowers would only give her ten minutes.

"Hang on, Cyril. I'm coming for you," she said, discarding her plan of acting at night for their escape. She had to act now!

CHAPTER 25

Escape

Magic from within Clotilda's hand chain wove Universeel into a dagger. She carefully turned Universeel around until its blade was to the enchanted shackles, cutting through the cuff around her wrists as if they were made of ribbons.

The clanking of armored footsteps echoed in the dungeon. Clotilda quickly withdrew her dagger into her hand chain and swept the shackles under the old blankets as she heard the approaching steps drawing closer. She sat at the far corner of the dungeon wall and faced her back to the cell door to hide her unbound wrists. She listened as she heard the footsteps stop by her cell and looked over her shoulders to see Ivan holding a food tray.

"Lunchtime," he said as he plucked a roll of bread from the tray, crowned it on top of the wooden cup of water, and placed it on the ground. "It's made with the finest ingredient," he said before he stood up and walked away with the empty tray.

Clotilda looked at the water and bread, feeling her stomach rumble. She gently rubbed her stomach, thanking Ivan mentally for the food. But she couldn't eat just yet, not with Cyril trapped and knowing Bandus would wake up from the sleeping spell very soon. She looked down at the bread again, immediately drawn to something protruding from inside it. She stood and walked to the cell door before picking up the bread. Her eyes widened as she realized the object buried halfway in the bread was the key to her cell. The finest ingredient, indeed!

"Thank you, Ivan," she said as she pulled the key from the bread and inserted it into the lock.

Clotilda slowly and carefully turned the key, trying to make sure the lock didn't click loudly and draw the attention of the prisoners or the guards. She opened the door, not all the way, but wide enough for her to squeeze through. She pulled the key out of the lock, stored it inside her pack, and pressed her finger against the keyhole, melting it down so that it looked like she used magic to open it.

Clotilda crept on the tips of her toes as she hurried down the dungeon, carefully peeking around corners to ensure it was clear. She followed the hallways by memory, retracing her steps toward Cyril's cell.

Voices from conversing prisoners caused her to cease her steps. She looked ahead to see that they were talking to each other from across the hallway. It was a single hallway with no other way to get around them. She bit the inside of her cheeks, knowing that the only way to get to Cyril was past these two prisoners.

She looked up at the ceiling, seeing the forest of wooden rafters overhead. An idea broke through her mind like the crack of dawn as she figured out how to get past them. She pulled her hair back into a ponytail with a leather ribbon she had brought and crept toward the wall, using one of the guard's wooden tables and an empty torch holder as her ladder as she climbed toward the rafters.

Upon reaching the rafters, Clotilda broke off the heels of her boots, not wanting to take the chance of clicking her heels against the wood and drawing the prisoners' attention. She stuffed the broken heels into her waist pack and made sure she was deep in the veil of shadows where the glow of the torch lights couldn't touch as she scaled over the rafters with soft and careful steps.

Guards walked down the hallway below her, halting her mission. She watched them walk away before continuing her climb. Guards infested almost every corner of the hallways, keeping sharp eyes on the more notorious prisoners, taking short breaks at their tables to eat their lunches, and conversing with one another.

A smile of triumph tugged on Clotilda's lips when she realized she had made it to Cyril's cell, but she looked around with nervousness when she counted twelve guards standing by his cell door, two of them being Ivan and Kay.

"I don't think Clotilda killed the princess," Ivan said as he brushed his silver hair away from his eyes. "I've known her since I joined the royal guard three years ago, and she has done so much for us. She even risked her life to save me from that Graffias Assassin spy," he said as he tightened his gauntlet hands into tight fists. "I would have been dead if it weren't for her."

"I care about her too," Kay replied. "I don't think it's fair either that a good soul like her should be sacrificed for the life of a spoiled princess."

"Stop talking about her, you two!" One of the female Dominus elf guards scolded them. "Clotilda has failed to protect the heir to the throne, and now she has to pay the price with her life."

"She's not a failure!" Kay and Ivan snapped in unison.

"Uh, you two are hopeless! You both have always had a crush on her since you joined the royal guard," the female guard rolled her eyes.

Clotilda's eyes widened. So the woman both Ivan and Kay had a crush on was her? She was flattered and smiled softly at them. Even after all these years of strictly being under the thumb of King Thierry, she didn't realize that she positively impacted some of the people here despite being so reserved, and she didn't know Kay and Ivan were attracted to her.

The former commander returned her attention to her goal, looking around for a way to distract the guards so that she could get to Cyril's cell. She held her hand behind her back, opening it to feel the warmth of fiery feathers forming into a small bird in her gloved palm. She glanced over her shoulder at the firebird, the little creature looking up, ready for her orders.

"Fly over there," she whispered to it as she nodded her head toward the direction of the far-off empty cells behind her. "Set everything in those cells ablaze."

The bird chirped quietly before it spread its wings and flew toward the cells where Clotilda told it to go with the speed of a shooting star. In a few moments, smoke billowed out of the two cells, curling like coils of serpents.

"Fire!" one of the female guards near Cyril's cell called out, causing all but Ivan and Kay to run over to investigate and try putting out the growing flames.

Clotilda dropped behind Ivan, snaking her arm toward his face, and pressed her hand against his lips. His muffled gasp caused Kay to summon his sword from his hand chain, but he froze as soon as he laid eyes on Clotilda, quickly dismissing his weapon as soon as he saw her.

"Commander?" Kay asked.

"Shh," she softly shushed him, placing her index finger against her lips.

"Do you have the keys to Cyr . . . I mean, the Manticore's cell?" she asked.

"Why would you want to free the Graffias Manticore?" Kay asked as he arched his brow.

"He's a friend. Trust me," she said with a smile.

"It's right here," he said as he pulled a key from his key ring and gave it to her.

"Thank you for your loyalty, my friends," she said as she accepted the key from Kay and removed her hand from Ivan's lips. She fished the key to her prison cell from her waist pack and planted it in Ivan's hand. "I melted the lock to my cell. If anyone asks how I escaped, tell them I broke free by using my magic."

"Best of luck, Commander. Get as far away as you can and be safe," Ivan said as he turned to her with a sad smile.

"I will. I'll miss you both. Please promise to check on my family and friends often and ensure they are safe for me."

"You have our word," Kay said with a nod, and he and Ivan saluted her.

Clotilda saluted them back before inserting the key into the lock to Cyril's cell and opening the door.

Clotilda made her way over to Cyril, who hung by his chains. He flinched a little at the sound of her light steps and jerked his head up to see her. Clotilda pressed her index finger to her lips to motion for him to keep quiet as she approached.

"I'm here to help you escape, Cyril," she whispered to him as she walked over with the key and began unlocking the first of his shackles.

"How did you escape?" he asked as he watched her.

"A couple of my troops helped me," she replied.

"I was planning on escaping with you tonight. But it's good to see you sooner," he said as he smiled at her.

"It's good to see you too. I'm sorry for all the trouble, but we'll get you out of here soon before . . ." Her words trailed off and she gasped sharply when she shifted her gaze to her legs.

"What is it?" he asked her in concern before following her gaze and seeing her legs disappearing.

"No! Bandus must have woken up," she said as panic bloomed in her voice.

"What?" Cyril asked with a growl at the mention of the mage.

"I must get you free before Bandus teleports me out of here," she said as she unlocked the shackles to Cyril's wrists and quickly moved to his legs.

Her body began to disappear faster, her fingers fighting to hold the key as if she were a ghost.

"Where is he teleporting you to?"

"He is sending me back to Cygnus, the village I grew up in before it was destroyed. I must hurry," she said as she freed his left ankle.

"Clotilda," she looked up to see Cyril kneeling to her. "I'll come to Cygnus tonight. Wait for me."

Clotilda nodded in understanding before magic enveloped her. Cyril and the dungeon around her faded into a blur as she was teleported away.

CHAPTER 26

Tranquil Dread

Blades of grass crunched under the soles of Clotilda's boots and broken high heels. Bandus's magic unveiled from around her, bringing her to the forest of Mysomatarian. She glanced up, squinting, and held her hand over her brows as she looked up at the afternoon sun through the spindly, woven diamonds of thc treetops.

Clotilda remembered running around and playing in the forest of Mysomatarian when she was a little girl, but this area was unfamiliar. She had never been this deep in the woods before and wasn't sure which direction to take to get to Cygnus.

"Bandus, where did you bring me?" she said out loud as she looked around.

Birds and fairies sang together in the flowering hedges and bushes, accompanied by the soothing rhythm of churning water from the river nearby. Clotilda walked toward one of the trees, removed her long glove, and pressed her right hand onto the rough bark.

When she went out on trips through the forest, her mother and father taught her that one of the powers elves have was the ability to identify the names of landscapes and see paths through the natural energy flowing through the trees and animals upon them. They ensured she knew how to find her way home if she ever got lost. She had only tried the ability once when her family taught her how to cast it; she hoped it worked after all these years.

"Life force that intertwines with all creations, grant me guidance to my home," she chanted the ancient words.

Energy surged through her as her life force intertwined with the forest. She rooted her feet in place, whispers of nonexistent words echoing in her ears. Her vision rapidly linked with the eyes of the forest, following along a path down the river, leading her to a lagoon and the long-forgotten ruins of a village.

Clotilda gasped softly as her mind returned to her body. She pulled her hand away from the tree and held it up as she looked at her palm, seeing the particles of bark sticking to her skin."It's time to go home," she said as she turned to the path she was shown and began her trek toward Cygnus.

Hunger took hold of Clotilda as she followed the path through the forest to find the river. She took a moment to pick a few berries from the nearby bushes along the way and popped them into her mouth as she continued her trek. She hummed as she ate the berries, enjoying the sweet and refreshing taste. This area was familiar to her because she recognized the river. She had only been to it once with her parents.

The young, ten-year-old Clotilda picked berries from the bushes. She gathered as many as possible until they piled up in her palms. She put some of them inside her pocket to eat later and carefully covered her free hand over the handful of berries. She spun on her heels and ran toward a clearing where two elves, one

male and one female, were standing beside an aquatic pegasus that bore some resemblance to Coralina and had a swollen, pregnant stomach.

"Mommy! Daddy! I got some berries for Coralina and her baby," she cheerfully said as she showed the berries to her parents.

"Well done, Clotilda," her mother said as she smiled. Her mother, Bathilda, was a battle priestess. She was beautiful like her daughter and had rose-gold blonde hair that grew to her ankles. Her skin was fair and shimmered like the surface of a pearl, and her eyes were deep blue like the ocean. She wore a long, elegant white gown with a long purple scarf around her arms and an amethyst choker around her slender neck with a Kraken-shaped insignia of the Airavata elven culture. "I hope you saved some for yourself."

"Yes, I did," she said happily, slipping her free hand into her pocket.

"I don't think you are supposed to put berries into your pockets, sweetheart," her father said as he and his wife looked down at their daughter with worried expressions.

"It's okay. I made sure that I ran carefully . . . aww," her cheerful face morphed into disappointment as she pulled out the crushed remains of the berries with her now juice-stained hand.

"Uhh, next time we go out again, we'll bring a basket along," her mother said as she empathized with her daughter.

"Okay. But at least I have these berries for Coralina," Clotilda said, the cheer returning to her voice. She ran around, stood before Coralina, and held the handful of berries up to her.

"Be careful. Make sure you keep your stained fingers away from Coralina, or she'll mistake them for food," her mother said with worry.

"Okay, Mom," she replied, holding her hand up to the aquatic pegasus with the berries and keeping her berry-stained one away from the hungry steed.

"We should return to the village. It's starting to get late into the afternoon," Cadmar said as he picked his daughter up by her waist.

"Aww, can we explore a little longer?" she asked as she wrapped her hands around her father's shoulders.

"We can't anymore," he said as he walked to Coralina's side and placed her on the steed's saddle. "We've traveled far from our village. If we don't head back now, we won't return before sunset."

"How come?" she asked with a curious tilt of her head.

"This forest has two faces. In the day, it's beautiful and safe to travel in. But at night, it becomes ravenous with dangerous beasts. This forest is called Mysomatarian, meaning Tranquil Dread."

"Really?" she asked as she felt a nervous shudder run down her spine.

"Don't worry, sweetheart," Bathilda said with a gentle pat on her shoulder to comfort her. "The sun is still out, so we are safe."

"That's right," Cadmar said as he grabbed Coralina's reins, and both he and his wife guided the steed as they began their walk back home. "All right. It's time to go home."

Clotilda watched the memory of her family dissolve away like mist. She stared in the direction of one of the forest trails. She glanced up at the afternoon sun and then back toward the path.

"I still have time before dusk," Clotilda said as she took a deep breath, summoning Universeel and continuing her trek.

The soles of her feet began to throb from walking on the rocky outcrop, and her stomach's loud rumbling caused her to flinch in surprise. She pressed her free hand against her stomach, knowing she needed more food besides the few berries she had eaten.

Pulling off her shoulder guard, Clotilda went to the river and scooped up some water. She carefully sat down on one of the small boulders near the river and held the shoulder guard with both hands. Fire licked through her fingers, heating the water in it. Bubbles erupted from the bottom of the shoulder guard, churning like a storm as the water began to boil.

Clotilda reached into her waist pack; fished out a pouch of teabags filled with berries, lemon slices, and edible flowers; and lightly dipped one into the boiling water. She slipped the teabag back into her pack and brought the water to her mouth, the herbal steam billowing around her face. She lightly blew the warm liquid to cool it off and took a small sip. She licked her bottom lip to catch any escaping droplets and glanced down to see fish swimming along the shallows. Again, her stomach rumbled as she looked at the fish. The thought of sinking her teeth into the fish's tender, scaly flesh made her mouth water. Setting up traps for them was the ideal choice for catching them, but the thought of waiting for fish when she needed to find shelter before nightfall and being as good at fishing as she was at archery caused her to change her mind.

"Maybe later," she said and shook her head as she sipped her tea.

After finishing her tea, Clotilda put the shoulder guard back on and ate a few berries from the nearby bushes as she continued her trek. As she ventured, her explorative eyes locked onto a familiar cave on the foot of a slope. It was the same cave she saw Cyril sleeping in all those years ago.

Clotilda walked over toward the cave, kneeling by the old remains of the fire pit to light it before her smile dropped when she noticed that the air was silent, like a tomb. She lowered her hand to the necklace of rocks around it as slowly as possible. She could hear it. Something was right behind her. She looked out of the corner of her eye but kept the crown of her head and back facing toward the sound of approaching tapping. The predator stalking her was getting closer, and it was hungry.

Clotilda remembered reading about this beast, recognizing it to be a sleator. A sleator was built for stealth, with its body shaped like a jackal, and its paws were like a tiger's, armed with sharp claws. From its head, down its spine, and to its tail, it resembled a scorpion, oozing with venom through the numerous barbs on its spine and its stinger. It was hard for prey to hear a sleator when it was on the prowl unless the prey happened to be an elf.

Clotilda listened carefully with her sharp hearing as she waited for the beast to come near her, giving it the confidence that she was oblivious to its approach. She coiled her fingers around the large stone closest to her. Strands of her hair slithered over her shoulders and brushed against her cheeks with the creature's breath. Her ears twitched when she heard its straining jaw muscles as it opened its mouth, ready to bite the back of her neck. Clotilda spun around, shoving the rock into the sleator's mouth until she felt it hit the back of its throat. The monster recoiled, giving her the space to stand up and summon Universeel.

Clotilda stood in a battle stance as she held her weapon, readying herself for the creature to attack. She remembered reading that sleators were too fast to outrun but were vulnerable to fire, and their scorpion tail was their weakness. The beast coughed the rock out of its mouth, snarling menacingly as it charged toward her. She held her weapon like a shield, jamming it sideways into her attacker's mouth. Its sharp fangs gnawled on Universeel, and its saliva burned with venom. It posed its tail into an attack, lunging it toward her. Clotilda jerked to the side to avoid the stinger while fighting to push the beast away.

A burning pain shot through her body. She yelled, looking down to see that the sleator's stinger pierced her lower left thigh. She grunted as she used all her strength to tilt Universeel and thrust it forward, slicing it through the creature's tail. The beast yelped in pain and collapsed to the ground, squirming. Clotilda grabbed the severed stinger, hissing through her teeth as she pulled it out of her thigh and tossed it to the ground. Seizing the opportunity, she charged toward the sleator and thrust Universeel's blades into its head, giving it a quick death.

The forest bloomed with chirps once again. Clotilda inhaled deeply through her nose as she pried her weapon from the sleator's corpse and looked at the fallen beast sorrowfully. Clotilda hated killing, but it was the only way to stop it from killing her. She took one of her long gloves off and tightly tied it around her upper thigh like a tourniquet to prevent the venom from spreading. She limply went over to the cave, lying herself down against the cave wall where she saw Cyril sleep. She placed her hand on the blood-stained blade of her weapon and cast her powers on it to ignite it in flames to melt away the blood and kill the bacteria.

It wasn't going to be comfortable, but she needed to get the poison out of her body. She died of toxins in the past, and they were not pleasant. She took a deep breath and brought the hot blade to her thigh, holding her breath in preparation as she sliced it over the puncture wound.

Her body was resistant to heat and fire, but that didn't mean she couldn't feel the pain from the blade. She cried out, groaning softly as blood oozed from the laceration. She pressed her hand against it to force some of the tainted blood out before she turned the hot blade to its side and pressed it against the wound to close the cut. She slipped her hand into the pack that held her healing blossoms and coated her injury with the flowers, healing it instantly.

Clotilda looked at the sky to see the sun nearing the western mountains. It was too late to travel anymore, and her strength was fading.

"I hope you were able to escape from the dungeon, Cyril. I'll wait here as long as I can. Please be safe."

Clotilda looked over toward the slain sleator's corpse. She got onto her shaky feet, trembling as she walked toward the body and kneeled beside it. She closed her eyes and held her hands together in prayer. "I humbly appreciate your sacrifice, and it shall not go in vain. Rest well until resurrection calls for you," she ended her prayer before carefully grasping the beast's ankles and dragging it back to the cave to prepare her first kill from the wild.

CHAPTER 27

Stillborns of the Phoenix

Fallen branches that Clotilda harvested near the cave crackled in the fire pit as she tossed them into the flames, and the aroma of cooking meat feathered along her nose, making her mouth water. She cooked the meat fillets with a skewer she made from a long, low-hanging branch. Clotilda slowly rotated it, changing Universeel into a dagger to check the meat's doneness.

"I hope this turns out all right. I never cooked sleator meat before," she said to herself as she continued cooking until it was well-done.

Removing the meat from over the fire, she tossed the stinger and the head into the fire pit and brought the cooked meat to her lips. She slowly bit into it, feeling her taste buds ignite to the warm juices splashing on her tongue. She hummed in satisfaction, feeling her hunger fade with each bite.

Clotilda untied the leather ribbon of her ponytail to free her hair and looked at the sun sinking behind the western mountaintops. It would be nighttime soon, and there would be a half-moon tonight. She wondered how

Cyril was doing—hoping and praying that he was all right. Then she thought of her family, friends, and Coralina. Were they okay? Was King Thierry going to go after them, thinking they helped her escape? Clotilda hoped King Thierry would listen to the story that she asked Ivan and Kay to tell him and prayed that they would be all right too.

After swallowing her food, Clotilda fished out her pegasus whistle and blew into it. She knew Coralina had acute hearing and could hear noises from far-off distances. But could she hear the whistle from out here? She blew into it again and prayed it would reach her trusty steed's webbed ears.

Once Clotilda had her fill of the fresh sleator meat, she burned the remains and skinned the fur hide of the beast for a blanket. She walked around the cave, setting up traps using the materials she found on the forest floor. She kneeled next to one of the traps she made and covered her ears as she set it off by yanking on the vine of a large trumpet-shaped blossom called fairy's bugle, which would create a loud sound for a few moments whenever something touched it.

Clotilda smiled at the success of her trap before the flower went silent, and she pried her fingers from her ears. Whatever tried to approach her tonight, the fairy's bugle would be able to warn her.

"If that won't wake me, I don't know what will," she said before returning to the cave.

Clotilda lay against the cave wall and threw the fur blanket over her as she prepared to get some sleep. She looked up at the fading gold and pink lights in the sky that began to dissolve into a deep indigo haze, signaling the coming of night. Nightfall was going to bring out the dreadful second face of the forest. Clotilda pulled the blanket to her chin and curled her legs to her chest, her mind becoming anxious about what dangers would be stirring after dark.

Clotilda's eyes shot open to the billowing sound of the fairy's bugles trumpeting. She quickly sat up, pushing the fur blanket off, and summoned Universeel. Straining her eyes, she saw something approaching through the darkness. Clotilda stood her ground, her muscles going taut like chains of a drawbridge, as she heard a loud snort. The tapping of claws drew closer, the glow from the campfire revealing the smooth fuchsia scales and feathers and the graceful folded wings of an aquatic pegasus.

"Coralina!" she smiled in excitement as she ran toward her steed. Coralina neighed gleefully as she galloped toward her master. Clotilda lovingly wrapped her arms around her steed's neck. "I missed you, Coralina. I'm so glad that you heard the whistle and came."

After reuniting with Coralina and silencing the fairy's bugles, Clotilda caught faint movements in the shadows. Her eyes slightly adjusted to the dark, and she knitted her brows in concentration as she saw a male figure standing behind one of the trees.

What she could make out with very little detail was that he looked like an elf and was wearing heavy armor. In addition, she noticed long branches or rods sticking out of his back, looking like he had a pair of broken, mangled wings.

"Cyril?" she called out, but something told her he wasn't Cyril. The male figure remained silent before turning away and fleeing clumsily with quick but unbalanced steps into the darkness toward the direction of her village. Curious, Clotilda turned to her steed, grabbed the reins, and tugged it lightly to encourage Coralina to follow.

"Stay close to me. Let's see who that is," she said as they cautiously followed the figure.

Remembering how she always ran along this familiar trail to play in the forest as a little girl, Clotilda and Coralina followed it until they came to a large forest clearing nestled near a deep lagoon, where the corpse of her village, Cygnus, lay.

Sadness swelled in Clotilda as she remembered the village in its former glory—the welcoming open gates of the surrounding wall, made of a waterfall with kindling fire on the bottom and floating islands of ice hovering over it, for the elven guards to stand on and keep watch. Now the flames of the wall were gone, and the waterfall was blackened water like a fountain of tar.

Clotilda and Coralina slowly walked through the wall's broken entrance and into the marketplace's veins that once displayed the passionate and devoted artists' works and studio shops.

Travelers from far and near came to the village, admiring the beautiful works of various art pieces and occasionally buying them to support the artists. Clotilda glanced sadly at the lifeless mouths of each shop they walked past, remembering the Lazarus and Airavata jewelers, tailors, sculptors, dancers, musicians, writers, and painters who shared their creations. She remembered befriending them, becoming inspired by their creations and giving her the drive to improve her musical talent.

She continued to walk down the silent market until the ashen remains of her home greeted her. Clotilda's heart shattered seeing her home in such a state, remembering how beautiful it looked before it was engulfed in flames. She slowly looked to the barren wasteland next to what used to be the village's apple tree orchard, which offered bountiful harvests for the villagers and a peaceful sanctuary for her to write her music.

Clotilda swallowed thickly as tears threatened to come, and she tugged Coralina's reins for them to walk away from the orchard when a glimmer of light caught her eye. A ghostly, white lion that looked like it was made of moonlight prowled the orchard before turning around to face her.

Her feet came to an abrupt stop as she stared at the lion. At first she thought it was Cyril, but she realized it was one of Cyril's ghost lions. What was he doing here? Did Cyril send him to find her? Was he telling her that Cyril was in trouble? The lion stared at her before turning a few steps toward the orchard, stopping to look at her as if telling her to follow him. Curious,

Clotilda tightened her hold on the reins, and they followed the phantom lion. Maybe he was guiding her to Cyril.

They walked around skeletal trees and occasionally looked up to see the starry night sky as they followed the ghost lion. Clotilda returned her gaze to the lion who had led her to a large rock outcrop. Much to her surprise, a patch of grass around it was green, unlike the rest of the ashen ground, and the rocks were brown and white with not even the faintest speck of ash on them. The ghostly lion scratched his paw in the rock pile at the mouth of the opening as if telling her to look inside before he disappeared like vapor. Clotilda cautiously released her hold on the reins before slowly approaching the outcrop. She peeked inside, her eyes widened, and her mouth dropped open when she saw the hidden treasures.

A wooden harp and piano that her mother and father gifted her, which she thought had been devoured by the flames that consumed her village, was tucked safely inside the outcrop. This discovery touched her. Cyril must have saved her musical instruments!

Her gaze soon dropped to a small tower of tomes on the wooden piano seat. She carefully picked up one of the books as if holding a newborn and slowly opened it to be greeted by columns of musical notes she had written. She glanced at the notes, seeing how her writing had matured from how it used to look back then, and felt nostalgia bloom inside her as she saw the first music sheets she had written when the Fossegrim was teaching her.

"Thank you, Cyril," she whispered as she carefully closed the tome and hugged it.

Clotilda's ears twitched as she heard a glass painting jar inside one of the village homes fall to the ground and break. She glanced back to the village and at Coralina, who was starting to snort uneasily. Clotilda tucked the journal into her pack as she slowly stood up.

Clotilda gasped when she heard a ceramic pot break. Coralina neighed nervously as she turned her head toward the village.

"Let's get out of here . . . !" Clotilda cried out in pain as two decaying arrows shot through the darkness and pierced her right thigh. Clotilda looked at the arrows, her eyes widening when she recognized the once golden, bird-winged Lazarus designs of the arrow were now rotten.

She grunted as she pulled the arrows out of her thigh before looking around to see an army of overlapping, shadowy figures moving through the corners of the ruins, the broken wall, and the forest edge. Clotilda took slow steps toward her frightened steed. She climbed onto Coralina's back, quickly snapping the reins when she saw a rain of rotten arrows showering toward them.

"Hurry! Take flight!" she commanded, and her pegasus quickly flapped her wings to get into the air.

The ash on the ground billowed and curled as Coralina lifted into the air, and the puncturing of arrows striking the ground caused Clotilda's stomach to churn. They flew out of the orchard until Clotilda felt something heavy grab hold of her right leg!

Rotting fingers dug into Clotilda's leg, causing her to cry out and look to see a decaying, bird-like, elven creature clawing up to her, with numerous broken arrows protruding from his back like skeletal wings. Clotilda summoned Universeel to get him off, only for the monster to snarl as he grabbed her right wrist with his bony, bird-scaled hands and yanked her toward him. She could feel his fingernails through the fabric of her gloves and pants, leaving red crescent moons on her skin that bit at her menacingly. Coralina neighed angrily as she struggled to stay in the air. The pegasus slammed her body roughly against tree trunks to get their attacker off, and she circled over the lagoon's shore.

Clotilda punched their attacker, straining as she tried to hold onto the reins. He climbed closer, and she planted her left hand on his face to keep him back. She glanced down at his neck, seeing a deep laceration on his throat that was oozing a black tar. Framed between her fingers were his dry and weeping black ooze eyes that used to harbor fiery orange irises that she inherited from him. Molting, decaying feathers sprouted from his rotten, gray flesh that was once sun-kissed, and his once red, braided hair was now messy and greasy. His armor, which he always maintained and cleaned with care, was tarnished and stained with brown blood smears.

"Dad . . . !" Clotilda sobbed, and she felt her heart break as she looked at the elven man she had loved since she was a baby, now a Hollow.

Her Hollow father growled and shrieked like a starving vulture, causing the ooze in his throat to gurgle. He sharply pulled her off Coralina's back, and they plummeted toward the lagoon. Clotilda grunted as soon as her back hit the sandy shore, and she firmly planted her shaky hands on the beach that engulfed her fingers like hungry quicksand.

Clotilda looked toward her father, seeing him slowly getting up. His movements were clumsy and broken, and she worried he might snap off his arms and legs. Cadmar turned toward her, his head cocking to the side like an owl with a broken neck. She tightened her hold on her weapon, preparing herself to stand up, only to hear bubbles gurgling from the lagoon behind her. Before she could turn her head to look, she gasped as multiple waterlogged, webbed hands grabbed her ankles and began dragging her toward the dark water. Clotilda swung Universeel's blades toward her captors, slicing through their fingers and causing shrieks to erupt from under the water. When some of the hands retreated, several more speared through the wake like regenerating hydra heads and snapped a hold on her legs.

Clotilda desperately sank her fingers through the sand to stop them from dragging her in, but it was useless. She looked at her father with pleading eyes for him to help, but he just stood there watching and cocking his head with a twisted smirk of anticipation spreading on his lips. Dread and panic swelled in her veins, and the water engulfed her as she was dragged into the lagoon.

The water's murky depths constricted Clotilda as she was dragged deeper into the lagoon. The half-moon's light broke through the wake, revealing submerged half Lazarus and half Airavata Hollows dragging her down, and an inky ribbon of blood from the arrow wounds on her thigh slipped past her toward the surface.

Being half Airavata, the Hollows had no issue breathing underwater like her and probably fled to the lagoon as soon as they transformed into Hollows. She did the same. When she transformed into a Hollow for the first time, she hid under the water inside the bath in the orphanage before being disturbed by one of the frightened orphans, causing her to attack them.

Clotilda grunted as she freed one of her legs and kicked as hard as possible to force her captors to let go. She hated herself for hurting her kin, but they were Hollows now. They didn't know what they were doing anymore and were as aggressive as rabid animals. She reluctantly struck them in their heads, finally getting them to release their hold on her.

Clotilda reached up to her choker, pulling it off to expose her neck to the water. Four small gills opened on each side of her neck, helping her to breathe. She yanked her gloves off, the small webs between her fingers growing until they reached the bottom of her fingernails. She pushed her swirling hair out of the way to see more Hollows swimming toward her. She stuffed her gloves into her waist pack, held onto Universeel, and began swimming toward the surface when she heard a loud splash near her.

She turned to see a male figure swimming toward her, his stardust silver hair flowing around his handsome face and his eyes glowing through the darkness. Her breath hitched, and her heart skipped a beat when she saw him. Cyril swam close to her, wrapped his muscular arm protectively around her waist, and brought her back to the surface.

Cyril pushed her to the surface before him, and they gasped deeply for air. Clotilda held him protectively, afraid that one of the Hollows would drag him down. Unlike her, Cyril couldn't breathe underwater, and the thought of him drowning scared her.

"Are you all right?" he asked in concern.

"Don't worry, I'm fine. But we need to get back to the shore! They're coming!" she replied as the gills on her neck closed from being out of the water.

Cyril nodded in agreement before they swam toward the shore.

Gurgling bubbles circled them like a noose. Cyril and Clotilda held onto each other's arms so they wouldn't get separated. Female Hollows charged toward them, shrieking like vengeful mermaids as they breached the surface and leaped toward them. Clotilda and Cyril summoned their weapons, swinging them toward their attackers, slicing the slain Hollows into clusters of seaweed before they sank beneath the wake.

Clotilda and Cyril sank their feet into the shallows as they reached the shore, kicking their legs into underwater sprints as they hurried out. Clotilda pressed her hand to her right thigh, trying to stop the bleeding as she struggled to stand up. She was losing her strength fast! She felt Cyril's strong arms slip behind her trembling knees and the other arm wrap behind her back before he scooped her up like a bride in her groom's embrace.

"Call for your steed, and we can get out of here," he said.

"All right," she replied, nodding before glancing up to see Coralina circling overhead. "Coralina!" she called out, causing the pegasus's webbed ears to twitch and look down at the two elves before gliding toward them. Coralina's snout wrinkled into a snarl when she saw Cyril, and Clotilda held her hand up to stop her steed from attacking him. "Don't worry! He's a friend!"

"Place your hand on her nose, and I'll teleport us out of here," Cyril said as he looked around intently at the Hollows surrounding them.

Clotilda saw the army of Hollows, including her father, charging toward them. She gently placed her hand on Coralina's muzzle before moonlight illuminated them. She tilted her head back to see Cyril basking in the half-moon's light, his veins glowing like moonbeams, like before during the crescent moon. His eyes glowed in lunar light before she, Cyril, and Coralina vanished.

CHAPTER 28

Recovery

The moonlight of Cyril's magic faded away from them as he completed his teleportation powers. Clotilda gently petted Coralina to calm her from the surprise of being teleported. Clotilda glanced around, seeing that they were standing in a courtyard, and saw a large kingdom before them. This castle wasn't Streng. It was larger than any she had ever seen and was made of white marble, with eight tall towers that looked like they could touch the heavens.

"Where are we?" Clotilda asked as she tilted her head back and marveled at the castle.

"This is the castle of Algieba, my home," Cyril replied with a smile.

Cyril gently shifted Clotilda as he carried her in his arms, and he walked toward the castle, with Coralina following close behind them. As they climbed a grand staircase toward the giant double doors of the entrance to the castle, Clotilda tilted her head back to see rows of giant, prowling lions and lionesses statues looking down at them in silent roars as they walked past them. Two Regulus elf guards, one male and one female, stood on each side of the doors, and their eyes widened as soon as they saw Cyril approaching.

"Your Highness!" they said in unison before they kneeled before him. "It's so good to have you back."

"I'm glad to be back home. It was a long journey, but it was well worth it," Cyril said as he smiled respectfully at his guards.

Clotilda glanced at Cyril with a surprised gaze. He was a king, but he was polite and respectful to his guards as if they were family members. King Thierry never did that to his guards, whether he had known them for a long time or had just met them. Seeing that kindness and respect was pleasantly refreshing, making her smile.

The guards stood up from kneeling, and their focus soon dropped to the female elf their king was carrying.

"Is she the maiden you've told us about?" the female guard asked.

"She is. This is Clotilda, and she'll be staying here with us for a while," Cyril replied.

"She's quite beautiful," the male guard said as he looked at Clotilda, causing her to smile at him bashfully for the compliment.

Cyril arched one of his eyebrows irritably at the male guard before softly clearing his throat to get his attention from Clotilda and gesturing his head back to Coralina, who stood by the foot of the staircase.

"Go ahead and escort Clotilda's aquatic pegasus to the royal stables with Sleipnir and get her comfortable for tonight."

"Yes, Your Highness." The male guard bowed before he walked down the stairs toward Coralina and gently patted her.

The guard grabbed the reins and tugged lightly to escort her to the stables, but Coralina held her ground and kept her stare on her master in concern.

"Don't worry about me, Coralina. I'll be fine," Clotilda reassured her with a smile. "These people are here to help us. Treat them with respect."

Coralina snorted softly in reply before she turned toward the male guard and obediently followed him to the stables.

"As soon as he's back, you two should get some rest. I'll have my ghost lions take over," Cyril said to the female guard. "But before you get some sleep, find Violyne and tell her to come as soon as possible."

"As you wish, Your Highness," the guard said and bowed her head with a smile before she opened one of the giant doors to the castle for them.

Clotilda felt like she was the size of an insect within the large arched hallways. The walls were made of white marble and decorated with numerous oil paintings that looked like the finest artists painted them.

"Your home is beautiful," Clotilda said as she looked up at Cyril, causing him to glance down at her with a smile.

She groaned softly as they climbed a giant staircase when she felt her adrenaline fade. The arrows had struck her femur, and the nerves were tender from the slightest movement.

"Take it easy. We're almost to your room," Cyril said softly.

"My room?" she asked.

"I had my servants prepare a bedroom while searching for you. That way, you would be comfortable during your stay here," Cyril said as he reached the top of the stairs to the fourth floor. He walked down the hallway until he came to two double doors that led to a bed chamber. He summoned a couple of his ghost lions, who gently pushed against the doors and opened them so they could enter.

Clotilda was taken aback as they entered the grand bedroom. The room was flooded with moonlight pouring through the arched crystal windows and the door to the balcony. There was a spacious wardrobe, an elegant vanity made of rose gold, and a standing mirror decorated with a frame of porcelain vines and flowers. Two tall vases holding elegant flower arrangements stood beside the door like guards, and a short walkway led to a bathing chamber. The bed was adorned with thick blankets and giant pillows that looked soft and inviting to sleep or jump on.

Cyril walked to the side of the bed and slowly lowered Clotilda onto the blanket. The soft, cool covers soothed the tense muscles in her back, and she felt herself sink into the bed with how comfortable it was. Her hair framed her head like a halo and draped over the pillows as she looked around at the murals on the ceiling and the crystal blinking at her like a chandelier as the lunar light shone through it.

"I–I can't believe you and your followers went through the extra effort to get a bedroom like this ready for me to stay in."

"Do you like it?" Cyril asked.

"I do," she said as she sat up and supported her weight on her elbows. "I appreciate it greatly. I'm just not used to staying in a room like this."

"You get accustomed to it over time. But as long as you are happy here, it's worth it."

"Thank you," she smiled politely at him.

Cyril returned her smile before sitting on the edge of the bed. Clotilda scooted a little to give him room to sit. She watched as he looked at the arrow wounds on her right thigh. Then he reached into his waist pack, pulling out a pouch. He opened it and scooped out a handful of healing blossoms, the Tears of Eir.

"Now, let's tend to your injuries so you can get some rest," he said as he gently placed the flowers on her wounds. Clotilda flinched a little from the pain, causing Cyril to look at her apologetically.

"Thank you, but don't you have healing powers?"

"Only during the crescent moon. Tonight is a half-moon, so it granted me the ability to teleport," he explained as he gently pressed his hand against her wound to encourage the flowers to heal faster.

"Oh, that's right," she muttered as she squinted her eyes in embarrassment. "I forgot about that. How do you do it?"

"I was born during a Celestial Shower. That is how I came into the world as a Celestial Born Regulus elf."

"A Celestial Shower? That's when the night sky rains, shooting stars, right?"

"That's right," he replied with a nod.

"During the full moon, what kind of power does it grant you?"

"Well, it grants me the ability to use its light as a weapon, but most importantly, it grants us Celestial Borns enhanced hearing."

"So that's how you hear those who walk on the land?"

Cyril nodded.

"Yes. Due to it being a full moon the other night, I could hear you. I woke up when I heard you fall and walk in the field outside of Streng."

"I'm sorry about that," she said and lowered her head bashfully, feeling bad that she disturbed his sleep.

"Don't be. I would have never found you if you hadn't done that."

Clotilda glanced up at him, her smile dropping when she noticed he looked deep in thought.

"Is something wrong?" she asked worriedly.

"Just thinking about all that's happened," he said softly as he kept his gaze on her healing wound. "I wasn't impressed by how the people at Streng treated you."

"Just the royal family and Bandus, but everyone was nice," she replied, hoping her words eased the irritated aura from the elf king.

"Still, you shouldn't have been treated like that," he sighed through his nose. "I should have come for you sooner."

"You're not at fault. The enchanted barrier of Streng prevents outsiders from seeing the capital and hearing anyone inside it. But a part of me wishes that I crossed the barrier sooner instead of keeping you searching for me all this time."

Cyril turned his gaze to her, their weary eyes meeting. They silently looked at each other before he broke the silence.

"It's in the past now. Whatever rumors you heard of me as the Graffias Manticore, I have no intentions of imprisoning you here. You are welcome to stay here as long as you wish and leave whenever you like."

"I'm not one to listen to rumors about people without getting to know them first. I appreciate you saving my life and bringing me here," she said sincerely, causing him to smile.

Once Clotilda's thigh was healed, Cyril carefully inspected her for more injuries when a knock erupted on the door.

"Come in," Cyril called out.

The door slowly opened to reveal a female elf peeking through the doors and stepping inside. She was an Airavata elf, her pearl-like skin shimmering in the moonlight like the ocean surface, and she had a light touch of makeup on her elegant face. She had a slender form that was close to an hourglass figure. She had long, pale-blue hair pulled in a braid that grew to her narrow waist, and her eyes were blue like aquamarines. Her fingernails were blue with orange painted on the tips like orange peels, and she wore a white lace gown that reached her ankles.

"You've called for me, Your Highness?" she asked with a bow.

"I did. We have a guest here. Clotilda, this is Violyne," he introduced the servant as she bowed to Clotilda in greeting. "She will be helping you with wardrobe care and anything else you need."

"It's a pleasure to meet you, my lady."

"It's a pleasure to meet you too," Clotilda replied as she smiled back.

"Take good care of her, Violyne. Help her get set up in the bathing chamber and ready for a night's rest."

"As you wish, Your Highness," she said and bowed to him before walking toward Clotilda and offering her open palm. "Come along, dear. Let's get you cleaned up."

"Okay," Clotilda said as she swung her legs over the edge of the bed. Her legs were still shaky from tiredness, but she steeled her muscles as she stood up.

Violyne wrapped her arm behind Clotilda's back to support her as she guided her to the bathing chambers.

Upon entering the bathing chambers, Clotilda was greeted by a large pool of water as clear as a mirror. The ground under her feet felt like a field of swan down even through the soles of her boots, and a mist-like steam curtained the air and rippled warmly against her skin.

"Right this way," Violyne said as she led Clotilda to the pool, and the water's surface was laced with pink flower petals. Violyne turned around until her back faced Clotilda. "Once you've changed out of your clothes, sit inside the water, and then we can get started."

"Sure thing," Clotilda said as she peeled off her bloodstained jumpsuit, Commander of the Royal Guard armor, waist pack, hand chains, and broken-heeled boots. Then, using her long hair to hide her bare body, Clotilda laid her clothes and armor on the ground and stepped into the pool. She sat down until the water reached her collarbone and sighed happily as she felt the warm water soothe her sore muscles. "All right, it's safe to look now," Clotilda said, causing her new lady-in-waiting to giggle.

"Silly thing," Violyne said as she turned around and cast her magic to summon a crystal pitcher filled with warm water. "Now, close your eyes and tilt your head back," she instructed.

Clotilda did as she was told and felt the water from the pitcher splash onto her head and run through her hair. Violyne grabbed one of the cleaning potions by the pool, poured a palm-sized rose potion into her hand, and scrubbed it into Clotilda's scalp. She instructed the former commander to tilt her head and close her eyes again before refilling the pitcher and rinsing her hair. Clotilda used one of the wash potions Violyne gave her to clean her body as the lady-in-waiting dried her hair with a towel.

"That was quite relaxing. I hadn't had anyone help me with bathing since my mother gave me baths when I was a baby."

"You are certainly easier to clean than my six sons were. They never held still."

"How old are your sons?" Clotilda asked with a smile.

"Five of them are in their twenties now, while my youngest is ten. Two of them followed in their father's footsteps to become soldiers, while the other three are studying to become mages."

"What does your youngest want to be?"

"He's thinking about being a writer."

"That sounds great!"

"All right," Violyne said as she dried her hands with a towel and bent down to pick up Clotilda's clothes and armor. "I'll take these back to my home and fix these for you."

"Are you sure you're okay with doing that?" Clotilda asked as she looked at the damaged clothing and boots. "They would probably take much work."

"Oh, it's fine. I've mended my husband's and sons' armor sets, so it shouldn't be a problem. I'll leave this at your vanity for you," Violyne said as she held the waist pack.

"Thank you, Violyne," Clotilda said gratefully as she watched her walk into the bed chambers and return to help her finish.

After getting cleaned, Violyne brought Clotilda a towel to cover up and helped escort her back to the bedroom, where Cyril waited patiently. Clotilda opened the bottom drawers of the wardrobe, carefully going through the soft fabrics of the nightgowns before choosing a long, pink-laced gown. She stepped behind the divider doors to remove her towel and into her new nightwear. Once dressed, she looked over to Cyril, who was leaning against the purple-painted wall with his hands on his hips.

"I'm ready for slumber!" Clotilda said as she stepped out from behind the divider, holding her arms out in presentation.

Cyril smiled back at her with a chuckle at her gesture as he walked over toward her.

"It looks nice on you," he said.

"Thank you. This one reminded me of one of the nightgowns that my blood mother used to wear."

"It's very nice. Now, let's get you to bed," he said, offering his arm to her.

Clotilda nodded in agreement as she linked her arm with his, and he escorted her toward the bed.

Clotilda slipped under the covers and lay on her left side as she rested her head on the pillow.

"Sleep well. I'll see you tomorrow," Cyril said with a tired but happy smile.

"You as well. Thank you, and you too, Violyne," Clotilda said as she returned the smile at him and the lady-in-waiting.

Cyril bowed to Clotilda before slowly moving toward the bedroom's double doors with Violyne close behind. He opened one of the doors, allowing Violyne to walk out before he followed and closed the door behind him.

Clotilda rolled until she was lying on her back and folded her hands on her stomach as she stared at the ceiling. Here in this new castle, everyone was so pleasant. Cyril was as friendly and polite as she remembered, but she still couldn't believe he was a king. Thierry was the second king she had ever met and served, but he acted more like a tyrant than a noble ruler. As much as Clotilda was polite and sweet toward the people in Streng, she knew she could be pretty cold to those she didn't trust, especially toward Bandus and the royal family. Being under their thumbs had made her close up. Not just to protect the Deity of Lazarus but to prevent unnecessary conflict with those she wanted to steer clear of.

Even showing Cyril a little bit of her humor, she appreciated that he didn't scold or degrade her. Bandus always hated it when she acted the way she was and did whatever he could to convince her to change, but not for the better. Even though there was a small pit of nervousness inside her about being in a new kingdom, the kindness of Cyril and his people put her at ease. Tomorrow was a new day, a new beginning. Cyril and his people were giving her a chance, and now it was her turn to give them a chance and share who she was with them.

Clotilda slipped her hands under her pillow, sighed softly as she turned to lay on her side, and felt the heavy weight of all that happened that night melt away, making her sleep soundly.

CHAPTER 29

The Recovered Strings

The sticky salt of her tears and blood stained her cheeks as she kneeled to the ground. Her mother, Bathilda, lay in a growing pool of her blood, trying to hold onto what was left of her diminishing life.

"It's okay . . ." her mother said weakly as she gently brushed her fingers over Clotilda's injured cheek. "I'll be fine, sweetheart. I'll be in the arms of the Hands of the Sea."

"Mommy! Don't die! Please don't go!" Clotilda sobbed.

"I'm so . . . sorry," Bathilda apologized with a sob. "Know . . . that . . . I love you so much, and I'm very . . . proud of you . . . my little musician . . ."

She spoke her last words before her hand went limp and collapsed on her daughter's lap.

Clotilda wailed as she looked down at her mother's lifeless body. Her cries ceased as she heard the screeching snarls of undead beings approaching them.

Cadmar scooped her up from behind and cradled her in his strong arms. She could smell the faint scent of decay radiating from her father's flesh as he was beginning to transform into a Hollow.

"Dad, wait! Cyril is in dang . . . !"

"We need to get you far away from here now," he said as he ran toward the burning stable.

Cadmar wrapped his blue cape over his daughter to protect her from falling, burning rafters as he escorted the panicking, pregnant mare out of the stables. He lifted Clotilda onto Coralina's back and placed the Seal of Serpentis in her hand.

"What is this, Daddy?" she asked as she looked at the gold, serpent-designed seal glowing in the light of the hot flames.

"The Seal of Serpentis will help you find the capital of Streng. Coralina will take you there, and no one will ever find you. Promise me that you will never tell anyone you are the Rune of Lazarus. You'll be in danger if anyone finds out."

"No, Dad! Come with me!" She begged, not wanting to lose her father too.

"I can't! With Coralina pregnant, I'm going to be too heavy for her. You're light enough that she can carry you without harming her offspring. Also, I am becoming a Hollow. I'll be as much danger to you as our attackers. You're a courageous girl, and I know you can do it," he said before he kissed her forehead and slapped Coralina's hip, causing her to neigh and open her wings, ready for flight.

"No, Dad!" Clotilda wailed.

"Good luck! I love you, Clotilda!" Cadmar said as Coralina galloped away and took to the air.

Clotilda felt the smoky air rush past her as she watched her father fight off the undead, enemy archers. She felt her heart sting and stomach churn as she saw arrows pierce his back. He fought through as he tried to return to his wife's body and stopped as the enemies surrounded him. Her attacker from earlier came from behind Cadmar and slit open his throat with the iron dagger still stained with her blood. Warm blood oozed from Cadmar's neck. He gurgled as he placed his hand over the wound and struggled to breathe before collapsing.

His limp arm fell to the ground and outstretched toward Bathilda's body, trying to reach out to his soulmate's hand before dying.

"Dad! Mom! Cyril!" Clotilda screamed as Coralina flew them further and further away, leaving them as the only survivors of Cygnus.

The morning sunlight flooded through the balcony of Clotilda's bedroom and basked over her sleeping form, causing her to stir. She slowly opened her eyes, the haze of sleep clearing to reveal the interior of her new bedroom. Clotilda's barely waking mind looked around in confusion, wondering where she was before the memories of last night flooded back.

Clotilda sighed as she slowly sat up, feeling something wet run down her cheeks. She gently brushed her right hand on her cheeks and pulled it away to see a tear coating her fingertips. She bit the inside of her cheeks. She thought about her father. Cadmar must have begun transforming into a Hollow after his wife was killed. She was the love of his life. He was a good husband to her mother and an excellent father to her. The loss of his wife and daughter was too significant. She understood the pain. The loss of her parents and music journal caused her to become a Hollow as a child.

"Mom . . . Dad . . ." she whispered sadly.

A knock on the double doors to her room caused Clotilda to jolt and quickly wipe her face with her hands to clear away the tears. She leaped from the bed, walked toward one of the doors, and slowly opened it. A Beetje elf girl she guessed to be in her late teens or early twenties stood by the doorway, holding a food tray. She was around four feet tall, had blonde hair the color of limestone that was styled in a low bun, her skin was sun-kissed with rosy cheeks, and her eyes were blue like robin eggs. She wore an elegant, lacey dress similar to Violyne's, but it was pale yellow like a daffodil in full bloom.

"Good morning, Lady Clotilda. May I come in?" the girl asked with a cheerful voice.

"Uh . . . sure. Please, come in," Clotilda said as she stepped aside and opened the door for the servant girl to walk in.

The smell of food wafting around Clotilda's nose caused her stomach to growl in hunger.The servant girl put the food tray on the small nightstand beside the bed, grabbed the pitcher, and poured an alabaster liquid into the chalice.

Clotilda studied the food on the tray, seeing a platter of juicy, herbed meat with a dark grill pattern and a porcelain stand with a greenish-blue egg on top. Clotilda recognized it as an Emerald Slitagon's egg, a small, greenish-blue wyvern known for roaming the skies over mountain springs. She remembered seeing Malvolia and King Thierry eating these eggs for breakfast while doing her kingdom duties, but she had never tried one. Next to it was a bowl of pudding that smelled of honey and blueberries. Clotilda's mouth watered as she sat on the edge of the bed, and the servant girl happily rested the food tray on her lap.

"Thank you so much for the food. It looks delicious," Clotilda said with a smile.

"Don't thank me, thank Chef Aldwin. King Cyril asked him to cook his favorite dish for you and to bring it to you. He hopes that you enjoy it."

"Give my thanks to them. By the way, where is Cy . . . I mean, King Cyril?"

She corrected herself, mentally reminding herself that Cyril was a ruler and respectfully addressed him by his regal title.

"The king said that he needed to catch up on some royal duties but asked me to tell you that once he finishes them, he would like to give you a tour of the castle."

"That sounds great! When will he be done?" Clotilda asked.

"Probably in the afternoon," the servant girl said with a shrug.

"I'm pretty patient, so he doesn't have to rush anything."

"I'm sure he'll appreciate hearing that. Anyway, I hope you enjoy breakfast, and be sure to be dressed and ready. I'm sure that once His Majesty comes here, he will be most anxious to show you around."

"I will make sure I'm ready," Clotilda said and nodded.

"Once you're done with breakfast, ring this, and Violyne will come here to help you get dressed," she said as she handed Clotilda a small aquamarine bell.

"I will. Thank you. What's your name?"

"My name is Canary," she said as she held the side hems of her dress and curtsied. "It was nice meeting you, Lady Clotilda. Call if you need anything."

"It was nice meeting you too, Canary. Thank you again," Clotilda smiled.

Canary curtsied once more before she walked out of the bedroom. Her petite, egg-yolk-colored fairy wings fluttered as if ready to fly as she closed the doors behind her.

Finishing her food, except for her drink, Clotilda placed her tray on the nightstand and stood up to make her bed. She fluffed the blanket until it was even on each side, stood the pillows up, and arranged them in order of larger ones to the back and the smaller ones in front. After smoothing down the blankets for any wrinkles, Clotilda curiously looked around the sunlit room. She picked up the cup from the tray, took a sip, and tasted nectar milk's familiar sweet and rich taste. She glanced down at the drink with a smile. Cyril must have remembered that it was her favorite.

She walked around with her cup, seeing her waist pack lying over the vanity chair as she neared it. Her reflection looked back at her in the large, oval-shaped mirror of the vanity decorated with a rose-gold frame of carved vines and lions.

Clotilda opened each drawer to find various cosmetics, perfumes, and hair accessories. She sniffed the small collection of perfumes and explored the wardrobe next to the vanity, rich with many elegant gowns, tops, pants, and jewelry of different styles and sizes that she felt excited to try on.

Clotilda explored the various paintings on the wall that she couldn't see last night in the darkness. Some were landscapes of forests and mountains, and some were portraits of people she had never met.

One of the paintings captured her full attention. It was the Cygnus village when it was in its prime. She stepped closer to the painting to see that the details were accurate as she remembered it. As she studied it, she noticed a rose-gold, blonde elf girl, who she realized was her, sitting in the apple orchard writing in her journal with her elf doll beside her. She stepped closer to the painting until she could see the delicate brushstrokes as she searched for the artist's name. A smile beamed on her lips, and her mind bloomed with the excitement of discovering that the artist was Cyril. All the paintings she saw last night were probably made by Cyril, too.

"My goodness. I didn't know that you are a painter, Cyril. They're beautiful."

Her attention from the paintings was torn away when she noticed a small room beside the divider. She peeked inside the hidden room and saw the wooden frame of a piano. Clotilda gasped softly as she recognized the musical instrument and hurried toward it to find herself in a small study room with a stack of her old music journals on the desk.

The wooden harp was tucked next to a writing desk and shelves with scrolls and books, with a pile of blank paper with an inkwell and quill perched on top. She placed her hands on the harp and the piano, hardly believing that she had just seen them last night surrounded by an igloo of stones and guarded by a ghostly lion in her ruined village. Her fingers glided over the keys, her nerves tingling, urging her to play. She pressed down on the keys, only to cringe when she heard shaky, loose notes.

"You are really out of tune, my friend," she said to the musical instrument as she opened the piano case and began tuning it.

Once her piano was tuned to the best of her abilities, Clotilda moved to tune her harp. She plucked the strings as she listened, hearing the notes becoming more fluid. She reached over to play the keys on her piano, smiling when she listened to the piano's vibrating melody restored after a century of not being played. She planted herself on her small piano seat, listening to the music playing inside her before she splayed her fingers over the piano keys and played the music from her heart.

Inspiration surged through her, making a slow but solemn melody leap into a triumphant beat. Inspired, she stopped playing, jumping from her piano seat and returning to the vanity where her waist pack was. She opened the pack and anxiously pulled out both of her books.

Clotilda rushed back to the study and grabbed the quill and inkwell. She opened one of the music books, grateful it survived the lagoon's water and was water-resistant. Clotilda began writing her newest pieces, humming the notes as she wrote them. She filled the page of the first part of the piece, turned to her piano, and used her left hand to play the rest of it, with the journal on her lap and writing with her right hand. Clotilda filled the second page before fanning her hand over it to dry the ink, then turned it and continued to write.

Clotilda sighed happily as she finished writing her creation, flipped five pages back to the beginning, and held the quill pen over the page to think of a title. She hummed softly as she thought about it before allowing the pen to guide her hand to form the name of her newest creation, *Awakening*, a piece inspired by how she and Cyril transformed into their Rune forms the other night and how they fought together.

Clotilda smiled happily as she carefully set the journal open on the music stand of her piano and placed the second one she found in her village on top of the stack of her other childhood music pieces.

She stood up from her seat and jumped in surprise when she realized she wasn't alone. Violyne stood at the mouth of the walkway to the study room and lightly clapped her hands when Clotilda discovered that she was there.

"Good morning to you, Lady Clotilda. Whatever you were working on, it sounded quite lovely."

"Thank you, and good morning to you as well," she said as she smoothed her nightgown. "How long were you there?" she asked, not seeing anyone when she ran out to get her waist pack.

"Not too long. I tried knocking on your door, but when you didn't answer, I opened it to see you were engrossed in your work."

"I'm sorry about that."

"Don't be. Your music is wonderful! Along with seeing King Cyril's beautiful paintings adorning the castle's walls like a portfolio so everyone can see them, hearing beautiful piano music fill the castle is soothing." Clotilda smiled as she heard Violyne's words. It was good to hear such a nice compliment, and knowing that she could write and play her music without worrying about bothering anyone made her feel at ease.

"Anyway, are you ready for me to help you get dressed?" Violyne asked.

"I'm ready when you are," Clotilda nodded.

"Glad to hear. Choose which dress you would like to wear today, and I will help you get it on and assist you with your hair and makeup."

"Will do," Clotilda smiled as she walked toward the lady-in-waiting, and they made their way to the wardrobe.

CHAPTER 30

The Kingdom of Algieba

Gold fabric fluttered like the wings of a monarch butterfly as Clotilda carefully pulled out a yellow dress decorated with small, green gems around the hip and the bottom hem of the gown.

"This dress is stunning," Clotilda said as she smoothed her hands down the fabric.

"I think you chose a fine gown, my lady," Violyne replied, turning around to give Clotilda privacy. "Just let me know when you are done, and I'll help you tie the back."

Clotilda carefully removed her nightgown, slid her arms through the dress's sleeves, and pressed the gown against her chest to prevent it from falling.

"All right, Violyne. It's safe to look now," Clotilda said as she turned around for Violyne to help her tie the corset. Violyne turned around and began tying the ribbons on the dress. "So, how long have you known King Cyril?" she asked.

Since I was twelve years old," Violyne replied as she continued tying the dress. "The first time we met, he saved my brother and me from a pillage troll. When that brute took us away from our mother and father, King Cyril and his Royal Huntresses chased after him and saved us."

"Your king is such a good man," Clotilda smiled as she listened to the story. She remembered reading about pillage trolls. They were known for being aggressive, giant beasts living deep in forests and for their vile nature of stealing villagers, especially children, and taking them to the woods to eat them. Knowing how brave and protective Cyril was, she felt her admiration for him grew stronger as she listened to Violyne's story as well as watched his actions. How he fearlessly protected those around him and boldly went out of his way to help her back in Streng inspired her.

"He sure is," Violyne agreed.

"So, when did you start working here in the castle?"

"I was twenty-two years old when I started working here. After King Cyril reclaimed and restored his kingdom, I volunteered to work as one of his maids. He accepted it, and my first job was caring for the girls and young women visiting the castle."

"Oh, was it some sort of school or training for the girls?" Clotilda asked.

"That too. But it was mostly because the king was searching for you. King Cyril spoke fondly of you for many years and had the capitals and villages send every Lazarus and Airavata girl and woman to his kingdom to train them and see if one of them was you."

"I see. I'm sorry," Clotilda said as she felt guilty.

"Why's that?" Violyne asked as she glanced up from her work.

"Because I made him search for me all this time. I must have put all of you through so much trouble."

"Were you aware that he was searching for you?" Violyne asked with one eyebrow arched.

“No, I wasn’t until he told me when he came to Streng.”

“Then you have nothing to feel terrible about. He found you now, and I can tell from last night that he was overjoyed to have you here.”

“I am too,” Clotilda smiled in reply.

“All right, that should do it,” Violyne said as she tied the corset. “Let’s finish your hair and makeup, and you’ll be ready.”

“Will do,” Clotilda nodded as she sat before the vanity.

Violyne carefully brushed Clotilda’s long hair, pulled it into a half-up, half-down style, and decorated the back with a cluster of small, yellow flowers. She helped her finish the elegant look with a light touch of makeup and a soft pink gloss for her lips.

“All right, my lady. You’re finished,” Violyne said as she put the makeup away.

Clotilda looked into the mirror, admiring the skilled hand of Violyne’s makeup expertise.

“It looks great,” she said as she turned around on the chair, careful not to damage her dress. “You do a better job with my makeup than I do.”

“I wouldn’t say that. I’ve just been doing it since I was a teenager,” Violyne said humbly.

“You did a beautiful job, so keep up the great work.”

“Oh, I will. I enjoyed it for the one hundred and fifty-two years of my life, and I will continue with it,” she said with a smile. “It’s already the afternoon. We should be seeing His Highness very soon.”

Clotilda’s smile widened, and her heart began to flutter with anticipation.

A knock on the door erupted the anxiousness in her, and Clotilda leaped from her chair. She jumped onto her bare feet, toppling the stool she was sitting on and causing Violyne to jump back in surprise.

“Oh, sorry! I didn’t mean to do that,” Clotilda said as she held her hand over her mouth in embarrassment.

"I know you're excited, but that doesn't mean that you can knock over the chairs," Violyne said with a giggle as she grabbed the chair and stood it back up.

"I'm sorry," Clotilda apologized once more.

Another knock caused Clotilda to take a step forward instinctively, but she held herself back from racing to the door as she looked back at Violyne.

"Go on, my lady. You don't need my permission to answer your bedroom doors."

With those words, Clotilda walked quickly toward the double doors before she grabbed one of the handles and pulled it open. Expecting to see Cyril, her smile dropped slightly when she saw that it was one of the male servants holding a tray in his hands with a letter lying on it.

"My apologies for the intrusion, my lady. His Majesty has asked me to deliver this letter to you," he replied as he held the tray to her, displaying the letter.

Clotilda felt nervous, wondering if something had happened and fearing that Cyril wouldn't be able to make it. Bracing herself, she picked the letter up from the tray, thanking the servant before slowly closing the door and holding the letter in both hands as she studied the brown envelope with a light-blue wax seal of the lion emblem of the Regulus elf culture. She tore open the envelope, careful not to break the seal, as she pulled the letter out of it and began reading.

Dear Clotilda,

I regret telling you this . . . but I need to catch up on some of my work, so I will be much later than I wanted to. Please forgive me. I need to complete some documents and a royal meeting, and I promise I will come to be with you as soon as I am done. Feel free to explore the castle; my servants will help you. All you need to do is ask. Make yourself at home.

Sincerely,

King Cyril.

Clotilda felt her heart drop to her stomach. Her desire to be with Cyril had to be postponed even longer than she wanted. She lowered her head sadly before carefully folding the letter closed.

"What's wrong? Did something happen?" Violyne asked in concern.

"No, it's just Cyril . . . the king will be late because he's busy right now."

"Don't be disheartened," Violyne reassured her with a gentle pat on her back. "As a king, he has many duties of running his kingdom and protecting his people."

"I understand because I served a king before. But . . . I just . . ."

"Miss him," she said, causing Clotilda to nod in response.

"Ever since I was a child."

"Don't worry. He's very hardworking, but when he makes a promise he knows he can keep, he will fulfill it. Trust him. So, what else did he tell you?"

"Um, he said he would be late meeting with us but wrote that I could explore the castle if I wanted to," she replied as she showed the letter to Violyne.

"That's our king for you," Violyne said as she grasped the letter from Clotilda and gently laid it down on the vanity table. "He wouldn't want you cooped up in your room. So let's begin the tour of the castle."

"Are you sure? Because I can stay here and read some of the novels while I'm waiting," she said, pointing her thumb over her shoulder to the study room.

"Of course, I'm sure," Violyne said as she opened the doors to the wardrobe and pulled out a pair of golden, ballet-styled slippers. "As I said, you have no reason to be cooped up here."

"I guess a little exploring wouldn't hurt," Clotilda said with a shrug.

"Here," Violyne said, holding the slippers out to Clotilda. "Put these on, and we can begin the tour."

"You got it," Clotilda smiled as she accepted the slippers, placed them on the ground before her, and lifted the dress hem to slip her feet into them.

Putting on her hand chains, she and Violyne walked out of the bed chambers to begin the tour.

Violyne showed Clotilda the closed doors of the servants' bedrooms as they walked down the numerous hallways of the fourth to the second levels of the castle and showed her a room with enormous doors that was Cyril's bed chamber, framed by two crystal statues, one lion and one lioness, in a motionless prowl that resembled the ones outside the grand entrance.

Violyne brought her to the royal kitchen to meet the head chef, Chef Aldwin, and his cooks and bakers, who greeted her respectfully.

From the kitchen, Clotilda was taken to the ballroom, and they made their way to the dining room. Clotilda opened the door and saw someone sitting in one of the chairs. His feet and legs lay propped on the long dining table, and he took a big bite of a red apple. Clotilda's eyes widened as she looked at the elven male. He was handsome, with his teal skin, red-wine hair, and deep purple eyes. He was also very familiar to her.

"Doric!" Violyne cried out in rage, identifying his name. "How many times do I have to tell you about putting your feet on the table," she scolded him before grabbing his booted ankles and pushing them firmly off the table.

"Feisty as always," Doric chuckled with his mouth full of the half-chewed apple. "I can't help it. It's a habit that doesn't seem to want to disappear," he said as he planted his feet on the table again, only for Violyne to push them off.

"Do that again, and I will string you up by your toes," Violyne fumed.

"Probably not such a good idea. If you're going to string me up, make sure I'm wearing my boots and don't touch my skin," he said calmly with a smirk before he took another bite from the apple.

"Doric?" Clotilda asked as she walked over to him. "I remember you! You're the one I met in the jewelry store the other day."

"Hmm," he mumbled before he met her gaze. "I sure am. I'm flattered that you remember me." He swallowed his food before he continued speaking. "Truth be told, I'm not a jeweler or a merchant. I used to steal jewels, but that's far in the past now."

"So, what brings you here?" Clotilda asked with a smile.

"I live here in this kingdom thanks to my good friend, Cy. He told me I could stay here if I didn't cause trouble, which is impossible sometimes," Doric said as he winked at Violyne, who rolled her eyes in irritation.

"If you're not a merchant, then why did you disguise yourself as one when we first met?" Clotilda asked.

"Cy was about to disguise himself as the merchant so he could give you that hand chain you're wearing," he said as he pointed to the second hand chain around her left wrist. "But I told him I owed him one and took his place. Although, I think it was a good thing I did. Because seeing that mage giving you a hard time that day, I'm sure Cy would have lost it and killed him where he stood."

"Yes. Probably a good thing," she said, remembering Bandus's insults that day. "After I left the market, I noticed you weren't at the shop anymore. Where did you end up going?"

"I was seeing where you were going. I turned invisible and followed you after you argued with the mage, and I was surprised to see you heading to the castle. I couldn't find you but overheard from the servants that there was a masquerade ball. I told Cy about it so he could see you."

"I appreciate that. I had a great time with him that evening."

"I saw that. I was at the ball too, disguised as one of the guests and wearing a crow mask," he nodded to her. "By the way, have you seen your musical instruments and music journals in your study yet?"

"I did. I was able to tune them this morning and play for a while. Did you help Cyril retrieve them?" she asked, ready to thank him.

"I did. I was on my way from Streng with my steed, Xavier, and we were bringing all your stuff from your house in Streng to Algieba."

"What? You mean you brought everything all the way here?" Clotilda asked as her eyes widened.

"I did. After Cy escaped from the dungeon, he told me to pack all your stuff and bring them here while he went out to find you. I lock-picked your house, packed everything, put them in a wagon I bought in Streng, and brought them all the way here," he said with a smirk.

"All the way here?" Violyne asked with a glare.

"Well . . . all right, I went as far as I could before Cy teleported Xavier and me to his castle after he rescued you. He retrieved your piano, harp, and music books from your fallen village after he brought you to your room, and after he teleported me and my steed back, we got them set up in your study while you slept. Your belongings are still in the wagon next to the stables. So the servants will bring your stuff to your bed chamber soon."

"I'll see what I can do to help them with that," Clotilda replied.

"So, what are you ladies doing anyway?" he asked, changing the subject.

"Violyne is giving me a tour of the castle. But unfortunately, King Cyril couldn't make it due to his duties, so he told us to start and that he would catch up with us later."

"Mind if I join? I don't have anything going on now, and quite frankly, I'm a little bored," Doric playfully pouted.

"I don't see why not," Clotilda giggled softly.

"As long as you don't cause trouble," Violyne said as she glared at him.

"No! I never do," he said dramatically before he threw the apple's core onto the table.

"Doric!" Violyne shrieked as the chuckling Doric leaped off his chair and fled with the angry lady-in-waiting chasing him, leaving Clotilda laughing as she watched the hilarious scene before her.

Following Doric and Violyne, Clotilda's stomach was sore from her laughing fit of watching the chase, and she carefully rubbed the tears in her eyes so as not to smear her makeup. She looked around in awe as she explored the kingdom's beautiful interior as she followed her guides. Like the rest of the castle, the hallways were well taken care of, and there were statues and paintings of many male and female elves and many other species on the wall, which she guessed were of Cyril's family and friends.

Two large wooden double doors with carvings of elven scribes and cascading scrolls with Regulus elven writing on them captured Clotilda's attention.

"Which room is that?" she asked as she pointed at it.

Her two guides looked back at her as they stopped and followed her finger to where she was pointing.

"That's the royal library," Violyne said.

"A library?" Clotilda asked with her eyes wide with interest.

"You like to read?" Doric asked with a chuckle as he noticed Clotilda's excited reaction.

"Oh, I love reading! Do you mind if I go in there and explore the collection of books?" she asked as she walked toward the library.

"You can't go in there right now, my lady," Violyne whispered, causing Clotilda to freeze in place. "His Majesty is probably in there working. He doesn't like being disturbed while reading or working on his documents unless it is urgent."

"If that's the case, I am stepping away," Clotilda said as she walked backward, creating distance between her and the library.

"You are a cute little thing," Doric chuckled as he watched her walk backward like a child trying to avoid trouble.

"Glad I was able to make you two laugh a little," Clotilda giggled with him as she stood beside them. "Do you like reading too, Doric?"

"No, not really. The only reading I did was for schooling and researching for my training. But that's the extent of it. Cy likes to read, though," Doric said with a shrug. "Of all the various rooms in the castle that he could be in, I always find him in the library. I wouldn't be surprised if he read all the books there."

Clotilda smiled as she discovered that she and Cyril shared a hobby they both enjoyed.

"Any genres he likes to read?" she asked.

"You'll have to ask him," Doric shrugged again.

"I was wondering, would it be possible to borrow a few books from the library?"

"You'll have to ask His Majesty first," Violyne said. "He deeply treasures the library, and all the books there are ones that his father and mother collected over the centuries before they died."

Clotilda went silent, and her smile melted away like the wax of a candle. A sympathetic sting of loss in her heart erupted as she realized Cyril was also an orphan like her.

The three elves perked their ears as one of the large doors creaked and swung open. Cyril appeared before the library entrance, causing Clotilda to stare.

The king of the Regulus elves wore a tunic made of dark indigo leather that looked like the evening sky, with silver threads resembling falling stars' tails. His attire was completed with a long white undershirt, elbow-length brown leather gloves, and two brown armbands around his muscular biceps. Deep indigo pants that looked like they had been dipped in squid ink hugged his sculpted legs, and he wore brown knee-high combat boots. His cape was long and flowed like an alabaster waterfall adorned with silver roaring lions. His hair shone in the afternoon sunlight, with the blades of his bangs framing the silver crown styled like vines circling his head, with lions opening their jaws to the celestial blue gem in the center.

Clotilda froze in place as if her skin had turned to marble. She had never seen Cyril in his royal garments before and couldn't help but admire him. But she felt a little nervous at the same time. He was very handsome, but he had a powerful monarch presence that demanded the respect he deserved.

Clotilda forgot to bow but was reminded when she saw Doric and Violyne kneeling before Cyril at the corner of her eyes. Cyril turned to the hallway as if ready to sprint, flinching slightly in surprise for not noticing that he had company. Clotilda and Cyril's eyes instantly met.

Snapping herself out of her distracted state, Clotilda quickly grabbed the hem of her dress and pulled it up slightly as she kneeled before him. She felt embarrassed. She forgot at that moment that Cyril was a king and mentally scolded herself for not remembering that detail. Clotilda shook her head in disapproval of her actions. Why was she acting so silly?

She could feel Cyril's gaze on her. She tilted her head slightly to see him through the blades of her bangs and felt relief bloom in her chest when she saw the corners of his mouth tug upward. Cyril gently shut the library door behind him and walked toward them, his cape billowing gracefully until he was in front of her.

"You can rise, my friends," he said softly.

"Yes, Your Highness," Violyne said respectfully as she slowly rose.

"Formal as always, huh, King Cy?" Doric said jokingly, causing Violyne to nudge him in the side with her elbow.

"Show some respect," Violyne whispered sharply at him.

"I am," he whispered back as he rubbed the side of his chest where she elbowed him.

The king chuckled at them before returning his attention to Clotilda, who was still kneeling. As part of her training as a guard, Clotilda was always told to kneel before any royal leader and not rise until they said so. She remained on her knee to show her respect to Cyril and would stand when he told her to. However, she witnessed something she would never see King Thierry do. Cyril bent down and held his upturned, gloved hand to her.

"You can rise, Clotilda. You're my friend too," he said with a smile that made warmth bloom in her chest.

Clotilda shyly looked at his offered hand before slowly accepting it. His gloved fingers wrapped around her hand, and he helped her back to her feet.

"Good afternoon . . . Your Highness," Clotilda said shyly.

"Good afternoon to you as well, my lady. I'm sorry that I'm late," Cyril replied.

"It's all right. I'm just happy to see you," she said with a smile, feeling less nervous.

Cyril's smile widened at her words and he quickly released his hold on her hand as if he had offended her by holding onto it for too long. Clotilda's smile dropped by his gesture, and she fought the urge to reach for it. Cyril cleared his throat.

"How far did you get with your castle tour?" he asked.

"Violyne showed me the kitchen, the hallway where the servants' rooms are, the ballroom, and the dining room, where we met Doric."

"Good. I didn't miss too much," he said before he turned to Doric and Violyne. "You two can take a break if you want. I can finish showing Clotilda the rest of the castle."

"As you wish, Your Highness," Violyne said as she bowed gracefully at him.

"Aww! Oh well, maybe next time then," Doric said in mocking disappointment before he gave Clotilda a friendly wink and walked toward the adjacent staircase. "I'll just rest my feet on the dining room table and eat more delicious apples in the meantime."

"Don't you dare!" Violyne growled and she chased after the laughing Doric as they ran down the stairs, leaving Clotilda and Cyril alone.

"Those two are very entertaining to be around. They're so funny," Clotilda giggled.

"They are. Their company makes the castle more exciting, and having them messing around is rather amusing," he chuckled before he cleared his throat again. "Anyway, I was able to finish what I needed to do for today. So . . . can I show you the rest of the kingdom?" he said as he offered his arm to her.

"I would like that, Your Highness," she said as she hooked her hand around the curve of his elbow, and they walked down the hallway.

"I appreciate your respectful nature, Clotilda. But when we are alone, you don't have to call me 'King' or 'Your Highness.' You can call me by my name."

"I'll make sure to remember that," she said as she looked back at him.

"By the way . . ." he paused.

"Yes?" she asked, noticing that he averted his gaze from her almost shyly.

"You look . . . beautiful," he said, causing her skin to flush.

"Thank you," she said as she wrapped her arm around his, feeling his arm tighten around hers as they continued their walk down the hallway.

No more words were exchanged, but they enjoyed each other's company and felt their racing pulses through their linked arms.

CHAPTER 31

Sharing Memories

Clotilda and Cyril's linked arms never separated as they explored the castle. He showed her each room, sharing the hidden historical gems of memories and the sentimental treasures within them.

He brought her to the throne room, explaining that it was where some of his meetings and strategies took place for planning defenses and the well-being of his people. Clotilda gazed around the colossal, empty chamber, where statues of lions and griffins were sculpted at each of the four corners, peering down at her. Loops of blue curtains hung from the ceiling like ribbons of streamers, and they were connected to a large, white crystal growing from the center of the ceiling.

Clotilda lowered her gaze from the ceiling and looked at Cyril's throne. The throne was made of marble with roaring lion heads as the armrests and had cobalt-blue cushions. The high seat was chiseled in the coiling vine designs and had the lion and lioness insignia of the Regulus elves at the throne's top center.

The expansive strategy table was adorned with old maps and markers of various shapes of figures and buildings. Clotilda stepped closer to the table and saw that the markers were posted on every castle, village, and capital on the map. The maps didn't have Streng on them, which didn't surprise her since King Thierry didn't want his kingdom to be marked on any map.

Her gaze dropped to a small figurine of an elven woman with long, elegant hair, a ballroom gown, and a sword. She carefully picked up the figure to study it closer.

"I made that figure of you while I was searching. All the markers you see on the maps are the places we searched, but none of them were where we could find you," he gently gripped the figure in her hand, which she allowed him to have. She watched as he placed it on the blank spot on the map of a large field, which she knew was where Streng was. "I should have known the place where I could find you was right under my nose the whole time."

Clotilda reached up and placed her hand on his shoulder.

"I understand that it may be difficult to think about, but please don't blame yourself for what happened in the past. Even though it has been years, I am very grateful that we have been able to reunite."

Cyril looked at her silently with a smile. He released his hold on the figure, left it on the strategy table, and offered his arm to her. Clotilda happily accepted it and followed him as they left the throne room to continue the tour.

From there, Cyril showed Clotilda the banquet hall and the guard rooms, with paintings of numerous criminals and villains hanging on the walls like wanted posters. She didn't recognize some of the villain portraits, but the ones she knew were of Delilah, some of the Graffias Assassins members, and one of Acanthus. Cyril explained that the paintings helped his guards understand whom to go after and for him to memorize the villains' faces.

After leaving the guard rooms, Cyril led Clotilda into his bed chambers, showing her around and the treasures within it. Cyril's bedroom looked similar to hers, outfitted with a bathing chamber and a study room where Cyril's painting supplies were located. Clotilda noticed a wooden canvas standing in the center of the study room with a new oil painting still drying. With Cyril's consent to look upon the painting, Clotilda slowly walked toward it. Afraid that sudden movements would knock the canvas over, she slowly approached it and studied it curiously, seeing that it was a painting of the Algieba castle.

Taking her time to study the art piece, Clotilda allowed her curious gaze to glide over the chamber to see numerous paintings covering every space of the marble walls.

"Did you paint all of these?" she asked as she slowly spun around, looking at the paintings surrounding her like the funnel of a tornado.

"I did," he humbly replied with a smile.

Clotilda slowly dropped her gaze to the ground to see a stack of paintings standing on the floor, leaning against the large writing desk.

"Do you mind if I look at these?" she asked as she pointed at the stack of paintings.

"You may," he said with a nod.

With a sense of awe and wonder, Clotilda lowered herself onto the ground and gazed at the paintings before her. She processed every detail of each canvas, pulling them forward to get a closer look at every landscape, still life, and portrait. As she examined each piece of art, Cyril's skill and passion struck her, and she felt a deep appreciation for his keen eye for beauty in the natural world and the imagined. Clotilda's eyes lingered on the brushstrokes and colors, and seeing his art inspired her to write more music. She hoped to capture as much detail in her craft as Cyril did for his.

She was greeted by a portrait of a male Regulus elf as she reached the final canvas. He was a Celestial Born like Cyril and had a long, styled, majestic mustache and beard wrapped around his strong chest, broad shoulders, and muscular arms crossed in front of his chest.

"Cyril?" she asked, causing the king to look at her as she carefully pulled the portrait from the stack of paintings and showed it to him. "Is this a painting of your father?"

"That's me," he said with a shrug.

"Really? I didn't know you had facial hair like this."

"It's one of the traditions of my people. Like all Regulus elf kings before, my father had a beard just like that. As a young boy, I wanted to grow one and style it like my father's when I grew up. The only difference was that his beard and mustache were golden-blond while mine was white and silver," he said. His smile faded before he continued. "But when I lost my kingdom and crown, the traitor who dethroned me shaved off my beard as a sign of disgrace and failure as a king."

Clotilda noticed his hands curling into tight fists as they hung by his sides. She heard the leather of his gloves strain from his firm grip. She glanced up and saw his gaze turn away from her, his brows knitting together, and his eyes looked down at the ground. She felt a pang of sadness as she looked at him in silence. Something terrible had happened to him in the past, and she couldn't imagine what he must have gone through. Her heart pained as she heard him say that he had failed, making her failure to protect Princess Malvolia seem insignificant in comparison.

Clotilda carefully placed the portrait back in the row of paintings before she stood up and stepped closer to Cyril.

"You're not a failure, Cyril," she replied softly, reaching toward his hand and gently wrapping her fingers around his tight fist to comfort him. "You never have been, and you never will be."

Cyril's scrunched eyebrows of concern and hidden fury softened as he met her gaze. His tightly clenched hand relaxed and opened to her gentle and caring touch.

"That means a lot to hear you say that. However, it did bother me when my beard was shaved off. It took a long time for me to grow it," he said as he arched his brow in annoyance.

"I like your clean-shaven look. You have a nice face," she smiled.

"I appreciate the compliment. But I will admit that not having a beard is much easier. Even though some of my friends keep saying I should consider growing my beard back," he said as he smiled at her.

"It's your choice, not theirs. But what matters is here," Clotilda said as she placed her free hand on his chest. "A true leader comes from within. When I saw you back at the library, how you carried yourself, and how you acted respectfully and kindly to others, I saw you as a true king. Something that I never saw in King Thierry."

Cyril softly took her left hand in his, bringing it to his lips and kissing it. Then he pulled away and gently tugged her toward the balcony.

"Come with me. There is something I want to show you."

Clotilda returned the smile, allowing him to guide her to what he wanted to show her.

Cyril approached the balcony and stood by its railing before she followed him and stood beside his left side as she looked at the view before them. She was greeted with a bird's-eye view of the kingdom. The tallest tower that housed the king's bed chamber reached the sky to the point that it looked like it could snag a cloud. Clotilda grabbed the marble railing and saw the castle grounds and the courtyard below.

The giant lion statues that towered over her when Cyril carried her last night were now the size of sunflower seeds, and the people below looked as big as grains of sand. A chapel stood in an emerald patch of grass, granting a sanctuary of prayer whenever needed. Clotilda wondered what the chapel looked like on the inside. She prayed in the playground of the orphanage and the chapel in Cygnus, but never before in a Regulus chapel.

"It's beautiful up here," she said as she glanced back at her companion.

"Being here next to the library is one of my favorite places in the castle. Sometimes, I like to stand atop the towers and watch the sunsets and sunrises."

"I can see why. Is it all right if I go to the chapel to pray?"

"Of course. I go there myself to meditate and pray. You're welcome to go there whenever you want."

"Thank you, Cyril," she said as she glanced down again.

Clotilda narrowed her eyes as she looked closer to the ground and saw a small building she could identify as the stables, with the wagon standing beside it filled with her belongings that Doric mentioned earlier. She wondered how Coralina was doing and how she was behaving with the rest of the steeds in there. Patches of circles with objects within them that look like training dummies, and a fenced area caught her eye.

"What do you see?" Cyril asked curiously.

"Is that a training ground?" she asked, pointing down at it.

"It is," he replied as he looked at her with amazement and rested his elbows on the railing. "You can see it and everything else in the castle grounds from up here?"

Clotilda nodded softly and gave him a bashful smile.

"My father and the Lazarus elves in my village could see from far-off distances like a predatory bird. The ability didn't awaken in me until I reached my teenage years. It served me well when I was in battle or wanted to see what was over the wall and beyond the enchanted barrier surrounding Streng," she replied as she folded her arms and rested them on the railing.

Clotilda felt her cheeks grow warm when she realized Cyril was looking back at her with interest and full attention. She glanced down to see that her elbow was close enough to brush against his. "If I recall, can Regulus elves see in the dark?"

"We can. Seeing in the dark was very useful for me over the years and spared me the use of a torch when I went into the sewers as a child."

"Why did you go into the sewers?" she asked, her expression morphing into disgust.

"Monster hunting," he chuckled at her funny expression. "I was eight years old when I learned a creature was hiding in the sewers and scaring the villagers. So, I decided to go down there and slay it."

"Oh no . . ."

"Yes. 'Oh no' is the best way to word it," he said, placing his gloved hand over his eyes in embarrassment. "I received a scar on my back from my encounter with the beast, and I was met with a furious mother and father when I was brought back."

"That must have been terrifying," she said in worry.

"The creature, not so much. But my angry mother and father . . ." he said as he rubbed his hand down his face and cringed. "That was the most terrifying."

Clotilda and Cyril burst out laughing.

"I can relate," she said through her fit of giggles. "When I did something my blood mother and father, or my hobgoblin mother and father didn't approve of, their anger made a griffin look like a harmless kitten."

"Your adopted parents are hobgoblins?" he asked.

"Yes. They run the orphanage back at Streng, where I was taken to. They adopted me and raised me as if I were their blood daughter. But they can act pretty funny when they get angry or irritated. But whatever you do, don't laugh at them when they are," she said as she pointed at him with a stern warning. "They will put you in your place if you do."

"Don't mess with them, huh," he repeated her warning with a smirk.

"Never mess with them! Rose Hip and Stump are not pushovers," she giggled.

"I'll heed your advice," he chuckled.

Clotilda's giggling died in her throat when she noticed the frown of regret on Cyril's face. She reached her hand over to him and planted it on his bicep.

"Is something wrong?" she asked worriedly.

"I'm sure that you miss your family by now. I'm sorry I took you away from them," he said with a soft sigh.

"You didn't do anything like that. You saved my life and brought me to your beautiful home, and the people here are so kind and welcoming. Of course, I will miss my loved ones, but I am happy as long as they are safe," she reassured him.

"Are you sure?" he asked.

"I'm sure," she said.

Clotilda's heart twisted as homesickness sank into her veins. As much as she missed her family and friends and knew she couldn't return now that she was labeled an enemy of King Thierry, they had their own lives and were safe in Streng.

"I want to stay here with you," she smiled warmly.

Clotilda looked toward Cyril and noticed his gaze was fixed on her. She could sense that the concern previously visible on his face had dissipated, and in its place was a glimmer of hopefulness. This subtle change in his expression profoundly affected Clotilda, causing her heart to skip a beat and a wave of excitement to ripple through her body.

Clotilda shyly glanced down at the castle grounds, her brows knitting together, when she noticed a male figure stalking along the chapel and approaching the castle entrance. Her hands tightly gripped the railing as she focused on him.

"What is it?" she heard Cyril ask.

"I see someone down there," she replied as she focused on the figure.

"Who is it?"

"I don't know. It's hard to tell. He's wearing a brown cape with a hood over his head."

"I'll inform the guards and summon some of my ghost lions to investigate," he said as he pushed himself away from leaning against the railing. "I don't tolerate intruders."

"Me too," she said with a glare.

"We'll put a hold on the tour of the castle grounds and resume once it's safe. Ready to go?" he asked, offering her his arm.

"I am," she said softly, linking her arm with his and following him out of his chambers.

The royal guards and Cyril's ghost lions searched the castle grounds to ensure no one broke in. But there was no sign of a brown-cloaked intruder. The search was unsuccessful, causing Cyril and Clotilda to feel uneasiness swarming in their veins as if infested by termites.

Evening set upon Algieba. Clotilda followed Cyril into the dining hall, where a grand feast greeted them. Her eyes widened at the beautiful plating of dishes on the dining room table that looked like they could be works of art instead of food. The long table was set for two, with one chair at the head of it and one on the other end. There were two of each dish, one on each side and mirroring the other. Cyril led Clotilda to the closest chair, pulled it out for her, and gently pushed it toward the table when she sat. He walked toward the other end of the table and sat in the chair across from her.

Clotilda looked around the table to see five different dishes. The first dish was a thick and creamy soup with a rich aroma of vegetables, accompanied by the second dish, a basket of golden-brown bread. The third dish was a large slab of herbed meat coated with a glossy gravy. The fourth was a long, thin plate with small drumsticks with sliced medallions of eggs laying in a pattern and drizzled with a ribbon of golden sauce. The last dish was a dessert of a delicate vanilla pudding that looked as light as silk and swam in a purple berry sauce that made it look like it was an island in a violet sea.

Clotilda marveled at the beauty of the dishes, and the smells that emanated from them made her stomach growl with anticipation.

"Your chefs did an amazing job with these dishes. They all look wonderful," she said as she looked across the table at Cyril.

"I'll pass your compliments on to them," he smiled.

"But the problem is . . . I don't know which one of these dishes I want to try first," she said as she laid her napkin on her lap.

"You're welcome to sample them all."

"I will. Thank you," she nodded with a smile, causing the elf king to smile warmly at her polite comment.

Clotilda scooped her portions from the dishes closest to her, and the servants aided her with bringing the other plates closer, which she repaid with polite responses.

The servants assisted their king with plating the food on his plate and poured his and Clotilda's drinking chalices with water and a rose-pink fruit juice. Clotilda took a sip from the juice, feeling the sweet liquid slide down her throat, thinking about how it was the best juice she had ever had.

Everything about the meal with the king and everyone's kind treatment of her was surreal and enjoyable compared to the previous kingdom she once lived in. She would never have thought in her eternal life that she would eat at a table with a king, let alone with Cyril. But she still thought of her family. What was Rose Hip cooking for Stump, Garth, and the orphans tonight? What kind of meal was Ignis eating? She felt her heart hurt a little as she missed them. But she was sure they were enjoying a good meal in their homes. She wondered if she could write to them but hesitated at the thought. If King Thierry found out that her family and friends were receiving letters from her, an enemy of his capital, there was no telling what horrible things he would do to them. She couldn't risk endangering them. As much as she wanted to write to them and let them know she was all right, it was better if she didn't.

"Are you all right?" Cyril's voice pulled her from her thoughts.

Clotilda met his gaze and reassured him with a smile.

"I am. I'm sorry, I got lost in my thoughts for a moment," she said, glancing down and pointing at her half-finished meal with her fork. "The food tastes delicious, but I don't think I will be able to finish any of these dishes, even if I wanted to," she giggled.

"Don't worry. Any leftovers are given to my servants and the villagers of my kingdom. They won't be left out," he smiled.

"That's very nice of you. I'm sure they would appreciate that," she smiled, captivated by Cyril's compassion.

"I appreciate my people's support of me being their king and everything my servants have done for my family over the years. It's the least I can do," he said as he stared into his drinking chalice.

Clotilda could see a heavy weight in his slitted pupils: tiredness, a hint of stress, and what looked like self-restraint. His troubles, whatever they were, bothered her just as they bothered him. There had to be something she could do to help him. She grabbed her chalice and held it in the air toward him.

"I want to make a toast," she said happily, noticing how his eyes rose from their downward gaze and met hers. "To all the good people who impacted us in our lives and the family and friends, both mortal and immortal, who inspired, supported, loved, and healed us. We will forever be grateful, and may the Father God bless them."

To her surprise, Cyril rose from his seat, walked around the table toward her with his chalice, and held it to her.

"I couldn't have said it better myself," he smiled.

She raised her chalice to his, and they chimed them together.

CHAPTER 32

Gratitude

The shelves of her study were filled with open journals of new pieces of music, and her inkwell was half full from it being used since the first day.

Clotilda lay on her bed, resting on her chest and stomach as she read the last few pages of one of her novels. She rested her head on her right hand, cupping her chin as she silently read. Her heart felt empty, and the familiar feeling of aloneness she had become accustomed to for years returned tenfold.

It had been two days since she was brought to the castle, but she felt empty despite the open opportunity to read her collection of books and write her music. She longed to be with Cyril.

During the first two days of her stay in the kingdom, Clotilda didn't have the opportunity to see Cyril in the mornings and the afternoons. They were only able to have dinner together, and even then, their conversation was interrupted by a servant who informed Cyril that he had to attend to some of his royal duties. As a result, Cyril was forced to leave Clotilda, much to his reluctance.

The day before yesterday, the servants helped get all her belongings into her bed chamber. Clotilda set up her second piano and harp inside the study with her other ones. Her collection of books was placed on multiple shelves, and she set up her clothing, jewelry, wolf mask, and makeup in her wardrobe and vanity. She found the apple blossom that Cyril had given her and the vase she had put it in and set it on her nightstand. The extra pieces of furniture were placed in the castle's storage room, and she kept most of her remaining belongings in chests in her bed chamber.

But even after completing the unpacking and organizing her things in her new room, she spent most of her day alone. Yesterday was miserable, and she dreaded that today would be a repeat.

Boredom spread through her body like an illness, but the worst feeling was the loneliness and longing to be with Cyril. She understood that he was a king and respected that he was a devoted leader, but she missed him greatly!

Reading the final page in her book, Clotilda closed it and placed it on the stack of five books she had finished reading. She folded her arms and rested her chin on them like a pillow as she sighed softly. She was used to being active and fulfilling a purpose. Cyril told her that she was welcome to leave the palace and explore the village of his kingdom, but she didn't want to do it alone. She wondered how he was doing, and the thought of working in the castle as a guard did cross her mind.

"There's got to be something I can do," she muttered, looking up at the late afternoon sun.

The blue gown she wore for the day draped over her hourglass figure and fluttered over the blankets of her bed like a wilted flower. Her thoughts soon turned to one of the books she read about the Regulus elf culture earlier today, about a band of elite female warriors called Royal Huntresses who fight alongside their king, hunt with him, and accompany him as his guards. It reminded her of her former role as a commander, and she would contribute to something and help Cyril for all that he has done for her instead of staying in her room doing nothing.

Clotilda slowly rose from her bed and made her way toward the doors of her bed chamber. She carefully opened one of them and stepped into the hallway. She followed the hallway by what she remembered from the tour that Cyril, Violyne, and Doric gave her and asked some of the servants if they knew where the king was. They told her he was filling out documents in the throne room. Thanking them for their guidance, Clotilda followed their directions and descended the staircases until she reached the throne room.

She gently grabbed one of the handles of the double doors and tugged on it to see if they were locked. As expected, they were. She pulled her hands away from the handle and walked around to see if there was a window for her to see through. Clotilda looked around until she saw an opening through swirling, golden vines inside the throne room that wasn't covered by the large curtain. She leaned to the crystal glass, not too close that her breath would fog it, as she peeked through it to see Cyril at the large table with generals, kings, and queens from other kingdoms. She looked over at Cyril to see something that made her heart sink. Cyril looked exhausted as if the weight of his entire kingdom had crashed down upon him. His eyebrows were knitted together intensely, emotions from frustration, anger, and concentration clashing together like battering rams as he tried to focus on his work.

"Poor Cyril," she said softly as she slowly moved away, returned to the entrance to the throne room, and sat down on the bench next to the giant doors as she waited.

An hour passed to the point that Clotilda's tailbone became numb. She walked around a few times in the empty hallway to wake her lower half and summoned Universeel to play quiet music as she waited. She sat back down as she played her music but could barely hear the melodies as her thoughts turned to worry. Why was Cyril so upset? Was there some confrontation with the other kingdoms that wanted to declare war on Algieba? Was there a difficulty with the trading? Was there an attempted assassination? Her worries as a guard caused her fingers to pause against the delicate harp strings and piano keys of Universeel. Clotilda couldn't stay in her room doing nothing! If she could become a Royal Huntress, she might be able to help Cyril and serve him. But would he be all right with that?

The loud click of the large locks snapped Clotilda from her thoughts, and she jerked her head up to the entrance to the throne room. The large doors creaked loudly as they swung open. She banished Universeel back into her hand chain and watched as the guests and attendants flooded out of the throne room, some glancing at her with curious gazes before making their way down the hallways. Clotilda scanned the crowd for Cyril, but he was nowhere to be seen.

Once the crowd was gone, she slowly and carefully approached the half-opened doors to take a peek but was stopped when she heard Cyril's quill pen tapping and scratching against paper.

"My king. I know you wish to see her, but you must complete these first," an unfamiliar female voice spoke from inside the throne room.

As Clotilda was still acquainting herself with the kingdom, she was taken aback by the unfamiliar voice she heard. She was curious to know who the speaker was, but at the same time, she was apprehensive that revealing her presence might disrupt the king's concentration.

"I'm well aware of that," she heard Cyril's voice in duet with his writing pen.

"You can see Lady Clotilda as soon as you are done," the woman softly reassured him.

Clotilda moved away from the doors and planted herself on the bench. Cyril looked busy, and whatever he was working on required his full attention. She could wait a little longer to talk to him.

Four minutes passed before Clotilda's ears perked to the heavy, clunking sound of Cyril's boots echoing off the marble floor as he approached the doors. She looked over to see the king emerge from the doorway. A long, drawn-out sigh slipped from his lips as he rubbed his gloved fingers through his bangs and forehead, pushing his crown up. Clotilda watched in silence as he straightened his crown. She wondered if she should wait to tell him about her request.

She prepared to get up and return to her room when Cyril's surprised gaze met hers.

"Clotilda?" he asked.

"Hi, Cyril," she said with a smile and a small wave.

"What are you doing here? Are you all right?" he asked as he approached her.

"I just wanted to check on you and see if everything was all right. Did something happen?"

"No, nothing happened. I just needed to catch up on some work."

"Were you able to finish what you needed to get accomplished?"

"Yes, it's finished. Just a lot of work that needed to be done."

"That's good. I got worried when I noticed you looked troubled while working."

"There's nothing to worry about. How long have you been waiting?"

"For a while," she replied, not wanting to tell him she had been waiting more than an hour.

"I apologize for today. I wasn't expecting it to be so long."

"No, don't be. It's all right. From what I saw, it looked like it was important. I hope everything went well," she said before she stood up from the bench and smoothed down the wrinkles in her gown. "Anyway, I'm going to make my way back to my room, and I'll see you later."

Clotilda noticed Cyril's exhaustion and decided to hold off on inquiring about her desire to become a Royal Huntress. She could see that he needed rest. As she turned toward the grand staircase to head back to her room, Cyril's voice caught her attention, causing her to pause.

"Is there something on your mind?" he asked curiously.

"It can wait," she waved it off with a smile. "You go ahead and rest, and I'll see you later."

She turned back to continue her trek, but Cyril's strong hand gently wrapped around hers, stopping her.

"Clotilda," he said, her heart fluttering at the sound of him saying her name. She turned around until she was facing him. "If there is something that you want to talk to me about, you can tell me."

Clotilda paused for a moment, feeling unsure of how Cyril would respond to her request. She knew that avoiding his question wasn't the right thing to do. Ignoring someone in authority was never appropriate. Gathering her courage, Clotilda carefully crafted her words in her mind.

"I-I've been thinking. I want to contribute to my stay here in your kingdom and wondered if I could become a Royal Huntress."

Her chest tightened in regret when she saw the shock in Cyril's eyes.

"Clotilda . . ." he said with slight hesitation. "You don't have to become a Royal Huntress."

"Why not?" she asked softly. "I want to help. I want to contribute to something. I trained for years to become a guard. That's who I am," she said, placing her hand on her chest.

"I don't want you in harm's way. So, my answer is no," he said sternly.

Clotilda was taken aback by his refusal, causing her eyes to widen and her heart to grow cold. Her throat swelled, and she bit her lower lip. A tense silence grew between them. Clotilda drew a shaky breath before she tried to pull her hand free from Cyril's grasp when he spoke again.

"I had a group of eight Royal Huntresses in the past before I lost my kingdom. On the day I was betrayed, Acanthus and his Battle Komodons captured me, and . . . they killed all my huntresses. I ordered them to run, but they didn't obey. Due to their loyalty to me, my Royal Huntresses tried to fight off Acanthus and his followers to save me. They were all killed right in front of me," Cyril panted a sigh of dread, and Clotilda could feel his hand tighten around hers."I have not had any more Royal Huntresses ever since. Even the thought of having new ones brings back those memories. I don't want to put anyone else, especially you, in danger again."

"I'm sorry," Clotilda said as her heart sank. "I didn't mean to reopen a painful memory from your past."

Clotilda felt terrible for Cyril that he had to watch the slaughter of his comrades. She could relate. She had to watch some of her troops die when they were trying to fend off invaders in the past. Even though she could resurrect them and erase their memories of death, seeing them dying around her scared her. Cyril couldn't bring back others as she could, and she couldn't bear the thought of what he had to endure, unable to restore those he lost.

Being his Royal Huntress was out of the question, but maybe there was something else she could do.

"Cyril . . . if by any chance . . . can I be a castle guard? Even if it is a small duty, I would be willing to do it. I trained for years to become a guard to protect others. I may not be Commander of the Royal Guard anymore, but I can't sit around doing nothing. It's not in my nature," she said softly. "I want to help as best as possible and repay you for how you saved me and everything else you've done. So I'm willing to offer my military services to you."

Clotilda could see Cyril slip into his thoughts as he gently brushed his fingers over his left cheek. His other hand held hers as if telling her not to leave. His eyes soon met hers again.

"I need time to think about your request," he said.

"As you wish," she nodded in understanding.

"Your Highness," the feminine voice spoke up, causing both king and former commander to look over to see a female Regulus elf carrying a stack of documents. The female Regulus elf stood six foot eight inches tall, surpassing Clotilda by three inches. Her long, knee-length hair was the color of spun gold and was pulled back in an elegant braid with violets woven into the locks. Her skin was lightly tanned, and her eyes were yellow like topaz. She wore a long, purple gown that matched the violets in her hair and gave her a strikingly regal appearance.

"I just need your wax seal, and then these will be ready for . . ." She paused when her feline eyes caught a glimpse of Clotilda. "Who is she, Your Highness?"

"This is Clotilda, the one I was looking for," he said as he introduced her.

"Is she," she smiled as she dipped into a bow. "Our king has been talking about you, Lady Clotilda. It's an honor to meet you finally."

"You as well," Clotilda replied as she bowed respectfully. "Your name is?"

"My name is Kefira. I'm His Majesty's advisor."

Cyril turned his gaze back to Clotilda before placing his free hand on hers, sandwiching her hand between his.

"I'll come to your chambers later and talk with you about your request," he said.

"All right, Cy . . . I mean, Your Highness," Clotilda corrected herself, remembering to address him by his royal title when they weren't alone.

Cyril reluctantly released her hand, turned to grab the stack of documents, and walked back into the throne room. Clotilda watched as he and his advisor disappeared into the throne room before she turned around in the dimly lit hallway, glancing up to the window to see that the sky had darkened into the evening. She grabbed the bottom hem of her dress and followed the torch-illuminated hallways toward the stairs. Clotilda felt tears well in her eyes. All her life, she wanted to be a guard and worked hard to become one, but to hear Cyril refusing her military help felt like a stab in the stomach. What was she going to do now? What was Cyril going to say about her request? Would he let her be a guard even if it was not a Royal Huntress? Her head throbbed at the thought. She rubbed her hand through her bangs and forehead to ease the headache as she climbed the stairs back to her bed chambers.

Upon returning to her room, Clotilda sighed deeply, feeling bad that she reminded Cyril of a painful memory from his past. She shouldn't have asked him about becoming a Royal Huntress. She would understand if he refused her to become a huntress, but if he were to say no for her to become a castle guard here, it would be like someone had cut her hands off so she couldn't play her music. She wondered what Cyril would say when he came to visit her but braced herself for the possibility that he would decline her offer.

Her skin felt like cracked stones, and the weight of a lonely day seeped into her like salt water on an open wound. Clotilda looked over at the bathing chambers, her body and mind longing for a comforting bath. She doubted Cyril would be here soon, and a bath was needed to help ease her mind.

"I guess it wouldn't hurt," she said as she grabbed a nightgown from her wardrobe and went to the bathing chambers.

Clotilda slipped out of her blue gown and carefully folded it as she laid it on the edge of the pool, along with her undergarments and hand chains. She slipped into the soothing waters and used the cleaning potions to wash her hair. She walked deeper into the spring toward the small waterfall flowing from a tall cluster of lavender crystals in the middle of the pool and combed her fingers through her hair as she rinsed it.

She sat down in the shallows and leaned against the pool's edge as she took another cleaning potion and rubbed it over her body. Clotilda rested her head on the pool edge as she tried to relax and rubbed the potion over her forearm. Clotilda washed her legs and feet before standing up and returning to the waterfall. She slipped under the waterfall and inhaled deeply as the water splashed onto her as she rinsed herself clean.

A sharp churning of water caused Clotilda's heart to spike. She looked around calmly despite panic building up inside her. Someone was here with her! She could sense it wasn't Cyril. Her gaze lingered on the hand chains beside her folded dress. She gritted her teeth, sternly scolding herself for not wearing her hand chains! She let her guard down, and it was a big mistake! Now she was vulnerable!

Clotilda charted a path with her mind on retrieving her hand chains when she felt rough fingers ensnare her scalp. Clotilda gasped in pain and shock as she was forced into the crystal-embedded cluster on the other side of the waterfall. The stranger's hand gripped her right arm and twisted it behind her back, causing her to grunt in pain as the bones cracked, threatening to snap. The crystals dug into her bare torso and left cheek as the stranger pinned her, feeling the gems pricking her skin like needles. She strained as she looked over her right shoulder, seeing the brown-cloaked figure.

"Shush," he said through the crashing waves of the waterfall behind them. "If you do as I say, I will spare your life."

"What do you want?" she growled, and her eyebrows knitted together into a glare.

"I've come to obtain what you stole from me," he said with a raspy voice.

"What are you talking about? I'm not a thief," she protested.

"I know you have it. I want it, even if I have to peel the skin from your bones to get to it."

Clotilda cringed, feeling the stranger's eyes raking up her body. She was grateful that her long hair offered her some coverage, but she felt violated. Her captor stepped closer and breathed into her ear. "Such a shame I would have to do that. You have grown up to be so beautiful . . . just like your mother before I killed her."

Clotilda gasped in recognition, and the scar on her left cheek burned from the memories of her dying mother, her father having his throat slit open, the iron dagger piercing her left cheek, and the tormented villagers who had fallen into Hollows. All that pain and death was caused by this monster, now standing behind her!

Clotilda closed her hands into tight fists, causing her fingernails to rake the crystals off the wall she was pinned against. She ignored the pain of her restrained arm and retaliated with her free arm, launching her left elbow into his jaw. She cringed when she felt exposed, rotten teeth against the skin of her elbow. Her captor released a pained cry from the blow before releasing his hold on her.

Clotilda seized the opportunity! She slipped past him and fled toward her hand chains. The hooded figure snarled as he pursued her. She grabbed one of the hand chains, realizing it was the lion one Cyril made for her.

"Come on, come on," she said through her clenched teeth as she fought to get the hand chain on as quickly as her soaked fingers could.

"Fighting back," she heard him say as he approached her. "Good. I like prey that fights back before I kill them."

Clotilda glared at him as she got the hand chain around her right wrist and attempted to reach for the other. Ropes of vibrant pink magic emerged from her hand chain, causing her to gasp. The lion heads of the jewelry growled as their eyes glowed, and ribbons of magic appeared from it to create a sword that had the same design as Universeel.

A glimpse of her enemy quickly approaching caused her to forget her curiosity for her new weapon and swing it toward her attacker. Clotilda hardly felt the sword's weight as if she were holding a baton and struck her attacker hard on the shoulder with it.

Waves of water splashed loudly as he collapsed. He gasped as he broke through the water and stared back at her in rage as he pressed his hand to his injured shoulder.

"You'll pay for that! The Deity of Lazarus is rightfully mine!" he snarled before he drew his iron dagger and charged toward her, unfazed by the restraints of the water.

Clotilda held her weapon in defense, bracing herself to fight back before a flash of white and navy blue stood in front of her protectively. Blades clashed together like splintering earthquakes—the iron dagger of her enemy and Cyril's large sword summoned from his right hand chain.

"Stay away from her!" Cyril snarled as he pushed the enemy back.

The attacker looked at the elf king, staring at him in recognition and with a twisted smirk underneath his soaked hood.

"Fallen King. It's been a long time since we last fought. I will take great pleasure in taking your Rune power and hers," he laughed sadistically.

Cyril growled as he stood in the knee-deep water, standing protectively before Clotilda as he fought. He delivered powerful blows with his sword to the point of exhausting his opponent. Each strike of his sword drew him closer to ending his enemy, but the hooded intruder disappeared before he could, teleporting out of the waters.

Clotilda looked around frantically for him, lightly gasping as she felt Cyril's hand securely wrapped around hers. He had his back facing her, and he didn't turn to look at her as he reached behind.

"Stay behind me and hold onto my hand. He can teleport. He might try to take you away."

She nodded in silence, taking deep breaths to ease her shaky breathing, and wove her trembling fingers with Cyril's, feeling him gasp softly at her action.

Clotilda perked her ears as she saw Cyril unfastening his cape. Cyril hesitantly slipped his hand from hers, and he stepped behind her. He kept his head turned, and his eyes averted to give her privacy. The weight of the warm cape spilled over her shoulders, and Clotilda could smell Cyril's scent feathering her nostrils. She closed the cloak around her, feeling bad that the bottom hem of his cape was submerged in the water.

"Are you all right?" he asked in concern as he slowly looked at her, ensuring she was completely covered.

"Yes, I am," she said softly, trying to keep her shaky voice steady as she spoke. "Thanks to you."

"Come. Let's get you out of here," he said gently as he wrapped a protective arm around her and helped her out of the spring, and they hurried out of the bathing chamber.

The castle guards hurried to Clotilda's bed chamber when they heard their king's calls and thoroughly searched her room and the bathing chambers. Clotilda sat on the bed with Cyril's cape still wrapped around her as she looked at her hand chains. She felt the bed dip and looked up to see Cyril seated beside her, tenderly wrapping his arm around her.

"I'm sorry you had to go through that," he said softly.

"It's not your fault. From now on, I'll wear my hand chains when I bathe."

"Did he hurt you?"

She shook her head in reply.

"It was him. He was the one who destroyed my village and tried to steal the Deity of Lazarus." She tightened her hold on Cyril's cape. "Do you know him? I heard him call you 'Fallen King.' Was he the one who stole your crown from you?"

"No, it was someone else. The one who attacked you is named After Walker. He was one of the opponents I had to fight when I was a prisoner in the Slachten Arena. He's an undead being known as an Aptrganga. He discovered the powers of the Rune deities and has been hunting after them ever since I escaped. He's very dangerous. But I swear. . . ." Clotilda heard his leather gloves strain as he curled his hands into fists. "If I see him again, for what he did to you, from the past to now, I will kill him!"

"Please, Cyril . . ." she tried to calm him, but she held her tongue as she heard him continue.

"Seeing what just happened furthers my confidence that I've made the right choice about your request," he said. Clotilda's eyes widened. "Tomorrow at dawn, I'll teach you everything I know about hunting, and I will be your trainer for combat in the ways of a Royal Huntress," he said as he met her gaze.

"You mean it? But what about your previous huntresses?" she asked softly.

"It's in the past," he shook his head slowly. "I'm not fond of the thought of you being in danger, but you being my Royal Huntress means we can be together. Besides, you will make a fine Royal Huntress with your impressive fighting skills."

"It means a lot to hear you say that," she smiled.

"So tomorrow morning, be ready for your first lesson," he said with a smile.

"I'll be ready," she said with a nod.

CHAPTER 33

Royal Huntress Armor

Despite another search through the castle and Clotilda's chambers, the royal guards couldn't find After Walker. Cyril made sure to have ghost lions guard her chambers, the rest of the castle, and the village, just in case the assailant tried to strike again.

Clotilda was tucked under the blankets of her bed, with Cyril's cape still securely wrapped around her. Her hair was slightly damp from the spring waters, and the locks streamed over the pillow as she lay facing the elf king resting on the blankets beside her.

Even with the guards willing to escort the king to his bed chambers, Cyril refused to leave and told them to rest for the night. Clotilda was relieved to have him here. She didn't want to be alone. Not with that murderer on the loose. Cyril's company eased her nervousness, but she wondered if he might return to his bed chambers after she had fallen asleep. Clotilda hoped he would stay, not because of After Walker, but because she wanted to be with Cyril.

"Thank you for staying here with me, Cyril. I'm sorry for all the trouble I've caused."

"It's not your fault," he said as he planted his left elbow on the second pillow and cupped his chin and cheek in his palm. "I want to stay here to make sure you're safe."

"I appreciate that," she said as she shifted a little under the comfort of the blanket and Cyril's cape. "Are you going to be comfortable tonight? You're welcome to slip under the blankets, or I can get you another one."

"Don't worry, I'm fine. I'm quite warm right now," he politely refused the offer.

"Okay," she smiled at him. "Can I ask you something?"

"What is it?" he asked curiously.

"I've finished reading the books in my study today. Is it all right to borrow some books from the library?"

"Of course. You can borrow as many as you want."

"Thank you," she smiled before she brought her hand to her lips to muffle a yawn.

"Get some rest," she heard him say before noticing him reaching out to her as if wanting to touch her cheek.

Clotilda felt her heart race and watched as his strong hand neared her. She had some loose strands of her hair draping over her cheek. Was Cyril going to tuck them behind her ear? She hoped he would.

Her heart sank slightly when she noticed his hand froze hesitantly before he closed it into a fist and pulled it slowly back, sighing frustratedly to himself.

"Your training is tomorrow morning. So, we need to get plenty of sleep," he said.

"I look forward to it. Sleep well," she said as she closed her eyes.

"So do I. Sleep well, Clotilda. May your dreams be void of any nightmares," she heard him say as a soft smile spread on her lips.

The rays of the morning sun poured into the bedroom and basked Clotilda in its warm glow. She stirred in her sleep and opened her eyes to be greeted by Cyril's peacefully sleeping face. She was surprised as she stared at him, sure that he would return to his chambers after she fell asleep last night, but he stayed. She smiled gratefully at him. She lay there silently looking at him, wanting to let him sleep a little longer.

She perked her ears as she heard a knock on her chamber doors. Then, as she sat up in bed, she noticed Cyril stirring.

"I'm sorry I woke you," she apologized, realizing that when she moved, it probably woke him.

"Not at all. Did you sleep well?" he asked as he stifled a yawn.

"I did. Thank you for keeping me company last night."

Another knock caused them to turn their heads toward the doors.

"It's Violyne," he said as he sat up. "She's probably here to help you dress for your huntress training."

"Oh, that's right. In that case . . ." she attempted to stand up to answer the door but was stopped by Cyril, who gently grabbed her hand.

"Wait until I'm gone before you let her inside. If she sees me here and you're wearing only my cape, she might think we did more than sleep last night," he chuckled softly.

"Oh . . ." Clotilda's face turned red like a pomegranate when she realized what he was referring to.

"I'll go back to my chambers and get ready. I'll see you soon," he said and gave her a wink before transforming into a falcon, leaping from her bed, and flying out of the large arched window.

"See you soon too," she whispered before she stood up from bed, wrapped a blanket around herself while taking Cyril's cape off, and hid it under the covers on the foot of the bed.

"Are you awake, my lady?" she heard Violyne call out.

"Yes, I am," Clotilda replied as she walked over and opened one of the doors to see that Violyne was carrying a black-and-blue leather armor set, matching high-heeled boots, and a necklace choker.

"You must be quite the sound sleeper," Violyne giggled.

"I'm so sorry about that," Clotilda said as she gave her an apologetic smile.

"It's not a problem," Violyne paused as she held out the armor to her, and Clotilda kindly accepted it. "His Majesty told me last night to bring you the Royal Huntress armor in the morning for your training. So go ahead and try it on. If it doesn't fit, I can get you a larger or a smaller size," she said as she made her way toward the bed and began fluffing the blankets.

Clotilda stared worriedly at the bed, watching as Cyril's cape slid out and fell into a crumpled mess on the floor. She felt her cheeks heat up, and she sprinted over to the bed and nudged the cape under it with her toe.

"Don't worry about that, dear. I got it. You go ahead and get ready," Violyne reassured her.

"All right," Clotilda said, trying to hide her embarrassment as she walked behind the divider and changed into her new armor.

The Royal Huntress armor was just as lightweight and comfortable as her jumpsuit. The leather-plated chest guard fit her like a one-piece swimsuit, providing a comfortable fit without being too tight. The chest guard, belt, elbow-length gloves, and thigh-high boots were decorated with claw marks and lion designs in blue, silver, and black, like Cyril's royal armor. The skirt had engraved leather ribbons that extended above her knees, and a long flowing train trailed behind her, brushing the ground. She finished getting ready by slipping two matching armbands on her biceps and a black leather choker with a blue pendant like a cat's eye.

Clotilda looked herself over in the mirror. Regulus armor is known for being the strongest and most durable of all sets. She felt comfortable and safe wearing it but had never worn armor that showed her legs and felt a little self-conscious about it.

"How's it going, my lady? Are you finished?" she heard Violyne call out from behind the divider.

"Yes. I'm all set."

"Good. Let's see how it looks on you."

"Sure thing," she said as she stepped out from behind the divider, showing her new armor.

"You . . . look . . . amazing! The Royal Huntress armor suits you," Violyne said excitedly.

"Thank you," Clotilda smiled as she gathered her hair, held the locks over her shoulder, and turned around to show the rest of the armor.

"It looks great on you. All we need to do is get your hair styled and your makeup on, and you'll be ready," she said as she walked over to the vanity, and Clotilda sat on the chair. "It's been so long since I saw this armor. You are the first to wear one in so many years."

"This is my first-time wearing Regulus elf armor. It feels sturdy and comfortable."

"Is it? What kind of armor did you wear when you were in Streng?"

"Dominus armor. It wasn't as strong as Regulus armor, and it did have a bad habit of being noisy when you walked in it, but it did serve its purpose," she said with a shrug as Violyne grabbed the brush.

"I don't see how noisy armor can serve a purpose, especially since we elves have sensitive ears." Violyne grimaced before carefully brushing Clotilda's hair, braiding the side locks on her temples, and pulling them back into a half-up, half-down hairstyle.

Violyne paused as she reached under the vanity, grabbed a silver makeup box with lion designs, and opened it.

"Now, to get you set up with your Royal Huntress makeup," she said as she applied it to Clotilda's face. A foundation that protected Clotilda's skin from the sun's harsh rays, a gloss that would keep her lips hydrated, and an eye shadow that acted as a visor so she wouldn't be blinded by the sunlight. "The king always hesitated about getting new Royal Huntresses, but whatever you said last night must have truly impacted him."

"He saved my life, and all of you did a lot for me already. It's the least I can do."

"We appreciate it. Now, I'm sure His Majesty is looking forward to seeing you. You better not keep him waiting—and take his teachings to heart," Violyne said as she walked toward the doors and opened one for Clotilda.

"You go ahead," Clotilda called out as she stood up from the vanity and approached her bed. "I just need to get something."

"As you wish." Violyne looked at her curiously before she shrugged. "As soon as you're ready, go to the king's chambers. I think he's waiting for you," she said before she stepped out of the room.

"I will," Clotilda said with a smile.

"Take care, and I wish you a good first training day," she said before she closed the door.

Clotilda listened carefully as she heard Violyne walking away before she kneeled beside the bed and reached under it. She quickly retrieved Cyril's cape from the floor and patted it gently to remove any stray dust before holding it behind her back. She carefully folded it and put on her hand chains as she exited her bed chambers.

CHAPTER 34

Family Ties

Curious male eyes followed Clotilda as she walked down the hallway toward Cyril's chambers. She shyly pulled some of her locks of hair over her shoulders, trying to hide her bashful blush as one of her male admirers wolf-whistled at her as she continued her walk.

As Clotilda turned the hallway's corner, her vision blurred, and she jolted back when she collided with someone.

"I'm sorry! Excuse me," she apologized as she looked to see whom she had bumped into. It was the royal advisor, Kefira.

"It's all right. I wasn't watching where I was going, so . . ." Kefira paused when she looked at her, and her eyes widened in realization. "Wait . . . you're Clotilda."

"That would be me," she said as she kept the bundle of Cyril's cape behind her.

"Why are you wearing the Royal Huntress armor?" Kefira asked. The slightly stern tone in her voice made Clotilda's smile drop.

"Cyril asked Violyne to bring it to me, and he said he would teach me how to be a Royal Huntress," Clotilda replied.

"You agreed to it?" the advisor asked with her eyebrows knitting together.

"I did. I used to serve the Royal Guard and wanted to offer my military services to King Cyril for everything he's done for me."

"I see," Kefira replied, with her frown softening. "Anyway, I better get back to my duties. I'm sure the king is waiting for you. Take care."

"You too," she said as she watched Kefira walk past her and down the hallway.

Clotilda waited until she could no longer see or hear Kefira's footsteps before releasing a long sigh, sensing the advisor's distaste toward her.

"Great . . . I'm making friends again," she said as she shook her head and continued her walk.

Clotilda could sense a fierce protectiveness radiating from the advisor. She didn't want to create any conflict with her, but she didn't know why Kefira acted irritably toward her. Was she a potential love interest to Cyril? Was she a family member? Whatever it was, Clotilda decided to leave it be. Kefira didn't look like someone to mess with.

The double doors of the king's chambers came into view as Clotilda continued her trek down the hallway. Her attention turned toward two male elves talking in the hallway. One was a stranger, and the other was Cyril.

Cyril looked well-rested compared to the tired state she saw him in at the throne room last night. He wore a black-and-blue tunic with three belts over his broad chest, lion-head design shoulder guards, black pants, matching long gloves, and armored thigh-high riding boots that made his sculpted legs look longer.

She watched as Cyril opened a letter the young male elf roughly handed him, the king looking none too pleased about whatever was written on it.

"This is an outrage! My mother and father have to send me all the way here so I could learn some 'proper manners'? Absolute rubbish!" the young elf said with a scowl.

Clotilda looked over to the young male elf, seeing that he was a Dominus and Seax elf hybrid. He had thick, dark-brown hair, grayish-beige skin, and ebony eyes. Despite looking attractive, his arrogant attitude reminded Clotilda of Bandus, which she found most unappealing.

"So the duke and duchess wish me to be your mentor?" Cyril asked flatly.

The young marquess rolled his eyes before looking over to his side, his eyes widening when he spotted Clotilda standing in the middle of the hallway.

"Who is that?" he asked, causing Cyril to look up from the letter, following the direction of where the young marquess was looking, only to have his eyes widen as soon as he saw her.

Clotilda bashfully smiled at Cyril. She was happy to see him but a little embarrassed that she had disturbed him. The marquess took a few steps toward her, only to be stopped by Cyril holding the letter outstretched in front of him, blocking him. The marquess stopped and looked at the letter like he had been slammed into a wall.

"My servants have breakfast ready for you," Cyril said politely yet sternly to him. "Go to the dining hall, and they will get you fed."

"Later . . . oof!" the marquess grunted as he tried to push Cyril's arm away, but the king slammed his hand with the letter against the boy's chest, knocking the air out of him.

"That's an order," Cyril said calmly, but Clotilda could sense protectiveness and anger in his regal demeanor.

The marquess frowned at him before slowly and reluctantly turning away and storming toward the dining hall. Cyril's expression softened as he turned to face her and walked over to her. Clotilda sank her head to her shoulders timidly as he approached.

"I'm sorry about that," he said as he slowed his walk toward her and stood before her. "He tends to behave like that whenever there is a new female face here."

"It's all right. I'm the one who should be apologizing because I interfered with your meeting with him."

"Don't be," he said as he folded his arms across his chest. "Calvin is my least favorite being to converse with. Even being the son of a duke and a duchess, he doesn't act respectfully toward his title or anyone he meets. His mother and father think I am a good 'role model' for him," he said as he rolled his eyes slightly. "They sent him here so I could mentor him, but it won't be easy."

"I know what you mean. I've had my share of students like that when I was trying to train them into becoming guards."

"Pretty bad?" he asked.

"Well, thank the Father God, many of my students were good and respectful, but the few I got who weren't, I immediately kicked them out," she said as she lightly kicked her right leg in the air, causing Cyril to chuckle.

"I might consider taking your example with Calvin. Anyway, I suggest you keep your distance from Calvin during his two weeks here. He enjoys fooling around with numerous women, and I don't want him to think you are another toy to play with."

"I'll stay away from him. If he does talk to me, I'll be polite to him, but other than that, I have no desire to be around someone who reminds me of Bandus."

"That's good to know," he said and sighed deeply through his nose.

"Here," she said as she slipped her hands behind her back and held the cape out to him. "I brought your cape back. Thank you for letting me borrow it last night."

"You're welcome. Glad it served you well," he smiled before accepting his cape, throwing it over his shoulders, and clipping it on.

"Shall we go and begin your training?" He smiled as he offered her his arm.

"Ready when you are," she said happily, linking her arm with his, and they walked down the staircase.

The doors to the castle grounds swung open for Clotilda and Cyril, welcoming them to the green carpet of grass with the chapel and stables standing in the rays of sunlight. Clotilda looked around with curiosity as she gazed upon the Regulus chapel, training grounds, and stables she remembered seeing from the tower.

Cyril walked beside her as they made their way toward the stables. He held the door open for her, a small gesture of courtesy that made her smile, and followed her inside.

As her eyes adjusted to the dim light, she saw three horses in the stalls. Her trusty steed, Coralina, was munching on a hay bale alongside Xavier, Doric's dracstal steed that she remembered Cyril had borrowed to escape the capital with her.

The third horse was unlike any she had ever seen before. It had eight legs, twice as many as a regular horse, and its body was sleek and muscular. The horse turned to look at her, and she felt an excited thrill run through her. This must be Sleipnir—the steed that Cyril mentioned was his when he brought her to his kingdom. Sleipnir was built with a strong, lean body covered with black and white scales and feathers resembling a sea serpent's graceful patterns. His long, white and black, two-toned mane and tail had raven feathers through the locks, and he had long legs like a wolf that ended with large hooves. He had large, folded wings, and his eyes were amber with slitted pupils.

Coralina's calmly closed eyes opened halfway, only for them to shoot wide open, and a happy neigh erupted from her mouth as she took excited steps toward her master. Clotilda giggled softly as the pegasus nuzzled her wet muzzle to her cheek, and she wrapped her arms around the mighty creature's scaly neck.

"I missed you too, Coralina. I'm sorry that I didn't visit you sooner."

"You got a majestic steed there, my lady," a male voice spoke up, causing Clotilda to break the embrace and look over to see a male Beetje elf standing on top of the wooden railings, brushing Xavier's mane with a horse brush. He stood around four feet tall and had a handsome face, a dark-brown beard, and a mustache with white and gray highlights, and he wore fine leather clothes, showing his rank as a royal stable master. He had green eyes with slitted pupils, indicating he was part Regulus elf.

"The aquatic pegasus is known for being the closest companion to the Airavata elves, just like the squirrels are to Beetje elves. She is a good horse and very gentle."

"She certainly is," Clotilda smiled as she looked at him.

"That's Drauphir," Cyril said as he stood beside her and introduced the Beetje elf. "He's the finest stable master here in the kingdom and does a great job caring for the animals here."

"I appreciate the compliment, Your Highness. Anything to help my cousin," Drauphir said as he bowed his head.

"Cousin?" she asked as she looked at Cyril with a smile, excited to learn that Cyril came from a melting-pot family like hers.

"Drauphir is my cousin," he returned the smile. "Just like you come from a family of Airavata and Lazarus elves, I come from a family of Regulus and Beetje elves. Drauphir here is the son of my mother's brother."

"It's a pleasure meeting you," Drauphir said with a charming smile before his red wings behind his back flapped.

"It's a pleasure to meet you too," she said and returned the smile before returning her gaze to Cyril. "I like how you have family here to help you rule your kingdom."

"That's what a family does. We support each other," Cyril replied.

"I like it. It reminds me of my blood, adopted, and animal family," she said as she patted Coralina's forehead.

“Drauphir told me she was a little nervous around Sleipnir and Xavier the first time in the stable. It looks like they are getting along quite well,” Cyril smiled.

“It’s good to see you making friends, Coralina,” she said with a smile.

“Coralina?” Cyril said in recognition, reaching out to the pegasus and gently petting her. “It’s good to see you again, Coralina.”

“She’s not the Coralina you met years ago in my village. This is her great-granddaughter,” Clotilda clarified.

“Really?” he asked in surprise.

Clotilda nodded with a giggle at his reaction.

“How long do aquatic pegasus live? I always thought they were immortal like Sleipnir.”

“I wish they were. They can live up to sixty years, longer than other mortal steeds. Coralina’s great-grandmother was forty-eight years old when she was pregnant with her last colt. My mother told me that she had four other colts, and their descendants live free in the lakes of the Mysomatarian and Sheratan forests.

After I came to Streng, she gave birth to a magnificent stallion. He was stubborn and had a fire in his heart that reminded me of my father. So I decided to name him Cadmar after him. At first he was hard to train, but he and I were close, and he rode me into several battles. Coralina lived to be fifty-eight years old. Poor Cadmar was devastated when he lost his mother,” she said sadly as she recalled the memory. “Afterwards, he mated with a gentle mare, and they had a daughter. Like I named the stallion after my father, I named the sweet colt Bathilda after my mother. Her father died just a year short of his mother’s age. But Bathilda lived to be fifty-nine years old when she died. But four years before her death, she gave birth to her,” she said as she gently patted her pegasus. “I named her Coralina after her great grandmother, to continue the lineage name,” Clotilda paused as she sank into her thoughts, remembering the mortal friends she made, like Duril, and how she lost them when they reached old age.

She looked at Cyril, seeing the same pain of loss and sympathy in his eyes.

"Did you try resurrecting them with your Rune power?" he asked softly.

"I did," she nodded. "I used my powers on her great-grandmother to resurrect her when she died of old age. But she was so weak," she said as her eyes burned with tears. She felt Cyril's hand gently rest on her shoulder, his touch comforting her. "Sadly, I realized that I . . . I had to let her go. I can resurrect other immortal beings when they are killed or die of illness. When it comes to mortals, I can resurrect them when they are killed or die of sickness. But when their life expires, I can resurrect them, but I can't give them immortality or eternal youth, no matter how long I've tried to find a way." She and Cyril were silent; even Drauphir had stopped brushing Xavier's mane to listen to the story. "Even though I've lost many mortal friends, it didn't stop me from befriending them."

"I do the same. Mortal or immortal, we are here for a reason. To have a chance to experience the gift of life. No matter how long or how short it is," Cyril said.

Clotilda smiled softly and slowly reached up to his hand on her shoulder.

"You're right. Even though nothing truly lives forever, the memories of all living creatures we treasure are truly immortal. As long as we don't forget them."

"That's right. Grant your loved ones immortality of remembrance," he smiled.

"I will do that." She rubbed the oncoming tears in her eyes.

CHAPTER 35

Training

Clotilda and Cyril led their steeds out of the stable and brought them to the training grounds. Sleipnir approached Coralina and stood beside her, sniffing her folded wing and face. The shy pegasus folded her webbed ears back submissively and stepped away, only for him to step toward her.

"Behave yourself, Sleipnir," Cyril said as he and Clotilda looked toward them, causing the stallion to snort back at him.

"I think he likes her," she said with a giggle.

Clotilda dropped her gaze to the hand chain around her left wrist, her thoughts turning to the memory of how it formed into a sword when she was attacked by After Walker last night. She looked up from studying her hand chain to see Cyril looking at her.

"Is something wrong?" he asked.

"No, I was thinking about what happened last night and what the hand chain you gave me did to protect me."

"I made the hand chain as a gift and a weapon to protect you. Since you were unarmed last night, it summoned a weapon for you so you could defend yourself."

"That explains why it didn't weave a weapon when I had Universeel summoned in the past," she said.

"There's more to that bracelet than just a weapon. That is what I am going to teach you first. So go ahead and summon two weapons from your hand chains, and then we can begin," he smiled.

"As you wish," she said as she summoned twin Universeels in both hands. "All right, what else do you want me to do?"

"Now that you have two weapons drawn, I'm going to teach you how to dual wield," he said as he summoned two swords from his hand chains. "We'll start slow and move faster when you get more accustomed to them."

"Will do," she said as she stood in a battle stance and held her weapons securely. "I'm ready when you are."

"Good," he smiled as he held his swords firmly in his hands, and both he and Clotilda entered the battle ring, ready for their duel.

As Cyril and Clotilda trained, he introduced her to their swords' offensive and defensive moves and showed her the best ways of holding her dual weapons and having her repeat actions until she memorized them. Clotilda focused on him and followed his instructions with her full attention and interest in remastering her dual blades. She felt her left arm become fluid while swinging her weapon, and the energy and strength became balanced as if she were playing her piano and harp.

Clotilda gasped as Cyril disarmed her of her weapons with his swords, her weapons shattering into fragments of magic before disappearing into her hand chains. But before she could resummon them, the tip of one of Cyril's swords pointed at her throat, causing her to freeze in place.

"You fought very well for your first training on dual wielding," he said as he pulled the blade away from her throat and dismissed his dual swords back into his hand chains. "Your attacks are skilled, but I saw some weak points in your defense moves. We'll polish that up later, so you are well-balanced with offense and defense."

"Sounds good," Clotilda said as she caught her breath. "So, what else do you want to teach me?"

"What I will show you next is the barrier that I cast into your lion hand chain," he said as he gently grasped her left hand and held it in his palm. "Now that you have the matching enchanted gems, it will offer you different abilities. One is an enchanted shield," he explained as he pressed his index finger on the pink gem.

"A shield?" she asked, intrigued.

"That's right. Like how you summon Universeel, you can call forth a shield to surround yourself or anyone nearby," he explained.

"How do I do that?"

"Simple, instead of thinking of a weapon, think of a protective barrier, and it will obey."

Clotilda glanced down at her hand cradled in Cyril's, narrowing her eyebrows as she thought of a barrier she was instructed to summon. The jeweled eyes of the lions glowed as a veil of pink magic rippled out of the gem and enveloped them in a large dome of magic.

"Well done," she heard Cyril's voice and turned toward him. "As long as you are in this barrier, it will protect you or anyone else inside it."

"This is remarkable! I wish I had learned it sooner," she smiled softly, knowing she had another ability to help protect Cyril and others. "But wait, must I be disarmed to summon the barrier?"

"No. Whether armed or not, you can summon the barrier whenever you like."

"That's good to know," she breathed a sigh of relief.

"It will serve you well. So, banish the shield, and then we can teach you archery."

"Archery?" she grimaced.

Despite her discomfort with using a weapon she wasn't comfortable with, Clotilda followed Cyril to the archery training grounds. She watched as Cyril summoned his bow and stood ready to arm it with an arrow. She looked behind to see Coralina and Sleipnir standing side by side at the edge of the archery grounds, watching with calm curiosity.

"All right, the targets are ready," she heard Cyril say, causing her to turn her gaze back to him. "Is something wrong?" he asked, noticing the embarrassed look on her face.

"This is . . . humiliating," she groaned as she slapped her gloved hand on her forehead and rubbed it down her eyes.

"What's troubling you?" he asked as he approached her.

"I am disgracing our elven cultures with this confession. I am dreadful with a bow and arrow," she sighed, dropping her hand from her face and slapping it against her thigh.

"Why do you say that?" he asked as he arched one of his eyebrows.

"I wish I was kidding. I'm comfortable with many weapons, including a slingshot, but when it comes to archery . . . I'm horrible at it. I end up making a vast garden of speared arrows in the ground instead of hitting the targets," she frowned.

Cyril chuckled softly before touching her shoulder.

"I'm confident you would make a fine archer," he reassured her.

"I appreciate your faith in me, but I'm unsure about myself," she said softly.

"Don't degrade yourself," he softly scolded her. "I'll teach you how to use a bow."

"All right," she said as she followed the king to the standing targets and stood where he was.

"You'll be fine. I have faith," he said with a wink.

"Thank you," she said with a nervous smile.

"All right. Summon your bow and draw it," he said as he walked up behind her.

"Uh . . . yes. Of course," she stuttered a little as she felt him stand close behind her, and she was sure they were about to touch.

With a gulp, Clotilda summoned Universeel in its bow form and drew the bowstring back, her hand chain's magic creating an arrow as she pulled the string fully back.

"Very good. Now breathe calmly as you aim for the target," he softly guided her, his patience putting her at ease.

Clotilda inhaled slowly as she aimed for one of the terra cotta jars perched on top of the rows of small columns before she let go. Her eyes screwed shut instinctively as she felt the string rebound, afraid it would snap in half. She opened her eyes, realizing that her arrow had not moved and was staying in place. At the end of the arrow, she could see that Cyril's fingers were pinching the feathered tail, holding the arrow in place.

"Your posture is where it needs to be. But you're hesitating," he said. "It's better not to shut your eyes when you fire an arrow. You might hit someone."

Clotilda gulped at the thought of hurting someone and glanced around to see the Regulus guards patrolling and the gardeners tending to the flowers growing along the castle wall. She would never forgive herself if she were to hurt or kill an innocent person with an arrow. She glanced over her shoulders to see Cyril, expecting him to be disappointed, but his expression showed only gentle encouragement.

"I'm sorry," she said softly.

"You have no reason to fear your bow. Try again. But this time, when you're ready to fire, breathe in through your nose." Clotilda took a deep breath as she was told. "Then exhale slowly when you release your hold on the arrow and keep your eyes open."

She exhaled through her mouth and felt him bring the arrow's tail to her fingertips.

"I'll try," she said as she wrapped her fingers around the end of the arrow. She aimed for the target, preparing herself to fire. She breathed in through her nose, held her arms steady, exhaled slowly through her mouth as she released her grip on the arrow, and kept her eyes open. She felt the feathers of the arrow brush against her cheek as it shot in the air, weaving through the air toward the jar. The arrow neared its mark, chipping the neck of the jar as it shot past it. "I missed it!" Clotilda said disappointedly as she lowered her bow.

"You did great," he smiled.

"But I didn't hit the target," she said with a shrug.

"Even though you didn't hit it, you shot perfectly."

"Thank you," she said, feeling a little better.

"Try hitting it again. But this time, aim more to the left and a little lower," he winked at her.

"All right," she said as she did what she was told—aiming the arrow where Cyril directed her to and both inhaling and exhaling before she fired. The arrow struck the jar, shattering it into large shards.

"Perfect!" he whispered as he slowly backed away from behind her. Clotilda smiled, and she breathed a sigh of relief.

"You did great! Why don't you try hitting those six targets down there," he said as he pointed at the rest of the columns of jars next to it.

"All right. I'll see what I can do," she nodded at him as she drew her bow and prepared to fire another arrow.

CHAPTER 36

The Third Rune

The bow began to feel like a part of her. Clotilda could draw the arrows more confidently, but her blood boiled for her lack of accuracy. She sighed deeply with a growl, lowering her bow after firing at her last target.

"If I ever master the art of archery, it will be a miracle!" she groaned.

"You'll get better at it as you keep practicing," Cyril reassured her as he walked beside her.

"I hope so. Out of the six targets I needed to destroy, I only hit three," she said as she held three fingers before dismissing her bow back into her hand chain.

"I think you did great. That should be it for today. We'll continue your training tomorrow."

"Are you sure you want to end it there, Cy?"

Cyril and Clotilda heard a familiar male voice, and they turned to see Doric sitting on one of the columns with his legs crossed and one of the target jars resting on his knee.

"I think you should end this first training day with something exciting." Doric shrugged.

"How long have you been here, Doric?" Clotilda asked in surprise.

"From the beginning to the end of your training. I was hanging around the forested area near the royal gardens when I saw you and Cy training. I didn't want to disturb you, so I used my invisibility powers to watch you without being seen."

"So, what brings you here . . . besides watching?" Cyril asked as he rested his hands on his hips.

"I'm just bored," Doric said with a shrug as he released his hold on the jar, allowing it to fall and break once it hit the ground. "I didn't feel like teasing Violyne this afternoon, so I thought I'd come out here and aid you in making the training with your new huntress more interesting."

"If you're thinking what I'm thinking, Clotilda is not ready to face another Rune right now, Doric," Cyril said sternly.

"Another Rune?" Clotilda asked, her eyes widening as she looked at the relaxed Seax elf."You're a Rune too?"

"That's right. I'm the Rune of Seax," Doric rolled his eyes. "Unlike you two, I didn't drink the waters from the sacred treasures. I obtained my power when I killed the Rune of Seax."

"Oh," she said as her smile dropped.

"It wasn't easy. After I killed the Rune, I obtained his power, which was one of the worst mistakes I've ever made," he sighed as he stood up from the column. "But enough about me! I will change into my Rune form, and you two can fight me."

"Doric . . ." Cyril said lowly.

"It's all right, Cy. She won't have to worry about touching my skin because I'll be armor-plated in my Rune form."

"What do you mean by that?" Clotilda asked.

"You'll see," Doric said as he winked at her.

"Listen," Cyril said firmly, his face morphing into anger. "This is Clotilda's first training day to become a Royal Huntress. She doesn't need to fight a Rune just yet!"

"Aren't you acting a little overprotective of her, Cy?" he chuckled as Cyril looked back at him with a glare. "Don't get me wrong. I can see many reasons why you would be protective of someone as sweet as her. But don't forget, she used to be commander of the Royal Guard, and seeing how she fights, there is a good reason she obtained that title."

"If you're saying I think she's weak, you're wrong!" Cyril protested.

"I'm not saying that. I'm just saying that she's probably had her fair share of battling many powerful enemies in the past, maybe a few Runes," he shrugged before he pointed his index finger at Cyril. "That includes you."

"Yes, but I didn't change into my Rune form when I fought her."

"Cyril," Clotilda said softly as she placed her hand on his broad shoulder, causing Cyril to look at her. "I appreciate you are watching out for me, but Doric is right. I have fought many enemies in the past. I look forward to this training with you because it will help me hone my skills and strengthen my weaknesses, like archery. I'll be fine. Besides, what better way to get stronger than face a challenge now and then?"

Cyril's stern face softened to her words, and he met her gaze with realization and understanding. The corners of his mouth tugged upward before he reached his hand up to her face, hesitation causing it to freeze in the air before he lowered it to her shoulder instead.

"You're right. I need to remind myself that you are no longer a little girl but a grown woman," he said.

"So," Doric said as he clapped his gloved hands, grabbing their attention. "Is Clo going to be fighting against me, or will you join her?"

"What do you think?" Cyril smiled as he summoned his dual swords.

"So two against one? My kind of odds. I will transform when you're ready. I won't hold back, so you better give me your all. One more thing," he said as he pointed at Clotilda. "As a Royal Huntress, your most important duty is to protect the king. So if Cyril is in danger, you must save him as quickly as possible."

"I will," she said as if accepting a command.

Doric smirked before his purple eyes glowed ebony, and glowing black runes erupted through his skin and spread down his skeleton. Clotilda summoned Universeel in a sword form and a second one from her lion hand chain as she stood by Cyril's side.

Doric groaned in pain as his clothes tore apart at the seams before disappearing, and his skin formed into a transparent exoskeleton billowing with dark mist, the color of squid ink. His hands trembled, his fingers fusing into sharp claws and pincers. His handsome face split open into a menacing, arachnid face with long, strong mandibles dripping with threads of saliva. His sculpted legs were divided into six legs as his body fully transformed into a giant scorpion, with gold designs that spread from his shoulders and down to his tail curling over his body with a large stinger, posed for an attack.

"You ready?" Cyril asked her as he tightened his hold on the handles of his swords.

"I am, my king," she said with a smile.

Cyril returned her smile before their feet moved in sync as they charged toward the Rune of Seax.

Doric opened and quickly shut his pincers like a pair of giant scissors. His hiss and hollow chirping echoed like a prowling scavenger in a catacomb. He launched his stinger toward Clotilda and Cyril like a catapult. The stinger pierced the air, and the two elven warriors quickly dodged it, hearing it spear into the ground, causing it to rumble under their feet. Clotilda and Cyril swung their swords toward the large pincers. Sparks were raining behind the blades as they struck the scorpion's armored body.

Clotilda multitasked by keeping her eye on Cyril, who was fighting off the scorpion claw while she fought off the second one. Her eyes shot wide as she watched the stinger hovering over the king and torpedoing down toward him. She swung her left arm toward the king, and the magic of her lion hand chain ribboned out of the gem and surrounded Cyril in the dome-shaped shield. The stinger ricocheted when it hit the shield, causing Cyril to look at her proudly.

"Look out!" he called out as his smile fell.

Clotilda shot her gaze over her shoulders, and her vision blurred when she felt a tight vice grip around her waist. Clotilda planted her hands down on the large scorpion claws as Doric brought her to his face, his glowing, black eyes looking at her tauntingly. She glared at him as she thrust her blade between the pincer holding her and grunted sharply as she tried to pry them open.

"Release her, Doric!" Cyril commanded as he ran along the spine of the scorpion and landed on the claws that held Clotilda.

Cyril put the two blades of the dual swords together and slipped them next to Universeel to help Clotilda break free.

Doric's claws opened wide, allowing her to climb out. Cyril helped her, and they leaped to the ground to face Doric again.

They prepared to attack in unison, but their focus on the battle was shaken when they heard the advisor calling to them.

"My king!" Kefira called out from the entrance to the castle, causing all three of them to look over at her. Kefira stood on the top of the stairs with her hands folded in front of her. She looked calm, but Clotilda could sense concern radiating from her. "A challenger has arrived! He challenges you to a duel for control of your kingdom! He's waiting for you in the throne room," Kefira spoke the last words softly before slowly spinning around and hurrying back into the castle.

"A challenger?" Clotilda asked as she looked at Cyril, noticing his narrowing eyes as he looked at the castle.

An intense silence bloomed between them before he dismissed his swords and touched her shoulder.

"Let's continue this fight some other time. I can't keep the challenger waiting," Cyril said before offering his arm to her.

Clotilda linked her arm with his, nervousness coursing through her veins like venom. She followed Cyril toward the castle, looking over her shoulders to see that Doric had changed back into his elf form, his dark clothing restored, and was following them.

CHAPTER 37

The Duel of Kingship

Servants, guards, and every royal court member gathered in the throne room, with the challenger walking in circles on the marble floor like a shark circling an injured fish. The strategy table had been cleared out of the way, opening the throne room until it looked almost as large as the adjacent ballroom.

Clotilda followed Cyril as they made their way to the throne room. Waves of people quickly cleared a path for their king to walk through. Clotilda nearly bumped into him from behind as he abruptly stopped.

"Wait here. This is something I need to do on my own," he said softly as he turned to her and placed his strong hands on the curves of her shoulders.

Loose strands of hair stuck to her cheek from her sweat as Clotilda tilted her head to look at Cyril. What did he mean by that? Who was this challenger?

"Good luck, my king," Clotilda said softly.

Cyril slowly and hesitantly lifted his right hand from her shoulder to brush the loose hair off her cheek. Her skin ignited as she felt his gloved fingers graze her cheek. He slowly pulled his hand away, and the other slid down her arm before he walked toward the awaiting challenger.

The challenger was another male Regulus elf. Judging from the height difference between him and Cyril, he looked eight feet tall and had an intimidating build. His full, long hair and beard grew to the length of his belt buckle and was deep maroon like cooked cranberries, and his eyes were green as jades. From how he stood with his arms folded over his broad chest and tilted chin, Clotilda could sense a pompousness radiating from him that immediately degraded any natural charm he had.

"So, you're the king of this castle?" the challenger asked as Cyril approached him.

"I am," Cyril replied as he stopped before his opponent.

"You don't look as tough as I thought you'd be," the challenger said as he unfolded his arms and walked around Cyril like a predator sizing up his prey. "Celestial Born is a rare breed of elf. But that doesn't mean that they're invincible. Taking your kingdom will be simple," he said, stopping behind and tauntingly glancing at the king as Cyril returned the glare. "Unless you want to back down now and forfeit your crown to me, I'll save you the humiliation."

"I beg to differ," Cyril said with a glint of anger. "I accept your challenge!"

"Good," the larger male smirked before he stepped away from the king and stood toward the onlookers. "Your king has accepted my challenge! The Duel of Kingship will begin!"

Clotilda felt a gloved hand rest on her shoulder and glanced back to see Doric standing behind her.

"Let's make our way up," he said as he gestured to the flying balcony above them. "We can watch the battle from there, and we'll be out of the way, so Cy doesn't have to worry about anyone getting hurt," Doric suggested.

"All right," she said hesitantly as Doric slipped his arm behind her, and they followed the crowd toward the balconies.

Clotilda squeezed through the crowd to the front of one of the balconies, politely excusing herself as she reached the railings, and glanced down to watch Cyril and the challenger fight.

"Excuse me," she heard a soft voice speak out.

She glanced down to see Canary carrying a small stool to stand on and placed it next to Clotilda's right side.

"Hi, Canary!" Clotilda said as she watched the little Beetje elf stand on the stool and glance over the railing.

"Hi there, my lady! You mind if I stand here?"

"Not at all," she softly smiled.

"We'll join you as well," she heard Kefira say as she stood by the railing beside Canary along with Doric and Violyne.

"Can you tell me more about the Duel of Kingship?" Clotilda whispered to Doric, who stood by her left.

"The Duel of Kingship is a law that all Regulus elf kings have to follow to protect the crown," Kefira answered. "If he doesn't accept the challenge, he's banished. That goes for the Duel of Queenship, which allows Regulus elf queens to fight in their husbands' place."

"What are the rules?" Clotilda asked as she glanced at the advisor.

"The first one to fall on the ground three times loses. The main goal is to tire out your opponent through injury or exhaustion. Then the winner will be crowned, and they can choose whether to kill the loser or banish them."

"How often do these duels happen?" Clotilda asked.

"It varies. Sometimes challengers come soon after a duel or don't come for years."

"A new Royal Huntress, I see," the challenger called out. Clotilda dropped her gaze, noticing that he was staring right at her. His lingering eyes caused her skin to crawl, and her brows narrowed in disgust. She looked at Cyril and felt an intense heat of protectiveness radiating off him as he noticed the challenger checking her out.

"She's a feast to the eyes. How about we step up the challenge? I declare Fractured Blades!"

"That's not good," Doric hissed through his teeth.

"What's Fractured Blades?" Clotilda asked.

"When a challenger or the defending ruler announces Fractured Blades before they start the fight, they declare the duel to become a death match." Doric's words hit Clotilda like a war hammer. "But it all depends if Cy accepts it or not."

"Once I claim your kingdom, your Royal Huntress will be mine too," the challenger boasted as he pointed at her.

"Not happening," Clotilda mumbled as she looked back at Cyril. "Please don't do it. Don't accept the death match," she softly prayed as she watched him.

Cyril glanced up at her, his frowning eyes softening as he looked at her.

"I'm waiting for an answer," the challenger called out impatiently as he stood on the other side of the painted design of the marble floor, like a boxer in the ring.

Cyril gave Clotilda a reassuring smile before he turned his attention back to his opponent.

"You won't be laying a finger on her," Cyril said as he summoned his dual swords. "I accept your challenge, but it won't be a death match."

Clotilda sighed in relief.

"What? So the mighty Graffias Manticore is a coward!"

Clotilda noticed Cyril flinch angrily at the sound of the title. She remembered their encounter with Delilah the other night and their conversation. Cyril mentioned how Delilah forced him to kill for her by using her pendant and how he was given the title, which Cyril carried like a heavy burden. She didn't know what he had to endure, but it was obvious that he hated being called the Graffias Manticore.

"Let's begin this fight!" Cyril said with a growl.

"The sooner I claim my prizes, the better," the challenger licked his lips as he summoned his sword. "I'll celebrate my win by laying with your Royal Huntress!"

"Clotilda's not a prize!" Cyril snarled, bearing his fangs as he charged toward the challenger.

The rage of battle stirred in Clotilda's blood, making her tense. The loud clashing of Cyril's and the challenger's swords thundered in her eardrums and rattled her instincts in preparation for the fight. She tightened her hold on the railing until she felt her gloved fingers digging into the marble, causing fine fragments to rain down toward the throne room. As she watched the battle, it was like seeing a lion fighting a saber-toothed cat.

The challenger hammered his sword toward Cyril, but Cyril used one of his swords to block the attack and knock his opponent back. The challenger quickly regained his footing and held his sword up to strike, only for Cyril to deliver a powerful kick in his chest, knocking him to the ground.

"That's one," Clotilda counted the first fall.

The challenger leaped back onto his feet before charging at his opponent again, dismissing his sword into his hand chain and falling on his hands. His body morphed into a large, red lion as he charged, roaring as he neared his opponent. Cyril quickly slipped past the charging lion, dismissing his weapons and transforming into a white lion. Cyril bore his fangs and sank them through the other lion's thick red mane, sinking his jaws into his opponent's neck. The other lion cried out in pain before Cyril lifted and threw him down.

Clotilda and the crowd watched with anticipation, and the king was able to pin his opponent on the ground twice. Cyril's victory was within reach if he could pin the challenger on the floor again. The challenger roared in rage, tearing himself out of Cyril's grasp, and threw his paw at Cyril's shoulder, his sharp claws ripping through his flesh.

"No!" Clotilda said as she heard Cyril yelp in pain, watching his blood stain his white fur as it streamed down his arm. The challenger changed into his elf form and firmly kicked Cyril in the chest, launching him in the air.

Cyril nearly stumbled to the ground as he landed and shape-shifted back into his elven form.

Blood dotted the floor as Cyril stood up, summoning his swords again, and swung them at the challenger. The sharp tip of the challenger's sword hooked onto the skin and fabric of his training armor and ripped it open. Cyril sharply grunted as he felt the blade lacerate his skin, pressing his gloved hand on the wound on the side of his chest to stop the bleeding before the challenger grasped his throat and lifted him in the air.

"No!" Clotilda called out through the loud protest of the servants and the royal court.

She stepped onto the railing to jump down and help Cyril when Doric's strong arm slipped around her waist and pulled her back.

"No, my lady! You can't intervene!" Canary called out, grabbing Clotilda's arm to help Doric hold her back.

"But he's in trouble!" Clotilda grunted as she struggled to free herself, and Violyne joined in to grab her other arm to restrain her.

"You must let the king fight on his own," Kefira joined in as she gently held Clotilda's shoulder. "If anyone interferes with the Duel of Kingship, then His Majesty will be disqualified, and he will be forced to surrender his kingdom to the challenger." Clotilda's struggles ceased when she heard the words. "King Cyril has fought many duels and reigned victorious for many years. Trust me, he'll be all right."

Hearing those words and sensing Cyril's supporters' unwavering faith in their king, Clotilda reluctantly stepped down and returned to watching the duel.

Cyril gasped for air as he glared at his opponent. The challenger's grip on his throat tightened as he lifted him higher in the air and slammed him into the ground. Clotilda flinched as she felt helpless. Watching Cyril getting pinned back-first onto the floor and bleeding from his injuries made her heart drop to her feet. She was a guard! She wanted to defend and aid him in this fight but couldn't. She had to force herself from intervening! She had to have faith in Cyril, just like everyone in the kingdom.

"Please . . ." she softly said, "Get up, Cyril. Get up."

Cyril's eyes, tightly closed from when he hit the ground, shot open, and he snarled as he glanced up at his opponent. Clotilda could see the fire in Cyril's eyes as he tightened his grip on the challenger's hand on his throat and pried it open. The challenger's bones crackled under his powerful grip, causing his opponent to grunt in pain. His hold on Cyril's throat loosened, allowing the defending king to return to his feet.

The challenger backed away as Cyril summoned his dual swords. The challenger called his swords and charged, but Cyril sliced through them, shattering them like glass and disarming him. The challenger stood in disbelief at Cyril's strength, then the king banished one of his swords and delivered a thunderous punch to his cheek. The challenger cried out from the pain, lost his footing from the punch, and collapsed.

With the third fall of the challenger, the crowd roared in cheers. Clotilda let out a long sigh of relief. She smiled proudly at Cyril, grateful he won and protected his kingdom, but she worried about his injuries.

"How is this possible?" the challenger yelled as he slammed his fist into the marble floor. "I trained hard so that I could defeat you!"

"You lost because you overestimated yourself," Cyril said as he approached the challenger.

He dismissed his sword and offered a hand to help his opponent up. The challenger sneered before ignoring his hand, pushing himself back up, and walking quickly out of the throne room and toward the castle entrance.

Clotilda watched as Kefira took the form of a dove and swooped toward Cyril, who was watching the challenger leave, shape-shifting back into her elven form as she stood beside him.

"He'll probably return for a rematch," Clotilda heard Kefira say to him.

"I'll be ready," Cyril said and paused as they heard the castle doors slam shut, signaling that the challenger had left.

Cyril groaned softly in pain and pressed his hand on his injured shoulder.

"Your Majesty!" Kefira said as she placed her hand on his back.

"It's all right, I'll be fine. I'll make my way to the healer's chamber," he reassured the advisor before leaving the throne room.

Clotilda watched Cyril walk into the hallway with trailing droplets of blood behind him. She excused herself as she walked through the crowd and entered the grand halls to help Cyril.

CHAPTER 38

A Growing Bond

Clotilda looked around for Cyril and soon spotted him climbing the stairs while holding onto the marble railing for support. Without wasting any time, Clotilda rushed through the hallway and ran up the stairs, skipping a few steps as she hurried toward him.

"Here. I can help you," she said as she walked beside him.

"I appreciate your help, but I'm fine," Cyril reassured her with a smile.

"I want to help you, just like you helped me the other night," she replied.

"You're planning on carrying me?" he said teasingly.

"I would if I could, but I don't think I'm strong enough," she said as she giggled softly, and Cyril joined in with a chuckle. "How far is the healer?"

"The healer's chamber is at the other side of the castle, behind the guard rooms."

"That's a long walk from here," she replied, worrying that Cyril might lose more blood and collapse before they could get halfway to the castle. She thought momentarily, her eyes widening when she realized she had left her waist pack in her room, but it was close to the stairs. This would save Cyril some of his strength. "Wait, I still have some Tears of Eir in my waist pack. Let's head to my bed chamber and see how much I have before we go to the healer."

"As you wish," he nodded as Clotilda gently grasped Cyril's arm, swung it over her shoulder, and held a steady arm on his back as they continued walking up the stairs.

With slow steps, Clotilda and Cyril arrived at her bed chamber. Clotilda looked around frantically until she saw her waist pack hanging from one of the rose-gold handles of the wardrobe. She helped Cyril to her bed and sat him down before hurrying to her pack and quickly opening it. Much to her relief, she had enough of the healing flowers to help tend to his wounds.

Clotilda quickly lifted the stool from her vanity and moved it toward the bed until it was standing before Cyril, and she sat on it. She scooped out a handful of the flowery vines from her pack, pausing momentarily as Cyril took off his chest guard. She allowed her hair to fall around her face to hide her blush as she gently tended to his wounds, placing the Tears of Eir on the claw marks on his shoulder and the laceration on his side while trying not to stare at his toned, muscular chest.

"I just realized something," Cyril said as he watched her.

"What's that?" she asked curiously as she met his gaze.

"This is the third time you've tended to my wounds since we reunited."

"The third?" she asked, only for him to reach into his pant pocket and pull out a small, neatly folded piece of fabric.

"My handkerchief. I forgot all about it. Thank you," she said as she accepted it and laid it on the vanity table. "Cyril, I'm sorry you got hurt during the duel."

"It was worth it. I wasn't going to let him get anywhere near you," he replied.

Clotilda dropped her gaze silently as she slipped into her thoughts.

Despite being at Streng searching for her, Cyril refrained from killing any of her troops or innocent lives. Even during the Duel of Kingship, Cyril refused to engage in a death match despite his opponent's boasting.

Decorating Cyril's chest were old scars from what looked like lacerations from swords or daggers. Reading the scars, they weren't from victims fending him off defensively. They were from attackers, maybe from the gladiators he had to face in the Slachten Arena and the challengers who wanted his crown. Cyril was a protector, not a murderer.

"The rumors were wrong," she smiled.

"What's that?" Cyril asked.

"I'm sorry, I was thinking out loud about the rumors of the Graf . . . I mean . . ." she hesitated, remembering how Cyril didn't like hearing his manticore title.

"It's all right. You can call me the Graffias Manticore if you wish," he said.

"I didn't want to call you something that offends you. I don't mean to disrespect you."

"You never have," he smiled at her, which caused her heart to leap. "What kind of rumors did you hear about me?"

Clotilda hesitated, remembering what Corinthia and Bandus told her about the Graffias Manticore when they were trying to prevent the women of the capital from crossing the barrier.

"Just rubbish about you being a bloodthirsty killer," she said and noticed how one of Cyril's eyebrows rose in irritation, not at her, but at the words she was telling him.

"I only take a life when hunting for food or out of defense. I don't like killing, but I will use my sword to stop a threat coming after those I care about."

"There's no need to explain that to me. You're a good man."

"I try. But when I fought in the Slachten Arena and was a slave to the Graffias Assassins . . . I spilled a lot of blood." He rested his elbows on his knees and yanked off his gloves as he wove his fingers together. "Anyone Delilah wanted me to kill, she used her necklace to control me, and I slaughtered them," he said softly. "I always thought the inner scars of remorse would never heal. I was a broken man . . . until I met you."

"You speak about how I impacted you when I didn't do much," she shrugged.

"You're very humble, Clotilda."

"I mean it. All I did back then was invite you to be my playmate and bring food for you, but that was it."

"You did more than that," he said, standing up from the bed.

Clotilda froze and tilted her head back as she stared up at him. Cyril stepped toward her, causing her to lean back with the stool until her spine bumped into the vanity. Cyril bent down and gripped the vanity table, caging her with his arms. Clotilda heard her pulse ring in her eardrums and leaned back until her elbows and forearms were propped onto the vanity table.

"What I said to Delilah the other night is true. I'm very grateful for what you've done for me. You've grown into a wonderful woman. You have a brave and kind heart. That's why I chose you." Clotilda felt her heart race to his words, and her breath quickened when she saw him lift his right hand. She felt his warm fingers graze the pulse point of her neck, and his thumb lightly stroked the outline of her jaw.

He slowly leaned closer to her, to the point that their bangs touched. Clotilda went silent, and a shiver ran up her spine as she felt his breath on her lips. She looked into his eyes, seeing conflicting emotions and hesitation. He froze, glancing down momentarily as if battling his thoughts. He leaned forward to her left cheek and pressed his lips against the scar. Her eyes widened, her racing mind barely processing what was happening. Cyril was kissing her! The kiss wasn't long, but it wasn't short either. She felt every branch of her nerves ignite into a frenzy. The elf king's warm lips enveloped the scar that once held sorrowful memories of loss as if he had kissed them away.

Cyril broke the kiss, slowly and reluctantly pulling away from her. He hid his eyes behind his bangs and pulled his hands away from the vanity and Clotilda's pulse.

"Thank you again for your healing," he said, his voice lightly laced with guilt as if he did something wrong. "I'll see you at the dining hall for lunch," he said before he grabbed his chest guard from the bed and began making his way out of the chamber.

"Cyril, wait!" she said as she leaped off the stool and sprinted toward him.

Cyril turned to face her and was greeted by her arms wrapping around him, and she pressed her body against his in a caring embrace. Clotilda tightened the hug, being careful not to touch his healing injuries. Her loving gesture caused him to lose his grip on his chest guard, which fell onto the floor. His tense body relaxed, and she felt his arms wrap around her and his fingers combing through her hair.

"You impacted me too. I don't want to lose you again," she said, looking up at him.

"You won't. I'm not going anywhere," he said with a smile.

Clotilda's thoughts whirled with her emotions like a crazed typhoon. What was this feeling she was experiencing? Is this just a crush she had since she was a little girl? Or was it something else? She loosened her hands around him as she thought about it. She needed to give it time. For years, she wanted to learn more about Cyril. Now was the opportunity.

Clotilda slowly pulled away, breaking the hug as she met Cyril's eyes.

"I have a question. I know we will spend time together during my training, but can we possibly do the same off the training grounds?" she asked.

"Of course," he smiled. "There is more to being a Royal Huntress than battle and hunting. You'll be able to act as my guard and accompany me with my royal duties," he said and gently placed his hands on her shoulders. "So you and I will spend a lot of time together."

Clotilda felt like she was going to burst!

"I'm looking forward to that," her smile beamed.

"I am as well," he said and paused as he bent down to pick up his chest guard and slipped it back on. "After lunch, I'll have to complete some of my royal duties before tomorrow. So you can keep me company while I am working."

"Can I help you with any of the work there?"

"If you want, but having you there is all I can ask for. Your training will take about a month or two, so I hope you don't mind putting up with me," he smirked.

"I was about to ask you the same thing about me," she giggled.

"I'm going to suffer," he sarcastically said, smiling back.

CHAPTER 39

The New Royal Huntress

Branches of trees brushed against their bodies as Clotilda followed Cyril through the woodland trail of the kingdom's forested training grounds. The sound of rustling leaves followed them as they raced toward an unknown destination. She hadn't been through this path that Cyril mentioned where they were heading, but she trusted him, and he asked her to follow him and be ready for the training dummies awaiting them.

Two months ago, Clotilda had felt uncomfortable using a bow, but now it had become an extension of her arm, no longer burdensome. A growing bond of trust with it was beginning to grow along with her new skills as a Royal Huntress. She was still getting used to it, but it no longer felt foreign. She could now shoot arrows accurately, and the satisfaction of hitting the target was immense. The Royal Huntress armor she wore felt comfortable, as if it had become a part of her skin. She felt confident and capable, ready for whatever challenges lay ahead.

The warm afternoon wind rushed past her ears and blew through her hair. Her heart escalated as she heard a tune pulse within her, and a smile spread on her face. This was the first time she had felt a storm of emotions in so many years: inspiration and happiness. But there was something else. Expecting this new emotion to falter, it had only grown stronger with every second she spent with Cyril. Clotilda monitored how her heart would beat faster every time she met up with Cyril and how she looked forward to embracing him with every hug they shared.

Straw-filled target dummies jumped from their hiding places behind bushes, marble columns, and rocks as they ran closer to them. Clotilda confidently drew her bow and aimed for the targets. She released her hold on the arrows with steady breaths, allowing them to shoot through the air like comets and directly hit the targets. She quickly shifted to the next approaching target, firing another arrow and striking it down. She glanced up at the treetops and aimed her arrow above, seeing one of the hidden targets hovering over them.

"I'm getting you this time," she said as she fired her arrow, remembering that last month when she rushed through the trail with Cyril the first time, she kept missing this lurking target. But not this time! The arrow shot through the air effortlessly, causing leaves to flutter and break off the branches. Clotilda's eyes widened as the arrow punctured a tree branch instead of the target.

"Oh no, you don't!" She said as her brows narrowed. She quickly fired another arrow at it. Again, the arrow rushed through the treetops like the first one, only this time, it struck the target. "Yes!" She cheered as she turned her attention to Cyril, noticing him looking back at her with a smile, causing her cheeks to redden.

Cyril came to an abrupt stop, causing her to halt to see that they had arrived at a fork.

"All right! This is the last part of your training," Cyril said. "We have one more challenge left."

"What do I need to do?" Clotilda asked, catching her breath.

"Unlike the other trails we went through last month, this path has enchanted targets. They will stay in one place, but they will be firing enchanted beams toward us. The beams won't hurt, but touching any of them counts as an injury."

"Where will this trail take us?" she asked curiously.

"This trail will take us to the forest lagoon. Ready?" he asked with a smile.

"Ready!" she smiled back.

"Good," he said as he summoned his sword. "Stay close, and best of luck."

"Thank you. You too," she said as she drew her bow, and her feet shifted as she readied to sprint into a run.

"This is it! Let's go," he said as he sprinted down the forest trail.

Clotilda kept a firm hold on her bow, armed with an arrow, and her focus strongly attuned as she followed her king. Her ears perked up as bushes rustled above the slope near them, and she heard the pulsing of glowing magic charging. She aimed her bow toward the top of the hill, firing her arrow when she saw one of the enchanted targets preparing to fire at Cyril. Her arrow struck the target, causing it to disappear into vapor.

Cyril's grunt caused her to quickly jerk her head to him, seeing that one of the enchanted targets had fired a beam of magic at him. She growled as she cast another arrow from her hand chain and fired a direct shot at the target.

"Are you all right?" she said, grabbing his shoulder and gently tugging him to a stop.

"Don't worry; I'm fine. It didn't hurt, but I felt the beam hit my arm," he replied.

"I'm sorry about that," she said as she looked at him with guilt.

"Don't let that make you stumble. You're doing great," he said with a smile. She smiled back, feeling her surfacing doubts melt away. "Let's finish this. I have something to show you when we get to the lagoon."

"What is it?" she asked.

"You'll see," he smirked before he resumed running.

"Wait? What? You get back here!" she said with a laugh as she followed him, hearing him laugh as he ran.

Clotilda and Cyril fired arrows at distant targets and summoned Universeel and his dual swords to destroy close ones. Clotilda felt a few of the beams hit her shoulder and right foot, but like Cyril said, they didn't hurt. But she mentally reminded herself that she needed to improve her dodging next time because if those were real injuries, she would have been slowed down.

Finally the forest opened, and trees parted for them as they came to a large lagoon. The lagoon reminded Clotilda of a garden fountain with its three-tiered bowls of rocks stacked on top of a vast waterfall and giant lilies that delicately floated over its smooth surface.

"Congratulations. Well done," Cyril said after he caught his breath.

"It's done?" she asked, hardly believing that her two-month training had ended so quickly.

"Yes," he said as he gently touched her shoulder. "Your training is complete. You are now a Royal Huntress."

"I have you to thank for that." She dismissed Universeel and hugged Cyril, feeling his arms wrap around her to return the embrace.

"I have something for you," he said softly, slipping away from her embrace and walking toward the lagoon. The soothing churning of water echoed in the air with the gentle flap of Cyril's cape billowing in the afternoon breeze. Clotilda watched him with curiosity as he kneeled at the lagoon, reached behind one of the rocks, and picked up a lotus-shaped crystal box. He stood back up and carried it to her. She gratefully accepted it when he handed it to her and held it with one arm as she opened it with her free hand. Looking inside, she was greeted by small shelves filled with beads of various precious gems of different sizes, rolls of sweet pea vines, color-changing potions, and jewelry tools. "It's a present for you for all the hard work you've done with your training and helpfulness around the castle."

"Thank you, Cyril. I'll put this to good use," she smiled in delight.

"You're welcome. There's one more thing I need to tell you."

"What is it?" she asked as she closed the jewelry kit.

"There's going to be a grand ball tonight in my castle, and I would like you to attend it with me, not as my Royal Huntress, but as my date."

"I'd love to!" she said, biting her bottom lip bashfully when she realized that she had never accepted an invitation to a date that quickly in her entire life. "I mean . . . it would be an honor, Cyril."

"That's great, and I have a new gown and some new jewelry awaiting you in your room. You're welcome to wear them tonight."

"I appreciate it, but you've given me so much. You don't have to shower me with all these gifts," she said as she gently placed her hand on his shoulder.

"I know. But I want to."

"Out of all the gifts I've received from you . . . you're the best of them all," she said as she met his gaze. He didn't respond to her words; he kept his eyes on her, and his hand reached up and pressed against his chest, over his heart.

The air was pleasantly quiet between them until Clotilda softly spoke again.

"Is there anything I can help prepare for the ball tonight?"

"You don't need to. But if you want to help, I have no complaints."

"I'll see what I can do," she said.

"It's already late in the afternoon. We should return to the castle and get ready for tonight," he said as they linked arms and began walking through the forest trail.

This foreign mix of emotions coursed through Clotilda with every beat of her heart as she stared at Cyril. For two months, she had gotten to know him. He became her best friend, and she became more attracted to him. He had treated her with kindness, gentle guidance, and respect and encouraged her to continue being a guard and a musician.

A realization sank deep into her bones as she thought of her decision to give herself and her heart time to process her feelings. This feeling was the most wonderful one she'd ever felt. She was in love with Cyril.

CHAPTER 40

Kefira's Secret

Cyril and Clotilda enjoyed lunch together and parted ways to prepare for the night. She made her way to her room with the jewelry kit safely in her arms and knew a good place to put it in her study. As she entered her bed chambers, her eyes caught a cascading ocean of delicate fabric on her bed. Her eyes locked on it as she approached. The soft fabric belonged to the most exquisite gown she had ever seen.

The gown was in the shape of a mermaid's tail and was red, yellow, and orange like the setting sun. The top and bottom hems were decorated with small, glittering yellow gemstones that looked like cinders, and the dress had a veil-like cape in the shape of bird wings that glistened like vapors of the cosmos. A choker of red garnets lay on the gown, along with a pair of red, elbow-length gloves, red slippers, and a rose-gold tiara with scarlet and green gems.

Clotilda placed the kit on the bed and carefully scooped the dress up as she marveled at it. Whoever created it was the finest tailor, and she admired the masterful threadwork. She softly smiled as she laid down the fabric with care and brushed the tips of her fingers along the jewelry.

"Thank you, Cyril," she said as she smiled softly, looking forward to wearing the gown as soon as she was done helping with preparing for the ball.

Clotilda made her way from her bed chambers to the ballroom, where she saw the servants hard at work with the preparations. Columns were being wrapped with garlands of flowers, servants swept and mopped the floors, and a row of maids kneeled by buckets of water and trimmed flower stems. She made her way toward them, offering her assistance. Accepting the extra help, the maids allowed Clotilda to sit with them, holding each branch in the calm waters of the buckets, using scissors to trim the ends, and putting them in a basket next to her.

Once each flower was cut, Clotilda helped arrange and put them into elegant displays and decorated them with apples, berries, and blue ribbons.

Upon finishing the last flower arrangements, Clotilda glanced at the ballroom doorway, noticing Kefira standing there watching her.

Since the Duel of Kingship, Kefira had not exchanged another word with Clotilda and spent most of her time standing from afar and keeping her stern gaze on her. Clotilda found it irritating to say the least, and she was unsure why the advisor had such a distaste toward her. But over time, she learned to ignore it, deciding that giving the advisor space was the best courtesy.

The melody of practicing music notes brought Clotilda back to reality. She looked at the musicians warming up as they sat in the orchestra box at the corner of the ballroom. Unfortunately, one of the musical instruments was out of tune, causing Clotilda's musical ear to churn as if scraped with a razor. She searched the orchestra, noticing a familiar face among them.

Canary sat upon one of the vine-designed wooden chairs with a lyre in her lap and timidly plucked the strings as she struggled to tune the small harp. Sensing her distress, Clotilda made her way over. She heard Canary's frustrated groans as she stood by the orchestra's box. The musicians ceased practicing upon seeing Clotilda and watched as she approached their struggling companion.

"You need some help there?" Clotilda asked, causing the little Beetje elf to flinch from being startled.

"Yes," Canary sighed sadly, letting the lyre lay on her lap. "I love playing the lyre but have so much trouble tuning it."

"Here, I can help you," she said as she held her hand out for the lyre.

Canary nodded as she handed Clotilda her lyre.

Clotilda held it with one arm and used the other to tune the loose cords. She paused for a moment as she plucked the strings of the instrument. She listened to each vibration and adjusted the ones that were rattling with horrendous sounds.

"Here you go," Clotilda said with a smile as she returned the lyre to Canary.

Canary happily accepted the musical instrument back and curiously plucked the strings, listening to the harmonious melodies coming from them.

"It sounds so much better," she cheered, running her fingers over the strings. "Thank you, my lady!"

"You're welcome," Clotilda smiled.

"Are you a musician too?"

"I am, sort of," Clotilda said with a shrug.

"You are? I had a feeling when I was watching you tune my lyre. Maybe you can play tonight for the ball."

"I . . . I don't know about that," Clotilda said shyly, having never played at a ball.

"It would be great to hear you play! Violyne and some of the servants have been talking about how they have been hearing your piano and harp music in the castle."

"Really? I guess sound travels well through a castle, after all," Clotilda shyly smiled as she combed her fingers through her hair.

"It would be great to hear you play! Especially for your . . ." A loud, intentional cough cut off Canary's words from one of the male musicians.

Both elven women looked at the male musician, noticing his stare at them, especially at Canary. Clotilda lifted a brow at him before she returned her gaze to Canary.

"Um . . . what was it that you were going to say?" Clotilda asked.

"It's nothing," Canary said with a smile after she sent the male musician an apologetic look. "Thank you again for helping me. I better start practicing."

"All right. Take care," Clotilda said as she waved farewell and walked away.

She glanced back at the musicians, wondering why one of them interrupted Canary. However, Canary's words planted the thought of playing music for the ball. Would that be all right? Would she have the courage to share her musical gift? She shook her head at the thought. Now was not the time to make last-minute decisions for playing music. She had a ball to help prepare!

Clotilda went to the kitchen, watching the royal chefs working hard at preparing the festive dishes. The air filled with delicious aromas that caused her stomach to growl and her mouth to water.

"It's good to see you again, my lady!" she heard Chef Aldwin say as he placed the bowl of batter down on the table and walked over toward her.

Whenever she wasn't training with Cyril, Clotilda sometimes went to the kitchen to hang out with the chefs and bakers and became friends with them, especially the head chef.

Chef Aldwin was a half Lazarus and half Regulus elf who stood six foot eight feet tall, with orange hair like fire and crimson eyes like a sunset with slitted pupils. He was handsome and clean-shaven and was dressed in a clean, white suit with the golden lion seal on the right side of his apron, a sign of him being the head chef.

"It's good to see you too, Chef. Thank you for lunch. It was delicious as always," Clotilda smiled.

"I'm glad to hear that," he said as he smiled at her.

"Chef Aldwin! We got the dishes ready!" one of the female chefs called out.

"Nice work," he replied as he turned to them. "I'll finish the batter. You go ahead and get going on making the frosting. We must ensure that everything is set for the ball."

"Yes, Chef!" they said in unison.

"I have a question, Chef. What is the celebration for the ball?" Clotilda asked curiously.

"Um . . . I don't know," he said as he looked to the side, avoiding her eyes.

"You don't know?" she asked as she arched one of her eyebrows.

"I need to get back to work. Take care, Clo," he said as he quickly returned to the table to grab a bowl of batter and continue stirring it.

Clotilda looked around to see that the kitchen was scrambling to get ready. It was strange. First Canary and now Chef Aldwin refused to tell her what the celebration of the ball was about. She looked up at the eight large hourglasses embedded in the walls, each filled with blue sand like tanzanite gems, seeing that it was already evening. Her curiosity for what the ball was celebrating would have to wait. She turned toward the stairs and climbed the steps, not wanting to get into anyone's way.

Reaching the top of the stairs and back into the ballroom, Clotilda looked around at the growing beauty of the festivities. Amazement hummed in her veins as she admired the decorations and arrangements the servants put together. Everything was beautiful and set up with care.

Figuring that she was able to help with what she could, Clotilda turned to make her way back to her bed chamber, only to jerk back when she saw that Kefira was blocking her path. Clotilda took a hesitant step back, but she held her stare with the older female.

"May I speak to you for a moment, Lady Clotilda?" Kefira asked politely.

The question pricked Clotilda's brain like the tip of a dagger. What did the royal advisor want to talk to her about? Does she want her to leave the castle? She hoped not. Clotilda wanted to be with Cyril and tell him how she felt about him.

"Yes, of course," she hesitantly said.

"It won't be long, I promise," the advisor reassured her with a smile. "We can talk in the throne room."

"All right," Clotilda said cautiously as she followed her.

The air between the two female elves was silent as they reached the throne room. Clotilda wasn't sure what Kefira wanted to talk to her about, but she felt dread at the thought that the advisor would tell her that she couldn't see Cyril anymore.

"So, what did you want to talk to me about?" she asked, bracing herself for what Kefira would say.

"I want to start by apologizing to you," Kefira said softly.

"Apologize?" Clotilda echoed, not expecting to hear that word from the advisor.

"Yes. I am so sorry for my rude behavior," Kefira spoke with sincerity in her eyes. "I've been distant from you for two months and haven't spoken to you. Throughout this time, I've been studying your actions and how you treat the king and others around you. I am very relieved to say . . . that Cyril has found the right elven woman to be his companion."

"You mean it?" Clotilda asked, eyes wide like an owl's.

"Yes," the advisor replied, as she softly smiled at her. "For many years, the king has encountered a few women who shamefully proved they weren't right for him. So I tend to be very protective of my nephew."

"Nephew?" Clotilda asked, surprised.

"Yes. King Cyril is my nephew. His father was my twin brother. He was a good king, a good husband to his wife, a good brother, and a good father. That is . . . until a challenger killed him," Kefira said as she bore her fangs.

"I'm so sorry," Clotilda said sadly when she saw the look of sorrow and pain in the advisor's eyes.

"That's in the past now," Kefira said and gently placed her hand on Clotilda's shoulder before she continued. "But you proved me wrong about you. You truly are the heroine who saved Cyril from death all those years ago, and for that, you have my eternal gratitude. I hope you can forgive me for being so rude."

"You are forgiven, Kefira," Clotilda smiled at her.

"I'm glad," she smiled with relief in her eyes. "Thank you again for allowing me to speak to you and accepting my apology. The ball will begin very soon, so take this time to get ready," she said as she turned to walk back to the ballroom.

"Oh, Kefira?" Clotilda asked as she reached out to the advisor.

"Yes?" she asked.

"What is the celebration for tonight's ball?"

"You'll see," Kefira gave her a soft smirk. "Violyne will be at your bed chambers shortly to help you get dressed for tonight. See you soon," Kefira said with a friendly wave as she left the throne room.

"All right, see you later," Clotilda politely said before she groaned softly as curiosity roared through her mind. "Darn, I'm so curious now! Oh well, I'll probably find out tonight," she said to herself before walking out of the throne room to go to her bed chambers.

CHAPTER 41

The Ball

Shedding the Royal Huntress armor off, Clotilda neatly folded and laid the set on the foot of her bed. Then she carefully scooped up her new gown and stepped behind the divider to get dressed.

The dress fit her perfectly. The fabric was smooth, like a cascading waterfall of red, orange, and gold, mirroring the sight of a blissful sunset. The ends of the veil cape were tied around her wrists, covered in red elbow-length gloves, and moved gracefully with every motion of her arms like flapping wings. The gown was light like a plume of feathers.

"My lady? Are you in there?" she heard Violyne's voice call out to her from behind the confines of the double doors, along with a knock.

"Yes, I am!" she called out.

"May I come in? I've come to help you with preparing for the ball?"

"Of course! Please come in!"

Clotilda heard the door handle click, and one of the doors swung open. The tapping of Violyne's slippers echoed off the marble floor as she walked inside.

"Are you dressed?" Violyne asked.

"I am," Clotilda replied happily.

"Then let me see! I'm curious to see the gown His Majesty gave you."

"Sure thing. I'll be right out," Clotilda said as she carefully grabbed the bottom hem of the dress and stepped out from behind the dividers.

Violyne stood patiently at the doors, dressed in a delicate gown. It was lavender, one-shouldered, and had rows of ribbons on the bottom and one on her chest below her collarbone. She had gold rings, including her wedding band, around all ten of her fingers, wore a long golden necklace around her slender neck, and had her hair pulled back in a braid. Violyne looked at Clotilda, her eyes fixed on the striking new dress.

"That gown is exquisite on you! His Highness is going to be excited to see you wearing it."

"Thank you, Violyne. I'm looking forward to seeing him tonight," she said bashfully.

"He's been saying the same about you. Come now, let's finish getting you ready," she said as she gestured to the vanity.

Clotilda nodded obediently and sat by the vanity.

Violyne carefully combed through Clotilda's hair with an enchanted comb, styling her hair in a low bun to show off the gown's open back. Next she aided Clotilda with putting the garnet necklace around her neck, plucked small red gems from a jeweled dish on the vanity, and laced them into her locks. She finished by painting a light touch of makeup on her face, eyes, and neck and sprayed rose-scented perfume on the pulse points of her throat. She concluded by painting the apples of Clotilda's cheeks with blush and red lipstick on her lips.

"You're ready, my lady," Violyne said with a smile as she packed the cosmetics.

Clotilda looked into the mirror, hardly recognizing herself. She wasn't used to wearing red lipstick, but it balanced well with the sun-kissed hue of her skin, the red dress, and the pink blush, which helped make it seem lighter to wear instead of overpowering or heavy.

"You did an amazing job. I feel . . ." Clotilda paused as she looked at her reflection. "Pretty."

"Pretty? You look beautiful. Now, there is one last thing to add, and you'll be ready."

Violyne reached for the rose-gold tiara embedded with red and green oval-shaped gems on the vanity and held it over Clotilda's head.

"Are you sure? It might be too much," Clotilda asked as she looked at the overall look.

"It won't. The tiara will not collide with the small gems in your hair and won't slip and ruin your bangs. I'll make sure of it," she said as she grabbed a couple of hair clips.

Clotilda watched as her lady-in-waiting lowered the tiara, feeling its weight rest on her head. Violyne secured it with the hair clips and hid them under Clotilda's locks so no one would notice them, then she slowly moved her hands away from the crown.

Clotilda couldn't believe she was wearing a tiara. This differed from the woven vines and flowers she made as a child while pretending to be a dryad or a warrior princess.

"Thank you again, Violyne," Clotilda said as she stood up from the stool and hugged her.

"Anytime," Violyne returned the hug. "Now we better get going. The ball is starting, and the guests should be here."

"Will do," she said as she slipped on her new red slippers and approached the doors.

Opening one of the double doors, Clotilda stepped into the hallway, her eyes opening in surprise when she saw a familiar male elf leaning against the wall in the hallway with his muscular arms folded. Cyril was dressed in the same clothing he wore when he reunited with her during the masquerade ball. But this time, he wasn't wearing a grizzly bear mask and a brown wig to hide his silvery-white hair. There were no more disguises, no shapeshifting. Cyril was going to be attending the ball as himself.

Cyril glanced over at Clotilda, his eyes widening and his mouth almost agape when he looked upon her. He pushed himself away from the wall he was leaning against and slowly approached her. Clotilda bashfully held her woven hands together and felt her stomach flutter as if she had a swarm of butterflies ready to burst free.

"You look lovely in that dress," he complimented as he stood before her.

"Thank you, Cyril," she said as she stood on the tips of her toes and hugged him. "You look very handsome."

She felt his arms tighten comfortably around her in response to her compliment.

"Excuse me, my king, my lady." Clotilda and Cyril broke the embrace and looked over at Violyne. "Everyone is waiting for both of your arrivals," Violyne said with a bow before she gestured toward the stairs.

"Shall we go?" Clotilda heard Cyril ask as she turned to him and saw his offered arm.

"Let's do it, my king," she said with a nod before she linked her arm with his.

The orchestra's music resonated through the castle. The fragrant aromas of freshly cooked food taunted the appetites of hungry guests. Everyone gathered in the ballroom like a sea of anticipation, waiting for their king to arrive with his Royal Huntress.

Clotilda and Cyril walked down the stairs together, feeling the eyes of his ghost lions watching them as they stood in place of where the Regulus guards stood watch. She hadn't seen the guards since early afternoon, wondering if they were also celebrating at the ball. Her mind soon wondered about Cyril and her feelings for him. Her hesitant mind was torn between telling him or not. She gently brushed her free hand over her left cheek, feeling the phantom touch of his lips pressing against her scarred skin. She thought about it long enough. There was no denying this feeling. This love was very much real! Clotilda tried to be brave in many battles in the past, but she wondered if she would be brave enough to tell him her feelings tonight.

They reached the foot of the staircase and walked through the ballroom doorway, greeted by a sea of guests. The melting pot of elves, goblins, Ice Jotnars, and many others turned to the newly arriving couple and bowed before them.

"You may all rise!" Cyril said as he gestured with his free hand for the guests to stand up. "Enjoy the evening! For tonight, we are celebrating the right of passage for my new Royal Huntress, Clotilda!"

"What?" Clotilda asked softly in surprise.

"This ball is your celebration," he smiled at her.

"Really? I wasn't expecting that," she quietly said.

She watched as the guests saluted her with respect before clapping.

Cyril grabbed two chalices as they approached the banquet table, filling one with nectar milk for Clotilda and one with fruit juice for himself. He gave her the drink, which she happily accepted.

"Here's a toast to you," he said as he raised his chalice to her. She in return raised her drink to his and held it as he spoke. "Thank you for your hard work with everything you do."

"You're welcome. Thank you for being my teacher."

They smiled at each other before lightly tapping their chalices together and sipping their drinks.

"So, what did you think of the surprise?" Cyril asked after he swallowed the sweet liquid of his drink.

"It surprised me. I was curious today about what the ball was celebrating," she giggled.

"I told everyone here that no one was to say anything about it. I wanted it to be a surprise."

"They did a great job. I asked a few people about the celebration, but they kept their lips sealed," she said as she glared softly at Canary, Kefira, and Chef Aldwin as they giggled at her as they attended the celebration.

"Good," Cyril said, taking another sip from his drink. "What were the celebration balls like when you were still serving King Thierry?"

"I never had any from him," she said with a shrug.

"You're serious?" he asked, his brows furrowing into a frown.

"I am. This is my first one," she said softly.

"Then what did he do for you?" he asked.

"Um," she paused. "He just . . . simply invited me to his kingdom, told me that I got promoted in rank, and told me to leave. But it's all right, Cyril. Back then, my celebrations were thanks to my friends and family. That was more than enough for me. Speaking of which," she said in realization. "My mother should be getting close to giving birth."

"Her first child?" he asked.

"Yes," she said with a nod. "She and my father have struggled to conceive a child for many years. Once they found a caring and skillful fairy alchemist, she was able to get pregnant. I still remember that glow of joy in my mother's eyes when she told everyone in the orphanage that she was expecting," Clotilda smiled. "She and father did a great job raising me and caring for many orphans for centuries. So I know they will make great parents to their child."

"That is a great joy to hear. But I can sense that you miss your family," he said softly, his voice laced with guilt.

"I do miss them," she paused as she touched his cheek. "But I am thrilled being here with you. I haven't been this happy in so many years."

"Are you sure?" he asked, placing his hand over hers that cupped his face.

"I am," she nodded with sincerity.

CHAPTER 42

Musical Confession

Peaceful music played as the guests piled their plates with the food from the banquet. Clotilda ate next to Cyril. They exchanged a pleasant conversation as they watched the guests. The appetizers and entrees were delicious, but Clotilda's favorite evening dish was the cake. The frosting was light like a cloud, and the berries and edible flowers were beautiful and added rich flavor to the dessert.

As Clotilda scraped the last of the frosting off her plate with her fork, she saw Canary standing in the orchestra box, waving for her to come over. Placing her empty plate on the table, Clotilda excused herself from Cyril and visiting guests and made her way toward the orchestra.

"You need something, Canary?" she asked.

"I was wondering if you wanted to play some music tonight."

"I would love to. But I need to ask first to ensure it's all right."

"It's perfectly fine with me," she heard Cyril's voice from behind her, surprising her as she was unaware that he had followed her.

"Are you sure, my king?" Clotilda asked as she turned back to him.

"I've wanted to hear your music for quite some time now. I faintly hear it in my castle, and some of my servants have talked about how elegant it sounds. I would be honored if you would play tonight."

Clotilda felt her heart melt, and the impulse to share her musical gift lit inside her like a nova. A piece of music played in her heart, one she had worked on since she realized her love for Cyril. Playing this piece will give her the courage to tell him about her feelings for him.

"I have this one piece of music I want to share with you," Clotilda said with a blush.

"Let's hear it," he replied—a gleam of curiosity lighting his eyes like stars.

Clotilda stepped into the orchestra box, politely excusing herself as she carefully approached the piano. At the same time, she was trying to avoid stepping on any of the musicians' feet and musical instruments. She lifted her gown slightly as she sat on the piano seat and rested her feet on the pedals. She took the opportunity to take her hand chains and long gloves off and brought her hands to the keys. She let them hover over the keys as curious eyes watched her. She closed her eyes to clear the creeping anxiousness, shyness, and fear of making a mistake as she didn't have the written music in front of her. She would have to play it by memory. She inhaled deeply, feeling the music play in her mind's ear and her heart. She thought of Cyril, the melody growing stronger, urging her fingers to rest on the keys, and she started to play.

Her fingers tapped on the keys like flower petals landing on a pond's smooth, tranquil surface. She pictured the scene in her memory of when she had first met Cyril. The rolling of her fingers on the piano keys mirrored the gentle rustling of apple tree leaves and blossoms. The music became uplifting as the memory of children's laughter graced her eardrums: a boy—a king in disguise, and a girl—a musician and future guard.

A smile tugged at the corner of her lips as she remembered the joyful memories and her fingers leaped into a march as she and Cyril reunited. Her body swayed with the music, her fingers racing over the keys triumphantly. The music led to when Cyril saved her from her fallen village, where the Hollow elves attacked, and her training with him began.

The melody softened, metamorphosing into a romantic harmony. She glanced over her shoulder to see Cyril watching her. His face was relaxed, but his eyes were fixed on her like a lifeline filled with emotions. Clotilda felt her throat constrict with the words of her hidden confession swelling in her vocal cords. She couldn't trust her voice yet. She hoped her music would give her the courage to say three of the most sacred words: I love you.

The muscles in her throat began to vibrate with the desire to say them. Her fingers slowed on the keys, the sweet music softly ending into a serene coda. She held the tune with her fingers down on the keys, inhaling deeply with a smile, the music within her brought to life through the love pulsing through her. She exhaled softly before retreating her fingers from the salt and pepper keys and letting her hands fall to her lap.

The sound of clapping filled the ballroom. She looked back to see Cyril, the first to clap before the other gathered guests, whom she had never noticed were circling the orchestra box. Even the musicians were clapping. She shyly looked around, hearing the guests compliment her, and saw that some of them were brushing their fingertips under their eyes to wipe away the streams of tears. She slowly stood up from the piano seat, bowing gratefully and thanking everyone before approaching Cyril.

"That was the most beautiful music I've ever heard," the king said with a proud smile, holding his hand out to help her out of the orchestra box.

"I'm glad you liked it," she said as she happily accepted his hand and held the bottom hem of her gown as she stepped out. "I . . . I wrote that music for you."

"For me?" he asked, nearly speechless.

She nodded softly in response as she kept her eyes on his.

After basking in Clotilda's song, the musicians began playing a soft harmony for everyone to dance. Clotilda saw Cyril's open hand held up to her.

"Would you like to dance with me?" he asked.

"I would love to," she said as she kindly accepted his hand, and they made their way to the dance floor.

Clotilda's smile didn't falter, and she felt her heart flutter from contemplating what she would do. There was no turning back now, knowing she would regret it if she kept it bottled up. She wanted to tell him, express to him just like she did on the piano.

Clotilda and Cyril danced close to each other to the point that their bodies were pressed together. Their arms embraced each other, and their hands were interlocked. She glanced down at their feet, her mind whirling as she thought of the words to say.

"This brings back memories," Cyril said.

"I'm sorry?" she asked, looking up at him.

"When we danced at the masquerade ball, I noticed that you glanced down at your feet a few times while we danced."

"I guess it's an old habit of mine. I've always been more confident with my fingers than my feet," she giggled.

"You soared tonight, Clotilda. Remember that you have so many gifts and kindness that should never be hidden again," he said softly.

"I will. It's . . . I haven't been this inspired to write my music in a long time. I barely had time to write or play my pieces when I was commander. I could only get past this by writing a few notes before I would have to put them away and focus on my duties. But now it's just pouring out of me," she said as she noticed that all the dancing men and women were twirling and spinning to the music, but she and Cyril only swayed back and forth in one place. "Ever since I took my first music lessons from Fossegrim, I could sense that there was my music somewhere in here," she said as she freed her right hand from his shoulder and placed it on her chest. "I think I finally found it. It broke free and spread its wings as I have, and I have my muse to thank for that."

Cyril smiled warmly at her as he placed his hand over his heart, touched by her words. "I need to tell you something . . ." she said softly, her voice slightly shaking. Cyril's hand tightly held hers in reassurance. "I was very close to you when I was little," she said, her eyes beginning to burn from tears. She swallowed a lump in her throat as she continued. "Even in memory, you've always been close to me. But it's gotten so strong during our two months together. That's why I . . . I see you as more than just a friend. I'm in love with you, Cyril," she said with a smile.

Cyril hid his eyes behind his bangs, and he pulled her into an embrace.

"I'm in love with you too, Clotilda." She heard his voice tremble slightly, the tremor in his vocal cords overwhelmed with emotions: relief, happiness, and love.

Clotilda felt as if her heart had burst and she had swallowed the sun. She tightened her arms around him, not wanting to let go of the man she loved and never wanting to be away from him again!

Clotilda and Cyril walked side by side as they made their way to her bed chamber, holding each other's hands with their fingers woven together. They stopped by the doors to her room, facing each other.

"Thank you so much for tonight, Cyril," Clotilda said softly.

"I'm glad you enjoyed it," he replied.

"I did," she smiled, noticing she and him were drawing closer.

She hesitantly reached up and gently touched his firm chest as she stepped closer. She felt his hands gently grip her shoulders, and her heart raced as he leaned closer.

Their eyes shot wide open, and they pulled away when they heard a high-pitched squeak.They dropped their gazes to see a messenger squirrel by their feet. Cyril gave Clotilda an apologetic look before he kneeled, petting the squirrel before allowing it to step onto his palm. He opened the capsule on the squirrel's harness and pulled out the small scroll.

"Who's it from?" she asked as she watched him read the message.

"I don't know. It looks like it's an urgent message," Cyril replied as he read it.

"Urgent?" she asked as she became alert.

"Yes. I'll take this to my advisor and see if she can find out where this is from and what the emergency is. Have a good night, Clotilda, just in case I return and you're asleep."

"You too, Cyril. I'll see you tomorrow," she said and turned to face the double doors, holding one of the handles as she heard Cyril's hesitant footsteps descending the hallway.

"Cyril!" she called out, seeing him abruptly stop and turn toward her. She wrapped her arms around his neck before standing on the tips of her toes and kissed his cheek gently. Then she slowly pulled away, shyly meeting his gaze. "You have a good night too. I'll see you tomorrow morning."

She felt his arm slip around her waist, gently pulling her back to him, and he gently kissed her cheek. He pressed his forehead against hers.

"Sleep well, Clotilda," he whispered before walking down the hallway.

She smiled softly and gently placed her hand on her cheek where he had planted the kiss. She wasn't sure what would happen between them tomorrow, but something told her their confessions tonight would be the starting point for something special.

CHAPTER 43

Temptation

Not knowing where Cyril was and not having any duties as a Royal Huntress today, Clotilda decided to spend the morning organizing the music in her study. She sorted her music alphabetically and placed the sheet music on the shelves beside her pianos and harps. She wiped down each shelf with a rag and was careful not to ruin her jumpsuit and boots that Violyne had worked hard to fix for her while cleaning.

She wiped her hand over her sweating forehead and smiled at her neatly organized workspace. With the study cleaned up, the urge to curl up and read a book called to her like an oasis in the desert. She walked over to the bookshelf in her bed chamber, noticing that she had read all the books there. She borrowed books from Canary, Violyne, and Doric, who unfortunately used the books in his bed chambers as a footstool. They didn't have any more novels to read, and she needed to return the ones she borrowed from Violyne and Canary, except for Doric, who told her she could keep his books since he wasn't a reader.

The royal library called to her. Clotilda remembered that Cyril had permitted her to borrow and read the books there. Deciding to check out and satisfy her curiosity about what kind of books were there, she stepped out of her bed chamber and walked toward the library.

Clotilda opened one of the double doors to the library, hoping to find a captivating story from one of the collections of books. She wondered how many she could borrow at once and thought of grabbing a stack of them. Clotilda walked into the library, her eyes growing wide in awe as soon as she saw what was inside.

Tall towers of books were organized alphabetically, large marble columns carved to look like trees held the ceiling up, and a mural of a historical battle scene caught her eye. She tilted her head up to marvel at the mural. The images were beautifully painted. The blue sky had feathered white clouds framing the sun, where a large gold crystal grew from. Flowers of various colors spiraled on the painted ground like waves of jewels, and creatures from Regulus and Lazarus elves fought together against a horde of pillage trolls. Fauns, Beetje elves, and fairies guarded a giant snapdragon flower surrounded by purple and blue pollen.

Clotilda remembered reading about the alliance of Lazarus and Regulus elves from Turquoise and how they have been the longest-known allies next to the Beetje and the fairies. This mural illustrated the union of old and new allies defending the fairies' sacred home from the trolls who tried to uproot the flower for the gems of magic they wanted to devour. New alliances and friendships were forged that day, and the teachings of natural healing from the fairies and the messenger squirrels from the Beetje elves were introduced and shared with many cultures.

Fossils of well-taken care of, and carefully preserved dragon bones stood up at the corners of the library. Some were posed in still sprints, flights, and aggressive attack positions, with gold plates with the names of each dragon species.

Clotilda smiled in marvel. She had never seen a library as beautiful and rich with books and history. She could see why Cyril wanted to be here and why it was precious to him.

"Beautiful . . ." she said out loud.

"It is," a strong male voice spoke.

Clotilda flinched in surprise as soon as she heard the voice. She turned around to see Cyril sitting in one of the chairs with a novel open on his crossed legs and a crystal chalice standing on a small table beside him. Guilt bubbled in her chest. She didn't mean to interrupt him, remembering how she was told that Cyril didn't like being disturbed while he was reading.

Clotilda backed away slowly, ensuring her heels didn't click on the marble floor. She reached for the door handle, her fingers barely touching it, when she heard Cyril speak again.

"You can stay, Clotilda. You're not interrupting anything," he reassured her.

Her hand froze, then she saw him looking at her from his novel.

"I'm sorry about that, Cyril. I came here to get some new books to read. I didn't realize you were in here," she said softly.

"You didn't do anything wrong," he said with a smile. "This library is for everyone in this castle. If they treat the books here with respect and care and return them after they are finished reading, then I have no issues," he said as he turned the page in his book.

"In that case, do you mind if I take a stack or two back to my room?"

"You may," he said with a nod.

Clotilda thanked him before walking over to the shelves, lightly brushing her index finger along the engraved, gold letters on the books' spines and carefully sliding them off the shelf. Cyril and Clotilda exchanged small words as she stacked each book that drew her interest and carefully cradled them with both arms. She asked Cyril about the mural, the collection of fossils, and the worldly goods decorating the shelves, and she learned that the mural was painted by one of his ancestors when they claimed the kingdom from a family of tyrants many years ago and that his mother and father collected treasures from their journeys to neighboring lands.

Clotilda placed the stack of books on the table's smooth wooden surface, and Cyril glanced up from his book to see what she had selected.

"Eight books," he counted. "You're quite the reader, Clotilda."

"I love reading! It's one of my favorite hobbies."

"Mine too," he smiled.

She glanced down at the book in Cyril's hands, her eyes widening as she recognized the illustrations.

"That book you're reading . . . it's been one of my favorites ever since I was a child!" she said joyfully. "Are you enjoying it?"

"I always have. I lost count of how many times I've read this collection of stories," he said as he rested the book on his lap and glanced up at her. "I don't usually admit this to anyone, but one of my favorite books has always been tales from my childhood. Even though my mother and father were busy ruling the kingdom, they still managed to read these stories to me every night before I fell asleep. I don't have any brothers or sisters, and after I lost my parents, things started getting lonely. I binged on reading because it comforted me and reminded me of my precious time with my parents. But even as an adult, I still enjoy them. I never tire of the stories, the lessons, the imagination, everything about them."

"I know what you mean," she smiled, remembering how she turned to these stories to ease the pain of loss during her stay in the orphanage and read them to the children before they went to bed every night.

Clotilda noticed that Cyril turned the page to an illustration of a ball, allowing her to relive the memory of last night and the scene of them dancing together. She felt her cheeks blush as she remembered wanting to kiss him last night.

Cyril closed his book before laying it on the reading table beside his drink. Then he stood up and walked over to her. Despite her heart beginning to race, Clotilda stood her ground as he slowly approached, stopping as soon as he stood right in front of her.

"Last night, did you mean what you said about me?" he asked her, Clotilda sensing the uncertainty in his voice.

Aware of how close he was standing, she could feel his breath, laced with the sweet scent of the juice he was sipping on.

"I did. I meant what I said to you, about how I saw you as more than just a friend and how I love you," she smiled.

"Then," he said as he drew nearer to her, closing the distance between them. "There's something I've always wanted to do with you. A temptation that I have been holding back since we've been spending more time together. If you'll let me," he said as he lowered his gaze, eyeing her lips.

Clotilda impulsively rolled her bottom lip into her mouth, sensing what he wanted. She found herself desiring the same thing. "I won't go any further without your permission. You can say no if you don't want to."

"I want the same thing," she said, feeling fire engulf her cheeks.

Clotilda watched as a spark of excitement lit in Cyril's eyes. She felt her heart flutter as his right hand gently cupped her cheek. She could see him studying her features as if seeing if she would turn her head away, but she didn't. He leaned closer to her, the tips of their noses touching and the nerves in her lips humming as she was under half an inch of his. She stared into his eyes, giving him her consent. Then, severing the last shackles of his restraints, he took a deep breath as if he were going to dive into a stormy sea and fluttered his eyes shut as he pressed his lips against hers.

Her heart skipped a beat. Clotilda's eyes widened, and a gasp caught in her throat. Cyril's lips were moist and desirable, and she could taste his breath with the intertwined nectar of his drink. Clotilda had never been kissed before, and it was incredible!

Her legs began to feel weak, unable to stand on her toes to draw closer to him, and she quickly brought her hands up to his shoulders, clinging to him like a piece of driftwood. Clotilda felt his left arm snake around her waist, pulling her closer to him, holding her as if he could sense the threat of her trembling legs, ready to collapse at any moment. He timidly traced his tongue on her bottom lip, asking her permission to deepen the kiss. Clotilda shivered from the contact and felt her blush spread down her neck. She fluttered her eyes closed as she parted her lips, welcoming him.

He anxiously slipped his tongue into her mouth, sighing as it brushed against her awaiting one. Clotilda timidly coiled hers with his, melting their tongues together. A soft growl rippled in his throat as he deepened the kiss. Her ears twitched when she heard the wet slaps of their connected mouths, moaning when he sucked on her tongue and nibbled on her bottom lip.

Clotilda's eyes shot open, Cyril's seductive kissing slowed, and his eyes opened when they heard a knock on the library door. Cyril reluctantly broke the kiss, their connected lips creating a soft, wet slap as they parted.

"Be right there!" he called out when they heard a second knock.

Cyril unwound his arm around Clotilda's waist, catching her when she stumbled slightly as her trembling legs tried to carry her weight. He securely held her to ensure she didn't fall before he fixed his shirt and cape, granting whoever was outside permission to enter the library.

Clotilda sat on one of the chairs, picking up a book from her stack of novels and opening it to hide her blushing face from the visitor, taking a moment to make sure the book she was reading wasn't upside-down.

Cyril opened one of the library doors and was greeted by his aunt.

"I'm sorry to bother you, Cyril. But we were able to find out where the letter was from," Kefira apologized.

"Who sent it?" he asked, causing Clotilda to look up from the book in curiosity, noticing the advisor handing him a new letter. But unlike the first one, the second one had dark spots that looked burned.

"The urgent letter is from the capital of Streng. King Thierry is dead, and the kingdom is under siege by a Fire Jotnar."

"A Fire Jotnar," Clotilda said. Her mind began to panic as she thought of the friendly fire giant, Ignis.

She remembered the protective rage in Ignis's eyes that day when she went to the market for apples, declaring hellfire if anything terrible were to fall upon her. The wrath of a Fire Jotnar was not to be tested. She wondered nervously if he had changed into his fire giant form!

The sudden realization that her family and friends were in danger caused her to stand abruptly, and her chair fell back and landed loudly on the floor. Cyril and Kefira jerked their heads toward her in concern, noticing that she was using the table for support for her trembling legs and her other hand against her mouth. Cyril rushed over to Clotilda, touching her back to soothe her.

"What is it?" he asked worriedly.

"It's Ignis," Clotilda said as she pried her hand from her mouth. "Ignis is the Fire Jotnar and a friend of mine. My family is in danger!"

"Don't worry. We're going to get them out of there. Kefira!" he called out to his aunt. "Prepare one of the military carriages! Pack it with healing potions, water, and weapons, just in case! Also, hire one of the mages and tell them we need their aid in teleporting the civilians and us from Streng!"

"As you wish, Your Majesty!" Kefira bowed before racing down the hallway.

"Where would we bring them?" Clotilda asked.

"They would live here," he said with a reassuring smile. "I promised you years ago that your family is important to me as they are important to you."

"Are you sure?" she asked, her eyes widening as she remembered him making her that promise.

"Yes," he gave her a nod. "There is plenty of room in my kingdom. We're probably heading to a battlefield. Make sure you are ready."

"I will. Thank you," she said gratefully.

"Anything for you," he said, pressing his warm lips against hers. The kiss ended quickly before she could return it, but it was sweet and gentle. Cyril opened his eyes and pressed his forehead against hers. "Let's get ready. I'll meet you outside near the carriage."

“All right. I’ll see you soon,” she said as she reluctantly parted from him and ran out of the library to get ready.

Clotilda raised her right hand to her face as she ran, brushing her index and middle fingers over her lips, basking in her first kiss with Cyril.

CHAPTER 44

Destruction of Streng

Securing the hand chains around her wrists and her trusted packs strapped around her leg and waist, Clotilda was ready. She steadied her nerves, controlling her fear of the unknown by hoping and reassuring herself that her family and friends were all right. Then, with one last look around her bed chamber to ensure she had everything she needed, she rushed toward the partly opened doors and ran out into the hallway and down the stairs.

Clotilda hurried to the main entrance to the castle, looking to see Cyril standing by the foot of the staircase, watching the guards board the military carriage and working together to pack it with the necessary provisions and saddling their steeds. She walked down the stairs toward Cyril, causing him to glance over his shoulders at her as she approached him.

"We're just about ready to leave, Clotilda. I had one of the guards go to the stable to retrieve Coralina and Sleipnir, and then we can get going," he said as one of the female guards brought their steeds toward them with saddles and reins already equipped.

"Your Highness," the female guard called out. "Yours and the Royal Huntress's steeds are ready."

"Great work. Help the others finish preparing the carriage, and we will go as soon as it's done," he ordered.

"As you wish, my king." She bowed to him before she made her way over to the carriage.

With the last supplies loaded, the Regulus guards boarded the carriage while others mounted their horses. Clotilda and Cyril mounted their steeds as the male Regulus elf mage, who wore an armored cloak and a lion skull carved out of silver on top of his head, chanted the spell to teleport them to Streng. Clotilda listened to the mage rehearse the spell, her hands tightening around Coralina's reins until they started to shake as she readied and braced herself for the unexpected.

Warmth washed over her knuckles when she felt a hand over them. Her gaze dropped to see Cyril's gloved right hand wrapped around her hands, gently squeezing them. She glanced up at him to see him smiling at her in reassurance. She smiled back, releasing her right hand from the rein, and placed it over his. They kept their gazes on each other as the mage's magic surrounded them. The kingdom of Algieba faded away in the veil of magic as they teleported to the kingdom of Streng.

Ribbons of magic faded around them like mist. The thick smell of smoke struck Clotilda's nostrils and the back of her throat, and her eyes began to burn. She brought her fist to her mouth to mute her cough. She blinked a few times to clear her stinging eyes and saw a large forest of licking flames engulfing the homes, buildings, and the castle of Streng. Coralina panted from the intense heat, and her scaly skin and feathers began to sweat. Clotilda patted her pegasus to ease her. They had to hurry! The smoke was dangerous, and they needed to get Clotilda's friends, family, and themselves out of there before they suffocated!

"Here," Cyril said, causing her to turn to him to see him holding a potion bottle with an amber-orange liquid swirling inside it like honey. "Drink this. It will protect you from the heat and the smoke for a few hours."

"Don't worry, I'm fine. I'm half Lazarus elf, so the heat and the flames won't affect me. You go ahead and drink it," she said and kindly refused it, noticing that Cyril's bangs were sticking to his sweaty forehead and his pale skin had become red from the intense heat.

"Are you unaffected by the smoke?" he asked her, still holding the potion to her.

"That I'm not," she replied hesitantly, knowing she had inherited her mother's water-breathing ability, not her father's smoke-resistant lungs.

"Drink this, please. I'll drink from it once you've drunk some," he said.

"All right," she caved as she accepted his potion and drank a little, leaving enough for Cyril. She returned the potion to him, watched him tilt the vial to his lips, drank some of the liquid, and poured a little into his hand.

"Give the rest to Coralina. It will protect her too," he said as he handed her the vial and leaned forward on the saddle with his arm outstretched, allowing Sleipnir to drink the potion from his palm.

Clotilda poured the potion in her palm like Cyril did and leaned forward in her saddle to allow her pegasus to drink from it. She felt Coralina's tongue lap at the potion and the tips of her fangs hook onto the fabric of her gloves. She glanced back to see the royal guards and the mage drinking their heat-resistant potions and feeding the carriage horses with them too.

"Let's move out!" Cyril called out to his guards. "We must go to the orphanage to rescue Clotilda's family! If any of you spot any survivors, don't hesitate to rescue them!"

"Yes, Your Highness!" the guards and mage said.

Cyril snapped the reins, causing Sleipnir to rear up and neigh before he jumped into a gallop. Clotilda heard Coralina's soft neigh and watched her steed stare at the departing regal horse.

"You like him, don't you?" she said to Coralina with a smile before gently snapping the reins, and the mare anxiously galloped over until she was next to the stallion.

The market streets were unrecognizable to Clotilda as they rode down them. The grass was burned into ash. Buildings were engulfed in flames and were crumbling, and the streets were crushed by several giant, burnt footsteps of a colossal Fire Jotnar. As they searched, they couldn't find anyone. The city was void of people. Clotilda felt dread fester an abyss in her stomach; anxiousness overwhelmed her, and she hoped everyone escaped! But how were they going to save Ignis once they found him?

The crackling of flames and the eerie silence was shattered as a loud, distant roar of rage echoed in the air. The steeds neighed in fright. Clotilda and Cyril leaned forward on their saddles and shushed their horses as they gently patted them. She felt a chill. That cry of rage was from Ignis; he must be getting closer from how loud it was.

Movements caught the corners of Clotilda's eyes. She jerked her head toward the direction of the movements, noticing three figures approaching them.

"Cyril . . ." she whispered to the king, seeing him look at the figures, and the magic from his hand chain softly crackled as he readied to summon his sword.

The figures drew hesitantly closer, weapons drawn and pointing toward the ground as they approached. Clotilda studied their appearing details through the smoke, recognition hitting her.

"Commander?" Corinthia asked. "Is that you?"

"It's Clotilda! Thank the Father God, she's all right!" Ivan said in delight.

"It's good to see you again, Commander!" Kay said with relief and happiness.

"Where have you been?" Corinthia asked as she and the guards approached Clotilda.

"I'll explain everything later. But right now, we must get to the orphanage and save my family," she said urgently.

"Who is he?" Corinthia asked as she looked over at Cyril.

"Wait, isn't he the Graf . . . ?" Kay asked as he narrowed his eyes at him.

"He's an ally," Clotilda answered him quickly. "All three of you board the carriage, and I'll explain everything."

Heeding their former commander's order, Kay, Ivan, and Corinthia boarded the carriage, and Clotilda and Cyril rode beside it as they continued their trek. At the same time, one of the female Regulus elf guards helped with tending to the burn marks that Ivan and Kay had on their arms and legs.

"Can you explain what happened and why Ignis is destroying the capital?" Clotilda asked as she looked inside the carriage.

"Certainly," Corinthia nodded as she scooted closer for them to hear her. "This whole turmoil started after your trial, Commander. The citizens became enraged when King Thierry declared that he would execute you. Your hobgoblin family, along with a crying and angry young faun, protested, calling the king a disgrace."

"Garth," Clotilda said the faun's name softly.

"Ignis was among them. He was so angry that he started transforming into his giant form when the king quickly ordered us to bind him in enchanted chains and lock him inside one of the tower dungeons."

Clotilda tightened her hold on the reins as she heard the story.

"When did he escape?" she asked, trying to speak calmly through her anger.

"Last night," Corinthia replied. "He broke free somehow, attacked the castle, and killed King Thierry."

"How many people are still here?" she asked.

"Not many now. The guards and I immediately began evacuating the people in the castle and town. We used the royal tunnels to lead them outside the kingdom and sent a few messenger squirrels to deliver our distress letters. We also saved some of the prisoners from the dungeon, but bizarrely . . . Bandus has disappeared."

"What do you mean? I thought his powers were drained from his bindings and he couldn't teleport," Clotilda glared.

"He didn't teleport. When we went to his cell, the lock was picked open, and he was nowhere to be seen," Ivan joined the conversation.

"That's impossible. Bandus doesn't know how to pick locks and has no spells to help him achieve that," Clotilda stated.

"Clotilda . . . if you want to search for him . . . ?" Cyril said, causing her to look at him, seeing a hint of jealousy in his eyes.

"That won't be necessary. It would be awkward if we encountered him, and he did some bad things in the past that I have never forgiven him for," Clotilda growled.

"But I thought he had a crush on you, Commander?" Corinthia asked.

"He had an unhealthy crush on me, and I am in love with someone else," she replied as she looked at Cyril, causing him to smile at her, and the jealousy faded from his eyes.

"Is that the orphanage?" one of the male Regulus elf guards asked, causing Clotilda and Cyril to look ahead to see the tall canopy of the orphanage tree bursting into flames and all the orphans standing outside in fear.

"No!" Clotilda leaped from Coralina's back and ran toward the orphanage.

Tree branches snapped like logs in a fireplace and rained toward the large group of children outside. They screamed and threw their hands over their heads to protect themselves. The gem of Clotilda's lion hand chain glowed, and she summoned a barrier over the orphans, causing the branches to disintegrate as soon as they landed on the barrier, protecting the children. The children glanced up at the force field above them before looking at their heroine. Their eyes widened in disbelief, and their jaws fell agape.

"It . . . it can't be!" one of the goblin girls said.

"Clo?" Garth asked as he gently pushed himself out of the crowd with the red novel in his arms that Clotilda gave him. "Clo! You're alive!" he said as he rushed over and hugged her waist.

"Thank the Father God you and the orphans are all right," she said as she used her right hand to return his hug. The rest of the children circled and embraced her as she gently patted their heads. Clotilda looked around, noticing that two hobgoblins were nowhere in sight."Where's my father and mother?"

"They're still inside," Garth said as he pointed at the burning orphanage. "Stump and Rose Hip told us to wait outside as they looked around to ensure everyone was out."

"Are all of the children here?" she asked.

"Yes. But Rose Hip and Stump haven't come out yet," Garth said worriedly.

"I want you all to wait here. I'll go inside and get them out of there," Clotilda said.

"I'll go with you," Cyril said as he walked over and stood beside her.

"Who is he?" one of the elf girls asked as she looked up dreamily at Cyril.

"This is King Cyril. He's the boy I've told you about," Clotilda smiled as she introduced him.

"Your boyfriend is handsome!" the goblin girl said as she pointed at him with blushing green cheeks.

"Did he save you from the dungeon?" Garth asked protectively.

"Yes, he did. But I'll explain everything later. Cyril and I are going to go in there and save my parents. Head over to the carriage and wait inside there."

"But it's dangerous in there!" Garth said.

"I'll be fine. Cyril will be with me, and we'll be out very soon!" she reassured them.

"All right. Take care of her, sir," Garth said to Cyril as he and the other children hesitantly stepped away from Clotilda and approached the awaiting carriage.

With the children away from the torches of raining tree branches, Clotilda dismissed the shield and looked up at the orphanage.

"I hope they're all right," she said nervously.

"I'm sure they are," Cyril reassured her.

She softly nodded before summoning Universeel.

"Let's go!" she said before she charged toward the orphanage with her soulmate running beside her.

They climbed up the stairs, entered the door as if entering the jaws of a dragon, and began their search.

CHAPTER 45

Tears of Lava

Tongues of flames licked the air around the two elves as they searched the rooms of the orphanage that were engulfed in an inferno. Clotilda and Cyril searched the main level first from the kitchen, the dining room, and the piano room where the piano had been moved. They checked downstairs in the cellar and the storage room before climbing the weakening staircase toward the top level.

"Mom! Dad! Where are you?" Clotilda called out as she and Cyril reached the top floor and searched each room. "Let's check the children's rooms!" she called out to Cyril through the roaring flames. "They probably went there! Be careful and watch your step!" she said as she hurried down the crumbling wooden hallway with Cyril following her.

Rose Hip's pained screams echoed through the roar of the flames. Clotilda flinched at the sounds, and her steps quickened as she hurried to the children's rooms.

"Hang in there, Rose!" she heard Stump's voice.

Clotilda quickly slipped through the door of the room, hearing a loud crash coming from right behind her. Clotilda gasped, worried for Cyril, and quickly jerked her head back to check on him. Cyril stood behind her, his head turning toward the doorway where a cluster of burning rafters rained down.

"Are you all right?" she asked, looking him over to ensure he wasn't injured.

"I am," he replied as he turned to her. "Let's keep going."

She nodded before she continued forward.

Smoke parted, revealing the two hobgoblins sitting next to each other in the corner of the children's room, wearing torn fabrics over their mouths to protect their lungs from the smoke. Rose Hip tightly gripped her husband's hand, sweat rolling down her ash-covered, green cheeks, and the fabric over her mouth fluttered from her labored breaths.

"Mom! Dad!" Clotilda called out as she hurried toward them.

The husband and wife turned toward her, their eyes widening as soon as they saw their elven daughter.

"Clotilda?" Rose Hip strained as she sat up. "Where have you been?"

"I'm sorry, Mom. But we need to get you and Dad out of here!" Clotilda apologized.

"Who is that elf fellow with you?" Stump asked.

"This is Cyril. He's a childhood friend of mine," Clotilda replied.

"Cyril?" Stump said as he helped his wife to her feet and squinted his eyes as he stared at the elf king. "You look familiar somehow."

"We'll talk later. We need to get you and your wife out of here right now," Cyril said as he scooped Rose Hip up and held her in his arms.

"I'm sure I've seen you from somewhere too," Rose Hip said, reaching up to Cyril's hair and grabbing one of the alabaster locks. "Wait a second! You're the one who saved me and my husband all those years ago when we were on our journey to Streng!"

"I knew it! I thought you looked familiar, son! I still can't believe you lifted my cart with your bare hands . . . !" Stump gasped as Clotilda scooped him up in her arms.

"You saved them before?" Clotilda asked Cyril.

"I'll tell you later," Cyril said before turning toward the hallway from where they came and stopping abruptly, seeing that it was blocked with burning beams and rafters.

"Oh great!" Stump said with a sneer. "Things just got worse!"

"I have an idea!" Clotilda said as she walked toward one of the chairs at the corner of the room. She grabbed it with one arm and hurled it toward the glass window, breaking it and causing it to fall to the ground below.

"What are you doing, Clo?" her mother asked.

"This is our only way out," she said before she pulled out her pegasus whistle from her pack and blew into it. "We'll have Coralina fly us out!"

"You know how much I hate being near that horse!" Rose Hip said as she jerked a little from the labor pains.

"Coralina is very sweet, Mom. You have nothing to worry about. Remember when I rode you back to the orphanage when you, Dad, and Garth came to check on me?" she asked as she neared the window, watching the flash of pink from Coralina's wings pulse as she flew close enough for her master to climb onto the saddle.

"Well, you talked us into it!" Stump sneered as Clotilda carried him to her awaiting steed.

Clotilda held Stump securely as she hoisted herself onto Coralina's back. She adjusted her stance to get comfortable, ensuring her feet were secure in the stirrups. Cyril took off his cape and draped it over Rose Hip in a chivalrous act to shield her from the flames. He then mounted the seat behind Clotilda, wrapping his arm around her waist to provide stability as they prepared to fly to the carriage.

A large shadow engulfed them. Clotilda felt her blood turn to ice, and she tilted her head back until her crown pressed against the bottom junction of her neck as she looked upon the fire giant standing in their way, looking down at them.

Ignis stood one hundred feet tall. Once restrained in stone bands, his lava hair and beard spilled over his broad shoulders and chest like an erupting volcano and pooled to the ground. His eyes were piercing yellow like a pair of suns, and his skin was gray and crackled like stone.

Ignis locked his eyes on them like a hungry hawk eyeing a mouse. Strings of magma and lava dripped from his lips as he parted his mouth, the inside of his throat glowing red and yellow in a pool of fire. Clotilda and Cyril tightened their hold on the hobgoblins and each other. Ignis regurgitated a flood of lava, the wake of molten rock pouring toward them.

"Move!" Clotilda commanded her steed as she tugged tightly on the reins, causing Coralina to flap her wings, flying out of the way as quickly as possible.

Lava covered the orphanage, melting it until it was a lump under the wake. Rose Hip and Stump glanced around the arms of their elven saviors, their gazes saddening at the sight of their destroyed orphanage and home.

"For one hundred and forty years, we've created and had that orphanage . . . now it's gone . . ." Rose Hip said sadly as she brought her hand to her eyes to hide her tears.

"I'm sorry, Mom and Dad," Clotilda said softly, feeling sympathetic for her parents and saddened to see the place she grew up in be destroyed.

Clotilda and Cyril looked down as they circled over Ignis. They glanced at the carriage, hoping he didn't see it. Clotilda studied the area, trying to find a way to get Cyril and her parents down to the carriage. Clotilda looked at Ignis, wondering how she could help him too. Fire Jotnars were known for becoming giant berserkers when they became enraged, but there might be a way to calm him.

"It's a risk, but I think it might work," Clotilda said as she turned to Cyril.

"What's your plan?" he asked.

"Ignis probably thinks I'm dead. If I let him see me, he might stop his attack and revert into his passive form and . . . oh no!" she gasped as she saw that Ignis had spotted the carriage and was charging straight for it. "Come on, Coralina!" she said as she snapped the reins, and they dove toward the giant.

Ignis reached behind, pulled a giant sword from its sheath strapped to his back, and lifted it in the air, ready to hammer the blade down on the carriage.

"Ignis! Stop!" Clotilda called out as loud as she could until her throat and lungs burned.

The giant's attack abruptly stopped, the blade hovering over the carriage, the sword's edge grazing its roof. The orphans screamed from inside the carriage as they looked up at the fire giant, and Cyril's guards armed themselves with their bows and fired arrows at the large blade. Clotilda pulled back on the reins, and Coralina quickly jerked up until they circled high over the fire giant again.

"It worked!" Cyril said as he watched Ignis glance around, looking for whoever called out to him.

"I need to get closer!" Clotilda said as she knitted her eyebrows together.

"Are you crazy, Clo?" Stump said as he looked at her with panicked eyes.

"In a way, yes, I am," she chuckled softly to her father. "I'm going to see if I can calm Ignis down. Hopefully, I can distract him long enough so he doesn't try to attack the carriage again."

"I don't want you to do this alone, Clotilda," Cyril said as he tightened his arm around her waist.

"I need to, Cyril," she said as she gently placed her free hand over his protective arm. "I have to try! I can't leave him here like this! He's my friend!"

"Ah! My water just broke!" Rose Hip said as she held her hand up to show the translucent shine of water on it.

Time was running out! There were no more errors or second chances. She needed to calm Ignis and get her mother to safety before the baby came.

"Stay here with them, Cyril. I'll fly us close enough that he can see me, and I'll try to calm him down."

"Clo, don't do this!" Stump said as she carefully sat him behind her, snapped the reins, and flew closer to Ignis.

"Stay here with us, Clo! Please!" Rose Hip begged.

"I'll be fine, I promise," Clotilda pulled on the reins and flew over Ignis. "This is good enough. I don't want to get too close to him and risk the lives of you, my parents, and their baby," she said and looked over at Cyril, who still had his arm around her. "I'll be all right. If anything happens, I can always use my Rune powers," she reassured him.

"Be safe and come back!" Cyril said as he gently kissed her shoulder before reluctantly unwinding his arm around her.

"I'll be back, my love," Clotilda said as she looked back at him with a smile before kissing his lips.

She jerked her head back to Ignis, seeing that he was ready to attack the carriage again.

"Ignis! Don't!" she shouted as she leaped from her steed's back and plummeted toward him.

The air rushed past her and against her body as she dove toward Ignis. Her hair flowed behind her, and her eyes watered as the smoky, hot air dried them. Ignis let out a thunderous roar as he raised his sword. She needed to stop him! Clotilda summoned an orb of fiery feathers in her palm and transformed it into a giant firebird. By her command, the burning fowl leaped from her hand, soaring through the air like a firework and striking the giant's face.

Ignis snarled before he steadied his sword and swung his other arm around to shoo away the firebird as it flew around his face. Clotilda neared the hovering, giant sword, holding her feet out and making the muscles in her legs taut as she steadied herself for landing. Her heels clattered on the hot metal of the blade, and her legs bent to the knee as she landed safely.

She grunted as she felt her heel slide slightly before standing up and hurrying up the sword blade. She planted her feet with each step as Ignis jerked his weapon a few times as he tried to swat away the firebird, unaware of the female elf approaching him.

Clotilda reached for the sword's handle and climbed up Ignis's muscular arm to avoid the streaming lava beard. Ignis succeeded in shooing the firebird away as it disappeared into a shower of ash. He returned his outraged gaze to the carriage and saw Coralina dropping off the last two civilians and the male elf helping them off. Ignis lifted his sword again, roaring as he readied his attack. Clotilda pulled herself over the curve of Ignis's shoulder before hurrying toward his ear, using her hoarse voice to call him again.

"Ignis! Please stop!" she called out.

Ignis abruptly halted his actions before slowly turning his gaze down to his shoulder to see a tiny, familiar elf looking up at him.

"Clotilda?" Ignis whispered in disbelief, his glowing eyes swelling with tears. The tears rolled down his cheeks, causing steam to hiss and erupt from his face. He slowly held his hand to her for her to step on. "You're alive!"

"Alive and well," she said as she stepped into his palm and held her balance as he lifted her to get a better look at her.

"I'm so happy to see you!" he said.

"Likewise, Ignis," she said softly as she held her outstretched arm to him and placed her hand on his lean cheek. "Let's get you out of here. Everyone is waiting for you."

Ignis smiled at her, displaying the toothy grin she had missed as his rage lifted and his body began to transform and shrink.

Clotilda held onto Ignis's thumb as he transformed back. His hands shrank so he could wrap them around her waist and hold on to her as they reached the ground.

Fourteen feet tall again, Ignis held Clotilda in a grateful embrace, a hug they had missed giving each other. Clotilda pulled away, looking over at Cyril, who gave her a proud smile, and his eyes filled with relief.

"What have I done?" she heard Ignis say softly.

Clotilda looked back at Ignis, who looked at the destruction around them. She reached out and gently grabbed his arm.

"Don't look back at it, Ignis. Starting right now, it's time to move on and leave this cage behind," she replied as she held her other arm toward the gray sky and cast her Airavata powers.

An orb of water formed in her hand, and she shot it to the sky. The rain came down on the capital, slowly diminishing the flames and clearing the air of the heavy smoke. Ignis looked at her and gave her a soft smile before gently putting her back down. Clotilda looked back at Cyril, nodding at him for the mage to teleport them back to Algieba.

The mage began casting his powers by Cyril's orders to return them to his kingdom. Magic engulfed everyone around them. Clotilda became overwhelmed with relief. She was surrounded by her friends, family, and the man she loved. She hurried over toward Cyril as the magic swirled around her like water, her body colliding softly with his as she embraced him. She felt Cyril's arms wrap around her to return the hug, her skin tingling as she felt his kisses on her skin and hair. They held each other close as the magic encircled them, and they teleported from Streng.

CHAPTER 46

Final Promise

Upon returning to Algieba, Rose Hip was immediately taken to the healer's chamber to aid her in childbirth. Stump came with her, refusing to leave his wife's side. The orphans, Garth, Ignis, and the former guards of Streng sat outside the healer's chamber while Clotilda stood by the partly opened doors with Cyril, listening to her mother's pained cries. She lowered her head and held her hands together in prayer, hoping all went well and that her mother and the child would be in good health. Clotilda relaxed as Cyril gently ran his fingers fondly through her hair. She heard another cry of pain from her mother and peeked through the doors to see Rose Hip lying in bed with Stump sitting worriedly beside her with his hand tightly wrapped around hers.

"I hope my mother and the baby will be all right," she said softly.

"They will. I'm sure of it," Cyril said.

Clotilda leaned her head against Cyril's shoulder, feeling his arm wrap behind her as he pulled her closer.

"Clo?" she heard Garth's voice and saw him standing by the door's frame. "Has the baby come yet?"

"Not yet. Keep praying for them," she replied.

"I will," he paused as he looked through the crack of the barely opened doors and then back at her. "Clo . . . I have a confession to make."

"What is it?"

"You've probably been wondering who freed Ignis, right?" he asked hesitantly.

"Yes, I was wondering about that," she said with a nod.

"The one who freed him . . . it was me," he said sheepishly.

"You?" she asked in surprise.

"Yes," he admitted guiltily. "I watched as the guards threw the enchanted chains over him to prevent him from changing, and they locked him away. Since he's your friend, I visited him during the two months he was held prisoner, and I couldn't bear to see him chained up like a wild animal anymore. So I freed him. But I had no idea that he would cause so much destruction. I'm sorry, Clo," he said as he tightly clenched his eyes shut, causing tears to roll down his cheeks.

"I probably would have done the same thing," Clotilda replied softly, causing the faun to open his eyes and look at her. "If I saw an innocent person or creature trapped, I would have freed them too."

"You would?" he asked.

"I would," she nodded.

The final encouragement from the healers and a last sharp grunt from Rose Hip caused the tense air to ring into life with the cries of a newborn. Clotilda felt her heart erupt into joy.

"A son! A son!" Stump cheered, which caused Clotilda to giggle in response. The two elves and faun moved away from the doors as they flung open, and the overjoyed Stump stood before them. "Our son is born!

Everyone come in and see him!" he said before leaving the doors open and rushing back to his wife.

Garth and the orphans hurried inside the chamber, followed by Ignis and the former guards of Streng. Clotilda took a few steps toward the chamber, stopping when she didn't hear Cyril's steps. She glanced back to see he was still standing by the door frame.

"Aren't you coming?" she asked.

"I don't think my presence is necessary," Cyril said, shaking his head as if dismissing himself. "I think this special occasion is for you and your family only. It would be awkward to have me in there."

"You're my family too. There's no reason for you to be left out," she smiled at him before walking toward him and gently grasping his hand. "Please come. I'm sure everyone would like to meet you, and you can see my new brother."

A touched smile spread on Cyril's lips, and he allowed her to tug on his arm and lead him inside the chamber, where her family gathered around Rose Hip's bed as they looked at the newborn.

"He sure is small," one of the orphan goblin boys said.

"Of course he's small," Rose Hip said as she rocked her son. "It would be challenging for me to give birth if he wasn't."

"He looks like he could fit in a dollhouse!" one of the elf girls giggled.

Rose Hip looked up at Clotilda and smiled as she carefully held her infant to her.

"Meet your brother, Ekhart." Rose Hip smiled.

"Ekhart," Clotilda said as she carefully accepted the baby. He was too small to hold in her arms, but Clotilda used both hands to cradle him. He fit perfectly in her hands like a loaf of bread and felt soft and fragile like a bird. "I was sure you would give the baby a wilderness name like yours and Dad's."

"I was thinking about it, but I think Ekhart is a more fitting name for him."

Clotilda glanced back at the baby, a smile spreading on her face as she looked upon the sweet sleeping face of her new brother.

"He's so beautiful, Mom," she said as she held him close and gently rocked him. "Hello, little Ekhart."

Cyril walked over toward Clotilda and curiously looked down at the child, smiling as he looked upon the infant.

"I'm glad you came to see this special moment, Your Highness," Rose Hip said, causing Cyril to look at her. "The first time I saw you, you didn't stay around for long. So I missed my chance to give you my thanks."

"My apologies for that," Cyril bowed his head to her.

"You have no reason to apologize. You saved my daughter's life," Rose Hip said as she gestured to Clotilda. "You saved mine, my husband's and our son's lives. I owe you not one, but five thank-yous."

"Any time," he said with a smile.

Clotilda felt Cyril's hand rest on her shoulder as they admired Ekhart before hearing Ignis's heavy footsteps approaching them. She readied herself to lift her brother for Ignis to see him, but Cyril's startled grunt caused her to cease her actions, and she saw that Ignis had grabbed Cyril's waist and hoisted him up as if he were a chalice.

"Ignis?" she whispered in shock. "What are you doing?"

Ignis had a protective frown as he held Cyril up until the king was at eye level.

"Who's this, Clo?" Ignis asked as he glanced down at her. "Is he your boyfriend?"

"He is. Can you please put him down?" she said, hoping he wouldn't hurt Cyril.

Ignis returned his gaze to the male elf and gave him a stern glare.

"Are you treating her well?" Ignis asked.

Cyril met the giant's glare with his calm but stern frown.

"As my equal," Cyril sincerely replied.

The two males held each other's glares before Ignis's frown softened, and he chuckled.

"You have the steel nerves of a dragon! That's good! Clo deserves a strong man," he said as he held his right hand to Cyril in a friendly gesture. "Sorry, I have to joke around a little."

Cyril smiled back before accepting the giant's hand and giving it a firm handshake.

"Pleasure to meet you, Ignis," Cyril said.

"Likewise. Continue to take great care of Clo, all right?"

"I will," he said before Ignis lowered him back to the ground and released him.

Clotilda carefully handed Ekhart back to her mother before she walked toward Cyril, who dusted his clothes with a few swipes of his hand.

"I'm so sorry about that, Cyril. I wasn't expecting Ignis to interrogate you like that."

"It's all right," he said as he smiled at her. "You have excellent friends."

"You're one of them, as well as my significant other," she said as she hugged him.

Cyril returned the hug as he scooped Clotilda's hand in his and kissed it.

Rose Hip slept soundly with her husband in the healer's chamber with their newborn son in a crib beside them. Rooms were set for the orphans, Garth, Ignis, Corinthia, Kay, and Ivan, as they settled in, ready for a good night's sleep. Clotilda wished each of them a good night before making her way to her bed chambers, leaving the doors open for Cyril, just in case he came by to visit.

Clotilda stood by the marble railing of her balcony and looked at the sky as it changed from teal to indigo. She counted the first stars appearing in the night sky and thought deeply about her blood family, especially her father.

Whispers of a woman startled Clotilda. She looked around to see if anyone was in the chamber with her, but it was empty. She gasped again as she heard the whispers again, realizing they were coming from within her. Were the whispers coming from the Deity of Lazarus? What was the deity trying to tell her?

A knock pulled Clotilda from her thoughts, causing her to turn to the door. Her heart fluttered when she saw that it was Cyril.

"Can I come in?" he asked as he held a couple of water-filled chalices.

"Of course, you can. Please come in," Clotilda smiled, causing him to smile back as he approached her and handed her a chalice.

"How are you doing?" he asked.

"Much better, now that you're here," she replied before taking a sip from her water.

"What are you thinking about?" he asked.

"A lot. I've been thinking about my blood father and the villagers that have fallen into Hollows, and . . ." she paused as she placed her hand on her chest. "This is going to sound strange, but I think the Deity of Lazarus is trying to talk to me. But I don't know what she's trying to say."

"I don't think it's strange. I can also hear the Deity of Regulus talking to me. But I don't understand his words," he said.

"Do you think it might have something to do with us transforming into our Rune forms?" she asked.

"Maybe," he shrugged as he stared into his chalice, lost in his thoughts.

"Are you all right?" she asked, touching his shoulder.

"I am," he said as he looked at her, noticing that his gaze was heavy with a question that needed to be answered. "Do you remember the task you gave me before I had to leave Cygnus?"

"I do. But that was only my silly attempt to keep you from leaving back then," she giggled.

"Promises are meant to be kept. I have one final promise to fulfill," he said as he stepped closer to her.

"You don't have to prove anything to me, Cyril. You're exceptional, and being with you is enough for me."

Cyril smiled as he placed his chalice on the marble railing and wrapped his left arm around her waist, and the other one cupped her left cheek. Clotilda put her chalice on the railing, their bodies acting on their own as they leaned toward each other, and their lips met.

Her nerves ignited in bliss when she felt Cyril's lips touch hers. He was no longer hesitating but confident, hungry for passion. She moaned in the kiss as she wrapped her arms around his shoulders. She tilted her head to the side to get more access, parting her lips for him as she felt him lick her bottom lip, and their tongues met.

"Allow me to complete this task for you, and then I can ask you something I've been meaning to ask you for a long time," he said as he broke the kiss.

"As you wish, my love," she said breathlessly.

Cyril brushed the loose strands of Clotilda's hair behind her ears before he kissed her, gently grabbed her hand, and led her out of the bed chambers.

The rings of the torches lit the training ground like halos. Clotilda followed Cyril to the inner ring of one of the fighting circles, her heart beating faster with every step. Once in the ring, she stopped once Cyril did, and he turned to face her.

Tenderly holding Clotilda's hand, Cyril looked into her eyes and spoke sincerely, "I have been thinking about this for a while now, and I believe it's time we put our skills to the test. I want to challenge you to a duel, not to prove who is better, but to see how far we have come in our journey. I want to see the growth we have both achieved and how we can continue to improve ourselves. But I also wish to fulfill my promise to you. What do you say?"

Clotilda met his gaze, her soul touching his as she looked into his eyes and smiled with a nod as she spoke.

"I'm always ready to face you in a duel, Cyril. You compel me to challenge myself, and I welcome it! I look forward to our battles and the chance to learn from the best, win or lose. I want to see how far we have grown, too, for I want to go on this journey with you and continue to grow and learn with you! I accept!"

"You've gotten so much stronger that it has pushed me to do my best when I face a challenger," he said as he released his hold on her hand and stepped away from her. He summoned his sword from his hand chain before he stood in a battle stance. "Give me your best, and I'll give you mine!"

"I will," she said with a nod as she summoned Universeel from her hand chain and stood in a battle stand of her own. "I will give you all that I can muster!"

She could see his eyes gleaming at her. The hopefulness in them moved her. They held their gazes until they raised their weapons and charged.

Their weapons collided like a clash of thunder. Their bodies swirled gracefully around each other as they fought as if they were dancing. They pushed each other and fought harder than they had ever fought. They dodged each other's attacks and tried to counter each one they had memorized from previous duels during her training with him. Clotilda seized her opportunity to swing Universeel's blade at Cyril, feeling the edge of his sword approach her. Then they froze as the battle ended.

Clotilda panted as she caught her breath, feeling the blade of Cyril's sword press lightly against her throat. She looked up to meet his gaze, her eyes widening when she saw that she had her weapon lightly pressed against his throat too. She had never been able to get her blade close enough to Cyril before until that very moment.

"A draw," she said softly in disbelief. Cyril smiled at her as he lowered his sword, and she did the same with hers. "I can't believe it," she chirped, banishing Universeel back into her hand chain.

"See," he said, banishing his sword. "You have gotten so much stronger."

"I have a good teacher to thank for that," she smiled at him.

Clotilda felt her heart skip when she saw Cyril gently take her hand in his.

"Now that the duel is over, I ask you this question." She gasped lightly as Cyril kneeled, her eyes beginning to sting with tears. "Clotilda . . . I have longed for a wife and a queen whom I can trust and live with for the rest of eternity," he said and cupped her hand with his other hand as he continued. "During these two months, I have fallen in love with you and want to continue learning more about you and growing this bond. Will you marry me?"

"Yes," she softly smiled as tears rolled down her cheeks. "Yes, I will! I have longed for the right man to be my husband, and you are the one."

Cyril stood up with overwhelming excitement in his eyes as he embraced her.

Clotilda wrapped her arms tightly around him. She had waited so long to hear him ask her that question, and she had waited to give him her answer. They held each other close. Their hearts beating together as one. They knew this was the start of a new journey together, one as future husband and wife.

ACKNOWLEDGEMENTS

I want to start by thanking God for his many gifts, especially for my family and friends. Thank you to my mother for home-schooling my brother and me, being one of my best friends, motivating me to continue drawing and writing, and being my first reader! Thank you to my father for his advice to follow my calling, his support and guidance, and for being my second reader! I'm thankful for my brother for his support and always watching out for me! I'm thankful to my Uncle Alfie for encouraging me to pursue my dream of becoming an author when, back then, I wasn't planning on publishing my stories. Thank you to one of my best friends, Mike, for being so kind and trustworthy and for helping me brainstorm ideas for my stories throughout the years. I love every one of you guys. Thank you for everything!

Thank you to Bookbaby for helping me throughout this journey and I appreciate everything you have done!

S.I. Verteller lives in the beautiful North West and has enjoyed writing and drawing since she was a little girl. She dreamt of being a published author since she was a teenager and plans to continue writing fantasy stories for the rest of her life! Rune of Lazarus is her debut novel!

When she isn't writing or drawing, she enjoys reading, especially classic literature, fantasy, manga, romance, watching anime, playing with her dogs, and spending time with her loving family and friends.